JON GEORGE

FACES OF MIST AND FLAME

TOR

First published 2004 by Tor

This edition published 2005 by Tor
an imprint of Pan Macmillan Ltd
Pan Macmillan, 20 New Wharf Road, London N1 9RR
Basingstoke and Oxford
Associated companies throughout the world
www.panmacmillan.com

ISBN 0 330 41984 6

1 3 5 7 9 8 6 4 2

A CIP catalogue record for this book is available from
the British Library.

Typeset by SetSystems Ltd, Saffron Walden, Essex
Printed and bound in Great Britain by
Mackays of Chatham plc, Chatham, Kent

FACES OF
MIST AND
FLAME

Jon George lives in Ipswich, Suffolk. He vaguely remembers acquiring a degree in electronics, but now it's his wife who programmes the video. Supposedly gainful employment has included: telecommunications research, pizza delivery, graphic design, and driving very quickly when ferrying doctors to emergency calls.

He currently rides his motorbike when the sun is out, drinks beer when the pub is open, is generally of a cheerful disposition, and has never fired a gun in anger. Sometime in the future he would like to fly in a two-seater WW2 Spitfire.

Jon's initial publishing success was with a succession of short stories in the independent press.

Video programming notwithstanding, Jon George can still change a plug.

For Lynda

Acknowledgements

In a fiction based on a real event, it is tempting to take liberties with the truth for the sake of narrative. I'm no saint – I *have* tinkered – but, out of respect for the men that took part, I endeavoured to portray the assault on Guam as realistically as possible. Since a full bibliography would run to many pages, I would just like to pass on my thanks to the many excellent historians who have taken time to chronicle WWII. I own most of your books. Any errors – deliberate or otherwise – are mine.

To the people on Guam who have ensured that their folk-tales have not been forgotten: thank you – your stories bewitch me. The same goes for those who relate the Greek myths.

When someone does whatever it is they're good at, the world turns a little easier, and no novel is ever possible without the input of experts. To my editor Peter Lavery, and the rest of the team working the coal-face at Macmillan: a big thanks. The same goes to John Jarrold. And Don Smith – historical aviation expert extraordinaire. And LG for her skills at proof-reading and her objective comments

Finally, I'd like to thank the two unknown young marines that hoisted a flag on a boat-hook on Guam's beachhead – under fire. Their grins, when cursing and panic would have been more appropriate, are frozen for all time in a photograph. Their picture overlooked every word I wrote.

I hope that they found their own little bit of peace.

PART ONE
THE STORY

ONE

Friday afternoon.

Serena glares at the lion, decides that either it or herself must cease to exist within the next two minutes, and so she utters a banzai scream and leaps towards the animal. Since she is a five-foot, three-inch pixie of a woman, and the lion is a waist-high stuffed toy, she calculates the odds are about even. As Serena – a paw in each hand – wrenches its front legs apart, hoping to rip the beast asunder at her first attempt, she swears at the top of her voice and enjoys the sensation of seldom uttered profanities rushing over her lips. The words are ones her mother would consider disgusting.

Bad girl!

She surprises herself with the originality of the language chosen, and decides she doesn't care. Serena realizes some impartial observer might assume that, instead of having just changed the geometry of time with her startling invention, the pressure of being a twenty-first-century mathematics professor has taken its toll on her, and that she is falling into the abyss of insanity. But Serena doesn't care. She is not a Cambridge Miss Jean Brodie.

Ah, shucks, and I'm only twenty-four.

The right front leg of Caliban the lion succumbs to physical forces it was not designed to withstand, so it parts company with the torso, and leaves entrails of foam streaming in front of

Serena as the release of her tension sends its head and body –
and her knuckles – flying into a wall.

Serena yelps, transferring Caliban to her other hand by the
scruff of his neck, flapping the injured hand to cool the graze,
then smiles and dismisses the pain . . .

And proceeds to bash the toy's three-legged remains against
the corner of a shelf with renewed frenzy.

A girl's gotta do what a girl's gotta do. Die you little shit! Die!

Pieces of Caliban fly around the room. The toy appears set
on maintaining a quiet dignity, but its inane smile is not fooling
her any more. One of them must cease to exist physically, and
the odds do not favour Caliban. Neither is the old, insecure
personality of Professor Serena Freeman expected to last, as she
wants to explode out of her previous shell into something new.
Each blow increases in violence.

At the age of just four, Serena Freeman could take two
random numbers of three digits chosen by an intrigued adult
and multiply them in her head faster than they could tap the
sum into a pocket calculator. (*Well done, Serena! Did you see that,
she's faster than I am! Aren't you a clever little girl?!*) At six she
could provide the square root. (*Wow! That's amazing!*) And she
understood calculus. (*Good god, girl! What's that?!*) And liked
chaos theory. And wrote music. And played the flute. (*Really?
Is that the time? I must be somewhere else.*) She was aware that
nobody of her own age, or any age for that matter, liked her
very much, but she had gone beyond wanting to be considered
cute. For hers was a serious intellect and gift.

At ten she took her maths and physics A-levels, and it
wasn't any surprise when she went up to Cambridge at the age
of eleven. She made the news: the nationals, with their journalists and photographers, broadsheet and tabloid, calling her
name – calling her names. On morning television: Shouldn't
you be in school? Ha, ha, ha. Evening television: Isn't it past
your bedtime? Ho, ho, ho. The late news: "And Finally . . ." As
she stood in front of the world's media (raven-coloured pigtails,

thick-rimmed glasses, flowered patterned dress, desperately wishing she were elsewhere), she was made to accept a lucky charm in the form of a two-and-a-half-foot-high stuffed lion. It came from some crone-witch of a politician who had long been deluded into thinking she photographed well with such jingoistic symbols. At that moment, Serena mentally declared that she would like to progress from being eleven years old in body, and to stop being an oddity in others' minds.

So, she tried to ignore the plaudits – and the envy. Some academics hinted that they thought she'd already done her best research by age fifteen. Others were honest enough to admit they were jealous of the grants she continued to attract. At seventeen, burn-out was predicted; at nineteen, outflanked and confused professors mooted suicide as her next career move. Perhaps sex would drag her down? But did she know what it was yet? That was the one she found difficult to ignore. It always made her blush, and squirm.

When it came to everything else, though, she began to fool them all. As an apparent aside to her work, she produced a series of mathematics texts for children that had since become *de rigueur* in classrooms across the country – mainly because she used examples that the children could understand from within their own world. With her guidance, they found learning fun. The publication of those books annoyed and astounded the other academics even more.

The lion itself had lasted five years past her nineteenth birthday, but those nerdy glasses, skirt and pigtails had long gone. That at least was a satisfaction, but she knew she still hadn't demonstrated the full extent of her intelligence.

Today will prove that genius, and nothing, but *nothing*, will stop her from becoming the person she wants to be.

Odysseus has worked.

Odysseus has worked.

Serena stands still. The stuffed lion is no longer stuffed, and Caliban is a formless mass of foam and floating motes. Only his head remains in her hand. In the space of only a few minutes, a symbol of childhood prodigy has been ruined – and if she continues any further, it will completely vanish.

That could be me.

As she rolls her shoulders and drags in a lungful of air, she catches sight of herself in her full-length mirror.

Caliban's not the only one that looks beat-up.

As Serena moves in closer for an inspection, she tries to ignore the continuing feeling that she is being watched. She also wonders if her brother Alex was right in suggesting that her home could be bugged.

Where would they fit one?

Her study occupies the large upstairs room of her Victorian house just off Queen's Road and the Fen Causeway near the centre of Cambridge. The room had once served as a studio for a relatively famous painter from the thirties, and was adapted to be filled with natural light. The north wall of the room consists of floor-to-ceiling sliding windows. These open onto a patio-balcony, itself being bounded by a filigree wrought-iron fence in need of some paint. On it stands a small octagonal pine table patterned with coffee mug stains, a slatted wooden deck-chair, and half a dozen dead plants in terracotta pots. This, in turn, overlooks a thicket of back garden containing a small, untended forest of iris, forget-me-nots, lavender and islands of red-hot poker. And, since a month ago, when the council felled a small, rotten oak in the park lying beyond the bottom of her garden, the balcony now provides a view of the river Cam and the cream-coloured stone of college buildings in the distance.

Serena runs her free hand through her hair, wipes the run of tears of excitement from her cheeks and sniffs.

You're okay, girl. You're just tense and paranoid.

The opposite wall to the garden view has two sash windows – both wedged open securely with candlesticks – overlooking the street. Through them, from outside, normal, everyday life makes a muted call. A group of students are still celebrating finishing their finals, while preparing themselves for the forthcoming May Ball that takes place in June (Serena likes these little oddities that university life throws up), with the pop from another champagne bottle, as laughter bubbles up along with it. A wasp cannot seem to make its mind up whether or not to fly into the room, and keeps bumping and buzzing the topmost pane in one window. Two sparrows squabble in the young ash tree leaning over into the street from the pavement – their prize a piece of crust from one of the many pies sold daily from the vegetarian stall down near the park. The tangy aroma from the vendor's hot plate has drifted on the gentle swirling summer air, and makes Serena lick her lips as she relishes her task. She craves familiar smells – craves normality.

It's only the terror, girl, only terror.

She sweeps her hand through her hair again, blinks away a last tear, pulls a grin, and throws herself a hip and a pout in the mirror's reflection. Her eyes appear to sparkle.

You're looking good, girl. Kiss-kiss.

Serena knows that her colleagues and students consider her a potential high-cheekboned, full-in-the-lip, catwalk clone for a Paris fashion show (if she ever were to desire a different career). This is much to her blushing consternation, but there are days when she likes the comparison – and the delusion that she would ever consider it as an option.

Looking good.

Fuller in the lips and hips than those waifs on the covers of the fashion magazines perhaps, but there is nothing coy about the intelligent flash of determination blazing in her eyes now. The childhood pigtails have long been cut back to a shoulder-length wave that curls into her neck, and the glasses are now rimless circles of glass crimped to plain gold wires. Her former Pollyanna dress style has become baggy black leather jeans, loose black cotton vest top, black silk bra and black silk knickers. Those last two are her secret, of course. So is the inspiration behind a little metal comic-inspired anarchy badge – a capital V within a circle – clipped to the rear of her belt.

Nah, I'm better than a stuffed toy. I'm The Pocket Dynamo!

She stares down at Caliban's head in her hand.

You poor boy. Ha!

Serena pulls at the lion's mane and it peels off in one go. Dropping the bald head and entrails, she wanders over to her desk, takes some envelopes and notes off a letter spike made from a pewter game figure (Chinese warrior pikeman meets cartoon designer), and grimaces as she rams the mass of woollen mane into place on his lance instead. For some reason, she thinks of Hercules and the Nemean Lion. His first task.

Nice new paperweight. And a nice way to mess with a hero's life.

Serena places her trophy on top of the envelopes and notes, and turns back to the board on the wall. She picks up one of the chunky marker pens from the tray that runs below the length of the board, contemplates the hieroglyphics that relate to Odysseus, and taps her teeth with the end of the pen. Serena has just tried out, in earnest for the first time, the experimental equipment that resulted from her formulae and she now has to savour the moment. It is the realization of an idea, a fantastic conception, developed to its conclusion from the form of symbols on this board, being conjured into the physical reality of a device she has already named after one of her favourite, larger-than-life Greek adventurers. Odysseus and Serena – mind over matter? She glances back at her trophy, which she sees as her Nemean Lion.

What if it was first, the first of the twelve? Like Hercules' twelve labours? Would that save me from this mockery of a life? Or will this?

She drums the display board with her fingers, then shivers. The feeling of excitement still tingles in her hands, in the depth of her stomach, and it flutters in her groin and breasts. She appraises lustfully the large marker pen and rebukes herself.

Naughty.

Serena rubs her nose. She can still smell the powder from the exploding navy shells, still taste the salt from the sea – and from her tears – and can still feel the concussions hissing in her ears. With a snap, she removes the cap from the pen, sticks the exposed end under her nostrils and takes a hit. The chemical nip obscures, for just a moment, some of those other smells that she knows she is always going to remember. Gore has an awful texture; it can remove the very essence of being. But it puts into perspective the loathing she has of the success forced upon her in childhood. As she replaces the pen, she shudders.

Some distance away from her, a camera fixed on a tripod clicks, and another photograph of her is taken. The motor drive rushes the film onto the next frame, and then the camera is ready to be used again. It is an expensive piece of equipment and its telephoto attachment is one of the most powerful available. The man using the camera doesn't really need to take yet another photograph of the woman he watches through the lens, but Professor Serena Freeman has a lovely profile.

But a lousy attitude to tidiness.

He wonders if she realizes she's being watched. Or listened to.

The room contains everything Serena needs to do her work, and also everything she needs to ensure she can relax. The latest brand of PC is tucked away in the corner to one side of the sliding windows, the screen saver showing Odysseus blinding the one-eyed Cyclops. There are shelves, full of books (textbooks and volumes of myths and legends) on the wall beside it, quite apart from those heaped on the floor. Against the wall with the windows opening to the street, are her full-length mirror, a music stand and flute (a cluster of music scores are scattered among the books on the floor), a hi-fi and CD tower, then the walnut writing bureau with its new paper-weight and three mountains of paper, one of them consisting of curling yellow post-it stick-on reminders. Their infection is clearly spreading outwards; a small glass vase that contains a silk imitation red rose has acquired three stickers already this afternoon. The large white board covered with equations takes up most of the last wall, and on the door, to the other side of the board, is a Boris Vallejo poster of a hulk male with muscles instead of clothes and a warrior woman with a fantasy body. She manages to have even fewer garments than the man does. Several plants, smaller living versions of those on the patio, struggle to do their thing in large pots either side of the door; each has a faded yellow sticker reading: *Feed me!* It is a room that estate agents might describe as having possibilities.

And in the middle of this room, moved from its normal position under the front windows, is a worn seventies leather and chrome chaise longue with an additional, and fearsome-looking, headrest.

Surrounding the chaise longue, on the exact points of a notional pentagon, are five sentinels – football-sized spheres, constructed of thirty-four interlocking triangular miniature loudspeakers, encased with a fine copper mesh – each on a two-foot-high tripod. Multiway electric data cables, daisy-chained together, connect each box to another, and all the units are emitting a low hum. It's the sort of oscillation that high-voltage power cables emit, but there is also a slow, underlying, resonant beat that they produce in sympathy with each other; and that's something that would not be heard from high-voltage cables. The multiway runs off to a skirting board and, after disappearing behind the shelves loaded with books, finally connects this system to the PC.

This, then, is Odysseus.

On the chaise longue itself, in direct contrast to the techno-logically brushed-metal finish and polish, is a red cotton bean-bag with cross-stitched Greek figures, and next to that is a turquoise-coloured, gold-banded fountain pen.

Serena bends down to the units in turn and flicks a chrome lever switch on each. It gives her something to do: she is putting off the inevitable. The resonant beat alters – rapid, and then slower – as the hum from each box ceases to contribute, and the low noise stops with the last switch flicked. Now there is only the murmur of Cambridge from the open windows.

She picks up the fountain pen, taps it against her teeth and closes her eyes. She thinks of her hero Odysseus and his ten-year voyage home after his defeat of Troy using the Trojan Horse. He was a long-suffering traveller whose adventures with all manner of fantastic beasts and mythical people was caused after a disagreement with the god called Poseidon. There was also Odysseus' enduring love of his wife – that was something else to consider. The romance seems so appropriate. She then thinks about the strange voyage that she has just experienced. Her body jolts at the memory.

As a harbinger of what was about to happen, it felt completely wrong. The ocean was calm (a slow, rise-and-fall of Pacific swell the only indication of movement), while, above the waiting hordes of assault craft, the isolated clouds looked thin and transparent. The surrounding colours were too close to her expectations of tropical paradise to suggest that anything could disturb the peace there. Vibrant Prussian blue indicated the deeper ocean, while near the shore of the island, the coral lying only feet below the surface caused the sea to shimmer with an abalone mother-of-pearl. The sky was cobalt. The blues of the ocean and sky met at the horizon as a sharp line, and the sun now rose fast above it. It was raising the temperature the higher it climbed.

Even this early in the day, there was too much warmth, and there seemed nowhere for anyone to escape the heat – or the experience of this calm disappearing. At a preordained time, loud noise shattered and annihilated it. In the sky, thick, new clouds were spontaneously forming. The navy had opened fire.

Inside their yawing landing vehicle, which seemed to be either an amphibious tractor or a tank to Serena's view, the huddle of marines tensed as they rode the Pacific swell in towards the island. The bow wave washed over the sides, the rotating tracks churned the water underneath into froth, and the men themselves watched intently as the shelling from the destroyers began to move up across the beaches and into the jungle beyond. Above them, the air was ripped apart with gunfire from the large guns on the supporting ships. The sheer cacophony made Serena want to shrink into a ball and wrap her arms around her head. Planes screeched, rushed in from the horizon, and strafed and dropped their bombs. The unfettered diesel exhausts of the floating tractors belched and coughed as the pilots increased their vehicles to full speed. The violence of noise around the craft was tremendous. Only the men remained quiet. The beach was fast approaching.

The man through whose senses Serena had experienced all this for less than a quarter of an hour, hiked his gun over his shoulder and adjusted the position of his camera, as he tried to catch a photograph each time another round hurtled overhead from a destroyer. To Serena, it seemed the naval guns from each ship were going berserk. Multitudes of shock waves constantly punched through the air. Men threw up; one man – no, a boy, even Serena could see that – had wet himself. A sergeant had laid his hand on the boy's shoulder. Serena thought the sergeant didn't look much older than the marine he was giving support to. She could not understand how most of the marines remained so calm.

Didn't they have any *conception of what was about to happen?*

Serena didn't think that it was anything like the Hollywood ethos of John Wayne. It wasn't even like the realism depicted in *Saving Private Ryan*. Spielberg may have got it about right in the eyes of the men who were there during the invasion of Normandy, but this attack on Guam was no film – it was *happening*, and she was *there*. And the thing that amazed her, the thing she could not work out, was how *anyone* could have been persuaded to take such a personal risk. She had already delved into the history of the man she had been "travelling" within, and there had been no indication that such a creative mind could have ignored what he must have imagined beforehand. Yet there he was – doing his duty. It was crazy. Where did he keep his fear bottled up?

Again the planes dived down from the heavens, and guns from the enemy on the beach returned fire. The lead plane exploded, its fiery pieces carrying on, splashing into the surf and crashing into the palm trees. There was nowhere safe to look. She couldn't avoid the utter carnage unfolding. Several vehicles, identical to their own, were now on fire. Floating infernos, they were still moving forward, men trying to climb out of them. The craft beside the one she rode in took a direct hit. She watched men disintegrate. One moment they had been living, thinking about what they were trained to do, thinking about their loved ones, feeling their hearts pound within their chests ... then they were no more. This was no Hollywood invention, no potential special-effects Oscar candidate. The marines left in the flaming vehicles were screaming.

A bullet slapped the side of the photographer's helmet and Serena was aware he was stunned into unconsciousness for a moment. Staggering, he gripped the side of the vehicle.

Serena finally found her voice.

This is impossible. No one can survive this!

Then the landing vehicle thrashed itself onto the beach.

They're going to die.

The men jumped ashore.

No. No. Stop. Please stop! Serena shouted out in terror.

The photographer stopped, paused, looked around.

Boom!

Shrapnel and weapon fire ricocheted and erupted into the place the man would have reached if he had not stopped. He would certainly have been killed – she was sure of that. So, it appeared to her, was he.

Serena stopped remembering.

Too late.

The smell. The sights. Then a sudden thirty or forty seconds of her incoherent jabbering to him about Hercules and about how much he reminded her of that ancient legend. Just at a moment when he needed all his faculties, too. And because, at that moment, she felt a sudden need to keep him alive. She thought of him as a total hero. If he died there'd be no point in heroes anymore – and then who would save the world?

God to hell, I hope I didn't influence him. Have I done something back then to alter the present? Oh, dear God, what have I done? How can I correct it?

Serena shivers, closes her eyes for a moment. She tries to ignore the tinnitus in her ears. But out of her memories comes an adrenaline rush. The excitement of what she has just accomplished, what she has *done*, hits her again. She emits a little squeak and, for no reason that she can think of, jogs on the spot. At speed. The desire to be reckless, first to show she is *alive*, makes her toss her head back and yell. She *has* to do something to express her excitement. She has invented something *amazing*.

She runs to a street-facing window, thrusts her head outside, and shouts, "Eureka!"

The students outside pause in their celebrations and then cheer, causing the sparrows to scatter.

Serena laughs. *It's so good to be alive.*

Half a mile away, in a small upstairs boxroom, the young man takes another photograph. He is still new to the job, wanting to make a good impression with his superiors. The removal of the one old and rotten oak from the park, by an MI5 team disguised as council workmen, has provided clear visual access to Professor Serena Freeman's study. He turns down the volume of the microphone hidden in her room as she shouts her joy again and again. The young man, not much older than Serena herself, has been watching and listening to everything occurring in the room over the last four hours, and he now bites his lower lip. Someone, somewhere in F-7 is going to be interested in what he has to report. This either signifies a breakthrough or a breakdown.

As he contemplates her pirouetting around her room, the young man remembers his brief, and bends back to sweep the telephoto lens over her wallboard. He notes what Serena has written on it: The Mathematics of Time. As he squints through the lens, he wonders if the concept behind those words somehow prompted the murder of a toy. Then he notices that Serena has stood back from the board and is now rubbing her nipples. Her secret spy instantly becomes voyeur, and he smiles to himself. The young man hopes he will be ordered to continue with this operation, and then ponders the magnitude of interest that will be unleashed when he makes his report. And he wonders if she realizes the danger.

TWO

"Jeez, that pisses me," Corporal Joe Plotkin says, glancing across at me. And he's hardly started to frown before the middle of his face contracts towards a bloody point, his helmet flips off with a metallic twang, and the back of his head explodes.

Th-zip!

Another bullet passes close to me.

Th-zip!

And another.

I instinctively shut my eyes and feel bits of Joe peppering my face. I don't dare consider what it is of him that I have to brush from my lips.

Love the ground.

I say it to the sky.

Love the ground.

I lie on my back, clutching my carbine to my chest.

Love *the ground.*

Th-zip! Th-zip!

Thwack!

A bullet hits something, or someone.

"Ahh! Corpsman! Corpsman!"

Over to my right Rifleman Frank Weinberg yelps, and cries out for a medic. Medic? This early in the landing? They'd have to be nuts to attempt to come in under this onslaught, particularly since the Enemy is specially trained to pick them out. The corpsmen can wait – especially for that bastard Frank. I wipe my lips again and hope that the bad taste in my mouth is to do with my current thoughts about Frank and nothing to do with Joe.

Pock! Pock!

More mortars coming in.

Whoo-bang! Whoo-bang!

They explode.

Close to me.

I grit my teeth. The Enemy is trying to get *me*.

The coral tearing at my back bites harder – and harder. Maybe it's because I'm trying to squirm into the depths of it. All this sand everywhere and I find a bit of coral. But I'm carrying too much equipment on my back. I try to pull some of it around to my sides so I can duck lower.

Love the ground, Nix. Love the ground.

I utter the Prayer:

Make it quick, if it's gonna happen, make it quick.

Oh, God, give me a decent foxhole, give me sanctuary.

I'll settle for six inches. Five? Four?

Oh, God, who do you have to screw around here for a hole to hide in?

I laugh to myself. It helps.

I remember to breathe. It also helps.

I open my eyes and look to my left. That *doesn't* help. It's another unbelievable sight to add to the catalogue of terrible memories I've accumulated in the last three minutes. With a reflex I'm getting used to again, I roll over onto my stomach, loosen the lens cap of my camera with a swift twist, wriggle into a suitable position, and take a photograph of Joe Plotkin. *Click.* Ugly immortality. No myth today. I lower my camera and stare for a long moment at what I've just photographed. Joe's still kneeling, his hands clutching the bodies of the other dead marines he'd pulled in front of himself to serve as a last-ditch barricade. He could almost be praying. Except he has no back to his head.

What an image. Though they'll never print it.

Th-zip! Th-zip!

More bullets.

I duck again.

Pock! Pock!

More mortars.

Frank shouts again. I look across at him. It would appear from the bloodstains as though he's been hit in the leg and shoulder. I even find myself hoping it hurts.

Whoo-bang! Whoo-bang!

The mortars whistle in and go off a few yards either side of me. I'm getting distracted – it's a lovely sensation. So peaceful.

Does it hurt, you bastard?

Rifleman Frank Chickenshit Weinberg was a seventeen-year-old Texan salesman before Dec '41 – somehow selling contraceptives and razors to barbers, traveling on a regular route around all those small towns that get missed on decent maps. His sales pitch must have been something special, or else those barbers were desperate. Frank's made up of the bits that God decided were rejects on other, more deserving folks: His body is Houston Cowboy big, but it supports a head that is child-sized. His hair is oddly streaked, like a raccoon's, and his boy's face is as conical as a ferret's – must have been caused by his Klan hood slipping forward and his face then just grew up into it. It was repugnant to listen to him describing what he wanted to do to any young black girl if he ever had the chance, before he wised up enough to keep his mouth shut around me. I've also seen him bullying the replacements, making out to be the big veteran. The chickenshit! He let four good men die at Torokina on Bougainville when he said he'd give suppressing fire – and didn't. Just kept his child-like head down instead. It's a surprise we didn't throw him to the sharks during the bloody long wait to come ashore here. We just couldn't prove it.

"Corpsman!" he calls.

I know they'll probably be too late if I leave it to them –

he'd let himself bleed to death meanwhile. I'm tempted, though, for a moment. I may be a combat correspondent for a newspaper, but the leatherneck ethos has now got under my skin – I consider myself a marine. I wriggle towards him – *love the ground, love the ground* – then reach across and grab a handful of collar. I yank him down the slope.

"Nix!" he croaks. "Thank you, thank you."

I rip open the bloodied remains of his trousers around the wound, realize he's carrying a corpsman's Unit 3 – *where did he steal that from?* – and I rummage around through the bandages, safety pins and drugs, then break open the kit I was searching for, sprinkle some sulfa on the ripped flesh and press a gauze dressing to it. I get Frank himself to apply pressure. He can do that at least to help himself. This wound isn't that bad, surprise, surprise, and the one on his shoulder only looks like a nick. He's smiling now. I reach into his top pocket and remove his five poker cards. He has a Joker – that's useful – the Ten of Spades, the Nine of Clubs, the Five of Diamonds and the Three of Hearts. He starts to protest, then stops. He must have seen the expression on my face.

"That's okay, Nix, you take them. You take them. I've got my million-dollar wound."

I want to remind him that *that* would entail losing a limb, but I settle for telling him that he isn't out of the woods yet. It gives me a small twinge of guilt as he falls silent and his eyes grow wide again. Then I remember what this little piece of caustic filth had in mind with that black girl back home, and I let him wallow in his fear. I also take the morphine jabs from the bag – a better marine than him will need them.

How the hell did he get into this unit? He has no esprit de corps, and Chickenshit Frank should have been transferred out a long time ago.

Th-zip! Th-zip!

Th-zip!

Jesus! That one was close!

Thwack!

Another bullet tears into the remains of Joe, and this time sprays something over Frank. He cries out, squeaks more thanks in my direction, then scrabbles back down the beach.

Thwack! Thwack!

What a mess. This particular Enemy must be using dumdums.

Shit.

There's no respect anymore.

Then again, perhaps that doesn't apply here?

So say hello to my bit of hell: Guam, July 21st, the year of our Lord, nineteen hundred and forty-four.

My ancient homeland.

Where the ghosts roam.

It's crazy, it's crazy.

I hadn't even got off the LVT Alligator and one was already whispering in my ear: a soft female voice that seemed shocked at what I was doing. Father would be happy to be proved right after all these years – his daydreaming son has gone cuckoo. But what does he know? And who *was* that lady? And where's she gone now that I need her comfort? Has she sunk back into the coral, or is she hiding amongst the palms? They are so fickle these phantoms of horror, and so transitory. Her ghost was a solid presence in my mind for a few tantalizing seconds and now has melted, suddenly, away. Doesn't she care? I'm here to see the Enemy being beaten . . . and she leaves me with one of my heroes: Hercules?

She has provoked too many questions. Are they real, ghosts? Or have they always been whispers of memory that invade the brain? And this one, has it faded back into the surroundings that it may call home? Because that is where the ghosts hide. I know, since my grandfather told me, much to my father's displeasure.

Th-zip!

Oh, it's so good to forget what's happening.

Pock! Pock!

I've got to stop this Enemy. I've got to throw them all off this island.

Whoo-bang! Whoo-bang!

My grandfather – one of those frontiersmen who are bears in human form – was Chamorro. He came to America from Guam at the end of the last century and stayed. Spain and America had been at war for two months when the *USS Charleston* sailed into port here. My grandfather was one of the cheerfully unaware welcoming party sent by the Spanish governor to bid hello to the warship. After hearing what was happening between the two countries, my grandfather jumped ship on the principle that he loved adventure, and on the trip back to America entertained the captain and ship's officers with glorious tall stories to earn his passage. At least, that's what he told me later. My desire to tell myths and truth must come from him. He used to love to tell those stories that he'd made up.

And old ones about Guam – where memories are ones of peace.

The folklore.

Long, long ago, he'd always start, fingering his red and white Cowry shell bracelet, in that slow, slow way he had, *Guam was an island in the Pacific inhabited by a multitude of gods.* His voice would lower and I'd have to lean closer to hear all the words of any story he told. This was a time, he continued, well before the one god of the Spanish; this was before religion was even *called* religion. And one day, in this long, long ago, the Chamorro – the native people – came to the conclusion that Guam would be a better place if they were to purge their land of the interfering deities. They asked themselves a simple question: *Who needs gods? They make too many demands. We don't need them,* they said. Oh, the follies of the Chamorro people then. Had they forgotten what the gods had given them? Couldn't they see that they were blessed? Guam was clearly overrun with idiots.

My grandfather smiled and continued.

Amongst all these ungrateful people though, there lived a girl whose name was Veronica, young, carefree, but wise for her years. She could not see the sense in what the other people had now planned, as she had kept a faith in the gods' powerful magic. And also because she wanted them to favor her. Yes, she was young, carefree *and* wise, in the way that the cautious are wise – Veronica always covered her bets. Of course, the gods soon heard of the plan, they *were* gods after all, but they also heard the warnings Veronica gave to her elders. This was the only pleasure they took from a situation that made the gods more angry than they had ever been. Therefore, when the gods made their minds up to rid Guam of its people, and to start again, they decided to spare only Veronica. So, in the hours before the gods began their terrible purge, they constructed a beautiful bridge, one made up of many colors, for Veronica to use to escape what they had planned for the other inhabitants. The gods warned her what she had to do, and when.

At the appropriate time, Veronica climbed up its slope and she escaped the violence and death that the gods unleashed on the elders and all the other Chamorro people. And she learnt a lesson that day; all myths being stories with a message. She had avoided the vengeance of the gods and she was wiser for it.

Veronica left a legacy for all the people that came after her. Even today, you can sometimes see the bridge that she climbed to safety upon. It has a beautiful name: the rainbow.

All myths are stories with a message; that's what my grandfather said to me – all myths are messages.

I kind of like that. And the fact that the one I've just remembered was about keeping faith. Keeping faith and keeping your options open. Like I must do now.

Remembering this story relaxes me for a moment, as I sneak a quick, distracting look at the rainbow spray the other LVTs (Landing Vehicles, Tracked – thank god for Marine nomenclature) are currently splashing into the air.

This is the sort of story that my grandfather instilled in me as a child – and which I use to offer explanations in my reports to my paper.

Keep the faith, keep the faith.

I have followed this same group of men from boot camp, all the way to their war in my grandfather's homeland, for the edification of the public. That's what my editor told me I had to do – to illuminate the readers with words and pictures.

And I also get to help these men as they pursue their war.

I get to invent my own good luck.

I had let the shell bracelet I inherited from my grandfather hang around my neck with my taped-up tags for a while, until someone pointed out the contradiction. Muffling my identification tags from making a noise – which might alert the Enemy in dense jungle – would be a waste of time if I let the shells tinkle instead. So I now keep the bracelet in a leather pouch, wrapped in a cloth. Like I safely keep the stories in my head.

Th-zip!

Damn!

Pock! Pock! Pock!

I squirm lower.

Whoo-bang! Whoo-bang! Whoo-bang!

"Jeez, that pisses me." What did Joe mean? Why was he annoyed? That wasn't like him.

Corporal Joseph Plotkin was a tough young man of nineteen, and one of the few marines I knew who did his job without ever making a gripe. He had that same appearance and smile that Sinatra has – a calm cockiness – and I'd personally seen Joe hold off three of the Enemy at Bougainville with textbook hand-to-hand brutality and technique, until I could get my weapon trained on the last one – the one that had nearly got him beat. He had come from Carthage, Missouri, where he'd been training to be an engineer, and he had approached the war with the same determination that had got him top grades at college. You couldn't fault his skill at being a marine; it was just his luck that had run out. Rifleman Frank Weinberg lives and Corporal Joe Plotkin dies. The opposition doesn't care, of course. The Enemy up ahead of me carries on firing bullets that fly close to my head.

Th-zip! Th-zip!

Haven't these assholes heard of the Geneva Convention? There are rules, and you can't just go around killing the opposition any way that you feel like. War has its guidelines: that's what the Boys of the squad I have been following were told. I was there. I took notes. I snitched smokes – Lucky Strikes. I swapped yarns. I thought everyone knew. Apparently someone forgot to tell the Enemy. This war in the Pacific is different from that in Europe; it has the sort of difference that Frank must have forgotten when he stole that corpsman's bag: the Enemy targets medics because they realize that marines will take extra risks to save them. That's the sort of mentality we're up against, so we have to issue *our* corpsmen with a sidearm.

What did Joe mean?

I'll have to look.

Th-zip!

Yet another bullet rings past my ear. It may have nicked me, as I don't know if the blood dripping down my chin is Joe's or mine.

What did he see?

Form the picture, Nix. Form the picture, concentrate. This Enemy may be useful. A Nemean Lion?

Joe and I were together as we hit the beach. Splashing out of that LVT, rushing to gain cover, we were seeing the same things, so I know I myself must have seen what Joe was checking. I must have a mental picture, a subconscious image, and the answer's there somewhere. I obviously saw it all before I hit the ground. Why did Joe feel the need to sneak a peek?

Huh!

Sneaking a peek? I remember how important it was for me to look at the ancient homeland on that mad recon trip. To get some perspective on the situation, I assured myself. Some peek. Some perspective.

I pestered the Brass (using the influence my newspaper

could give), because I wanted to *see* my grandfather's homeland. For years, I had had a problem even pointing to Guam on a map, but I did feel that in some way I was coming home. I may be a Yank but, then, a large number of Uncle Sam's forebears sailed over in some boat or the other. It's sometimes nice to see which port they waved goodbye to. I saw mine first by air, under fire.

The first sweep was at several thousand feet. We were in a B-24 Liberator, an F-7 conversion job for long range photo-reconnaissance, with a plethora of cameras in the bomb bay. I had been told that the heavy additions gave the planes a tendency to break their nose wheel fixings and collapse – hence they were reassuringly referred to as Flying Dumbos by the 20th. That cheered me. I was, of course, superfluous. The pilot, J.J. Jnr from Pekin, Illinois, at twenty years young, knew exactly what he was doing and considered me extra weight. Extra marine weight at that. (The USAF men on the base were fiercely loyal to their own correspondents and could only see as far as the uniform I wore. A toad where a bird should sit, he'd said. His crew agreed.)

I snarled silently at them all. They didn't understand the significance of Guam to me, or what I felt I had to do.

They continued smiling as, one after the other on that long flight, they told me stories of their gung-ho Captain and the surprising number of crashes he'd survived. He gave me the notion – in looks and actions – of him being a disgruntled cherub drunk on some mad juice. I swear the man cackled when he announced we were nearing the target. Somehow, or so it seemed to me, J.J. Jnr from Pekin, Illinois, managed to pause his plane in flight on that first pass, just to give the Enemy an extra long look at his machine with its lithe wings, its stubby body, its excessive weight. To give them time to adjust their AA sights and fire a few experimental rounds that he could laugh off.

"You sad sons of bitches! Can't you shoot?"

J.J. Jnr from Pekin, Illinois, kept that plane straight and level and high and, even though we were inside, I thought he let the wind blow his words back to me rather than use the intercom.

"Goddam Brass! Goddam marines!"

It didn't seem to matter that I was from the *New York Picture Post* – I was dressed in the uniform of the marines, so I'd have to put up with the jokes.

Pop-pop-pop went the guns below.

I couldn't actually hear them. It may have just been the blood in my ears.

I hate flying.

My first sight of the old country was a bit unsettling from the air. Guam looked like a giant: a giant distorted green footprint surrounded by blue. Two hundred odd luxuriant square miles of myth and legend, running from the southern plateau of the heel (covered, my grandfather said, by scrub forest, bunch and sword grass), thirty miles on up north to some other mountains – the sight of them causing a tingle to shiver through me. There were lots of Enemy down there, I realized. I wanted to jump down there among them, with my carbine at the ready and a dagger clasped in my teeth. I didn't tell the crew this fantasy – they'd had enough jokes at my expense concerning my ancestral feelings. And my appearance.

In most people's eyes, when a grown man of twenty-six stands five ten in his socks, has the build of a grizzly bear, a thick bull jaw and a linebacker's forehead, he isn't supposed to have any intellectual thoughts beyond Neanderthal. It's supposed that I could not be burdened with verbal dexterity, that I could not have any concerns with the philosophical. People blinded by that sort of misconception tend to congregate in bars drinking strong liquor – like I do – and are forever picking fights with me. It gets worse when they discover my wealthy background.

Pop was actually born a Yank. In honor of becoming a US citizen, grandpa changed his surname to his French wife's maiden one of Lafayette and dutifully set about the task of producing little Americans. My father had therefore been born

American and didn't want anything at all to do with where his ancestors came from. He wanted to embrace the American Dream differently to his own father's approach: he left his childhood behind and went into adulthood with laughs, drinks, and enjoyment at all costs. J.J. Jnr from Pekin, Illinois, may have carried the air of an annoyed cherub, but my Pa did it bigger and uglier, and twenty years earlier.

My father made his fortune after the Great War and got married and was producing offspring (me) before the first Armistice. I don't know if it was the drink, my grandfather, or the sheer delight in making a statement about hope reborn, but I was christened Phoenix.

Pop, though, had a lust for money. In the space of five years he had become somewhat of a press baron – not as big as Randolph Hearst, but he moved in the same circles. It was during this time that my sister Alice was born and, as if to celebrate that event, he began a hobby of playing the stock market. It turned into a career and I was given long explanations of forecasts and techniques – even as a child – which I can still remember. Even at the craziest height of the speculation, he showed his skill by getting out before the crash. He did have a certain touch, a *style*. He had become his own man, something different from what his father had envisaged.

Grandpa had always been on at him to reinvest something back into the country by way of a company that *produced* something. The logic aired on both sides would leave me gasping. I myself was left with a curious fallout: I was a rich kid whose hero was an old man who told stories, but whose own father never seemed to be there at the important moments.

Is that a rich kid's moan? Sure seemed like I was the only one like that when I was a child. Alice seemed to cope – indeed, she flourished. She could do no wrong in my father's eyes. But me? Where, as a boy, do you get your confidence from, if not from your father? It was Grandpa who took me out for long hikes in the country and who taught me the craft of living off the land. I sometimes got the feeling that Pop was kind of envious of it all. Go figure: he could have joined us. Whether it was that that eventually made him send me away to boarding school, I don't know, but Grandpa's lessons were something that couldn't be taken from me – more so when I went to Yale. I became the son he felt he'd lost somehow.

In September '39 I decided to prepare. I thought, if we were going to get into something, it would be sensible to get myself associated with the best. There had to be some part of the services that I could excel in. I had no idea what I was getting into when I saw that poster for the marines. Something that would give me answers? At the time I didn't realize what I would have to do to find them.

When my father heard of my plan, he promptly proposed a different one – he could get me a job as a journalist at one of the papers he still held controlling shares in. I think his intention was to keep me away from trouble. I perceived this as manna from heaven, took the job, got qualified, left the paper to remove myself – and the editor – from my father's interference, and signed on as a war correspondent for a less prestigious publication. I persuaded them I had this great angle of following a group of young soldiers from induction onwards. They jumped at the chance, so I still ended up with the marines.

At the end of that first pass over Guam we banked in a long swoop, and then we came back in again, lower – much lower. I felt even more like jumping out to take the bastards on.

The northern plateau looked an insane place to launch an attack. It was thick with tropical rainforest, and the glimpses I caught of the few gaps in-between showed a matrix of vines and twisted undergrowth. I could imagine trying to hack a way through them, and how hard it would be, even with good weather. I did ponder if any of the Brass had even considered the weather in this part of the Pacific – from July to November you can expect the clouds to open up for some time during the course of every single day. That pushes the humidity up, and makes the heat worse. Our uniforms would turn to mould if we landed in the north – just as they did at Bougainville.

But I had to agree that the beaches on that part of Guam seemed to offer the best approach to the island. As we flew further south over the western ridge – with another tingle – the crew gave up joking and let me look in peace at the places where I suspected the 3rd Marines might land. Asan Point? I couldn't wait. As I gazed down at the unbroken coral, the colors diluted into underwater Veronica rainbows, I wondered how I'd feel once I'd crossed them and made land.

I now wish I hadn't gone on that reconnaissance trip – being on that plane caused me to think too much about God and death.

Pock! Pock!

Here they come again!

Th-zip! Th-zip!

Whoo-bang! Whoo-bang!

It'll be best if I give in to my terror.

It'll be okay, surely. The Boys know I'm The-Great-Writer-In-Residence, they're the professionals. Uncle Sam pays them to do this job. I can leave it all to them, and they'll let me tell the story.

Pock!

Ba-ba-ba-ba-ba!

Ba-ba-ba-ba-ba!

A Browning Automatic adds its cry. Someone's getting organized and is responding to the mortars.

Whoo-bang!

The mortar lands nearby.

Ba-ba-ba!

Yes, I'll leave it to the Boys.

Leave them to make the push forward.

Who the hell could have predicted the Enemy would work out where and when we'd land?

Ha, ha, ha.

I find sarcasm helps sometimes.

They must have hidden in tunnels, caves, somewhere safe, as we hurled in destruction from the ships. It didn't seem as if they wasted a single second, not even a heartbeat, before they swarmed out of the rice grass, the hideouts, the palm trees, as soon as the barrage was lifted from the beaches. And just in time to get their guns in place again. Their guess as to where we were going to make our landing must have had something to do with the fact that we've been pounding exactly the same locations for the last month. Spoiled the surprise element somewhat, I think.

Yes, leave the Boys to it.

Well, not Weinberg, now. He's out for the count in this fight and he's heading straight for a corpsman as soon as one is fool enough to come get him. Nor will Joe Plotkin be helping – *he* may have had the stomach, but he's got no head.

Did I just think that?

And Corporal Robert Bitten, our man trained with the backpack flame-thrower? Dead – just there. One of the many bodies in front of Joe. Never had a chance to get inland and don his tanks that are, I suppose, still in the LVT. No more listening to New Orleans blues when we're bored and need a lift. Awarded a Bronze Star at Bougainville, and now he'll get a Purple Heart for his grave. He was only nineteen, and I'm the Old Man at twenty-six. He looked up to me, like the rest of the Boys. He'd even have made a tune for that – he'd make up a tune for anything. At least he's at peace now, and doesn't have to live with this fear that we all face, this gut-sweat of a gamble about whether we're going to get through the hour, let alone the day. Damn, I've just realized, two of the three Fire Teams of our squad are now missing their corporals – combat hardened men – in the space of minutes.

Whistle – crash!

Fuck! That shell was close!

Least it's not me. It's all about odds, all about luck. There's no skill to being a dead hero. Just stand up and charge at the enemy anytime.

Is that what I'm going to do?

I'll take Joe and Bob's poker cards when I have the chance. They won't need them now. I stare back at the other guys squirming on the beach behind me. Who's next to take a spin on the old roulette wheel?

Sergeant Alfonso "Rici" Federici is locking his eyes with mine. Rici's a king-rat second-generation Italian from New York – one of those short-fuse rockets that you light on July 4th. With his deadpan expression, he could pass for Buster Keaton after a year of calisthenics and body-building. His sister sent me an old newspaper photo of him, taken when he'd won a poetry competition at high school.

"What's funny then, Nix?" he had asked me, as we sat in the mess hall, me choking on a mouthful of food.

"You know that film *The General*, that Buster Keaton made? The one with him driving a train in the Civil War?"

Rici cocked his head to one side and put his fork down. I'd made a reference to Buster before.

"Yes," he said – just as the man himself would have said, if his films had sound.

"Remember that photo of him his girl has? Taken when he's sitting in front of his engine? Remember the total lack of expression on his face?"

I passed Rici the clipping. I swear he damn near mirrored Keaton again, as he looked back at me from across the trestle table. But my camera was out of reach.

"Nice of your sister," I continued, "don't you think? Rather sweet."

Rici had left me under no illusions as to what he'd do to me, courtesy Lieutenant officer or not, if I ever made that clipping public. Or if I ever attempted to date his sister. And I believe that at that moment he meant it, since the anger in his eyes was fearsome. Only the next second and he was laughing at himself. But that's Rici – burn bright, burn high, burn that temper away. He had made Sergeant within a week of starting his training. We're pod-peas, him and I: the pair of us are brawn with brains – we could run a country. He's the Squad Sergeant and I'm assigned to his Fire Team. And I like him. We're buddies.

Ba-ba-ba!

Ba-ba-ba-ba-ba!

His eyes jerk left and right. I follow his gaze. Rici wants me to notice something.

What I see is the Boys.

Which one of them does Rici want me to pay attention to?

Or does he mean all of them?

I look, harder.

Rifleman Henry "Hank" Springsteen from Monterey, California – a jack-in-the-box starved for a month and then fed only coffee. Twenty, the face of an angel, piercing ice-blue eyes, and the most perfect white teeth I've ever seen. He quivers in his sleep.

Ba-ba-ba-ba-ba!

Ba-ba-ba-ba-ba!

So that's who's got it together.

Hank's closest friend, Automatic Rifleman Jim Landu, lies beside him, with his Browning Automatic Rifle – his BAR – at the ready, eye down the sight. Hank's Assistant Rifleman to Jim. Jim's a calm seventeen-year-old kid from Utah (he lied about his age), who once had curly ginger hair. He shaved it all off prior to our first landing, where he then demonstrated that he could kill better than most. No one in the squad called him a kid after that. Jim and Hank have a dangerous hidden completeness about them – two young men doing their job without much complaint.

Th-zip!

Thwack! Thwack!

Joe's body is being ripped apart.

Apart from the four guys Chickenshit Frank let get it, we lost the rest of the original guys due to a worm infection at the other island jump we made. The rest of the men in the squad are replacements. Van Zandt – Johnny – comes from Tampa in

Florida. He's the BAR man in the Fire Team that Joe headed. Known as Vizi, he, like Hank, is twenty years old. He's the boy you'd always pick last in the team at High, and is the one who'd end up winning the game in the ninth. Vizi did something in construction: one of those sky-walking mad-monkeys that bolts together the steel girders twenty-five storeys high. He says he's engaged to five women.

Riflemen Ron Clemons, Barney Tallent and Assistant Rifleman Bill Scott all come from Cincinnati. The odds are so remote, the rest of us kid them that they knew each other as boys and wanted to hold hands to get themselves through the war. They are all under twenty. We call them Chico, Harpo and Groucho when they're together. We demand autographs when we're bored.

The last of the Boys in the ragged line on the beach is the New Mexican, Automatic Rifleman Amos Clearmountain. The Chief denies his ancestors were even Indian – let alone at Little Bighorn. No one believes him. Amos is twenty-two and used to punch cows. He found the irony of being an Indian cowboy great fun.

That was the sum total of the Boys before we landed.

Rici and I are running one Fire Team (and the squad), with Amos on the BAR and Frank as his assistant. Joe was running the second Fire Team, with Johnny "Vizi" as BAR, Bill "Groucho" as Assistant and Ron "Chico" as Rifleman; and Bob – flame-thrower trained – had been in charge of BAR Jim, Assistant Henry "Hank" and Rifleman Barney "Harpo". We packed a punch. The Boys, I called them in my reports to the *New York Picture Post* back home.

And here we all are, those of us still alive, wondering if we're even going to get off this beach, let alone worry about the *banzai*.

The *banzai* is the most interesting defense technique the Enemy has yet devised. It's anything but a co-ordinated plan. The ideals of Bushido as I once read about them, now corrupted by their High Command, are alive and well and firing at us. *No surrender! Love the battle!* That's Bushido as the Enemy sees it today – nothing like it was meant to be. Send the troops off to their noble deaths and hope they take a few of us with them. It's a sight to see them, full of *saki*, rushing straight at you, yelling, shouting, firing, screaming, slashing with those long bloody swords and bayonets, man to man. Talk about fear. It's something to look forward to, for this squad. And the other two squads that make up our platoon. And the company. And the division.

Too much, Nix. Think small. Think: this moment – not the future.

I get a carbine with my camera and notebook. That and grenades, Colt 45, hunting knife, machete, bandoleer and belt with magazines, entrenching tool and at least a dozen other things to help me kill other people, help me stay alive and help me report the war.

Where am I?

Rici is still looking at me. I know what he's thinking.

Pock! Pock!

We must move, mustn't get stalled. We must get off the beach. It's the Boys' best chance – we must keep moving. Rici's thinking about *all* the Boys.

Pock! Th-zip! Th-zip!

I decide that it will be best if I just lie here and wait, let the war pass me by. I've done my five minutes' worth here, so let some other person do what has to be done. Let me go home and win fabulous prizes for my writing, and appear on the cover page of *Life*. I can write about the legends of my grandfather's island, and put it all into wondrous context with the way the whole world's developing. Oh shit, I'll settle for God just letting me get to find that girl that I'm going to marry.

Let me live!

I jump up and run screaming at the cluster of palm trees. There's something about this particular Enemy that makes my charge worth it. It's only about twenty yards, but the bastard has taken two of the Boys and about five other marines already.

I do the cross-step shuffle – just as coach Baker taught me at Yale.

Give me a touchdown, God, and let me get out of here!

Th-zip!

Zing!

Another nick: my left thigh. I can't believe I'm doing this. Then finally I see what Joe had noticed before he died.

What a nerve indeed.

This Enemy is sitting cross-legged at the entrance to a small bunker made of logs and palm leaves, a cigarette in one side of his mouth, with no protection from the invading hordes except for the jaunty way he has his cap planted lopsided over his forehead.

His cap. That's it. That's my Nemean lion's mane!

He's looking at me, with a stiff smile. He's so surprised at my move, so stunned at my high-step college duck and dive and lunge and twist, that he's fumbling uncertainly with his next magazine.

Touchdown. The cheerleaders scream, the crowds yell. Rockets are fired.

Someone barges past me.

This Enemy adds to that strange din of men screaming, that's been echoing as an undercurrent to all the bangs and thuds, as Sergeant Alfonso "Rici" Federici, my close buddy, lunges his bayonet right into this Enemy's face. I seem to find time to notice that his cigarette isn't lit. I scream along with him and recognize that Rici is making sure of the job with a couple of extra ripping bayonet swipes, though that first blow must surely have killed this Enemy.

I let my heart start again and I take a breath.

So does this Enemy. He shouts something visceral and accuses me with his remaining eye.

Shit.

Rici gives it to him in the face again – and again. One for all our friends. There's been a lot of them taken down since we hit the beaches.

God bless America.

The Enemy waves his arms about as his hands reach for the bayonet.

Rici kicks them away. He drives his bayonet into The Enemy's chest. He pulls it out and repeats his actions.

I see a sign nailed on a nearby tree as I turn away from Rici's fevered work. It's beautifully distracting: "Welcome, Marines! USO that way." Clearly a joke from a UDT – the Navy's Underwater Demolition Team – left there during the previous week of breaking holes through the coral for our landing.

Rici has really got a rhythm going. I can hear it. Above the bangs. Above the roar. Above the gentle swish of the surf.

Yes, I think, welcome indeed.

Touchdown. Touchdown. Touchdown.

Glory be.

I touch Rici's shoulder, deciding to pull my temporary Lieutenant's rank.

"I think he's dead, Rici."

He looks down at his creation. Then he nods, grunts, and moves on.

One down, God knows how many more thousand to go.

Men are still screaming their strange song.

God, let me live. Please.

I pull the bloody cap from the shattered mass of head, as a souvenir. I'm still thinking about Hercules. That female voice that scared me shitless in the LVT, as we came in, she mentioned the Greeks. That was a lovely girl's voice, one I'll dare not tell the other men about. Is it my turn to find my breaking point? Hercules. His twelve tasks. Is that my way to get through this? Pretend to be a legend? I wonder why I ignored all the risks when I rushed forward just then. I hadn't even drawn the sidearm they let me carry.

I take a photograph of the result of Rici's "work", then scribble a few words about how I feel in my notebook.

I write: Some part of me has died today.

Why?

I hurry after Rici, trying to remember what the hell those other eleven tasks were that Hercules was obliged to perform.

And what happens if I can't?

THREE

The Greeks thought of him first – in the same way that they dreamed up all sorts of civilized inventions, and they knew him as Heracles, meaning Glory of Hera. When, in 146 BC, the Romans invaded Greece, they also started to steal myths and legends from their neighbours – in this process they renamed the hero Hercules.

And that's the name that most people now recognize, for, notwithstanding its origins, it sounds good. Heracles might be historically accurate but, for most people today, Hercules has that ring, that sense of rightness, that image of courage, strength and definition of a hero without whom there would be no great exploits for them to gain inspiration from. I don't think *he* worries too much that he's remembered by this second incarnation. And why should he? Hercules is too busy doing what other immortal heroes do – interfering with people's lives for his own reasons. He's having the time of his eternity. And perhaps, sometimes, he even takes a moment to think about his origins.

The ancient Greeks may have lost their architecture, literature, theatre (their whole way of life in fact), but they bequeathed us an aspiration no amount of unprovoked violence can ever remove – a natural craving most of society is aware of, not only those perennial goals of success and prosperity that drive the majority, but also deeper moral ambitions that priests, sages and mothers frequently talk of: comprehension, fairness and benevolence.

And then they gave us their heroes.

Hercules was a love child. Well, that was the way his father bragged about it – his mother might have given another interpretation, but the records are rather vague about this, though she had good cause for it. His mother was the lovely wife of a Theban general and Hercules' father was not her husband. Hercules was sired by none other than Zeus, the king of those ancient and noble Greek gods who had made their home on Mount Olympus; and it was this king of the gods, acting on his usual feelings of lust, who seduced the woman while in the guise of her husband. To give the story its own particular twist (and to gain obvious pleasure for him, and a somewhat more dubious gratification for his misled victim), Zeus prolonged the length of that night by three. This is what you are able to do if you are a god.

Zeus' wife, his own sister Hera, certainly wasn't happy. Since she was the protector of women and marriage, she concluded that an earth inhabited by mere mortals would be a better, and less annoying, place, without the result of her husband's infidelity. There was also the small matter of her being his sister. (The gods have their own scale of morality and justice. Do what I say, not what I do, is their general mantra. Sibling rivalry and envy can be treacherous when you happen to be married.) To remove this irritant, Hera did what she considered necessary when the boy was born. Though maybe she should have pondered further; after all, Hercules *was* the son of Zeus, king of the gods.

Anyway, Hera wove a spell, and sent two serpents to kill the baby. But Hercules had none of it: he strangled the pair the instant they eased into his bed (an up-turned shield; every baby hero should have one), and gurgled to himself afterwards as he played with his newly dead toys. Hera grimaced, folded her arms and sucked at her lower lip – promptly setting the mould for mothers, and their concern for wayward children, in perpetuity. Maybe there was more to this offspring from her husband's loins than met the eye. What next?

The die was cast. Hercules was destined for an eventful life.

Now, after many youthful adventures (in which he had acquired the fighting skills that would serve him so well later on), he conquered a barbarian tribe. His reward was marriage to the princess Megara. (In those days it was assumed that princesses would agree to such arrangements. Megara wasn't too upset – she liked the twinkle in Hercules' eye.) They soon had a number of children. Life was good, they were happy; there was honey, wine and olives, and lots of laughs. But Hera had not forgotten. She had a plan: one that would result in atonement.

One day Hercules returned home to find a man about to kill Megara and their children. After some quick and nifty arrow-work, the assassin lay dead. Another notch – or so Hercules thought – on the bow. Time to celebrate. Time to pay homage. Time to offer a sacrifice to Zeus. Hera pounced.

She conjured Hercules to go temporarily psychotic. Even in terms of the cunning that the gods often employed amongst mortals, it was a vicious trick to pull, for though Hera was protector of women and marriage, she was prepared to sacrifice Megara's feelings. (Perhaps Megara seemed *too* happy for the likes of Hera.) It was a horror to behold: in the depths of this insanity that his father's wife had put upon him, Hercules believed his children were not his own. He believed the man he'd just killed had fathered them. And his madness told him that it would be necessary to kill them too.

Jealousy is a cruel God.

Hera looked down upon the carnage, thought about her husband's infidelity, and felt it was all worth it. She removed the spell.

Lucid again, Hercules was grief-stricken, and so ashamed at the course of his actions he decided that suicide was the only cure to his misery. His childhood friend Theseus did what friends are supposed to do, and calmed him down, then told him to seek advice on what to do next from the oracle at Delphi.

If the oracle were to instruct suicide as a means of atonement, then so be it. Hercules reluctantly agreed, though he wanted to tear out his own throat there and then. His beautiful Megara! She hates him now. His beautiful children – what they must be saying about him in the underworld.

So Hercules went to Delphi. He performed the ritual purification of himself, sacrificed a goat, and then he approached the oracle. The priestess inhaled deeply the fumes that rose in wisps from the stream running through the cavern and she chewed on the laurel leaves. As she screamed the screams of the possessed – for Apollo now spoke through her – she proclaimed that the oracle had one solution. It instructed Hercules to seek out a certain King Eurystheus, and to perform any task he saw fit to ordain.

Hera was happy. Because, initially, Eurystheus dreamed up ten tasks for Hercules to attempt. And then increased them to twelve.

Power is an interesting weapon to wield.

These tasks are what are known as The Labours of Hercules.

"Your first task, Hercules," announced Eurystheus, rubbing his hands in the manner of someone who has time and power to waste, and certain gods to impress, "is to show me the skin of an invincible lion. I must stress this: I want to see the pelt of an animal that cannot be wounded by any weapon. There is one such creature that menaces the hills and countryside around the town of Nemea. This lion's hide is proof against any metal or stone; spears and arrows bounce off its back, even the fiercest slingshot doesn't even bruise it. No man has ever stood up to it and won. Quite a beast, huh? And a bit of a nuisance. Think you can do it? Think you can bring back its pelt to show me you've killed it?"

King Eurystheus settled back onto his throne. He was a small man, and reminded Hercules of an overgrown toad. An overgrown, overfed and unhealthy toad, observed Hercules further – a toad of a man whose legs couldn't touch the floor when he was sitting down.

Hercules gave the king what is known in the questing profession as the Hero's Glint – stone, ice and flame. He continued staring as Eurystheus grimaced and crossed his legs. Hercules nodded and assured the king that he believed that he, Hercules, was the man to defeat this lion. Or he would die in the attempt. To himself, as he left the throne room, he made a mental note that his soul depended on it.

So Hercules set out on his first adventure, in the classic Greek hero way: with high resolve, a steady arm and clear eye, and it was not too long into his travels before he came upon a small town. The journey over the last few days had been long and hot – something was missing, Hercules realized that. A man called Molorchus, a poor and humble labourer of all trades, whose son had been savaged to death by the lion only a few days before, offered him lodgings in that small town. And it was this lowly man who quietened Hercules' unease as they washed away the dryness of the day with wine.

As they began to drink, Molorchus was impressed and pleased by the nature of Hercules' initial task, and he decided that a sacrifice was necessary for a judicious and happy quest. Even a lowly labourer in ancient Greece knew what was needed to achieve good fortune. Hercules smiled, and let out a long sigh of relief. He had just formed a better idea than his host, and was happy that he now knew what had been missing. As Molorchus put down his goblet and began to hurry towards the small stable which housed his few goats and sheep, Hercules requested that he postpone the sacrifice for thirty days.

"If I return here by that date with the lion's pelt," he said, "then we will both of us offer up a sacrifice to my father Zeus."

Molorchus stopped and looked over his shoulder, then nodded acceptance and promptly he turned to refill their goblets.

Hercules reached for the wine that Molorchus held out to him.

"On the other hand," he said, pausing before he drank, "if I should die, dedicate the sacrifice to me – as a hero."

Molorchus smiled, and nodded again.

So, a little while later, Hercules arrived in Nemea and, without any of the usual preliminary discussions with the locals as was the custom, and without any hesitation about what he was there to achieve, he began his hunt through the low hills around the town. As the townspeople watched him preparing to stalk his prey, their silent expectation spread out like a subtle hush. A possible saviour to their woes had just passed through their town – and he had a strange look in his eye.

A pungent texture drifted on the breeze. Hercules paused and surveyed the land around. The whole area was littered with the gnawed and shattered bones of many creatures. He recognized some as being human.

"This fearless animal is going to be easy to track," he said to himself. "Bloody paw prints and a trail of carnage."

A deep rumble echoed around the little valley. The noise of a massive animal scenting trouble? The rumble turned into a roar, and Hercules strode towards the source of it.

The Nemean Lion was huge: at least twice the size of any lion Hercules had ever seen. Its mane was as black as Hades, its teeth would not have looked out of place on a sea-monster, and from its paws protruded claws too large to retract fully. It moved as if it were the lord of the Underworld, with complete menace in its prowl – one lazy rolling stride after another. Clearly there was nothing it feared. The Lion stopped to roar at Hercules again, the sound echoing throughout the valley.

Even though King Eurystheus had warned him that this beast could not be killed with any weapon, Hercules let fly with a number of arrows. They flew true and hard, but all they did on hitting their target was ricochet every which way. The lion's tail swished at the points of impact; it was as if dealing with a troublesome fly. Hercules hung his bow and arrows back over his shoulders. He then demonstrated the qualities that made him a hero, by using his head *and* his brawn. Taking his club in hand, Hercules followed the lion towards its den, which he noticed had two entrances. Hercules first crept around to the furthest one and blocked it up. Having thus cornered the wild beast he entered the cave through the remaining entrance.

Inside the confined space the stench was even worse. But Hercules couldn't worry about that, being aware that he was being carefully watched. He first let his eyes become adjusted to the gloom, then stepped forward, deeper into the lion's den, his sandal-boots cracking on bones strewn across the floor.

When the lion roared again, it sounded ten times worse than out in the open.

Hercules gripped his club.

The lion roared once more.

Then there was a sudden movement.

Its monstrous bulk hurtled towards Hercules in a sinuous, fluid charge. The lion's mouth was wide open, its teeth bared, its eyes bright despite the gloom. It rushed towards him and leapt.

Hercules swung as hard as he could with his club, and brought the blunt, heavy end of it onto the beast's head with a savage blow. The lion crashed into him, he staggered back and they fell to the ground together. Hercules rolled quickly away to one side, then got up on his hands and knees to check if his plan had succeeded. For the moment he was safe; the lion was stunned. Before it could come to its senses, Hercules grabbed the lion's throat between his huge arms. As the beast came to, shaking off the effects of the blow, it realized the predicament it was in. With a snarl, it began to buck and writhe, again and again making slashing lunges with its terrible claws. But Hercules held on as the huge paws smacked and ripped at him, the lion struggling to turn its head and savage the hero, but to no avail. Slowly, Hercules choked it to death – the animal that no weapon could harm.

Thirty days after he had left the small town, Hercules arrived back there with his prize – the entire carcass of the lion slung over his shoulders. He discovered Molorchus about to make a sacrifice in honour of Hercules himself, having assumed the hero had died in his quest. Overjoyed, Molorchus would have continued the same ritual, but the killer of the Nemean Lion remembered the pledge he had made, so the two men made their sacrifice to Zeus instead. Shortly afterwards, and after several goblets of the rough wine Molorchus kept specially for those who appreciated it, Hercules hit upon the idea of flaying the beast using one of its own tremendously sharp claws. When it had been dried and cured, Hercules wore it as a cloak – more effective than normal armour, since no weapon could damage it. Scooping out the brains, he used the head as a rather unusual helmet. They were fitting trophies – the first of many, vowed Hercules.

Eurystheus wasn't happy though. He pouted and kicked at his throne.

He then decided he would have to invent something harder for Hercules to do next.

FOUR

F2/6836/11/103   TOWROPE TELEPHONE TRANSCRIPT

DATE ▪▪▪▪▪▪▪

TIME 13.36

SUBJECTS:

FREEMAN, ALEXANDER "ALEX" (A)

FREEMAN, SERENA (S)

A: Hi, you've reached Alex Freeman. I'm sorry I'm not
available to come to the phone, if you'd like to leave
a—

S: Alex, Alex — shut up with the fake answerphone voice,
you know it doesn't fool me anymore — now listen.
Listen to me! (ITALICS ADDED) I've done it!

A: Serena? Stop *screaming*. (ITALICS ADDED) What are you
going on about?

S: I've done it!

A: Stop shouting, girl, or I *will* (ITALICS ADDED) put the
machine on. Now, you've done wha—?

S: It works! I *was* (ITALICS ADDED) right!
SLIGHT PAUSE IN CONVERSATION

A: What were you right about, Sis? That women never get
to the point? Or would it be too sarcastic to ask

whether it is the formula for winning the lottery
perhaps? The Chaos solution to—?
SLIGHT PAUSE IN CONVERSATION

A: Hey! Are you *serious*? (ITALICS ADDED) Your (EXPLETIVE
DELETED) *machine*? (ITALICS ADDED) Holy (EXPLETIVE
DELETED) Odysseus *works*? (ITALICS ADDED)

S: Yep! Isn't that great? It was incredible, Alex – just
the same as physically being there. Seeing everything, seeing *everything*. (ITALICS ADDED) And the
sensations, the sensations were – well . . .
SLIGHT PAUSE IN CONVERSATION

S: Alex, it was truly breathtaking. Beyond anything I
could have hoped for, like being on a roller coaster,
it was insane, insane – like watching "Saving Private
Ryan" on acid. Total involvement. Another world. It's
more than I could have asked for, Alex, much more.
You're just there; you're *there*. (ITALICS ADDED) Do
you know how this affects how we can look at the past?
It's like I told you when I first thought of the idea;
the beauty now is we can go and check anything. Imagine the implications for history buffs like yourself,
Alex, or *any* (ITALICS ADDED) researcher for that matter. Go find Boudicca? See the Brontës? Pankhurst?
Woolf? And that's just the women. Think of the big
moments. The Magna Carta. Nelson at Trafalgar. Gettysburg. Wouldn't you want to be there when Lincoln
gave the Gettysburg address? Oh, my *God* (ITALICS
ADDED) Alex, ancient *Greece?* (ITALICS ADDED) Imagine
getting the verbatim on Plato! I can't wait—?

A: Serena?
SLIGHT PAUSE IN CONVERSATION

A: *Serena?* (ITALICS ADDED)

S: Mmm? What?

A: I know you're excited, and yes, it sounds great, but
I'm the first person you've talked to, right?

S: Of course stupid, do you think I'd—?

A: Remember what I said *not* (ITALICS ADDED) to do if it actually worked? Remember what I said about the telephone?

S: Oh.

SLIGHT PAUSE IN CONVERSATION

S: Yeah, okay, Alex. I can't see why I should be worried about your concerns over secrecy – they're so abstract, this isn't politics – but – okay, let's meet then!

A: Let's. The tea shop near Kings?

S: In an hour? I've just got to write down a couple of things before I forget.

A: *You* (ITALICS ADDED) forget something? Ha! You can remember everything – even me telling you not to ring. I bet you did it just to wind me up. In an hour?

SLIGHT PAUSE IN CONVERSATION

S: I'm so excited! So will you be! I promise!

A: In an hour.

CONVERSATION ENDED BY A.

DIGITAL TAP*

REFER TO GCHQ RECORDS FOR FREEMAN, ALEXANDER.

CURRENT STATUS ORANGE ONE

*ADDITIONAL INFORMATION

DIGITAL TOWROPE TECHNIQUE USED AS RESPONSE TO

INITIAL TRAWL.

Serena sits at her PC. The windows of her room are still open to the warm Cambridge summer air of the early afternoon, but the noises from the outside world are submerged beneath the loud music from her CD tower. It is Mozart's Concerto for Clarinet and Orchestra – K.622. Some musician friends of Serena – Annette's ex-keyboard player Christian, for instance – say to her that having Mozart's work catalogued by number is appropriate, as he wrote his work in that style: *by* the numbers. And why hasn't she tried Bach, if that's the sort of thing to set her bells ringing? That's a *real* mathematician's composer – puts Mozart to shame. Serena tells them (and, in particular, Christian) that they should wash their mouths out with soap and hopefully choke at the same time. Great music is great music. And anyway, she adds, who is this upstart Beethoven they keep talking about anyway? Or Chopin? Her friends may know how to tease her, but they are aware there is a limit. She'll never let anyone dismiss Mozart "The Man" by merely saying he was a great classicist, and not adding that he was also *the* greatest. That argument would be short and loud: Mozart *is* The Man.

Out of the many isolated, yet individual, talismans that were formed in her youth, Serena's love of Mozart's music was one of the few that she allowed to continue the transition into the life she now leads. While she appreciates the mathematical principles that prevail within any piece of music (it doesn't take much to notice that even a child hitting the table with an eggcup to amuse itself tries to do it in *time*), such cold analysis is not for her. No, it is the recognition that there is a spark needed from some place else to move the soul, a little something extra; and she considers it fact that some lucky people are destined to be given the chance to dance to the glorious vortex of flame that is imagination. God – whatever He, She, It, may be – granted such a gift to Mozart.

Ever since, at the age of three, she heard his music being played on The Last Night of the Proms, she has been entranced by his magic. She has every score – from K.1, his Minuet and Trio for Piano, in G, 1761, to K.626, his Requiem Mass, 1791 – now stacked on three shelves. On her flute, she has played those of them that were written for that instrument, and she has re-listened to *all* of the collection in her head. She has memorized whole symphonies and finds her ability to replay them in her head an advantage, because her mental playback seems to be of a higher quality of recording than her disc collection. Serena knows she can't put the same feeling into playing the pieces as she might like to, but, hey, she tells herself, she *is* an expert in mathematics, and there are other dazzling gods in the musical field who are able to interpret Mozart for her.

They are the conduits to God's soul.

Because music affects mood.

And music is sound.

As she prepares herself to work, the notes from the clarinet cascade and flow, and hesitate and repeat in just the right places. The strings of the orchestra act as chorus as they wait for a new verse, with every intention of supplying perfect balance to a different variation from The Voice of God, as given to Wolfgang himself. These days, Serena has to listen to Mozart while she works, or else she plays something by The Beatles. To her, The Beatles were as good, in their way, as The Man was. She can argue just as easily with passion about them, but for the moment she needs a tonal background of delight – and no words. She has to try to forget her recent sensory experience that may change the world, and now put down her observational results in written form.

Scientific method. Be precise. Leave no room for query.

She'd been so excited on the phone. She'd *had* to tell someone.

So be precise.

But who'll believe me?

She writes quickly.

To understand how Odysseus works, it is first necessary to understand the three interconnecting sciences behind Transcranial Magnetic Stimulation (TMS), Psychophysics and, lastly, the principle behind – and the results achieved from – the United States of America's Central Intelligence Agency's (CIA) "Operation Stargate".

Firstly: TMS is a non-invasive medical, and psychiatric, technique that supersedes the barbaric and blunt methods used in the recent past to cure illness of the brain and mind. Compared to the surgery, drugs and severe electrical treatments that were, and are, employed in finding solutions to alleviate many of the circumstances that influence brain function, TMS offers the potential to move into a far more refined future.

The usefulness of TMS lies in the discovery that a strong, and rapidly changing, magnetic field directed at the skull could produce electrical effects in the neurons of the brain and produce non-voluntary action in the subject. This was found to be of help, for example, with neurologists attempting to ascertain whether nerve-link function existed in, say, the toes. The magnetic pulses of the TMS device caused the toes to curl if the pathway was intact, if the appropriate part of the brain was stimulated. With the advent of improvements that increased the rapidity with which the magnetic pulse could be alternated, interesting effects were noted. Not only is it possible to produce a reaction in a particular part of a patient's anatomy, it was found that Rapid Transcranial Magnetic Stimulation (rTMS) can alter the whole range of brain function: sight, smell, taste, touch, and hearing. Even memory and mood can be affected. Temporary in nature, these changes diminish quickly after the course of rTMS has finished.

This discovery, rTMS, forms the foundations on which Odysseus is built – in tandem with Psychophysics.

Psychophysics is no New Age invention; the word was first coined in the mid-nineteenth century. In a way that is resonant (pun intended) with so-called offbeat thinking today, scientists were of the opinion that it would eventually be possible for the state of mind of an individual to be scientifically measured using technology. We have made advances towards doing so, as many are aware, by monitoring brain activity with an electroencephalogram (EEG). The Victorian scientists concluded that a person's thinking and state of mind could be influenced by certain noises. It is an idea that has been around for some time.

That sound can in fact do this is now well established.

Even to the extreme.

In the late fifties and early sixties, a scientist discovered the correlation between very low-frequency sound (being well below the range of human hearing) and the onset of nausea. His ideas were based on a suspicion that an outbreak of illness and headaches in his research establishment was a result of an engine vibrating in a duct. All matter has a fundamental natural frequency, known as the resonant frequency.

A wet finger on the rim of a glass of water causes the glass to oscillate at its resonant frequency, thus generating the musical note that can then be heard. This is the physics behind opera singers shattering wine glasses; they generate the necessary resonant frequency that causes vibrations in the glass which cannot be sustained by the mechanical properties of the glass itself. It was concluded that the engine in the duct was producing a frequency of the same order as the resonant frequency of the brain. To demonstrate the theory, a huge piston-operated organ pipe that generated a note of about 5hz (five cycles per second) was built. When the experiment was initiated, the spasms of illness brought on by only a few seconds' exposure could last for up to a day. And so, while a generation of Directed Sound Energy Weapons were born (some have been designed for crowd control), a proven connection between sound and physiology had been established.

Serena sits back in her chair, stretches her arms, then places them behind her back and pushes her closed fists against each other. Ribs and elbow joints tinkle. Then, while she continues staring at the screen of her PC, she leans to her left and reaches over to her CD tower. Mozart has finished. She removes the disc, places it in its case and slides The Man back into his place on the rack. Still without looking, Serena then runs a finger down the other CD case spines of her music collection. She pauses, the finger goes back one slot, and the other fingers of that hand help to withdraw the case – she has so good a memory that she can remember something she read in a newspaper four years ago. As she still considers the words in front of her, she opens the case and sets the disc in motion. The title track from *Sergeant Pepper* fills the room. It is just one of the many recordings she has by The Beatles.

Forget tone – I need words now.

Her argument for having them alongside Mozart is at once simple and complicated. In her opinion – and she knows some Rolling Stones, Nirvana, and Steps fans might disagree – The Beatles were gifted by God as well. While she thinks that George Harrison was that extra polish, that extra sparkle, that fate had decreed should be added to a combination already shining – the two main component parts of Lennon and McCartney added up to an entity greater than just one plus one. And that sort of mathematics fascinates Serena.

It's the people – relationships.

It is those sums of human existence that Serena has fostered in her work, and which led her to make the developmental steps she has taken up till now. From the simple constructs of her childhood – where one plus one was equal to two – she made the mental and aesthetic jump to realizing that one idea added to another idea causes a star to emerge. Some lucky people can manage this lateral train of thought by themselves; others – like Lennon and McCartney – need each other to germinate artistic solutions. And this sort of thinking – where answers are ambiguous, are neither fixed, nor exact – prompted Serena, and others in her field, towards scientific investigations into chaos. And, once again, music, and its effect on mood, was where scientists looked. In the same way as a mountain peak may have a variety of changes in height before reaching its summit, so music has patterns that rise and dip. And these patterns are important. One case study Serena came across took a score by Bach and altered it slightly by refining the structure, taking away the sudden changes. The result was perceived as being dull, and lacking the life of the original. When the reverse process was used – the changes accentuated slightly – the outcome was distortion and random noise. Serena, and many others, had come to the conclusion that life needs a little disorder and it is this, the so-called chaos, which makes life enjoyable – and which opens doors to making discoveries and affecting change. Alex had proclaimed to Serena that the status quo dislikes mutations of thought, but they are necessary for life. She agreed with him.

However, while Serena had felt at one with the mathematics of chaos guiding her life and accepting of some of the decisions made for her, her brother Alex had been the other side of the coin – rebelling against authority. And it was his endless questions about what is right, what is wrong, what is truth and what is fiction, which enabled Serena to join the mental threads from music and mood into the building of Odysseus. She simply wanted to know Truth – like Alex.

She nods her head in time to the music. And continues typing.

Lastly: Stargate. This was an attempt to ascertain the viability of using so-called psychics to describe objects or locations by means of mental visualization – primarily as a tool for espionage. The perfect spy, in other words. This technique is otherwise known in parapsychology as Remote Viewing. The cessation of this program was made public by the CIA in 1995 and it caused a furore. Why? Because what if the results were valid? Even once?

At the end of the sixties and the beginning of the seventies, the US intelligence services became aware of reports that the Soviets were engaged in Extra Sensory Perception (ESP) research. First ignored as hokum, or at least as a sideshow to the messy professional business of the Cold War, the CIA's suspicion that there was perhaps a reason to at least look at the phenomena was enhanced when sources began to report a massive increase in funding by the Soviets. Personnel within the CIA began to ask questions. Perhaps the Reds had achieved a break-through? Or was it just a ruse – a bluff to ensnare the US into wasting millions of dollars?

When the initial program was given the go-ahead in 1972, it was provided with the name Scanate (SCAN by coordinATE) and, with funding from the CIA, a research institute began its experiments. Using the absurdly simple technique of asking a person to describe what their mental vision and impression was for a number of locations around the globe (having ascertained that the individual had no prior knowledge of that place), the institute were able to winkle out, for further training, viewers who demonstrated the right potential. The pass mark was said to be sixty-five per cent.

After various mutations and amalgamations with Army Intelligence, Scanate reached its last incarnation as Stargate in the early nineties. By now thousands of remote-viewing experiments had taken place – costing many millions of dollars – and the reason the CIA was prepared to allow expenditure to continue was that they apparently had had some success. In 1995 a team was engaged by the CIA to evaluate their findings. Despite the statisticians reporting that the remote viewers were correct fifteen per cent of the time, their recommendation was to abandon Stargate. A month after the final report, the CIA itself recommended to Congress that it should suspend funding.

The money stopped.

No one in Congress apparently bothered to point out that fifteen per cent was an extremely thought-provoking statistic; even one per cent would have been interesting. If – even once in those twenty years – a remote viewer had been proved to be correct, wouldn't that fact have sufficiently serious repercussions on our knowledge of ESP?

So the question that extends from these three ideas is this: how do you induce a state of mind that facilitates the perception, or indeed the reality, of time travel?

I call it Odysseus.

Odysseus is a coupling of five loudspeaker and magnetic resonance units – positioned on the imaginary points of a pentagon – whose outputs are controlled, via a PC system, to the specifications of the author's mathematical program. (The units consist of thirty-four interlocking thin-film triangular loudspeakers, the whole surrounded with copper mesh for protection, while inside are the elements required to generate the enhanced Rapid Transcranial Magnetic Stimulation – rTMS – component.) Each output unit produces a range of sounds and magnetic flux that interact with each other within each unit, and within the pentagon arrangement, to produce beat frequencies and flux harmonics that have a local point of action within a two-centimetre sphere at the centre of the "pentagon". (Odysseus includes a headrest to restrain the head of the Chrononaut: the remote "time traveller", in the resulting field.) The wave structure so constructed by the Odysseus program is designed to induce in the Chrononaut's brain a state of mind identical to those observed in psychic trance – using the electroencephalograms results as measured in "Operation Stargate" – and to produce a perceived localized space/time anomaly, via rTMS, to enhance the state of perception. If the Chrononaut is thoroughly focused on destination and historical personality, by researching as much information on the subject as possible, before initiation of Odysseus, this mindset assists the speed of the operation greatly. The desired date and time are programmed at the initiation of the program, together with three essential mathematical constants of the five formulae needed for each speaker. (This precaution, incidentally, came from a conversation with an engineer at the firm that made the speaker units, who discussed methods to prevent commercial industrial espionage for prototype inventions.) The Chrononaut can then home in on a chosen subject at a chosen time. It is presumed that accuracy will improve with use; but only further experimentation will confirm this.

A word of warning. It is necessary to be clear that the mechanisms that influence the brain patterns may affect the mind in an, as yet, undefined manner. Though rTMS has been shown to have no long-term effects, its combination with psychophysics is an uncharted field. One's perception of what is reality, what is invention, and what represents the true past, may be distorted and twisted together in consequences unforeseen. The risks to mental and physical health are unquantifiable. There may be other, as yet unidentified, inherent risks and consequences.

Serena stares at the last paragraph she has written.

How can I observe myself to check? That's silly.

She sits for several minutes pondering this question.

Has my desire to do similar tasks as this man Lafayette has decided to do – at your suggestion, girl, at your suggestion – been prompted by using Odysseus? Am I being affected already? Am I exacerbating an existing personality disorder? Will I induce psychosis in myself in the same way as hallucinogenic drugs would? Can I even remember what the rest of the Twelve Labours of Hercules are?

Shit. I've only copied the first one.

Serena shuts down her PC, pushing the buttons hard and glares at the paperweight on her desk, adorned with its Nemean Lion hairpiece.

No problem.

As she leans over to switch off her CD as well, she smiles

grimly to herself at the coincidence of The Beatles being in the midst of singing *Lucy in the Sky with Diamonds*.

Umm – there just can't be a reference to LSD in that title, can there?

John Lennon is abruptly cut off from continuing his thoughts about the girl with the interestingly patterned eyes.

Serena walks down the road, checking her watch as she does so. The partying students have gone; the only evidence that they have been there is the wire cage that contained a champagne cork, which itself lies in the middle of the pavement along with the foil that had originally surrounded it. The sparrows have moved on as well, and the zephyr that pretended to be the wind has shifted – there is only the grass-dust smell from the park mixed with an edge of traffic fumes. The sun has bleached itself of any colour and is a hot, white hole in the sky. It glints off any shiny surface it can find. As a result, the crumpled champagne foil on the pathway is a golden nugget. Serena squints and cups her hand around her wristwatch's face. For a moment she remembers Phoenix doing exactly the same as the boats roared into life. The smell from the vehicles in Barton Road suddenly takes on a different meaning. Serena refocuses: she slaps at her wrist and begins to jog.

Done it again, she says to herself.

Alex hates people missing appointments; even if they are impromptu arrangements between brother and sister to discuss seismic changes in science and mathematics. Serena sometimes wonders if it has anything to do with the disability he sustained only a few years before.

Guilt upon guilt?

Especially, as Serena unexpectedly feels, for a moment, a sense of joy that it is *she* who is able to run, and not her brother burdened with his crutch. (He lets it hang off his elbow when he gesticulates and he aims it like some sort of inverted gun by its strut when he is making a point.) Serena is convinced that he only hates *herself* being late.

Their sibling rivalry started at an early age – when she was five and he was ten. One Sunday Alex had come into the room their parents had allocated as The Study whistling the theme to *The Dam Busters*. He had both hands raised to his face in the familiar symbol of World War II RAF pilot's goggles – thumbs and forefingers circling each eye – and found Serena completing his maths homework. For years after, Serena would re-enact in her mind what happened next. Alex had gasped. He had dropped both hands to his open mouth – and gasped. What Serena was doing was in direct contradiction to The Law. Both their parents were teachers and deemed education as the one true escape, and the only path to strike out on – but you had to make the effort on your own.

At home David and Lesley Freeman were benign tyrants. Enjoying the barest interaction with other adults, they both spent each working day in their respective schools in the town, moulding classes of children into fit replacements for society. They didn't see it that way of course – they did their best for the individual sparks they occasionally saw flicker in the class-room – but then David and Lesley were having to deal with bulk rather than quality. It blinded them sometimes to the way sparks can light fires. Their technique to cover the range of talent placed under their charge was to carpet-bomb with knowledge, and woe-betide any child who dared to contradict them without a good argument. This clear vision was not reflected by the way that they ordered the rest of their lives however. Their family lived in a small semi-detached in one of the better catchment areas of town. The jamboree contents of the house were a mixture of aboriginal art and Jim Morrison memorabilia, shelf upon shelf of books, pine furniture in myriad variety, and huge Triffid plants that somehow lived on fresh air only. In her early teens at university, Serena would eventually conjure up the image of her parents as bumbling Nazi caretakers of some compound, innocent of any crime –

they were only obeying the dictates of current thinking on how to bring up both a genius and a normal child.

As Alex stood at the door, staring at the scattering of books and paper, Serena banged the tip of her ballpoint into the page of a jotter and looked up.

"Finished it for you." She giggled at her brother's stance.

Before Alex could make any other sound, their mother's voice broke into the atmosphere that was building up as a flash of purple across Alex's face.

"That's good, Serena, but perhaps next time you'll let Alex try for himself. And, Alex, don't take advantage of your sister like this. Please do your own homework."

She ruffled her son's hair and she turned to her Sunday cooking chores in the kitchen. Alex didn't even smooth his hair down – he just approached Serena, with his fists clenched.

It took Serena a long time to understand why Alex had become so angry. And thereafter she would always associate the smell of roast-beef dinners with the one and only time her brother had hit her. She eventually came to realize that the maturity of adulthood has its foundations in memories.

Childhood?

Alex winning the one hundred metres at the school sports day; herself walking the same distance with her egg in a spoon, wondering why everyone was laughing at her slow, cautious progress. Alex scoring a hat-trick of goals in an inter-county match; her spending a painful hour on the hockey pitch with her trainers fitted on the wrong feet. Alex, frustrated, throwing his pocket calculator into the garden pond; Serena enjoying the interaction of its ripples on the water's surface, wondering about the mathematics involved and curious as to why Alex found mathematics so hard. Alex could never disguise his rage, so he reminded Serena of The Incredible Hulk.

"Don't make me angry. You wouldn't like me when I'm angry."

The Hulk was great in his own avocado way, but Serena leapt from one fancy-panted superhero to another during those early years of finding out that she viewed the world differently, and it was difficult for her family to keep track of who was flavour of the week. The range of heroes built up from her raids up to the loft where her father had laid to rest *his* childhood, till he tried to ration the comics and posters out to her. To no avail. His posters were snatched from his fingers and tacked one upon the other on her bedroom wall, their occupants' chisel jaws squaring up to each addition that would become their oblivion. Superman lasted a month, blasted away by the kryptonite power of The Silver Surfer, who in turn was flicked from his board when Serena discovered Spiderman. And then Peter Parker donned his webbed suit for the last time once Captain Marvel jumped into view. Captain Marvel was just what the girl ordered. He was – to use the parlance of the age when the poster was originally printed – 'neat'. Serena was told that her interest in them seemed 'different, for a girl', as her sexist father put it. 'A stupid waste of her time' was how Alex put it.

Something had changed between them after the homework incident; something had altered Alex's attitude towards her. Then, after three days of sullen silence, he bounced back into her life. Now it became a total encouragement for her to succeed. He became a constant cheerleader; pushing, cajoling, pressuring. He waved her on from the sidelines – seemingly wanting her to win the academic race their parents had set her upon – while he himself desired nothing more than to become a great sportsman. For the next few years he was up and out jogging by 6.30 each morning. His weekends were spent in some form of competitive sport as he pushed himself to become better, faster, stronger. But, strangely, always with one eye on what Serena was doing. Even as he struggled with his own A-levels, two years after she'd triumphantly passed hers, he became her ad hoc press-bodyguard while her parents expounded their teaching doctrine in front of the cameras. He drove her to conferences after he'd passed his driving test; bought her biographies – the sporty rival child discovered something intellectual.

Then Serena discovered *The Dark Knight Returns*, and all hell was let loose. Post-apocalyptic Batman gets his act together with a female Robin (young, street-wise and willing to learn The New Way – Serena loved her). Grim and gritty. And then, in the blink of a tired eye, Neil Gaiman's collection was discovered in a shop inhabited by curiously dressed young people and Serena turned to *The Sandman*. Serena suckled hard on her new-found joy, because there she was: a fourteen-year-old in her final year of university, while still expected to be all pigtails and giggles and Alice dresses, but absolutely in tune in her mind with the flowering rebirth of comics. She cut her hair, ordered a new set of glasses, and bought herself some black jeans.

The older students – those of a normal age for university – had found her a problem that they were generally unable to counter. They themselves were accustomed to the educated, the clever, the groomed ability to argue at an early age, but Serena was off their intelligence scale – even at Cambridge. Most therefore chose to ignore her. The "most", in this case, generally meaning the young men, their ego knocked off-balance by a child. The young women, on the other hand, allowed her sisterhood of a sort.

Then, two months before her finals, she published her first schoolbook text for children. Even her "sisters" were thrown by this new twist in her popularity – while they were experimenting with sex, here was Serena providing educational solace for the future consequences of hasty fumbling. It took some of the pleasure away to know that someone much younger than you was already thinking of your children.

By the time she graduated she had become an outcast. She drifted into some research think-tank and was left in an office to "do her thing". She quietly matured on her own.

Her salvation came a few years later with appointment to a post at Lady Murray. This was a small college that catered for women who had missed the chance of a university education in their teens. These women became surrogate mothers, Earth

Women, coming from every corner of the globe, and they clubbed together and told her dirty stories – in graphic detail. It was one of them who had told her about the Greek myths. They became an answer, superheroes that had stood the test of time.

So the potent mix of ancient Greek myth, modern graphic-novel legend and earthly female practicality had wrought its spell on her – she became totally dissatisfied with what remained of her parents' expectations for her. She started looking for something different. And found it with a chance remark from her brother. They had been talking about her career and her place on the academic ladder, when her brother Alex commented about how times had changed, how things could now happen if you set your mind to it. He'd actually been referring to female emancipation, but it set that train of thought in action . . .

Serena stops in her tracks. There, in the window of a shop catering for tourists with a frightening variety of nick-nacks (His and Hers fit-in-your-pocket teddy bears, scented candles covered in glitter, postcards of Cambridge that are neither historical nor recent), stands a very squat and very repugnant-looking china frog. The ornament is adorable in its way.

"The Lernaean Hydra," whispers Serena. "Hercules' second labour."

She goes into the shop.

Serena smiles at a camera. It is forty minutes later. And the phone is ringing.

Sod you, Alex. I'm busy.

The brand-new digital camera stands on a tripod – more technology on legs. It was expensive, yet another weight to add to her expanding credit-card bill. Contrary to popular belief, the salary for being a don in Cambridge is quite small, the perks and prestige being supposed to compensate. Serena herself would settle for another twenty thousand a year and the University could keep its esteem to itself – that or she'd seriously have to think about an offer from an American campus.

Serena is now squatting cross-legged in front of the camera, a hand outstretched, the palm supporting an object she has purchased. She has already taken a photograph of the paperweight with the Nemean mane fastened on top. Now it's the turn of the china frog. Just before the bright explosion of light, she remembers to smile.

The phone continues ringing, in the background.

Classified Secret

PLEASE SIGN RECEIPT PROVIDED BY COURIER

DO NOT ACCEPT IF TAMPER BAIL STRIP IS BROKEN

RETURN TO A4 RECORDS WITHIN FORTY-EIGHT (48) HOURS

F2/6836/09/22

TRANSCRIPT (ABRIDGED) OF INTERVIEW WITH DOWNEY, CHARLES BSc HONS HEADMASTER RTD. OF LITTLEMAY HIGH SCHOOL, CAMBRIDGE. SUBJECT: FREEMAN, ALEXANDER. FORMER PUPIL.

Page 3 of 8

CD: (CONTINUED FROM P2) . . . and it got to the stage where he was in my office every fortnight.

Q: So in essence, what you're saying is that you thought he was a complicated child?

CD: Of course I am – and he had to be. Consider the facts: Alex was never a dim child, far from it, and he should have had it all: intelligence coupled with a superb ability at sports, he was a natural leader. But off the football pitch he was weighted down with the burden of his sister. Can you imagine what it must be like having a prodigy in the family? Add to that the attention the media started giving her and you've got Alex on your hands.

Q: What sort of things were you seeing him about?

CD: His so-called practical jokes mostly.

Q: Which were?

CD: Oh, he was quite inventive, I'll concede that. We had a Spanish language teacher start here – originally from Brazil I think, so hated the cold – and she was always making sure the windows were shut tight in winter, to keep in the heat. You must know the sort of classroom windows I mean – they hinge near the bottom and swing inward about five degrees?

Q: I remember.

CD: Well, Alex came in early one morning . . . (PAUSE) . . . I assume it was him, and he didn't deny it afterwards when I accused him. Well, he went into the classroom early with a glass cutter, scribed around the edges of each pane, and then opened the windows very carefully. You can guess what happened?

Q: Please, for the record.

CD: The class came in – with Miss Costas in tow – and the first thing she told the children by the windows, was to close them.

Q: They slammed them shut?

CD: They slammed them shut, yes. Twelve panes of glass fell out with the impact. Blatant vandalism.

Q: And how did you punish him?

CD: We still had the cane then, dear boy.

Q: So it was practical jokes then? A reaction to the situation he found himself in at home?

CD: Well, it was not only those pathetic pranks that concerned me. It was his blatant disregard for authority that was the main insult. I thought that'd be the part that would interest you.

Q: How do you mean?

CD: I wasn't born yesterday. If you're a freelance writer doing an unauthorized biography on Professor Serena Freeman, then I'm a cuckoo. You're doing a background check on him, aren't you?

Q: I'm sorry, I don't know what you mean.

CD: I'm ex-army – a captain in the paratroops – I know a
     Positive Vet when I see one. Don't worry, I don't
     mind being asked. (PAUSE) Has Alex Freeman done
     something wrong? I always thought he was a potential
     subversive.

Q: That's an interesting choice of word.

CD: He became politicized very early. I thought the
     bloody Reds had converted to our religion, rather
     than still being able to attract barrack room law-
     yers like Freeman. As far as I'm concerned he was
     always heading for trouble. A restless mind, you
     see? I do know how children can turn out. 'Give me the
     child till he is seven and I'll give you the man.' I
     didn't get the chance, as the man he must have become
     was formed before he came into my realm. And if he's
     anything like I think he is – then I'd also have to
     ask questions about his sister.

Q: Why's that?

CD: Genes, dear boy, genes. Alex Freeman's bad blood
     just rose earlier, that's all.

Q: Maybe I'll mention that in my book.

CD: You do that son, you do that – if you still insist on
     sticking to your story. And don't forget, if you
     think he's a danger, just imagine what *she* (ITALICS
     ADDED) could do. Those bad genes combined with that
     intellect – in a *woman*. (ITALICS ADDED) That's why I
     pay taxes, because . . .

(REMAINDER OF INTERVIEW PRIMARILY TAKEN UP WITH DOWNEY'S
PERSONAL VIEWS ON THE STATE OF THE NATION. BUT HE HAS A
POINT. PROFESSOR FREEMAN IS A FAR GREATER THREAT THAN HER
BROTHER IS – *FAR* GREATER.)

FIVE

Bad news is wildfire.

And its effects can produce similar long-term changes in attitude and approach to life.

To say that King Eurystheus was startled to hear, days before Hercules even returned to the city, that the hero had fought, let alone killed, the Nemean Lion is an understatement. He made some less-than-regal comments and stomped around the palace a bit. After he recovered from the initial shock, and began to turn things over in his mind, he felt that little whisper of fear that rulers are apt to experience now and then. It is the King-of-the-Castle Syndrome: the child's game whereby you have a potential to be knocked from your high position. The vortex of wildfire bad news had left a scorch mark.

Eurystheus hurried back to his throne room. He sent out an edict, and a number of his biggest soldiers to back it up, that Hercules was to be prevented from entering the city of Mycenae. Then he looked around for even more protection. Always one for a different spin on a principle (it was something Hera appreciated in him; though maybe not quite in this context – the gods themselves preferring good attacking ideas, rather than defensive ones), Eurystheus arranged for an enormous bronze jar to be cast. He then half-buried it in the gardens of his palace and stored his best weapons and armour inside it – in case he needed to retreat should Hercules decide to breach the city gates.

As he stood in his jar, thus setting the trend for over-zealous safety officers for centuries to come, he rubbed his hands in the time-honoured fashion of one who is satisfied with a job well done, and it occurred to him to take one final precaution. He spun his inspiration further by issuing his subsequent orders to Hercules via a herald.

Even delivering bad news can also provide work.

"Your next task," said the herald, reading from a tablet, "is to kill the Lernaean Hydra."

The herald was standing to attention outside the city gates, dressed in his best black and gold ceremonial armour, and he addressed Hercules' forehead. (The herald had been told that it both gave the appearance of authority and intimidated people. Every day before reporting for duty at the palace, he would practise out-staring his pet cat. It was a good day for him if the cat lost.) The herald cleared his throat, even though it was completely unnecessary, and continued in the clear, rather loud, deep voice that he also had to practise – and which caused the cat to regard him with apparent disdain.

"Ahem. It is known that this foul and *ghastly* beast, on an almost daily basis, slithers out of the dank and loathsome bottomless swamps near Lerna to set early-morning ambushes close to its den, and then hunts voraciously throughout the countryside for the rest of the day if it fails to secure prey. It is a *dangerous* pestilence on the environs and particularly on the unwary wayfarer."

When, as the herald did, you stood tall and broad and had used your useful connections to get the career you wanted, it's a bit of a blow to find yourself having to deal with someone who is even taller and broader – and, being the son of the king of the gods, far better connected. The man before him had the air of someone who had already seen battle, yet had shaken off the experience as a mere trifle. He was relaxed, tanned, had muscles in places that the herald didn't have places, possessed the calm, chiselled features of an artist's model, and at this instant, was stroking his tidy beard thoughtfully. You take the opportunities your position allows, thought the herald. For a moment he stopped reading aloud, looked Hercules straight into the eyes this time and raised one eyebrow.

"Be warned," he continued, "that this *gargantuan* creature, spawned from a union of two gods, whose body resembles nothing less than a giant, foul slug, has *nine* serpent heads, one of which is immortal. This is a progeny conceived by gods, remember. Oh, and its breath is so poisonous it is reported that the smell kills any living thing that has the misfortune to inhale it. Curious how one would know that, hum?"

The man glanced up again and smiled with the thin smirk of one who is only passing on a message.

"Good luck," he said, finally.

Hercules smiled the smile of someone who is in total control of what is about to happen within the next few seconds. He squared his shoulders, punched the herald on the nose, then headed off.

Aside from the small point of being harassed by a slimy monster that made a habit of eating its own residents and any visitors, Lerna had a lot going for it. Cool sea breezes to ease the heat, rich soil for the farmers, wealthy religious tourists (the ones that survived passing the swamp), and the place was just down the road from the nightlife of Argos. So Hercules decided to arrive in style in this cosmopolitan town. He persuaded his nephew Iolaus – a young man still basking in the glow and glory of victory in the Olympic chariot racing (presents from everyone, an exemption from taxes, and free meals every day) to act as his uncle's charioteer chauffeur.

The clean-shaven Iolaus donned the golden armour that he'd worn in the races – he thought it complemented his fair hair – and proffered a hand to assist Hercules board the chariot.

"You need help there, old man?" said Iolaus.

Hercules reached up, clasped Iolaus' hand firmly in his own, squeezed a little harder than Iolaus had been expecting, and grinned at his nephew.

"I think we're going to get along fine," Hercules said.

He grasped the front rail, adopted his best hero pose and thrust his arm out in front of him, his forefinger pointing the way.

"This way, please," he said, still smiling, "and stop play-acting for the girls."

He then dropped his arm and placed his hand on his hip. Iolaus bit the tip of his tongue, forced himself to look ahead, and whipped the horses into a quick trot.

The pair soon arrived at the swamp near Lerna and, as Iolaus reined in the horses, the two adventurers studied the home of the Hydra. It was a dirty little part of the world: the trees had rotted away to mouldy stumps, the ground was more mud and filth than earth, and pools of stagnant water lay everywhere. There was also a mist, floating in a layer just above the surface of the swamp, that moved slower – and was of a darker colour – than the snorting clouds the horses rent the morning air with. An unpleasant odour added an extra dimension.

"Loathsome," said Hercules. "He was right."

Iolaus raised an eyebrow.

"My friend, the herald," explained Hercules.

Iolaus looked around, nodding his head.

"I left home for *this*," he said. "Thanks for asking me along."

"Not the prettiest place, I agree," a female voice added.

The pair turned around.

Apart from Iolaus, Hercules had some other help that he hadn't told his nephew – or King Eurystheus – about. The goddess Athene had joined them. It pays to be connected.

"May I suggest," she said, "that the best way to get the Hydra's attention would be to shoot flaming arrows into its den on the island over there?"

Iolaus grinned at her. Hercules flicked the young man's ear.

"Come on, boy," he said, "and thank *you*, my lady Athene."

Athene smiled back at him.

"Any time," she said.

Iolaus stared at them in turn and repeated his words: 'I left home for *this*. Thanks for asking me along.' He jumped down from the chariot and started to search for kindling.

Hercules adjusted his cloak, made from the Nemean Lion, wrapped straw around the tips of his arrows, lit them in the fire Iolaus had constructed, and let them loose towards the island den. The blazing arrows cut through the dank cloud of the swamp's mist and exploded in showers of fire at the entrance to the monster's lair. Hercules carried on fitting the arrows to his bow and sent them flying over the mire.

The Hydra stirred from its lair and appeared outside. It was bigger than Hercules and Iolaus had expected.

After a pat on the back from Iolaus, Hercules took a deep breath and held it, then ran towards the hissing nightmare. He figured that if he didn't inhale the poisonous breath of the Hydra, he'd be all right. The mammoth, mucus-oozing obscenity reared up at his approach, each serpent head turning to face him, and each of all the nine was spitting foul venom. Hercules didn't pause – he ran straight towards the nearest snarling head.

No sooner had he seized one long neck in his mighty hands though, than the Hydra coiled another around one of Hercules' legs ensuring that there would be no escape for him. He was trapped. Hercules set to work to prove otherwise. Unfortunately he soon discovered that as he smashed asunder a head with his club, two more grew to replace it. This was a small problem the herald had forgotten to mention. To add to Hercules' woes, just as he thought it couldn't get worse, while he wrestled with his trapped leg, a large crab from the swamp scuttled up and nipped his toe. Not only was this a total surprise, but it was a savage enough nip to make a normal man scream. Hercules didn't have the privilege, at that moment, so he smashed the crab to pieces with his club and then managed to gesture to his nephew Iolaus for help.

Iolaus did the only thing he could think of and ran up to him with a burning torch. Hercules nodded approval and made a downward jabbing movement with his free hand. Fortunately, Iolaus understood. Hercules clubbed one head of the Hydra to a mash of nothing but shattered bone and gristle, Iolaus cauterized the wounded remains of its neck with the fire from his torch, thus sealing the mess to prevent the growth of replacement heads. As the pair of them continued with this exercise, the stumps of the necks bucked and twisted, to no avail.

The toxic fumes issuing from the serpent's mouths began to thin as the number of its heads diminished. The last head, the immortal one, Hercules severed with his sword and buried from view under a rock. Iolaus sealed off that wound too. Unable to breathe, the rest of the Hydra finally lay dead. Satisfied, Hercules dared breathe his first lungful of air for five minutes and, becoming aware of a stinging taint on his lips from the dispersing mist, had the bright idea of dipping his arrowheads in the Hydra's blood. Each one would now be instant death to any living thing they touched, let alone impaled. Hercules and Iolaus then bid farewell to Athene and they headed home, triumphant.

"I'm sorry," said the herald, this time standing well back from Hercules' reach, "but King Eurystheus isn't impressed. He says you had help."

The man nodded towards Iolaus, then took another step back, keeping a fixed and firm expression.

He carried on. "The king also asked me to tell you that, well, actually, when he thinks about it, all you did was kill some big water snake. So I'm afraid this won't count as one of your ten labours."

The herald nipped back behind the city gate, and instructed the guards to shut it promptly.

Hercules rent the air with curses.

From her heavenly position on Mount Olympus, Hera

smiled to herself. This was going better than she had hoped, and she would decide what to do about that traitor Athene later.

After some thought over a number of days, Eurystheus became more devious in his thinking and he took a delight in that, because, for all his fear of Hercules, the king was having fun. It was great to be a king in those days – your subjects knew to keep their distance whenever you smirked. So Eurystheus issued his latest edict: Hercules' next task was to catch the Hind of Ceryneia. Not to kill the deer, no, as that would have been too easy for the likes of the sort of hero that could kill the Nemean Lion: Hercules had to bring back the Hind alive.

"And, I'm sorry to say," the herald added quickly, "she happens to be sacred to the goddess Artemis." He spread his arms wide and shrugged. "So," continued the herald, "you'll have to be careful when you bring back this hind of Artemis, she might get upset with you. And," he consulted his tablet of instructions, "it's larger than a bull apparently, its hoofs are crafted from bronze, its very horns are made from gold, and it runs like the wind. Quite an animal, isn't it? It'll be difficult to catch. And, as I believe I warned before, it's Artemis' pet."

He took his, now customary step back, smiled his herald's smile, and strode back into the city to give his report to Eurystheus, who was waiting crouching in his pot, armed to the teeth.

"Damn," said Hercules. He set off on his hunt.

The Hind itself was easy to track and Hercules soon had it in his sights, and apparent reach, but how to ever catch it without killing it? It seemed to taunt him. At his every leap and bound to seize it, for mile after mile, the Hind skitted away, light of foot, running ahead, and its evasive dance would end, only a little further on, as it lowered its head again to eat. Still, of course, with a wary eye on its pursuer. So this pursuit carried on, longer than Hercules had anticipated.

The days became weeks, the weeks became months, and, as sand trickled through the glass, the months became a year. By this time, even the Hind was getting tired – Hercules had been relentless in his chase – but the animal still had a trick or two to reveal. To escape, it headed for a mountain, and then on to a river bank. For the first time in a year, the Hind began to disappear intermittently from Hercules' view as it pushed its way in amongst the reeds. It seemed now that the creature had the upper hand. Was this how it would all end, in failure?

Hercules was tired of the chase himself. But after a year of pursuit, he had found time to figure out a possible solution. So he stopped running after it and put the string to his bow. Keeping his eye on the elusive target, he took an arrow that had not been dipped in the Hydra's blood and let fly a cunning shot. It sliced through the reeds and caught the Hind by surprise. The arrow nipped together its forelegs, preventing its further flight, but causing the animal little pain.

The goddess Artemis was furious and put in an immediate appearance. As Hercules hoisted the animal onto his back, she confronted the hero.

"What, in the name of Zeus, have you done?" she cried out, her hands on her hips, her angry face only inches from his chest.

Hercules shrugged his shoulders, but held on tighter to the Hind. It squirmed uncomfortably and looked down at its mistress.

"Necessity," Hercules explained. "The oracle has told me to perform any labours that King Eurystheus dictates. You can't argue with what is ordained – besides, the animal will soon recover from such minor wounds."

Artemis looked the hero up and down as she wondered what to do with him. She remembered what Athene had told her about him, and found herself gazing at him with a different eye. He had that aura: a bit of a brute really.

"Okay," she said, turning away and looking over her shoulder, "I forgive you, but handle the Hind carefully."

Hercules nodded, and headed back to Mycenae – and a rather surprised Eurystheus.

(It perhaps doesn't need to be noted but, after a year with the hero away on his quest and looking as though he would fail, the herald was less surprised than his master, but more consumed with hatred, when he saw Hercules return with the Hind. He couldn't even bring himself to speak. Which was just fine with Hercules.)

SIX

W Day. 08.46. Green Beach.

I charge through the undergrowth that's only yards from the surf-line – flinching at every incoming mortar explosion and every rifle crack – to get off the beach. We have to move; others are following us in and they'll need room to deploy. The extra items of kit I decided to add to my supplies make their presence known to me after my rolling and squirming on getting ashore. They bang and knock against my body – the additional canteen of water I've got strapped on hitting me hard in the kidneys – but I can't let them bother me. It's move, move, *move*.

Glance right.

Glance left.

Check ahead.

Check ahead.

I grunt and gasp with every rapid stride forward. Clumps of long sword grass whip at my legs, and already there are small cuts in parts of my uniform.

Glance right.

Glance left.

Move forward again.

I ignore the bullet nick on my thigh – I can deal with it later. God knows what will happen to those guys who converted their leggings into illegal shorts because of the heat on the boats. Perhaps they'll be arriving later in the day when there may be less imperative to run and duck. But that was their choice, their gamble. On an assault like this, it's all about how you bet, how you see the throw of the dice. I have Joe and Bob's cards in my top pocket now – I nearly forgot them in my haste to follow Rici. I've lost sight of him, but I hear him grunt and yell out.

"Grenade!"

For a second it is visible in the air ahead – he's given it quite a heave. Then there's a kind of silence right in amongst the hell-noise of chaos everywhere, as time slows to a stop – as it sometimes does in action. Then there's the crack. And a scream. That's another Enemy out of the way.

Rici appears out of the jungle, some twenty yards in front of me. He signals to me that it's okay to bring the squad up and he gives me the hurry-up sign. I turn and beckon the Boys forward. Henry and Jim (Hank and Babe), rise to move at a crouch, Jim keeping his BAR horizontal and aiming inland, and they weave themselves off the beach towards me, trying not to trip over the dead. They are acting as one and offering each other protection. Henry does a jink to the right, Jim goes with him. Jim stumbles and Henry steadies him.

I have a different image of them at this moment.

I can see Jim running across the yard of his farm to tell his mother some news; the chickens scatter and the dust raises from his worn boots, a patch on his overalls flapping in need of a stitch or two that his mom will do later. The sun catches his eyes and they shine. I also have a vision of Henry: he's running out from the ocean and up onto a beach, somewhere in his home state of California. His worries about making it as an actor have been put on hold, and he is simply enjoying himself. He's with friends, they've got a barbecue ready, and the surf is crashing in. A girl waves to him. Life, for him, for that moment, is easy. He's tanned, his blond hair is wet and slick, he jogs with ease, the knife scars have faded, he's the embodiment of health. He's laughing and smiling.

I readjust back to reality – Henry *is* laughing.

I frown.

"What's up?" I ask him, reaching out to touch his elbow as he passes me. He doesn't stop laughing, nor does he answer me. Jim – three steps behind – jerks his head to his right.

"Can you believe it?" he says to me. "It's nice to have the spare time. Show me where to sign up for that deal."

Henry laughs out loud again.

I look down the strip of beach to where Jim was indicating. Two grinning marines are lying less than five yards from their landing craft. They have raised the Stars and Stripes on a boat-hook, and are having their picture taken.

Am I necessary to this war? Everybody else seems to have cameras. My newspaper doesn't really need me: they could cut their budget if they put out a request in the small ads. Hey, your country needs your pictures. Dead Enemy shot gets double rates.

The marines carry on smirking as bullets flick the ground around them.

Th-zip!

Th-zip!

I mentally raise my hat to them – and to the man taking the photograph. That's the power of photography: forget the war, guys, just say cheese. People are doing strange things today, as they always do when coming ashore, and I take a glance at the men disembarking, watching out for any other titbits I can write about. It's like a disturbed ant's nest: men are jumping, leaping, ducking, shooting, throwing grenades – creating and unleashing their personal maelstrom in the fiercest way they know.

I nearly miss Vizi jostling past me.

Johnny Van Zandt is whispering foul obscenities (he and Joe Plotkin would spend a large amount of spare time together in drunken binges), then the expression on his face hardens. He grits his teeth, slows the sweeping of his BAR, and he suddenly finds time to apologize for banging into me.

"I'm sorry, Nix. Didn't see you there."

For once, I notice he has his chin strap done up. His helmet must be playing hell with his hair. He gives a quick jerk of his hand that could be a salute.

Killing can make you very polite.

The rest of the squad follow him in a rush, ready to fire, ready to do whatever they're here to do. The Cincinnati Marx Brothers – Ron, Bill and Barney – all have a look of absolute terror and bewilderment in their eyes: this is their first taste of combat and they've discovered the difference between training and reality. I nod and wink at them.

"Hey, guys," I say, "enjoying your Day at the Races?"

It's a poor joke, but it has the effect I intended. Though they've heard it so many times, they manage to take a deep breath and grin back. Some of the terror leaves their eyes. Barney – Harpo – is the first to regain his cool. He was assistant to a ball-wrecking crew back in Cincinnati, so he is probably more used to bangs and heavy crashes. He was the first of the three of them, yesterday evening, to shave the sides of his head and leave only a four-inch strip on top.

"Happy birthday to me," he says.

I shake my head.

"That's good, Harpo," I say to him.

Barney flips me the bird – Esprit de Corps.

Amos brings up the rear and he has the same look about him as Van Zandt – he's planning on putting *his* training to good use. The Chief pats my shoulder firmly to urge me on. The thump makes me feel like I'm being rounded up. I realize he is chewing tobacco and I move to one side to give him room to spit. God, we're so polite.

"Come on, Nixy," he growls.

I move . . . I get past the tree-line . . . I look back again. The Marines of the 21st continue to emerge from their landing craft, and then stampede forward and inland, converging on the Enemy.

I'm off the beach.

Thank fuck.

I glance over my shoulder yet again – and gawk.

Behind me I leave a version of hell that no amount of photography is ever going to capture correctly. On the horizon, sitting between the beautiful blues of sky and water, are the slim destroyers. They are pounding round after round over our heads and towards the ridge line. That low stuttering whistle has become a comfort: it means that there may be one less Enemy waiting for me up ahead. On the intermediate stretch, where the ocean turns coral, the rest of the LVTs are swarming and jostling to find an open place to hit the beach. Nearly two hundred open-topped water-tanks are churning up the foam; the men in the two cone-turrets of the landing craft that possess them are firing into the gap in the shattered palm groves where their vehicles will crawl inland.

Some get hooked on rises of coral and are stuck fast. Ideal targets for the Enemy.

I look away from the mortar fire falling down upon them to the LVTs that are moving forward. All I can see are rows of helmets, faces, shoulders and weapons held close and vertical. Minimum space aboard. The LVTs are producing an orgy of noise – their combined diesels corrupting my mind into thinking, for a moment, that I'm in some sort of mad farmhouse-tractor rally. They battle with the beach and thrust themselves as far up it as they can – giving their cargo more of a chance, making room for what will follow them.

Behind them are the DUKWs – those ingenious amphibious trucks – ready to move in with their 105mm howitzers. It's good tactics to get the medium artillery onto the beachhead early; it gives us an extra punch, makes us feel we're getting the strength in. If we're lucky, we'll see some "Zippo" M4 Sherman tanks after that. But that's still the future. I'm thinking too far ahead. I must concentrate.

Boom!

Shit!

A DUKW takes a direct hit. It becomes a fire-cloud of carnage. The silhouette of a marine – arms and legs outstretched – arcs into the sky.

I turn away and—

Oomph!

I trip and fall. Wasn't careful, wasn't looking. That changes. I'm looking darn good now. I'm flat on my chest, and less than a foot from me is a yard-long coral sea snake – red, yellow, black. Nature couldn't give any more obvious signs that it's as poisonous as hell, even if she tried. The thing must have slithered here to escape the racket we were causing in the shallows. I think I'm more surprised than it is, because I'd been assured that there were no snakes on Guam.

The Lernaean Hydra – Hercules' second task.

It writhes, a forked tongue tastes the air, and the snake begins to rise up.

It's going to strike!

Before I can think anything more I grab the first thing that comes to hand – a large coconut – and slam it down on the snake's head. Its now headless body squirms and jerks – just like Joe Plotkin's – then is still.

Good – I'm making the best of my opportunities.

I ask the snake's forgiveness – as my grandfather had taught me, and I start breathing again.

That's the right way, isn't it, Grandpa?

We were way up in the hills outside of Asheville, North Carolina, my grandfather and I, hunting deer, when I was taught the sanctity of life. I was twelve then. It was early fall; the leaves of the beech, chestnut, maple and oak trees enjoying that moment of being glorious in their gold and yellows. Colors that, in the distance, merged as if some artist had lost his mind and gone wild with his water paints – the sort of inspired outburst that produces stunning pictures.

As we crept along the trail, me trying to hold my Springfield rifle in the correct manner my grandfather had shown me, a few of the leaves were starting to drift down. I had been taught, a long time before that trip, that you never swept them away if they fell into your face – you just moved on as before, another beast in the woods that didn't make any sudden movements. I felt as though we could have been early settlers, out gathering food for our family; or even farther back, as Indians providing game for our hearth. This was the America that my grandfather had come to love – he told me that he felt honest here in the mountains, that it was impossible to tell lies to yourself, let alone others; that this was where the heart of the country could be found. I felt at home too. At home in such an enormous land. And I was terribly excited; being taken on the hunt meant I was growing up.

The air held a mountain freshness that I had come to relish; the morning was not even halfway through. There were no clouds. The wind wafted the smell of forest fruit that was ready to be eaten by its inhabitants, with a slight musty texture that hinted of deep sleep and hibernation. It was a hunter's breeze. All about, there was the undercurrent of suggestion that the mountains were about to undress and retire for a hard winter, and the animals were leaving easy tracks in the moist earth as they hurried to stock up on their stores and protective fat. The inherent threat in this atmosphere was that during the next season, only the strong would survive, as Nature dictated. That freshness was a hint of the sharp knife of winter.

Our pursuit had lasted three hours before we caught sight of the animal my grandfather had been tracking, and I had felt tired for the last two of those hours. We were much higher in the mountains than I had ventured before. As we reached the brow of a small rise, the animal itself came into view. It was a big, whitetail buck. We edged behind the cover of a red berry bush, and I realized that my grandfather was nodding at me slowly. I knew what he meant: he was allowing me to take the shot.

I looked at the buck, fifty, sixty feet upwind and tried to calm my heart. Keeping my eye on the animal – grazing, cautious but unaware – I slowly raised my rifle to my shoulder, the added rubber boot on the stock nestling into me as it had in practice, and I eased the safety off. The buck stopped eating and raised its head. I took a deep slow breath and aimed. The foresight of the Springfield drifted out of focus as I squinted down the barrel, but the animal itself stayed sharp, as my grandfather had said it would. I held my breath. Squeezed the trigger. The buck's eyes found me at last and it looked straight at me. At the moment it began to jump, my bullet hit it – a clean body shot. Nothing fancy, nothing clever, just a clean, efficient body shot – probably the heart.

As the buck's legs crumpled, unable to compete with the weight of death, the animal collapsed. We ran over towards it, that fresh mountain air filling my lungs, those golds and yellows flashing overhead, the leaves brushing my face. I was totally awake. I was alive.

I bit my lip. The animal lay on its side showing me death; its eyes were open, tongue was lolling to one side with saliva dripping from it; and the chest of the beast was matted with blood that made my nostrils twitch. I felt a sudden rush of shame and looked across to my grandfather. He gazed back at me, then knelt down and patted the buck's head.

"I'm sorry," he said to it gently, "but thank you."

He looked up at me, a sly smile on his lips as he noticed my confusion.

"Do you feel guilt?" he asked.

I nodded.

"Good," he said. "Never, *never*, kill anything without a reason, understand? This will fill our bellies for the next few days, and we've earned it. I'll show you all that you'll need to do to prepare it. But you understand the lesson?"

He stood up and clasped my shoulder.

"You may think that life is easy," he said, "but it's the other way around. It's death that's easy, Phoenix, and it's the living that's hard. I know there may come a time when you'll think back and consider that what I've said to you today is so much Grandpa nonsense, but don't forget this lesson. Never kill anything without a reason. If it's for sport, instead of the pot, so be it, but never lose sight of what you're doing. It's a life you're taking, so ask forgiveness afterwards."

And as I stood there, a slight tremor coursing through my limbs, the smell of new blood in my nose, he began to butcher the deer methodically. And, as he did so, he told me about the Legend of The Coconut Tree – about how the death of a young girl brought the fruit to the island when it sprouted from her grave.

"Life can spring from death", my grandfather said, slicing into the haunches of the whitetail buck. "Remember that in times of crises."

He smiled at me. "That is also how Guam was given the gift of the coconut."

I throw the one still in my hand aside, apologize to my Lernaean Hydra yet again, and clamber after my squad.

God, I could use a drink myself – a stiff rum, laced with spices. A big, fat quadruple, followed by another.

Pock! Pock!

I'm off the beach.

Whoo-bang! Whoo-bang!

My grandfather taught me how to kill, and here I am, at last, fighting for his history.

I'm off the beach.

We regroup and catch our breath. Losing three men so quickly means we'll have to make some adjustments, though slight. Ron takes over from Frank to give assistance to Amos with his BAR; Johnny and Bill merge with Henry, Jim and Barney to make a top-heavy Fire Team. I make a quick assessment of the situation we're in and check for the ever-present danger of Enemy. Around us grow swathes of thick, lush undergrowth, patches of more tall grass and countless palm trees, with more of them retaining all their fronds than those near the beach. I'd forgotten what it is like to be in jungle – even if it does look as if Barney has been busy here with his Cincinnati wrecking ball. The cloying moist smell of the chaotic jungle floor mixes with the stench of LVT fumes, cordite, and the aroma of pork, which I know isn't pork. This is indeed a different land to that which I grew up in. The nearest American equivalent I can think of is the Everglades – but without the expanses of water.

I glance around, check that beauty doesn't hide a beast.

There are so many delicate shades of green where the plants still survive. The sunlight catches broad leaves, turning them yellow and transparent. Bamboo fights its way above the shining lower vegetation. These plants could have grown up overnight, for all I know. It is also several degrees warmer in here, and moisture seems to hang in the air.

In places the earth has been ripped to pieces with the last few weeks of bombardment – today's barrage has simply stirred some of it around a bit. Smoke and steam rise from craters everywhere. Even here, just off the beach, the quality of sound has changed – the trees, the plants, the actual land itself having taken some of the sharp edge off the explosive thundering. The snap-crack of rifle-fire begins to filter through from the left and right, as others are moving forward. In front of *us* the ground rises sharply. This beachhead we're trying to establish is bloody narrow, and my first impression is that the Enemy appear to have taken root behind the ridgeline, so we'll have to figure how best to form an attack. I scan the area again, trying to make a judgment. We're not in danger just at the moment. I notice Amos is still near me.

"Hey," he says.

He then reaches over to me and flicks my breast pocket.

"You didn't wait, did you, Nixy?" he says. "What have you got?"

For a second I wonder what he's referring to. Then I grin as I pull out the cards. This is not the time to be doing this, but we're all catching our breath. A moment of light relief will help. I fan out the cards, glance at them, and pull my best wouldn't-you-like-to-know smile. The Chief comes and looks over my shoulder. I don't mind, as I'm doing great in the Dead Pool

Poker game. With the five cards I already had, plus Joe's, Bob's and Frank's, I've nearly half the deck from which to make a hand. This isn't how it was expected to happen, but I'm not complaining. Bob had an Eight High – the Eight of Spades over the Six of Spades, the Four of Hearts, the Three of Diamonds and the Two of Clubs. Joe had a Queen High – the Queen, Seven and Three of Clubs, the Six of Diamonds and the Deuce of Spades. I was dealt a high Pair, a couple of Aces – Spades and Diamonds – along with the Queen of Spades, Jack of Hearts and Eight of Diamonds. So, with Frank's cards that made up his Pair of Tens, I put together a full house – aces over Queens with Frank's Joker as one of the Aces – and rip up the remainder of the cards.

"They all had lousy hands," Amos comments. "I had them well beat, so did you. Says something, don't it? Bad luck?"

He sticks out his lower lip and shrugs his shoulders.

For a moment I consider the fact that he may be right, but I quickly dismiss such nonsense. Some of us had to have lower hands. There are more Jokers out there, not that I want to collect them, but they're out there still. Amos grunts and shrugs again. I've never noticed before how often he does so, and how he does it – slow, relaxed. I tell him I don't care that he's seen what I hold.

"Nixy, I'm tempted to put a bullet in you myself," he says.

I put the lovely full house back into my pocket.

I must be leading in the Dead Pool Poker – I'd put money on it.

I laugh to myself. After all, Dead Pool Poker started as a joke.

We were back in camp, just a couple of hours before setting out for Guam, and Corporal Joe Plotkin had been his usual efficient self and had finished writing his letters home ages before the rest of us. Joe had gone off to walk around a bit in that relaxed stroll of his, chewing the fat with anyone who'd care to. Then he had come back to join us and began sharpening his knife and bayonet to what, I presumed, was an engineer's idea of perfection. Then, in a quick movement that seized our attention, he pulled a few bucks from his pocket and began folding and unfolding the notes.

"This will be a great help where we're going," he said. "Anyone fancy a bit of a gamble?"

"Bears haven't stopped shitting in the woods, have they?" suggested someone.

Joe said nothing for a moment. He knew how to time things, did Joe, and hung us out – silent – until just before we lost interest.

"Well," he finally said, those blue Sinatra eyes peering out of narrow, enigmatic slits, "how about something different?"

Everyone stopped himself from what he was doing, sat up, and took notice.

It took us over an hour to argue out the rules.

We each put in fifty bucks and were then dealt a five-card hand. Since there were initially twelve of us, we had to rob other decks of their Jokers to make up the right numbers. Ranking was as per any normal game found anywhere that card schools form. (This is what took up most of our time, since everyone seemed to belong to different card schools.) From the lowest: high card, one pair, two pair, three of a kind, straight, flush – the arguments about the order of those last two you wouldn't believe – full house, four of a kind, straight flush, royal flush, five of a kind; Jokers wild. If anyone ended up with five Jokers they'd win the pot. Cards to be kept in breast pocket. Why? The reason was to do with the added incentive that if you were taken out of the game, anyone from the rest of the squad would know where to look to acquire your cards. These extra cards could then be used at their discretion to improve their hand; those discarded were to be destroyed. (Not kept to one side to be traded, swapped or sold; they had to be ripped up and put beyond use, in honor of the person who had been forced to give them up.)

The money was held by yours truly in my other breast pocket – taped, waterproofed, folded tight into the silver cigarette case Alice had given me for my birthday: seven hundred and twenty bucks to the winner. That's the game of Dead Pool Poker that Corporal Joe Plotkin invented.

A sergeant from 2nd Platoon had come up to Rici just as I had tucked the cigarette case into my jacket pocket under the watchful eyes of everybody.

"We're off," he had informed Rici.

Joe had smiled his smile, and was the first of the queue of men that had then to come up and pat the pocket where I'd hidden the money.

Game on – 'cause there's no other game in town. Just ask those who have gone before. We may have invented a stupid distraction but, sometimes, as the saying goes, if you don't laugh, you'll cry. And there's enough to cry about out here, always enough horror for everyone in a war.

We were told the stories, no, told the *facts*, while waiting in Guadalcanal. Some of it was down to a Guam islander who had taken his skiff, sailed off to safety and reported what was happening. The Enemy had invaded Guam on December 10th 1941 – just three days after Pearl Harbor – and they hit an outpost of American territory that had been ill prepared for such an event after years of neglect considering its strategic importance. The fight lasted a little over six hours; how could it have been otherwise when there were five and a half thousand Enemy pitched against a defensive force of less than three hundred? And that's when it started: that's when Americans discovered what the Enemy was capable of, face to face.

That's what boils my hatred.

A marine, waiting with others while the CO negotiated surrender, either suffered from jitters that caused his face to twitch, or he swore – not aware that one of the Enemy had picked up the basic insults used by Americans. The man didn't last long. The Enemy got pissed – he thought the marine was showing disrespect – and sliced his bayonet into him.

The occupation had started. East met West.

The islanders, undoubtedly some of which must have been

my long-lost relatives, suffered in ways that make me want to cry out. The one that escaped in his skiff had other stories that were passed to me via my newspaper.

Imagine one scene. Cave entrances in the interior of this tropical island of my fathers, outside of which stand two groups, men and women separated. It's late in the day, humid, the insects buzz and crawl. There are men wearing uniforms, their rifles fixed with bayonets, and the officer carries a long sword – the symbol of his rank. He gives an order that the two groups are to go into separate caves, and pass the night there while he decides what to do with them. So thirty-odd men and the thirty-odd women file into those dark and dank openings, wondering what is going to happen to them in the morning. They have done nothing to deserve this aggression; they look questioningly at their captors and see nothing but hate and contempt.

The island men make themselves as comfortable as they can, murmuring reassurances to each other, forcing smiles and poor jokes to their lips. Then the grenades spiral in through the dim light. They explode with echoing cracks and men gasp and scream and die. And as the survivors stagger and grope around, there is a command directed at them.

"Come out!"

As the first man reaches the humid, insect-singing, insect-crawling exterior, there is a soft, slick swishing noise and his decapitated body falls, shivering its last.

"Come!"

They still respond to the command.

Swish! Soft and slick, soft and slick.

"Come!"

Some manage to move evasively at the last moment – they are cut, but do not die.

The officer grows bored, gestures to his men. They go into the cave to finish off the living. Then they move on to the cave with the women. There they repeat the scenario, add rape to their crime, and leave none alive. Only their screams tell their story to the male survivors.

This is a war about stopping people doing terrible things to other people.

We have to react to barbarians and accept the cost of our actions. There will be tragedy and sadness.

The men I have seen fight, the men I have fought alongside, all think like me: I see dead Enemy as dead Enemy, dead marines as comrades I miss, but at least they're not me, yet. And that's how *everyone* thinks. It is unlikely that any of us will see the Pacific campaign to its natural end: standing on the steps of Tokyo's City Hall. I'm beginning to wonder how much someone can take. At the wire though, at the conclusion to the game – it's luck, pure and simple. Luck.

So, with all the carnage I'm watching, photographing and participating in, with all that history of recent blood on my forefathers' land, Dead Pool Poker seems an angry laugh at Death – it's an allegory about the chance of life. I like that.

Joe Plotkin handed me the money to keep safe, because "you're a rich bastard, Nix, and won't need to steal it. If you win, you'll see the Boys are all right. And if you take one, you know we won't cry about you – sir."

As I patted the money, I told Joe the facts of life.

"Fuck you, Joe – I'm the squad's main drunk. It'll only take me ten days to drink my way through this lot – they teach that sort of stuff in journalist's survival school. It means I'll never die and rot away, because I've been pickled in alcohol since I was a kid."

Then we got the final order to board our ships to start our journey.

W Day. 10.14. Green Beach. First rise of ground inland.

Pock! Pock!
Whoo-bang! Whoo-bang!
Th-zip! Th-zip! Th-zip!
We're trapped, pinned down. Bullets, crying like high-

pitched insults, zip and ricochet over our heads. And it seems the Enemy is simply throwing all their mortars over the edge of the cliff towards us in one go. Rici is issuing orders from about thirty feet to my right. It's the same type of staccato Italian bark he uses in his father's restaurant. The squad is spread out, squirming on their bellies through the jungle mush. I assist Rici by shouting at Barney, standing about four yards behind me, to get down.

"Tallent – take cover, you fucking idiot!"

He jumps, his whole body jolting at the sound of my raised voice, and he throws himself forward, kisses the ground, and then struggles to turn his head towards me. His face is pale, and I think he's been sick.

"Thanks, Nix," he says.

Ba-ba-ba-ba-ba!

Snap-crack! Snap-crack!

I wiggle my fingers at him and point at Rici, then cup a hand to my ear.

Barney nods, as he understands, and struggles once again to turn his head, this time towards Rici.

Whoo-bang!

Another mortar explodes close by.

"Colonel Butler has ordered us to stay here," shouts Rici from a hole he liberated three minutes ago. "We'll wait for the reserves to join us – they won't be long – then we'll circle around this piece of shit."

He jerks his thumb at the cliff, whose rock face is nearly vertical. Every one of us hate it; we know we should be moving, making ground, because becoming stalled is the worst thing. We must get ahead of our fear; make our own luck.

Another mortar comes whistling down from the heights. I squeeze further into the shattered palm I am taking cover behind, and pull my helmet down further onto my head. A shower of earth patters over me. I hear Barney Tallent swear – at least he isn't whimpering – so I can ignore him for the moment. I then realize I can roll over and look back the way we came up. It will give me something to do while we wait, and I can check that the reinforcements are indeed on their way.

Perhaps get a photograph? Work out what to do next.

I can leave Rici to sort the Boys out, so I stare at the ocean. Someone down there is doing their part: it looks as if in a few moments' time, more tanks will come ashore. The beach is crowded, but everyone will make room for the Shermans. (The Boys still refer to them as M4s – but I like the other name.) Heavy armor is heavy armor and I can't wait to hear those engines grunt into life, and hear some other shells heading for the cliff top. Facing a tank, even the weak old things that the Enemy uses, is absolutely terrifying. It's a metal Trojan horse: great to be safely behind, a fury to face.

Th-whoop!

Another DUKW explodes, but the marines who were inside it are already wading ashore. I don't think anyone caught one. The black smoke curls upwards, riven with a bright magenta flame. There are sparks of white – ammo exploding. It adds to those Hieronymus Bosch visions of hell that Tom Wakefield took delight in showing me reproductions of in Cambridge. Like the artist's triptych *Garden of Earthly Delights*, in particular the right panel contemplating the darkness of The Fall into the pit of hell, with its cracked, white egg on tree-trunk legs. The horror of it.

Thanks, Tom. You knew, didn't you?

That fantastically visceral vision of damnation was something to reflect on, and try to ignore, while I waited with the others on our extended layover at Eniwetok prior to today. And I, like everybody else, had plenty of time: fifty-two days. W Day had been pushed back because of the ferocity of the Enemy's defense of Saipan. Apparently no one in Brass had considered the obvious: that if we thought that place so important, then the Enemy might think the same, and do everything to stop us. What they did to the marines there at Saipan gave our replacements food for thought. It stirred *my* imagination as well.

So we endured, we waited: a month and a half in a floating LST (Landing Ship Tank) oven which rolled in its own peculiar see-saw motion and gently broiled and sucked away our strength. Rici and I had commandeered one of the many jeeps lashed down top-side and settled in – space on the deck became prime real estate and the guys who'd already seen some action were the ones quick off the mark. An old soldier always takes every opportunity to catch up on his sleep.

And the officers soon had to find ways of stopping lethargy taking hold. We were briefed, then briefed again ... then briefed and briefed again. Men became able to recite what they were being told, some of them moving their lips in synchronization with the officer standing before them, their hands clasped behind their backs as his were. We did calisthenics, and we then took our weapons to pieces and cleaned and inspected them, and then we did calisthenics again and then we were briefed, then we had chow and then a kit inspection.

And when even the officers' ingenuity ran dry, we played cards. I wrote letters to my mother and father and Alice, made up stories to send my grandmother, and sent Tom dirty poems for him to recite over a glass of warm beer. I never once told him I was glad he was still alive, because that would have been the worst sort of curse, and was contrary to everything I believed. Then we did calisthenics, and were briefed, and miles away the navy continued its job of firing round after round into the beaches that awaited us.

The barrage the navy and air force provided must have been something to see: our landing points erupting under high explosive – bittersweet. The reason was simple: every day that we waited meant another bombardment would take place, either from the ships themselves or from air-strikes. All the main armament of the Enemy would be targeted – like his airfields and anti-aircraft positions – and as the fight in Saipan began to draw to a close, more battleships, destroyers and carriers were brought into the equation and unleashed a colossal amount of shells and bombs. This was great in terms of trying to reduce the number of Enemy we'd eventually have to fight, but it also gave them an extremely good idea where we were intending to land, and they could thus prepare for us. All we had to do was try to survive the wait and the heat. That was all: waiting and enduring the heat. You can't underestimate the wasting effects of sweating non-stop; it drains the body and the mind, it stops you thinking straight, it—

Snap-crack!

—I jerk my head around to one side. Barney Tallent is looking right at me, his eyes wide, his body prone, one hand in the act of reaching for a dead marine's water bottle. He tries to say something to me, but another bullet smacks into his face, ripping his jaw off. He splutters, chokes, then reaches into the air, clutching at nothing with his fingers. I start to struggle towards him, to grab his ankles and pull him back, calling for a corpsman as I do so. Then I stop, as another two shots have found their mark, and young Barney Tallent has become a statistic. The Cincinnati Marx Brothers have been reduced to two.

I do some useless swearing – then stop. A hand appears from the undergrowth and latches onto Barney's left ankle. I lean forwards, ever so slightly, to get a better look. It's Amos, and I know what he's after. Sure enough, after he's turned the shattered human remains around, he reaches into Barney's breast pocket. He removes the cards, glances at them and looks over at me.

"I wish he'd gotten hold of that bloody bottle . . . I need a drink," he says, licking his lips.

I lie back against my hiding place again.

I need a talisman. Something to give Luck a push in the right direction. To make my own luck, make my own luck.

I lie here and think again of that lovely female voice I heard in my head, about how it means I must be going mad, yet how

I don't care about it. I think of Hercules and his Labors and I smile when I think it would be nice to undertake them all, so as to give this insane adventure the perspective it deserves. I've done the first two; and I seem to remember the next had something to do with a special deer that belonged to one of the Greek gods.

The Hind of Ceryneia – that's it. Where in Hell's name am I going to find one of those on this island? And why does the thought of not being able to manage that send a quiver to my bowels? Ha! That's why I remembered earlier about hunting with my grandfather – the deer!

I hear Rici shout. "Move out, guys – the Second Battalion's arrived. And keep low."

I check my weapon, check my camera, then I squirm through the undergrowth, trying not to look at Barney Tallent with his wide eyes and the open space that was once his mouth.

Make your own luck.

Find a deer.

W Day. 20.45. Ridge overlooking Asan River.

We've finally made contact with the 2nd Battalion on our left, and the 1st of the 9th to our right. The squad is dug in for the long night ahead; Amos is already bragging about his Dead Pool Poker hand, hinting about mine, and I'm thinking about telling him to shut up because I still haven't spotted a deer. Which isn't going to be likely, anyway. So this desire to find one is really stupid, but it occupies my mind for several minutes at a time.

I've seen and heard an awful lot of things today that I wish I hadn't. Being in combat hardens you to the gruesome and unexpected, but I haven't slid back into the callous way of it all yet, not in the way the other veterans from Bougainville have. I look and listen for sights and sounds that my morbid curiosity assures me are out there. Yes, I can still see and hear some of them, so I'll have to try and think of something that I can equate to a deer. I lick my lips as I think of rum.

A few moments later, the dusk approaches, I am gazing down on the beachhead, assessing what we've done so far today – a day I doubt many of us are going to see the end of. Rici is beside me and we are sharing a water bottle.

"Were we really there?" asks Rici, jerking a thumb at the view.

The narrow strip of beach is even more crowded than when I last checked. There is the wreckage of damaged vehicles slowing progress, and the never-ending shuttle of ones still functioning that weave between them. Stranded LVTs are scattered on the surf line from Asan Point to Adelup. There are groups of wounded men taking shelter beside them, and every now and then Rici and I watch them cower as another mortar round comes down upon them. They wait, while we watch. Squads then marshal themselves and plunge into the undergrowth, to make progress and to make room, as we did. And still more equipment and men are arriving – the navy is doing its best to off-load every single supply item as soon as it can. They'll soon be bringing in the Army, as our back-up.

"Why don't the Enemy make some sort of thrust?" I ask. "It'd be the best way to throw us off. I don't understand that – its stupid of them. Haven't they learnt from their mistakes?"

"Don't pick holes, Nix. We could still be down there."

He rubs his chin and passes the water bottle to me.

"Thanks," I say. I take another swig; water without alcohol never tasted as good as this previously. The humidity and heat are taking men out in droves; Rici told me earlier that there are some marines whose sole job at the moment is to ferry barrels of water from the beach up to the line. I even hear shouts demanding that someone gets a move on with fetching the water. The man hollers back that he's doing his best. Exhaustion is dangerous – in an attack, it's bad enough not having the maximum strength of manpower due to battle casualties, but to lose any because they already spent six weeks on a boat and are currently trying to operate in a steam oven is a bad oversight. It is something that *we'd* been stupid not to realize, even after Bougainville.

"They've taken Chonito," says Rici.

I look over to the cliff to our left. As I watch, a marine with a flame-thrower braces himself and squirts an arc of fire at a cave entrance. It's brief in duration. The marine moves nearer to the entrance, concentrating his fire in another burst. He must have heard something from there.

"Seems they drew the short straw," I mutter.

The 3rd had been on Red Beaches to our left, and they'd caught the brunt of the flanking fire from Adelup Point: the Enemy had been able to aim their weapons straight down the entire length of the landing – if they missed one marine, there was a good chance of catching another. For a while anyway – our tanks had shut them up once they'd got into place. All we'd had to do was encircle this rise and exchange a ferocious amount of ammunition with a well-dug-in position from the next slope. That was all. All we had to worry about was thick undergrowth, while the 3rd had open ground and steep inclines to deal with. Target practice for the Enemy – a cliché turkey-shoot.

I take another swig of water. I think about rum.

"You seen any deer?" I ask Rici.

He scowls.

"You wanna eat venison, Nix? In this heat? Mama, save me from this fool. Have I spoilt you so much with my father's cooking? Don't you ever think of anything apart from your stomach?"

"I could murder a drink."

"You've got the bottle – which I notice you're still holding on to."

I pass him the water bottle.

"I mean a *drink*," I say.

"Well, brew it up yourself."

I smile at Rici's reference to my habit of constructing a still for moonshine at any opportunity. It's crude and it's ugly, and it's rawer than an open wound with lemon and salt on the side. Any marine who sees it is usually impressed; the quantities it produced are tiny and rough beyond imagination, but the thought is there.

"Here, have this," says Rici. "You can't afford to build a fire here, anyway."

He hands me a hip flask.

I stare at it. "You've had this all the time?"

He shrugs his shoulders. "I knew you'd need it sometime."

I unplug the cap, hesitate to savor the moment, then take a slug. It's my favorite rum. Thank god for Rici. It clears the muck of the day from my mouth, sends a thrill across my shoulders and down my back, tastes of memories of Cuban bars and dark-eyed women, and smells of wood-smoke and spices. It's glorious. It's the first of the day. I go to take another slug, but Rici gives me the eye. I hold his stare and just take a little sip, screw the cap back on and pass the flask back to him.

"Dehydration's not a good thing," he suggests.

But we both know the real reason.

When Rici met my sister Alice for the first time, she demonstrated to him clearly that our family is addicted to drink whenever they want to enjoy themselves, but she then told him that I'm the worst. It's like life to me.

I stare out at the beach again. I hate this waiting.

W Day. 23.36. Ridge overlooking Asan River.

It's night, it's cold and isolated banzai attacks have started. I can hear them in the distance. God help us if they start coming in packs: it could end up as hand-to-hand combat in the dark. Which is something to be avoided. But that's what the Boys are paid for, I suppose. I hear another Enemy cry out from his own personal hell, and the answering thud from a grenade – muzzle flash is something to avoid at night, it points to where you are.

I find myself considering that these demons emerging out of the forest could be the taotaomonas that my grandfather told me about – the ghosts of my ancestors, angry at being disturbed. But I doubt it. *We're* here to help Guam, not invade it. I lift a fist of dark earth to my nose.

Rici hisses at me.

"What the hell are you doing now?"

"Do you know how Guam was created," I ask him.

"What?"

He obviously doesn't, so, with the backdrop of banzai hollering and crackling bullets, with the pleasure of still being alive as I sprinkle the cold dirt from my fingers, with this chilling night air invading my lungs, with that memory of that mouthful of rum, I tell him. I don't think he wants me to, but I go ahead anyway. I tell him we were created out of the very earth.

"We're all made from it," I say.

"Some storyteller your grandfather was," says Rici. Pale teeth appear in the gloom as he smiles in my direction.

I couldn't have been more unprepared.

I am about to answer him, when one of my taotaomona ghosts comes crashing and screaming through the blackness. In the instant I get to react, I notice the Enemy is carrying a bottle, waving a bayonet and has a pouch slung over one shoulder. He's carrying more than most, and he'll probably have what I want – they're quite common trinkets. He's already too close, so, too late for a grenade. Rici and I both bring our carbines to bear, but I change my mind and I'm up and out of the foxhole, in a running crouch, ignoring Rici's warning calls, shouting at the Enemy, making him veer towards me, making me his target. When the Enemy spots, he screams. He brings his rifle up.

Snap-crack!

I beat him to the first shot.

The Enemy stumbles and begins to dance, as others in the squad zero in on him.

Ba-ba-ba!

Ba-ba-ba-ba-ba!

I stop. I let their onslaught do its job. The Enemy collapses less than two feet in front of me. I jump forward and ram my own bayonet into him, to make sure he stays down. And again I plunge it into him. And again. I can't understand how I've ignored that first rule: stay in the foxhole, stay in the foxhole.

"What the fuck was that?" calls Landu.

"Just a ghost," I reply, picking up the Enemy's bottle. It still has a large amount of *saki* left in it. This Enemy either couldn't take his drink, or it was his second bottle of the night.

"Jesus," answers Landu. "I'd hate to have met him when he was alive."

Rici and I laugh – he's come out to join me – but then he whispers in my ear.

"What the fuck is this all about, Nix?"

I decide not to answer, and instead I pull the Enemy's body nearer to the lip of our foxhole. There he'll give us more protection – and make it easier for me to search him. I deserve a reward for the stupid risk I took. As I grab his blood-wet collar, my fingers become entangled in something. At first I think it's a part of him, then I look closer and see he has an object slung on a thin wisp of leather around his neck.

This is not happening. I was right! I was right!

"What's that?" asks Rici, putting a hand on my shoulder as he leans closer to get a look.

"It's a netsuke."

"A what?"

"It's a netsuke. They use it on their kimonos. Kimonos don't have pockets, so they hang things off their sashes with a cord that has a bead and a toggle on the end to stop the pouch, pipe, purse, whatever, from slipping off. The toggle is called a netsuke."

I weigh it in my hand. It's heavy.

"What did they do to you in England to get you to learn all this stuff?"

"They let me read."

"Hmm, looks like ivory." Rici bends even closer and his hand clenches my shoulder. "Hey! It's your deer you were talking about."

I again look down at the carved animal I hold in my hand.

"It sure is," I say. "It sure is."

God, this is a quick way to lose your mind.

I put the netsuke carefully in my pocket, trying to ignore my thoughts.

We then drag the body back to our foxhole, jump in, and Rici adjusts the position of the dead Enemy to give us the best protection. He then nudges me out of my obsessive thinking as he gestures to the bottle, and we pass it between the pair of us, waiting to see what the rest of the cold night has in store for us. At least the exertion and alcohol will keep me warm for a while.

A deer, a bloody deer. What's next? What's next?

SEVEN

Bank Holiday Saturday.

"Why have we come all the way out *here*?" says Alex. "I could get the same olfactory satisfaction in a public toilet."

Alex adopts his I'm-tolerating-you-but-I'm-close-to-breaking demeanour, so Serena looks back down at her route map of Colchester Zoo to avoid answering him. It has taken them over an hour to get here, even with Alex pushing his revamped Saab well over the limit. The weather is hotter than yesterday and the noon sun resembles a blinding white disc. It is a perfect day to be on holiday.

A perfect day to seek out an unusual photograph. But can I persuade Alex to be patient?

The zoo is swamped with visitors; the crowd appears to consist of family units that think a visit to the zoo demands clothing more appropriate to the beach, and there are also a large number of couples walking hand in hand – which surprises Serena. A strange place for a romantic assignation, she thinks, or is it some primeval link to get the lust juices running?

The people move slowly, no one above the age of ten seems to be in any hurry, and there are few unhappy faces. It has the atmosphere of any seaside promenade in Britain. And, in place of waves lapping a beach and gulls crying in the sky, there is an amazing racket and variation of noise that has nothing to do with the sea. Instead of being lethargic and sleepy, the zoo animals seem to be trying to outdo each other in the vocal stakes – as though seven different wildlife programmes are being simultaneously broadcast over a huge PA system. Serena has to pause and listen. Their rhythm is basic: call–respond, call–respond.

She is disturbed from her thoughts as an old keeper passes by, broom and bucket in his hand, appropriately whistling the theme music to *Animal Magic*. With a well-practised ease, he ignores Serena and Alex both. He appears to be ignoring everyone, Serena thinks. He has a different rhythm to his walk – more purpose. For a moment a breeze picks up, but all it does is waft around the watery tang from the Aquatic House, Lemur Island and the ponds from the Spirit of Africa section and mix it with the Rhino Outdoor Paddock. Serena is certain she knows where all the varied smells are coming from, because there are about ten zillion signs telling people where everything is. She wonders why she bought the map. The breeze moves the smells around again, and Serena smiles to herself.

"It smells of Africa," she comments to her map.

"How would you know?" says Alex. "The farthest you've ever been is to the Isle of Wight."

She looks over the top of the map. "You *know* I was in Paris only last week, Alex. And Stockholm the month before."

"That place stinks too," he replies.

She stares at her map yet again, even though her first glance had committed it to memory. When she finally raises her head, Alex is leaning on his crutch, adjusting his sunglasses, and Serena follows his gaze. Three small children of indeterminate sex are chasing each other around in circles; one face is painted as a tiger, another as a leopard, the third as a zebra. The kids scream and snarl and dart between other children grasping their ice creams close as *their* mothers look around for other parents to frown at. Immediately behind the face-painted children, two of the real articles pace to and fro behind thick glass partitions – a tiger in one, a leopard in the next. Between the children and the tiger, a man of about twenty – skinhead, white

T-shirt, 501's – leans with his back against the glass. The zebra-child treads on his foot as she avoids the leopard-child, and the man yells out, bending down to stroke his injured foot. Alex laughs out loud, and carries on doing so, even when the man glares in their direction. Alex then hobbles to the tiger's enclosure, ignoring the injured man who is still frowning, points his aluminium crutch towards the glass, and calls over his shoulder to Serena.

"This tears me apart," he says. "Look, they've gone psycho being here."

Serena goes over to her brother and links her arm through his. She watches as the tiger marks time: back and forth, back and forth.

"They're trapped," Alex continues, "just fucking trapped."

A nearby mother tuts and hustles her charges away.

"I know," says Serena.

Just like you.

And she cannot stop herself from patting his hand. She feels it stiffen under her fingers. Serena knows it has been a bit of a calculation to bring Alex to a zoo, but there is something here she has to do. Alex has been into animal rights for a long time and now here he is in The Tower of Babel. He must want to set them all free, she thinks, whatever the consequences.

What is the human impulse to cage animals? Curiosity – the desire to see something different? Or a subconscious desire to exercise their power – to demonstrate that the human race is the superior one?

Alex lifts his free hand to his sunglasses, wiggles the frames on his nose, and then does a Roger Moore with his eyebrows – the right one down, the left raised. Serena wonders if he is acting the fool on a greater scale today than he usually does because of his experience. The day before, he had come around to her place, three hours after she had stood him up – and had had the world thrust in his face.

"I *did* have the opportunity to be elsewhere this evening," he complained as he stood at her front door.

Alex then made his way to Serena's upstairs room and stared down at the five units comprising Odysseus. He gestured with his crutch. "What are these then?" he asked.

Serena ducked to his side and kicked the crutch away, before he knocked anything out of position. It took him a moment to regain his balance.

"Huh?" he said. "Is it pick on a cripple week?"

"Don't bleat and don't touch. They have to be set up in extremely precise positions . . . well, not to within micro-metres, but they're a sod to get right. Now just sit down."

Alex sat in the middle of the couch, put the crutch to one side and folded his arms.

"Okay," he said, "entertain me."

Serena went over to her PC, loaded a program from a CD and keyed in a number of values. She then moved from unit to unit, switching each one on.

"You remember the basic principle I explained to you?" she asked.

"Ah-huh." Alex was looking around, frowning as each unit added to the strange background hum that he felt building.

"So," said Serena, "can you think of a person, or a place, at an exact time?"

Alex smiled. "Dallas, Texas, November the twenty-second, nineteen sixty-three. The Dealey Plaza. The man standing beside Zapruder – the guy who took the film of what happened. I've read every guess there's ever been about that bloody grassy knoll. Now give me an answer if you can."

Serena paused.

"Alex," she said, "take that silly look off your face. You have to be serious about this – it'll be quite a shock. And if you think it's some sort of trick, it may affect you in certain ways . . . oh, I don't know, like a bad trip from LSD."

"So it *is* a hallucination, then?"

"Let's not have that argument now, Alex. Can you concentrate for me, please? Shut your eyes, make yourself comfortable.

Move slightly back, put your head just there, and then don't move."

Alex sat further back into the seat and nestled his head into the backrest.

"That's it," said Serena, "now think about this person. Think hard."

She waited until she felt Alex was doing as he was told and then she began to run her program. And studied her brother, closely.

Odysseus began its start-up routine. From each unit came sounds of varying pitch and volume, and, after a moment, the program began in earnest, causing sound waves to merge and interact. Alex soon showed signs of interaction with the system.

The slight up-curl to the sides of his lips faded away. He brought a hand to an ear and rubbed a finger around its ridges and curls. Then he did the same with the other ear. As it resumed its original position, the hand froze in mid-motion. A wan colour had replaced the normal healthy glow in his cheeks, then he let both arms drop to grip the sides of the couch. He now leant forward a little, and Serena – ready for this reaction – tapped some adjustments on her keyboard.

When Alex's eyes snapped open, Serena knew he wasn't seeing the room anymore. He was somewhere else, somewhere he had earlier fixed his mind on. His head twitched slightly from side to side, up and down and he began breathing hard.

"My God," he gasped.

"Stay quiet," Serena instructed him. "Just watch."

His eyes widened.

Serena could nearly see the scene herself. The separate triangles of grass, the pool, the office buildings housing the County Records and Criminal Courts, the Texas School Book Depository, the knoll, the triple underpass. The bright sun. The throng of people. In her own head, she ran the twenty-six-second-long Zapruder film as a mind video.

The lead motorcycle escort sweeps around from Houston and

approaches down Elm and the cop on the bike takes centre stage until Zapruder realizes the president is not immediately behind. The silent film jumps to where the camera picks up the Presidential Lincoln, and there is Kennedy and there is Jackie and there is Governor Connally. With the jiggles of a home movie, history unfolds towards one of its major climaxes. *Kennedy leans to one side and clutches his chest. Connally reacts to his own injuries, inflicted at about the same time.* It has not just started; this assassination has been in progress for several seconds. There is confusion in the open-topped car. *John Fitzgerald Kennedy slumps further as the car nears the cameraman.* You have to hold your breath. Then come the results of the shot that showed the world sudden death in all its gruesome frankness. That is what happens when a head explodes. (That is what happened to Phoenix's friend, Corporal Joe Plotkin.) A red spray of mist. And a President dies. *Jackie tries to climb out of the accelerating car.*

"No," Alex said, "no. Oh, my God!"

Alex's body jerked rhythmically, as if he was trying to jog.

Serena interrupted the running of the program, realizing her brother was becoming too involved with what he was experiencing. She got up quietly from her chair and went around to each unit, switching it off.

Alex didn't say anything immediately. He just sat there, shaking. He looked terrified.

It had been easy to persuade him to go to the zoo with her, the next day.

But now she had to keep him here.

Serena knew he had been merely indulging her when he'd tried out Odysseus. He had given her a date he was well familiar with, one he was certain he could focus on without any additional prop concerning person or era. And even a name for the one man whose senses he wanted to experience the events through.

She thinks he was convinced by the experience.

He has still not told Serena what had happened for him,

what he'd seen or who'd pulled the trigger. But at least he now *knows* who fired the fatal shot, and exactly how his hero had died. And the truth about Oswald. Today Alex has to play the jester to allow his mind to encompass what had happened to him yesterday. And, because of using Odysseus, Serena herself feels obliged to fulfil a number of tasks once completed by a Greek hero . . . and perhaps by an American combat correspondent? Serena and Alex are both breaking out of cages.

Serena knows Alex has a thing about freedom – it is what defines him, what literally shaped him. The crutch he uses was not acquired as the result of a sporting accident; it is evidence of the type of violence her brother hates.

The injury is three years old.

On a May Day protest, a police horse had trampled him to the ground. The noise of his leg breaking caused even the police officers that were nearby to wince. Alex spent four months in hospital, the police never apologized and Alex never made one complaint about the pain he was in. That incident defined her brother.

Ten minutes later and she has located what she sought.

"Hercules' third labour," explains Serena.

They are standing in front of an enclosure that quite a few people are hurrying past without giving a glance. The animal stands, in the shade of a tree, in a posture that suggests it is daring people to get close.

"The muntjac will do," Serena says.

The deer in the cage is small, dainty even – standing about two feet high at the shoulder. In proportion it is similar to any other type of deer, thinks Serena, but in some ways it would have made Michelangelo very happy – if he'd ever decided to carve a gargoyle. Two short, pointed antlers rise from its head. With their bony sheaths surrounding the lower part of the horns Serena thinks they look as though they've just, that moment, erupted from its skull. And it seems as though their roots have shot out the other end, for two tusks hang down from the animal's jaws. And every now and then a long tongue slides out and licks its eyes. It stops and lowers its head in their direction – and barks. Just the same as an Alsatian would.

"Jesus," comments Alex.

"I liked the idea of photographing something that can bite back," says Serena. "That's why we came here."

She goes and stands near its cage, her arms folded, and adopts a nonchalant look. Alex mutters under his breath and raises the digital camera Serena has given him earlier.

"Say cheese," he says.

"Crackers," she says.

The flash triggers itself, even though Serena stands in bright sunlight. Alex slowly inspects the camera and scowls. Serena goes over to him and takes it from his hands.

"Thank you," she says.

"I'd like to go home now," says Alex.

"Three down, nine to go," says Serena.

"I may have to leave the country."

As they turn away to leave, the muntjac starts to urinate.

"Missed your cue," Serena calls out to the little deer.

And she saunters off to the waiting car with the animal barking at her retreating back.

Classified Secret

PLEASE SIGN RECEIPT PROVIDED BY COURIER
DO NOT ACCEPT IF TAMPER BAIL STRIP IS BROKEN
RETURN TO A4 RECORDS WITHIN FORTY-EIGHT (48) HOURS
F2/6836/24A/67

Ref. Telephone enquiry

This department would like to thank you for bringing this matter to our attention and wishes to take this opportunity to report our current thinking on this question, so as to clarify any future discussion and/or decisions.

This department feels it appropriate to continue referring to the material as Odysseus, in deference to the achievements attained in the field of mathematics by Professor Freeman.

The following sections are the compilation of a number of previous briefings prompted by investigations into national security and passed to a Government think-tank of academics of various disciplines. The obvious threats – nuclear, biological, terrorist, subversives – were not to form part of the remit of this group; they were charged with considering more esoteric and/or unforeseen circumstances where the defence of the realm was affected. They were essentially instructed to let their imaginations take them wherever it would – so long as what they discussed remained within feasible bounds. One, initially bizarre, concept resulting from their meetings was the manner in which non-intrusive time machines might affect society to its detriment.

The first extract, reproduced here, is from a lecture given at their fifth meeting, where this possibility was originally mooted, by one of the physicists.

"Most people give little thought to the nature of time. Time, in everyday life, is considered fixed.

Since the beginning of the twentieth century, when Einstein produced his Special and General Theories on Relativity, physicists have known that time is *not* fixed. Experiments have confirmed Einstein's assertion that most people's view of time being fixed is false. The passage of time is dependent on a variety of factors, and they *do* affect it. Here are the two main attributes. One: scientists proved a part of Einstein's theories in 1971 when atomic clocks were flown great distances, at a constant speed, around the world. When compared to identical clocks that had remained static on the ground, the clocks on the aircraft were shown to be running many nanoseconds behind. This result was exactly what was expected from Einstein's Time Dilation Effect equation after the following secondary factor had been taken into consideration.

Two: according to Einstein, the greater the mass, and the closer an observer is to it, the slower will be the passage of time. This effect was verified as early as 1959 at Harvard University, where time differences were noted between the top and bottom of a tower.

Over the years, multiplicities of experiments have confirmed the fundamental soundness of Einstein's equations.

And for the purposes of this discussion, it should be noted that there is no restriction in the celebrated theories that exclude time travel. The simple fact is that there is no rigorous objection to travelling forward in time. (Travelling back in time does not contravene Einstein's equations either, but it does lead to questions on paradox by the nature of physical presence. These problems disappear if a non-intrusive method of time travel is used. If a more in-depth examination of this phenomenon is required, then refer to addendum.)"

If Professor Freeman has indeed sidestepped the normal lines of thinking of how to achieve time travel, this department would like to state some of the obvious implications discussed at the same think-tank meeting when considering the use of a device to observe the past.

As a tool of surveillance, it would be beyond anyone's wildest dreams; the sheer importance of information discovered, for example, by overhearing what is said at the political or military meetings of foreign, hostile or friendly, powers is incalculable.

Public knowledge of such a device must be stringently denied. The potential for civil disruption is self-evident. Some aspects of the implications are outlined below.

Politics:
Political parties would be able to monitor opposition plans, opposition members, and even dissident members of their own party. There would be a possibility that mainstream politics would formally homogenize.

Economy:
Industrial espionage would initially be rife. It is possible that such actions would trigger a world-wide depression.

Religion:
The West's predominantly Christian beliefs have the potential to be shattered. Suppose Christ was shown to be African?

Crime:
Such a device would be a stunning instrument to use against criminals. One line of thought does ask the question: if there is no crime, why have police?

Relationships and people:
With the prevalent instinct for nostalgia, it is felt that many people would become "Past Junkies" – wishing to observe, at first hand, the era of history that they are fond of.

It is this department's conclusion that the intrusion into private life by Odysseus will undoubtedly provoke an adverse reaction. In our opinion, the consequences of public disclosure will result in anarchy – Odysseus presents a cultural earthquake that would change society beyond recognition. Odysseus is power beyond knowledge.

It is recommended that Odysseus be classified as Delta Secret with immediate effect, and that we obtain Odysseus at all costs.

Classified Secret

PLEASE SIGN RECEIPT PROVIDED BY COURIER
DO NOT ACCEPT IF TAMPER BAIL STRIP IS BROKEN
RETURN TO A4 RECORDS WITHIN FORTY-EIGHT (48) HOURS
F2/6836/24C/95

This department has considered further the viability of
the acquisition of Odysseus: our conclusions are that
Professor Freeman's co-operation is unlikely. Compul-
sory acquisition, or theft, of the equipment remains the
best option. The question of Professor Freeman's ability
to build another will need to be addressed. Consideration will also have to be given to the possibility of
global publication if she is only harmed during the operation and not removed from the equation.

A D-notice to be served to the media should be prepared
in advance.

EIGHT

Hercules was duly given his instructions for his fourth task: to bring back to King Eurystheus the Erymanthian boar – alive. It was obvious to Hercules that the king was beginning to specialize in excessive requests. He had forced the hero to trap the Hind of Ceryneia, instead of killing it, and now he was making him do the same with an animal that was substantially bigger and rougher. Under a bright midday winter sun, and resisting a bitter wind that carried the crisp smell of snow, Hercules placed his hands firmly on his hips, cocked his head to one side and addressed the herald.

"Isn't that the giant wild pig that's been gouging the life out of the people and countryside around the Erymanthus mountain?" he enquired of the king's representative.

The smaller man nodded, let go the hem of his red cloak that he was clutching tightly around him, and raised his hands and eyebrows in the classic gesture of I-know-but-what-can-I-do? "The beasts you are expected to deal with are never average, are they?"

For a moment, the only sound to be heard was of empty trees crackling in the wind. Even the crows that had started their winter flocking in the towers of the palace gates ceased making their din.

"How observant," said Hercules, "and thank you for reminding me." He suddenly smiled a grim smile.

The herald dropped his arms, and his cloak flapped in the wind. Hercules turned to go and then paused. The herald stopped breathing again. Hercules looked back over his shoulder.

"I'll be in touch," he said.

A grimace, intended as a smile, remained fixed on the herald's face for several minutes afterwards, and the wind now blew his cloak up and about around his face.

The crows screeched.

A week later and Hercules was nearing the place where the boar had last been seen, when, on a whim, he decided on a detour to enjoy a little relaxing time with his old friend Pholus – a centaur who lived in a cave up on the mountain. As you may know, centaurs have the heads, arms and upper torso of a man springing from the shoulders of a horse, and Pholus was a thoroughbred both as a man and a stallion. Black of hair and black of coat, he cut the perfect figure of the wicked rogue who makes friends of men and is a seducer of women. Centaurs were pretty popular, it seems, if a little prone to arguments. Hercules told all who cared to listen that his friend, the centaur Pholus, had style – and Pholus had been saying the same about himself for years.

When he spied Hercules in the distance approaching along the mountain track, Pholus immediately stoked up the fire, raided the pantry and busied himself in his large kitchen. By the time the hero came walking up the bridleway to the centaur's combined stable–house, Pholus was ready to present Hercules a meal fit for a hero: large char-grilled steak sprinkled with tarragon and crushed black pepper, mushrooms in garlic butter, bread fresh from the oven. Pholus ate his own steak raw – centaurs were a mean bunch.

As good friends are wont, Hercules and Pholus felt close enough to be brusque with each other

"Wine? Are we having any?" asked Hercules.

Pholus did not miss a beat. "Ah," he replied, "unfortunately all I have is what is left in the communal jar, and the other centaurs won't like it if I allow you to drink from it."

Adopting an air of resignation, he held the large jar aloft, but made sure that when he placed it back upon the table it was within Hercules' reach.

"Tough," said Hercules, snapping up the jar in his hands and uncorking the top. "We both need a drink."

He breathed in its aroma and poured himself a large glass of magenta liquid, while smiling to himself. Hercules loved the sound of wine gurgling out of a jar. "There's no finer sound," he said.

"Except for 'here's some gold and the keys to my cellar' uttered by some rich merchant," said Pholus, as he suddenly discovered he now had a glass of wine in his own hand.

Pholus didn't care about the two of them using the communal jar, but he knew that the other centaurs would when they returned; they considered themselves to be the best sort of partying people and they saw their liquid refreshment as something sacred. As the other centaurs started approaching about an hour later, Pholus reminded Hercules that when a centaur took offence, he took it to heart. That always meant a fight to the death.

"It's my fault," said Pholus, "so I'll help here. Let's go meet them."

As they went outside, to find the other centaurs galloping speedily towards them, it could only mean that a certain goddess had already put a word in their ears about what was happening back home. Twenty centaurs began putting arrow to bow as they headed up the mountain track, the frozen earth beneath their hooves now flying up in great clods.

In the short, swift, deadly running battle that followed, Hercules managed to kill many of the attackers – those arrows dipped in the Hydra's blood seemed able to fell anything. One after the other, those splendid warriors staggered and succumbed. But Pholus was so intrigued that such a small missile could down his mighty comrades that, as Hercules pursued the last of them, Pholus went over to one of the slain that lay all around. Tragically, the arrow he extracted was still slick with a centaur's blood. It slipped from his fingers, nicking the skin above his hoof as it fell to the ground.

"Hercules!" he called out. But it was too late. By the time Hercules had rushed over, his friend also lay dead. There was nothing he could do there – except go around to all the centaurs recovering his arrows.

After burying his friend, it was a grim hero who set out to complete his task.

The snow that had been threatening all week began to fall.

There was no time to waste.

Hercules only paused to watch for a moment after he'd found the boar. He studied its bulk, the humped and muscled shoulders covered with a thick coat of bristle, the huge tusks sticking out at its mouth, and the sharp-looking cloven hooves. Then Hercules stopped looking, and charged into the thicket where it was rooting and scavenging about for food, and set after it when it fled – the boar recognizing death personified when it saw it.

Around and around the mountain the pair ran, their passage cutting new paths through the undergrowth, the violent sounds of both hunted and hunter thunder-storming around the valleys – causing the locals to become dry-mouthed and short tempered. But this was no ordinary hunt: these circuits of the mountain continued day and night until, worn out, the boar attempted to hide in the same thicket where Hercules had found it. The man himself had guessed what it intended, and crept closer to the animal, regaining his own breath. When Hercules saw the boar's flanks still rising and falling rapidly, he smiled and crept even closer. Hercules filled his own lungs to the brim, then boomed out a huge battle cry. This frightened the boar so much it leapt straight into a deep drift of snow, which prevented it from escaping.

Hercules then jumped onto its back, his massive hands becoming entangled in coarse bristles, his fingers digging into the lava-rock muscles. The boar snarled and roared, attempting to turn its head and sink its tusks into the hunter, but Hercules held firm. After hours of tussle, Hercules managed to wrestle the beast into a net he had earlier set up. He stood back as it writhed and bucked, but slowly its struggles ceased and its giant pink eyes glared up at its victor – who grinned and leaned forward to its ear.

"Apple sauce," he said, and waited as the boar renewed its roaring and rodeo prancing.

"Job done," Hercules added to himself.

"Next," said Hercules at the city gate.

"I'll go tell the king," said the herald.

"That would be nice."

The herald ran off to the palace, shaking his head and cursing, wishing the gods would rid him of this devil of a man.

But the smile on Hercules' lips slowly faded – all he could think about at that moment was Pholus.

NINE

W. Day. 23.53. Ridge overlooking Asan River.

My grandfather told me that there were plenty of pigs – feral ones – to be found on Guam. (They made tasty eating, he said.) Since every animal on this island appears to have been destroyed, or has saved its neck by getting itself the hell out of *our* hell, I have no idea where I can get my hands on one to complete the next task. I try to think of viable equivalents but, apart from taking on a notably fat Enemy (of whom I have seen precisely none so far), there's not many options open. That makes me feel nervous. And I don't like the sensation. I suddenly think of the night my grandfather talked of the French pig – it may give me ideas.

That was the year of my life when I learnt so much, when I started to grow up – when I was twelve. It happened in the middle of the night, during high summer – some weeks before I was destined to shoot my first deer. Grandfather had taken me along to spend the night on Montauck Point, Long Island. He liked to listen to the waves; it brought back memories of his homeland. We had the tiny bay to ourselves, with the old lighthouse standing guard on the small cliff. Grandfather had bought some fish from the lighthouse keeper for our supper – and we had hours yet before the tide would force us to move. The weather had been so warm for the past few weeks that we hadn't had to get under our blankets – so we rolled them up as pillows to lie on, still fully dressed. The embers of our fire had faded into the sand, and now we were left with just the sea and the surf.

With that regular unhurried beat that the ocean has, the waves rolled in; big, powerful breakers that hissed whispers of storms and sights seen earlier in Europe where I deemed their birth to be. They hit the beach with the sighs of ancient men and gave up their last with flecks of foam and hollow splutters. And as they melted back into the surge, their brothers would rise up and follow them in – echoes upon restless echoes. I stared up at the stars and listened to my grandfather's interpretation – it appeared that there were stories in the skies as well.

"You have to use your imagination," he had said. "Try to picture what the ancients saw. See that group of stars there? The box with the zigzag off to one side? That's the Great Bear, or the Big Dipper. And if you make a line upwards from the two stars on the right-hand side, you'll find the Pole Star. If you know where that is, you should never be able to get lost."

I looked to where he pointed and I located the star.

"It's a constant," he explained. "The heavens revolve around it. Now that's a security, something that's solid, something to hang on to – and it's millions upon millions of miles away. Now drop your eye down to the Great Bear again. See that squashed box? That's the body of the bear; that zigzag is its tail. Those less bright ones? The legs."

And for a moment I pictured my version of an animal onto that constellation; and it was a giant of a beast. My grandfather pointed out more: Draco the snake, Perseus clutching the Gorgon's head, and then Hercules. He told me of the last one's heroic labors – all twelve of them. I made my grandfather repeat them to me. My grandfather, for whom the stories of his homeland were akin to his soul, had for some reason taken up learning about the Greeks. Maybe he loved the idea that their stories could be depicted in the night sky.

"They'll be there for generations to come," he said. "Whatever silly, stupid, or heroic and brilliant things a man might do, it does him good to look upwards once in a while. All the vast emptiness of that void gives a person pause for thought."

The waves thumped on the shore, the slight wind blew in the smells of the sea, and I looked up at the stars winking in their infinity. It was just too big to comprehend.

"It frightens me," I admitted.

My grandfather reached across and took my hand. "Don't be scared – just hold on to the stories. Enjoy them. Use them as protection."

A particularly large wave crashed onto the beach, and the tremor ran up to where we lay. My grandfather laughed at it.

"All that way from France and that's all you have to say?" he said to it.

As if in reply, another wave rolled in hard.

"Ah, you want your child back, don't you?"

For a moment I was confused, until I realized he was talking about my grandmother and the country of her birth.

"Well, you'll have to wait."

I heard him turn towards me. "Hey," he said, "you know I told you about that pig Hercules was sent to capture?"

"Ah-huh." I feigned interest – Hercules had become my favorite hero.

"Well, in France, I hear tell they once hung a pig – for committing a crime."

I laughed.

"No, I'm telling the truth. I think it had escaped from its pen and killed a child, so the good residents of the town stuck some clothes on it, took it to court, pronounced sentence, then took it away and strung it up by its neck."

He turned back to the stars. "People do strange things sometimes," he added.

Then he told me about the Lady of Fonte River – just to scare me.

The Lady of Fonte River is the ghost of a Chamorro woman who died in tragic circumstances, and, it is said, whenever the night is moonless, or when the skies turn black with storm-clouds, she returns. She stands at the water's edge, dressed in her bridal clothes, her hair streaming in the wind. If you are unlucky enough, you will hear her screams.

I withdraw back into our foxhole. For a second, all I can hear is someone breathing. Then Rici speaks. "Well, thanks, Nix, that's just what I wanted to hear. Bad luck, ghosts and pissed-off women. You sure know how to pass the time. Any chance you get paid for this?"

He pulls his collar up, his helmet down, and he huddles further into our lair. I hear him scratch the stubble on his chin.

"That's okay," I say, even though I'm tempted to burst out laughing. "I've got lots more stories. My grandfather was fond of telling them."

"While he was making the moonshine or drinking it?"

"You insulting my drinking credentials?"

"Nix, if you could just take the bottle out of your mouth for long enough, I'd discuss that with you sometime. Sir."

"Fuck you too, Rici."

He grunts a laugh.

I turn the netsuke in my hand. Even in the dark Rici sees the motion – he must have bat blood in his veins. But then that's combat: it sharpens up the senses.

"What's with that thing, Nix? Some sort of trophy?" he asks.

I know why he's asking, and that he's being a little crafty. A marine doesn't loot for the sake of greed – though quite a number do – it's just that acquiring some trinket, some small item that you can carry easily, denotes an inherent belief that you will survive. Your subconscious is saying that you will emerge from the other side of war to be able to enjoy what you have acquired. So Rici's trying to discern my state of mind. I have a moment of inspiration and decide to face this question head on.

"I'm calling this one of Hercules' twelve labors – represent-ing the Hind of Ceryneia."

I think I hear him swear under his breath. "You're kidding me. The Hind of what?"

I turn it over in my fingers once more, then tuck it into my pocket, along with my Enemy cap.

"That's what I said: one of Hercules' twelve labors. I think I've accomplished the first three: the Nemean Lion, the Lernaean Hydra, and now the Hind of Ceryneia. I've been trying to work out the others I still have to do."

I *know* he's swearing now. "Ah, fuck, are you going nuts on me, Nix?"

His voice is lower, meaning he is serious.

I give a short laugh.

"I haven't a clue, Rici. It's just an idea I got from . . . well, it's just an idea I developed."

I dare not tell him that I feel so scared on this assault, feel that my moment will come any time soon, feel that I'll try *anything* if it only gets me out of here – even go mad (in other people's eyes) and listen to voices in my head. No marine, even with Rici's sensitivities, would tolerate my conviction of having an ancestral conversation with that woman, *my* woman, on the beach. But it *does* confuse me.

"I thought I needed something to get me through." I surprise myself – I didn't think I could confess that to him.

Now Rici laughs out loud. Some of the other men in nearby foxholes ask to hear the joke.

"You think I'm ready for the mental hospital?" I say to him.

"Sure," he says, "anyone would be crazy if they thought there was a chance of living through *this*."

I laugh too.

Grandpa died shortly after I'd graduated, while I was still in Cambridge, England, with my friend Thomas Wakefield the painter, whom I'd met at Yale. Tom is some sort of blond, blue-eyed Englishman who has forsaken his aristocratic inheritance to follow his own dreams. I'd been glad he was there for me at that time, as he gave me the encouragement to complete a little project I'd had in mind for some time. Before I returned

Stateside, I finished writing a story entitled *When the White Hummingbird Sings*. It was about a man's quest – an allegory on the situation the world was facing, and I thought my grandfather would have approved of the intention expressed within it. He was in my mind when I wrote it.

The day war broke out in Europe I had stood at the foot of his grave. Tom had sent a telegram to me, saying that, as we had predicted, Chamberlain had misjudged the tyrant Hitler, and that there were some things that even he, the great Thomas Wakefield, could not walk away from. He said he was intending to take up a position in the RAF to help in the coming struggle. And as I knelt down by my grandfather's grave – me a big hulking kid with a passion for art, writing and the mysterious – I thought I could hear in the winds that blew through the gravestones an echo of the storm that would draw America into the war. At least I was prepared for it.

And for that I have to thank Tom. That summer spent in England in 1939, I had been sitting out on the balcony at his home, which he'd bought and converted into a studio in Cambridge, drinking a good malt from Scotland, with my feet up on the wrought-iron railing, and I was counting how many people were out using punts on the Cam. Though they were some distance away, the tops of their poles and the occasional head were easy to spot, and the summer warmth had ensured that there were many who wanted to enjoy a day on the river. I was up to reckoning thirty-two, and meanwhile on my fourth drink. Tom was talking to me from inside his studio, as he finished a watercolor sketch for some oil painting he planned, and we were dressed English-casual, trousers and open-topped shirts, though he had smudges of color on his. And he was killing his whisky with soda and ice; I was more used to drinking than he was. I thought it gave me an edge in our conversation, as we discussed Hitler through the open French windows.

"If it's front-page news," said Tom, "we are *definitely* in trouble."

I looked over towards him. He stood at his easel, his hair tousled, cleaning a brush in a glass of water – the Artist at Work – as he spoke to me. The water in the glass began to turn milky-blue. I picked up the paper from the balcony floor.

"So," I continued, "von Ribbentop went to Moscow yesterday and signed a deal with Molotov. It would seem that the foreign ministers of Germany and Russia are apparently planning to carve up Poland again."

I threw down the newspaper.

"Now Adolf and Joe are friends, I don't think there's *any* doubt that we're in trouble."

"We?" asked Tom, coming out onto the balcony to join me.

"It'll be war in Europe, and sooner or later we'll have to come in." I jabbed a thumb at my chest. "Whether it's Hitler attacking our ships, or Japan deciding to extend its frontiers in the Pacific – *we'll* get involved."

Tom studied the remains of ice in his drink.

"Jolly – good – show," he said facetiously.

I raised my eyebrows. Had there been venom in his tone?

"Really?" I said. "You want to play at soldier?"

"And you?" he continued. "Ever since you got here you've been raiding every library for its books on Japan. It would appear that we both know we're going to have to fight at some time. That's why I took flying lessons, and now I intend to join the RAF. I just don't have to be happy about the killing."

I passed him my now empty glass without saying anything. He paused before taking it, and then he went back into the studio. I sat there impatiently and found myself thinking about the prospects of war and its consequences. Japan had been up to its neck in an expansionistic policy, and what it was doing in China beggared belief. In Nanking, in '37, they'd massacred over three hundred fifty thousand people in one month. Most towns in the States don't have a hundredth of that figure for a population. Three hundred fifty thousand – who'd speak on their behalf? There I was calling myself a journalist, but I wasn't really helping to let people know the facts; I wasn't reporting it live. I should have got into the Spanish Civil War, to make a stand against this rise of extreme right-wing thinking, but deep down, even during the late thirties, I knew I was eventually going to be needed elsewhere. My future – and my country's – lay in the Pacific.

There were some things that you *had* to fight for, extremely nasty people that you had to stand up to – and one of them was Hitler. And for us Americans, more than likely, it would be the Japanese. I wondered how long it would be before we would call them "the Enemy".

I'm glad I spent that pivotal afternoon the way I did. I know it made the arrival of *the* telegram that evening more of a shock, but at least I could later reflect on the last warm days of peace. The telegram informed me that my grandfather had died. For the rest of the night Tom let me tell as many stories about my grandfather as I could, while I drank myself into a disgusting stupor.

Months later, as I was taking steps to skip from my father's newspaper, and his continuing interference in my life, I pitched the idea to my prospective editor that I follow a bunch of new recruits into combat in the Pacific. The editor (Eric Jackson – bald, old, jowled and jaded) seemed intrigued, as it was then early in 1940, and among the population there was only the merest undercurrent of feeling that we might get called in to help out the Brits again. There was none of the battle fervor that would follow Pearl Harbor. He gave me a thoughtful look as I sat on the corner of his desk, drinking the long rum he'd proffered me when I'd come into his office and playing with his gold cigarette lighter. I was being very brave in touching it – the lighter had been a gift from President Roosevelt himself and Eric was known to eat cheeky young upstarts like me for mid-morning breaks. (I may have grown and put on my father's, and my grandfather's shoulders, but I was at least forty years his junior, and he had my grandfather's strength of gaze.)

"You're that certain, are you," he asked, "that we're going to have to go to war with the Japanese?"

I nodded and took a slow pull on my drink. It was good rum. I seem to find good rum wherever I go.

"It'll be on two fronts," I suggested, "but the Pacific will be mainly ours."

He massaged his huge jowls. "I thought your father was trying to jimmy you into politics?" he said.

"He is."

"Without any success?"

"Not so far."

"With his weight behind you, you could end up a senator in ten years. Don't you fancy that?"

"We all have our dreams, and that's not mine."

"What is, then?"

"To write. To tell it as it is."

He smiled. I shrugged.

"Yeah," I said, "the same-old same-old. Okay, I want to have fun, I want to be able to drink hard drink like this, I want to write trick stories." I hesitated. "I want to show how our boys become our nation's heroes. I want to show I'm human."

Jackson sat up. "Well, Lafayette," he said, "you're still young. And you've got a rich kid's chip that's so big it'll . . ." He paused. "It'll take you far. So, I'll give you the same carrot and stick which I give to all the young Turks that walk through my door and drink my drink and play with my lighter. Go and earn my approval. Earn it on something that will dazzle me with your intellect, your insight, your inner conflicts – or lose it. And, I warn you, you wouldn't want to lose my approval."

He held out his hand for his lighter.

So I did the one thing that I could think of. I went up to Canada and talked to the enlisting American boys that were getting in on the action before any declaration of war was made at home. Some wanted adventure, some were just restless – most could read the runes and wanted to give themselves a chance of survival by getting good at fighting before they were forced to. I was tempted at times to join them myself, but I was stopped by the inclinations I'd had in England, and the look that Jackson had given me in his office that day. My destiny lay in the Pacific.

Throughout the rest of 1940, and through early 1941, I sent back articles to the *New York Picture Post*. And I had to start to use a camera properly. I took shots of everything: I wanted to get across that they were just ordinary boys on a mission – which they were. By March 1941, I'd done enough to win over Jackson; even learnt how to make a judgment call on what pictures to take. I received a telegram from him that read simply: CEASE SENATOR RACE AND START WITH ME. I went back to New York immediately and spent the rest of the year chasing up stories about how we were "helping" the British, and how we were gearing up for war in Europe. Until December 7th.

Even though I had been expecting it, as the news came in on the wire, I felt like I'd been kicked in the stomach. Or lower down. It was an insult but, as tactics go, it would take some beating. There we were, a God-fearing country enjoying our day of rest (the world takes a break when America takes a break, right?), settling down to that stretching of time that is Sunday afternoon. We were mostly comfortable, mostly satisfied, and mostly innocent. Then Death came to visit, riding on many sets of wings. It was as if someone had strolled up to that apple pie cooling on the window, unbuttoned his fly, took out his pecker, pissed on the pie and handed it back, expecting us to eat it. As surprises go, Pearl will take some beating.

Eric Jackson was tuned into NBC in his office, and I happened to be there with him when the call came through. He went to his drinks cabinet and poured us both double-doubles. We knocked them back in one, then he started telephoning, calling out, and generally marshaling his troops. As I stood watching him work, he paused once and stared at me. We said nothing.

I gave it a week, then went to seek out the volunteers I wanted to follow. Remembering the poster I had seen, I headed for the marines – and their boot camp.

Some of the war correspondents from the bigger papers, *Life* for instance, were given the rank of colonel, as befits the nation's respect for the idea of free speech, I suppose. That, or the conviction that truth is the best propaganda. But I wanted to act alongside the privates – to do as they did. Then, when it occurred to me that in the services there are some advantages to rank (I could possibly acquire some space for illicit booze), I accepted "lieutenant", and played down the film-star role that the Brass wanted us journalists to participate in. I swore I would only follow these guys if I could do exactly as they did. And boot camp was where they weeded out the chaff, the marines being considered an elite.

They took men from the cities, the big towns, the small towns, and places that only a few hundred people knew existed. They took the clerks, the butchers, the gas-pump kids, the foundry workers, the longshoremen, the mechanics, the farm workers. They took them underage if the recruits could lie convincingly, and had the enterprise to fake their documents; they took them underweight if they had the ingenuity to stuff themselves with pounds of bananas. They took them from the poor, the rich, and the poor again. But they only took the best. In that first day of wandering around the camp, I saw men I reckoned could complete the course while standing on their heads, yet didn't last beyond nightfall; and I saw boys I thought would start crying if you shouted at them who took it all with a smile.

I met a man called Alfonso "Rici" Federici who didn't avoid my look, who laughed at the same things I did, who gave me a run for my money on the courses and who made Sergeant by the end of the first week. Out of the many volunteers that I observed, I decided to stick with this man as long as I could, as he seemed to represent Mr Average Joe America. We could get along, I realized. And we both felt the responsibility of our age and our position. Besides, it was easy to work out from those days of training which theater of operations he was destined for. He didn't mind that I called his men "the Boys".

It was appropriate marine-type sarcasm. A change had occurred within them – it included awareness of the magnitude of determination needed for the job ahead. Every other one of those marines on that course, those that came out the other side, had seen their personality taken apart and reassembled so that they could work as a unit, as a team, as an effective fighting force. To win, they had to pull together, act with one single thought. A nation had been mobilized.

After a stint in Hollywood, where I'd watched a jungle training film being made (to show everyone what to expect in the tropics and how to fight there), Rici invited me to join him on a weekend pass to New York. He said he'd stand me dinner at his father's restaurant. So on the Saturday evening I met him on the corner of Mulberry and Spring, and we made our way down the street, taking in the sights, sounds and smells. I recognized the magic in the people there that comes from a community at ease with itself – New York is New York, and for their security each immigrant population has gravitated to its own little imitation citadel of memories of the old home. But whether it's Chinese, Italian, Irish or whatever, there's vibrancy to be found in their hearts. I know there are places where the poverty is crippling, but I'll still assert that if you listen hard, you can hear a heartbeat. Some people will do their utmost to keep their souls above the line of desperation. So, as I absorbed this place that was Little Italy, with the cobbled streets, the tenements, the rows of small restaurants and bakeries, I felt transported.

I watched Rici greet and embrace his friends. This was where he'd grown up, and he was popular. A couple of old, old, women made blunt comparisons between the two of us and we nodded, smiled and laughed along with them. A party crowd, several drinks ahead, jostled us. Young women assessed us, but they had many other choices. Rici and I both commented on the number of men in uniform. Then, just after passing Grand Street, Rici took my elbow and asked me if I was ready for the meal of my life. I found we were standing in front of *Da*

Federici. Its large windows drew the eye in to a black and white checked floor, functional tables set in rows, people in animated conversation as they ate. As we went in, a wonderful aroma swirled out of the open door.

I was introduced to Rici's father (Rici as he would be in thirty years' time), who gave me a bear-hug and kissed me on both cheeks. He stood back and said he was honored to meet the famous writer – his only son had already told him so much about me. I glanced across at Rici, who rolled his eyes. I was then introduced to Mama Federici and her seventeen-year-old daughter. Signorina Federici and I enjoyed one of those special moments that rarely happen between men and women. We both knew straight away that we'd be friends, but that would be that. I knew she would be breaking hearts for years to come, and I knew I'd enjoy watching the fun, if I had the chance. After Mama Federici had again kissed me on each cheek, we sat down to eat.

I'd eaten Italian many times, but that night it seemed as though Rici's father had done his best to bring the real Italy to America. The food was amazing. For an appetizer, Papa Federici served up fresh squid in a light batter, covered in a sauce comprised of a mixture of spices that zinged in the mouth. It was cooked to perfection, melting on the tongue and causing expressions of bliss in the people around our table. I reckoned Papa Federici couldn't surpass that, but he did. The main meal was pasta – spaghetti with prosciutto ham, egg yolks, oak-smoked pancetta, pecorino cheese (smuggled in, God knows how, from Sicily) and onions. We washed it down with a bottle of chilled house white. The whole meal was an assault on the taste buds – a sensation that caused shivers down my back.

And through it all, as Signorina Federici and I joked with each other, Rici just sat, and ate, and put up with us. Life was good and the war now seemed the ephemeral invention of some callous magician whose spell had been weakened by our friendship and simple things like a great meal. I now knew why Rici had wanted me to join him that night. He was saying goodbye to all this and I understood, as we were like brothers already, that Rici knew that whatever happened (if he even returned home after the war was finished), our lives would somehow be different. We were putting our childhood behind us there. This meal was The Last Supper – the fattening of the pigs before the slaughter. As I caught his eye, Rici and I raised a glass to each other in a silent toast.

"Do you think you'll live through this?" Rici asks me again.

As if to underline his question, a sniper puts one between our heads.

Th-zzzzip!

The angry whine and buzz of it makes us both jump simultaneously. Rici springs from his crouch and brings his carbine up. I do the same.

"Did you see the flash?" he asks.

I shake my head. "No," I say, willing the Enemy to appear from somewhere, "maybe only something behind that thicket. Too far to lob a grenade."

"Hey, Nixy," calls Amos from his hole nearby, "can I come over and get your full house, or did that Jap miss you?"

I don't even look at him as I cuss him.

"I won't miss your fat Apache ass if you don't concentrate, Chief."

Th-zzzzip! Th-zzzzip!

Two more shots whiz over me. It's getting personal.

Is this because I haven't got a pig yet?

Thwack!

Another bullet hits the dead Enemy that Rici and I had positioned in front of us. I have an impulse to count him as the pig I need so badly, but I instantly dismiss the idea.

Don't fool yourself, Nix. Shit.

"Hey, Landu," calls Rici, "did you get that flash? We can't get a fix here."

There was no reply.

"Jim?" I shout. "It was 'bout fifty yards on up, did you see it?"

Muzzle flashes and a ba-ba-ba, ba-ba-ba, from his foxhole answers me. Ahead in the blackness someone shouts something in Japanese.

"I think I did, Nix," says Jim.

I hear Hank snigger.

But the Enemy keeps on shouting. And then he begins to get louder. I realize he's doing the same as my imitation taotaomona ghost from earlier. Rici and I both hear the crashing in the undergrowth at the same time and we let loose a volley. So does most of the squad. This time the shouting stops. The Enemy must have taken about thirty rounds. Less than the first one. We're saving ammo – or getting sharper.

"Feel free to go check him for bits of Hercules," says Rici.

"It's the tasks he did, Rici, the *tasks*."

"Well, he's there if you want him. But I'd suggest waiting 'till daylight this time. Don't go death-hero on me – we've got all night to get through, remember? Here, have your ration."

He holds out his flask of liquor. For the first time, in a long time, I hesitate.

"No thanks, Rici," I find myself saying. "Give me another hour."

I turn and peer into the black undergrowth, and listen to the pock-pock-pock of some Enemy mortars away to the right.

"Huh," says Rici, "you got religion now?"

"Amen, go in peace my son."

I lick my lips. Temptations, temptations. I must take hold of the situation for a time at least. I have to think about pigs. But it is an urge that is the very devil. Drink has been so important to me for a number of years.

A number? It seems like forever.

It's a legacy that my father and grandfather bestowed upon me when I was ten. I have mixed emotions about that moment. I go back there in my mind on many an occasion. I can't say if I'm happy about my end of the deal or not.

It was Thanksgiving dinner 1929, the stock-market crash was just over a month old, and my mother was carrying in the turkey. She had dismissed the two maids and housekeeper for the day, so that they could enjoy their time at home with their own families, and she herself had been cooking all morning. Mother pushed the door shut with a foot and came towards us – with the grace and mystery of a Pre-Raphaelite model, her dark hair up, her cheeks aglow – gripping the sides of the dish that held the turkey. It was a huge bird, a whopper: golden, with flecks of orange hinting at those glorious crunchy bits I loved. The steam that rose from its flanks jolted my taste buds into a frenzy of activity. Its size befitted the room in which it would be eaten.

The table, in the hall-sized space that was our dining room, was set with the best silver, the plates filled with the usual trimmings to accompany the bird, and the candles had just been lit. For all the formality of the setting: the landscape paintings, which my father had chosen; the arrangements of flowers on the expensive cabinets, which my mother was always in charge of; the seating for the meal had been completely ad hoc. Only minutes before, I had raced my sister and grandparents for a seat. My grandmother could still outpace me – her long white ponytail swishing in my face as she turned this way and that, her arms outstretched, to prevent me passing, and her laugh infecting me too much to run very hard. Grandfather outflanked us both. In the end, I sat next to my sister Alice, opposite my grandmother and my father, with mother's being the chair nearest the door she had just closed. Grandfather stood at the far end from my mother, with prong and knife poised, awaiting the bird. Father was sniffing the cork he'd pulled from a bottle. That moment is a slow-moving memory: it held such portent.

I didn't realize the atmosphere had subtly changed. My grandmother refused to play footsie under the table with me as I reached across with my toe, and for a time I wondered what I must have done wrong. Then I sensed some unspoken communication between my father and my grandfather. A switch had been thrown: some vague electrical circuit of human psyche had been energized. The obvious tension between the two men constricted my throat.

Father appeared happy enough. As he played with the bottle, dressed, as was his wont, as though he belonged in the last century – waistcoat, necktie, waxed moustache and only missing a Colt revolver on his hip – he was smiling more intensely than usual. As the financial world imploded with a giant intake of stock-market breath, all my father wanted to do was stand on top of the world and laugh. He'd been shrewd, having a savvy awareness of the situation, and had got himself out and realized all his assets back in July. The great cloud of despair that was now thundering into the lives of the world's population would hardly touch him – or his family. The forthcoming Depression would provide ideal opportunities for expansion – that was the way *he* saw it. As he poured the wine, he glanced at his father. I caught the look in his eye, and it spoke of triumph.

I had never seen my grandfather lose his temper, but he came close that day. Grandfather had always made it plain that the one personality trait in his son that he couldn't stand was his gloating pride. He said it made him feel sick. And that day, when mother placed the turkey before him, he paused before giving the blessing and stared at my father. Then he spoke, still locking eyes with his son. My grandfather gave simple thanks for the food in front of us, and a wish that the peoples of the world would be able to take this economic blow and that they too could find some sort of happiness. He then began carving. But it wasn't his normal careful ritual – on this Thanksgiving he attacked the bird with a passion. Again and again he sliced into the turkey with savage knife movements. He was brutal: each cut was imbued with a kind of hate, a kind of panic. The violence with which he slashed at the meat caused everybody at the table to look away, except my father.

He studied my grandfather for a long moment and then turned to me.

"There comes a time, son," he said, in a tone that suggested nothing out of the ordinary was happening, "in every boy's life when he has to take the step towards growing up. The world is a tough place, and the people that run it have to be tough as well. I think it's time you learned how to drink."

My mother started to say something and my father turned to face her, his hand reaching out, his mouth open to speak, but he was halted by the sound of my grandfather ripping the legs off the turkey. The sound was terrible. We all turned to look, and listen. It seemed as if the fully cooked bird was attempting one last strangled call. Off came the legs, then the wings. Finished, grandfather stood there, wiping his hands on his napkin, a smile on his lips. He was breathing heavily.

"That's right, Phoenix," he said, "take a drink. And raise it in a toast to this feast we have before us."

He pushed his glass towards his son, and my father filled it. And then my grandmother's, my mother's, and mine. I stared at it. A big, tall glass, filled with a liquid that hinted at the golden color of the turkey now being dished up onto our plates. I saw, in its wonderful attraction, that it was an easy way to escape the mad game that my father and grandfather were playing. Up until that instant, I had never really thought about the many glasses of wine that had been drunk at that same table in my presence. Bubbles clung to the edges of the glass, causing the light to dance deep in its heart. And I knew, with all the certainty that a boy on his first steps to adulthood will ever be able to muster, that in that alcoholic vessel was a world that would alter the one I was living in at the moment. I knew I would change – for the better. It was a savior I didn't realize I needed. As I reached out to it, I found I had lost my fear of the tense atmosphere in the room. Let the adults argue and compete, I didn't care. A drink was whispering my name. The first of thousands: the first of many changes for the better.

I hear Rici move. I glance over and see he's taking a piss. The black undergrowth suddenly becomes attractive again.

"God, that looks like hell," he mutters.

I turn back to him, feeling my eyebrows knit together as I frown.

"If you need a medic," I say to Rici, "give a call, 'cause I'll be damed if *I'm* looking at your pecker."

"The beach, Nix, the beach. Looks like the army are on their way in."

I shift around further and look down. Every now and then, a star shell lights up the landing area. It's even worse than when I'd watched it earlier.

"Shit, it's really packed down there," I say.

The army is having a bad time. The tide has started to come in and the soldiers now have to jump over the side and wade inland. The beach is too crowded to let the boats get nearer.

"Some of 'em look like they're carrying half the world on their backs," I continue.

Rici grunts. "Isn't that a job for Hercules?" he asks.

"Atlas, it's Atlas. I thought you poets knew things like that."

"Nix, that jibe of yours always comes with a comment about my sister. You try for her and I'll kill you."

"Try, try, try. Ya-boo, I need my drink *now*."

He passes me the flask, I unscrew the top, raise the container to my lips and I sip the nectar – glad that I've managed to hold off a few minutes – meanwhile I watch the activities on the beach. The Enemy provides the light. That and the mortars from the ridge at our backs. The rain they are providing is hot and lethal. No relief from thirst.

It's easy to see that the men now coming in must be on their first operation – they're carrying far too much equipment. The first rule is to get in quick, and then off the beach at an even faster pace. You can't do that with an extra fifty pounds strapped on your back. They must be cursing down there; the army likes dry land, not sea, sand and coral. Still, they're getting ashore. And if they've got fresh water with them, they'll be welcome. I pass the flask back.

"You were right," says Rici, leaning close. "I can't understand why the Japs don't attack."

A bazooka lets rip to our right, closely followed by three or more other retorts. Tank fire adds itself to the din. We turn away.

"There," says Rici. "I spoke too soon."

"It's not *us* that's getting it," I say.

"Amen to that."

"Nice to see I'm spreading the Word – and glad you've seen the light."

"Shut up, or I'll sing you a song."

"I'm shaking in my boots."

We both quit yapping and hunker down. Anyone looking at us would probably have assumed that we were just a pair of hard-nosed fighting machines. Not that one was a brute who'd won a poetry competition at high school and was permanently concerned about the virginity of his younger sister, or that the other was a writer trying to hold on to his sanity by emulating a Greek myth. I decide to risk sleep. Perchance to dream. Hopefully of Thanksgiving and that first ever drink.

I dream.

It's night in the park-sized garden down in the Everglades, and it's the Fourth of July to beat all the Fourth of Julys; it's better than all the rest put together. Everybody I meet tells me so. It's a good crowd: everyone I've ever known is here – including the guys I've seen killed in action. We chew the fat, swap yarns, and they tell me they like my stories. I tell them they have great taste. And every so often we stand up and gawk at the entertainment. The firework display is the best that any man has ever seen. Rocket after rocket after rocket exploding with glorious colors of blue and gold and red, sparkling in a pure black sky, making fountains upon streams upon clouds of shimmering stars. The rat-tat-tat of the giant Chinese firecrackers in the distance gets the children screaming and jumping and hollering, and we men just stand around looking good in our tuxedos, as we search through the shoulder-high yew maze we find ourselves in, trying to find our way back to the bar. I know it's only a party, but I could really use a damn good belt of bourbon. For some reason, even though I feel uneasy about being in this maze, I have this strange intuition that the host of the party would be upset if I cheated and climbed onto the top of the hedge to get a better idea of where the exit was. Still, he throws a terrific party, does Hercules.

I look over towards him, sitting regal in his lion's cloak on a throne made from all the bones of animals he's killed. He's so noble and wise and gracious, and has surrounded himself with horned demons and powerful gods and wicked Minotaurs and the cheerful Jason and his poker-playing Argonauts. All of them are drinking the finest wines, all of them are setting aside their quarrels for the night; everyone is enjoying the spell that his party casts. The host appears bemused with it all.

Is that how you see him? Is that how you see Hercules?

That's how he is to anyone who cares to look. He'd make a great fullback – poise and strength. I don't think the coach would go for the cloak, though. Or the spear. Or the bow and arrows. Anyway, who are you? Who's speaking? Where are you?

It's me. My name's Serena. Didn't I tell you that before?

Nice name, one that I know from somewhere. My grandfather's stories? I don't know. But what's in a name? A rose would smell as sweet . . . These two houses of Capulet and Montague . . . Why should I be thinking of Shakespeare just now? No, you didn't tell me before. Ah, I remember you now; you were with me on the beach this morning.

Yes, that was me.

You surprised me. But it was worth it. You have a lovely voice, Serena.

Thank you. I've been thinking, while watching what you're doing, and I've decided it's okay to talk to you, as you're obviously dreaming.

Really, how do you know? Are you one of Hercules' friends? Are you a goddess? Tell me, do you have the immortal power of dreams? Is that your secret? I wish I could see you. Are you a goddess, Serena?

I try to think I'm a normal woman.

But you wouldn't mind being treated as a goddess?

I wouldn't complain if men got down on their knees to me.

In homage or enslavement?

Both if possible. Are you volunteering?

I don't know if I dare.

I think you've got enough courage to do anything – even to treat me as a goddess. Now stop making me laugh.

Ah, you have such a wonderful laugh, but do I detect the old worship-but-don't-touch routine?

I've been taught to keep some mystery about myself.

That's basic woman stuff, isn't it?

That would be telling – no clues, sorry.

Feisty? I fall in love with feisty women all the time. It's in the blood.

Oh, yes? So, is this how you romance women? Is this how you sweep them off their feet? And does it work?

It's my dream.

Oh, yes, sorry, I forgot. You'd do it differently if it wasn't your dream?

God, yes. We'd bust out of here, borrow a good car and drive into town. Doesn't matter which town, I know all the really good restaurants on the East Coast, and we'd have wine, definitely have some wine, a great big glassful each, and we'd have pasta as our main meal. Yes, pasta would be good, so it'd have to be an Italian restaurant. I know some terrific Italian places. They may be allies with the Germans, but Rici has convinced me that their food still tastes the best in the world. We'd get his sister to cook.

That sounds wonderful. But why do I get the feeling this sister is special to you? Don't you want to run off with *her*?

Ah, that's nothing to worry about – this is a dream, remember? Besides, I've only met her the once. Rici made the mistake of showing me her photograph and I got to meet her at his father's restaurant when we had some leave. I've been goading Rici – telling him she's cute – ever since. I only do it because he's in love with my sister. Rici's sister's pretty, but I'm sure she'd pale beside a goddess like you. If only I could see you, then I'm sure you'd win me over.

When did you become some sort of prize, to be won?

When my grandfather won me.

Pardon?

I'll explain some time. Do you still want to bust out of here? Come on, it's my dream, so it gets to be my treat. We could have some fun: catch a film, or try looking up that new kid Sinatra? I've heard you ladies go a bundle on him. Rici's sister loves him. Then we'd go and eat, listen to some mellow music. Yes, go somewhere with some quiet music. Anywhere away from these fireworks. They're too noisy, too hard on the ears. Don't you think so?

It's good that you're still alive.

Well, yes, I have to agree with you about that, that is good, but I think I'm happier about it than you could be. So, am I doing my best film-star line for a goddess, or are you some sort of ghost, then? Ghosts I can understand, at least.

If you want to think of me like that, then go ahead.

A ghost with a beautiful voice. Did Romeo make a comment about Juliet's voice? I can't remember. Hey! I'm a fool – you're English, aren't you? I've just realized you're English.

I'm sorry it's so obvious.

Don't apologize. I told Tom how you Brits always use "sorry" to fill in the pauses in conversation.

Tom? Are you talking about your friend Thomas Wakefield? The painter you lived with in England before the war? The friend that was killed during a raid over Holland?

Tom's not dead – he's flying those wooden Mosquitoes right now. His last letter hinted as much. Hey, how did you know I lived with him in England? You are some ghost. And filled with the myths of the Greeks? Interesting. I have lots of questions to ask – and you'd answer them, wouldn't you? Isn't that so? Isn't it?

Hello?

Isn't that true?

Hello? Hello?

Are you still there?

Yes. Yes, I am. Phoenix, listen, I'm just a figment of your

imagination, I'm a ghost. Treat me as nothing but a ghost. You should take everything I say with a pinch of salt.

Like the Twelve Labors of Hercules you suggested?

Oh, God.

You go ask Hercules, he's just over there. I've done three of his tasks already. I'd have a chat with him myself about them, discuss tactics – if I could only get out of this maze. We're never going to get to that restaurant if I can't get out of this maze. I think the next task has something to do with a pig. Is that right? You'd know, wouldn't you? Completing the tasks was your suggestion, after all.

Was it? I can't remember.

A ghost with a defective memory – that's a nice spin I could use sometime.

When? In your stories? Yes, think about your stories.

That's right. I think ghosts and spirits and myths must be in my blood. I've heard that some people think that ghosts are a place's surrounding memories. That's a nice idea, don't you think? A home holding memories? I've recently decided to believe in that. Are you a memory, Serena? Are you a ghost of one of my ancestors, come to warn me of my fate, disguised as a message in a dream? Ah, I remember, you say I'm dreaming. Then this isn't Florida. Yes, I'm dreaming, aren't I? Can I dream we make it to the Italian restaurant?

Yes. Yes, you can. Travel well, Phoenix.

Travel well – I wrote that once.

I know. And yes, in answer to your question, it's a pig. The Erymanthian Boar – that was Hercules' fourth task.

You sound worried. Is it going to be dangerous?

I don't know. I don't know if I should tell you these things. I – I . . . Travel well, Phoenix, travel well.

My friends call me Nix.

I'll remember that, Nix.

I think I'll watch the fireworks some more, Serena. If I can ignore the sound, I may as well watch. Maybe I'll even see if I can solve this maze. I want to find the bar – yes, I could drown in drink now. And maybe grab a bite to eat? Then teach some of these slobs how to eat food properly. God, there are some noisy eaters around here. They're making me hungry. Just listen to them. Serena? Are you still there? Serena?

I give up calling and try instead to find where the food and drink are. It's infuriating, because someone is sure enjoying himself or herself. Slop, slop, slop – that's all I can hear. Slop, slop, slop.

W Day +1. 05.01. Ridge overlooking Asan River.

I wake up with a jolt. The dark is fading, fast, as it does at equatorial latitudes, and objects are melting into focus through the jungle mist. I blink, swat a couple of crawlers from my face, and poke the sleep from my eyes. Color is beginning to emerge from the blacks, from the deep browns and from the muddy purples of the undergrowth. The mist moves slowly, following its own course down the hill, and I spot the odd movement from the Boys. Then they are covered over again – the morning fog thickening for a moment. I shiver, and I can't decide if that's because I think I feel cold, or whether it's something to do with my recent dreams. I lick my lips, to find that the mist tastes of salt and cordite. There's a roar above me and I suddenly find myself ducking down, and I wince at the sound. A rapid barrage from the navy is being flung over our heads. It's a wake-up call to the Enemy, as well as to me. I wipe the sleep from my eyes again and notice Rici is smiling at me.

"Two hours, you bastard," he says. "You owe me."

I nod and blink rapidly. I breathe out, and suddenly become awake, so alert that those few hours of troubled sleep are a memory already. Something is moving out there in the under-growth. It's in front of me, not to one side. And it's nothing to do with the Boys. I bring my carbine up, squint down the sight and take up the tension on the trigger. Then I drop the barrel and feel myself gawking. Thirty yards in front me, amid the mush of jungle litter, is a pig. A genuine, honest-to-God, sent-to-me-from-my-dreams pig. And it's eating: slop, slop, slop. I watch as it raises its head for a second, I listen as it snorts and grunts, then I choke as it shoves its snout back into the belly of a dead Enemy – probably the same one from the night before. By the noise and fury of its feasting, this Enemy must make good eating. Before I can stop and rationalize the whole idiotic situation I find myself in – I decide I have to take this opportunity. I raise my carbine again.

I'm back in the hills with my grandfather. I take aim. I hold my breath. The sight wavers. I start to shake. I take another breath. I talk to myself to stop the jitters.

Concentrate, Nix – it's number four.

I take aim.

Number four. Number four.

I take aim. I start to shake again. I try not to—

I begin to squeeze the trigger. A clean body shot is what I want. Nothing fancy, nothing clever.

Do it!

I take aim. I try *not* to tremble. I—

The shot rings out and the pig crumples down without a sound, its head disappearing into the gore of its repast.

I breathe out again.

Done it!

"Hey, Nixy!" calls Amos. "Why'd you go kill my mascot? He was fattening himself up nicely."

I lean back against the side of the foxhole.

"You all right?" asks Rici.

I stare at the dead pig, and the dead Enemy. I listen to the bangs and the booms and the whine of incoming mortars, and I stare at the dead Enemy again, with that dead pig nestled in his lap.

The Erymanthian Boar!

Pock! Pock!

"Incoming!" shouts Rici.

Whoo-bang! Whoo-bang!

I cower. For the first time since we hit Guam, instead of

crouching, I cower. The Erymanthian Boar is out there in front of me.

Pock! Pock!

"Rici!" I shout, even though he's only five feet away.

"What?" he answers, as he pulls his helmet down further, over his face.

"Rici, I think I'm going mad."

He laughs and nods to where my Erymanthian Boar lies dead.

"Who'd be able to stay sane here?" he asks.

"But that's the Erymanthian Boar!"

Whoo-bang! Whoo-bang!

"I wouldn't even care if the damn thing sprouted wings and took to the air," he says. "If that's the stupid pig you wanted, then so be it. Whatever gets you through, Nix, whatever gets you through."

More mortars crash nearby.

I hunker further into my foxhole and pray to the goddess of my dreams, requesting – fervently begging that she'll stay beside me. I figure this day is going to be a long one. I'll need all the help I can get.

Whoo-bang! Whoo-bang! Whoo-bang!

Even if it means going mad.

TEN

F2/6838/20/07   Team C Report (partial)

08.32   Subject was seen to exit her home along with her
        brother. After a delay of some minutes, involving
        a heated discussion, they got into the brother's
        car and proceeded to drive out of the city. It was
        noticed the brother's general demeanour became
        sullen after a bout of apparently swearing. He
        constantly broke the speed limit, sometimes by
        an excessive amount. -

09.03   Subject travelling East on A14 towards Bury St
        Edmunds. No conversation noted between parties.
        Speed, at times, above ninety miles an hour.

10.21   Subject enters Touch-May farm, situated at Blaken-
        ham. The only exhibit subject appeared interested
        in was a collection of Vietnamese pot-bellied
        pigs. After some discussion between the parties,
        brother photographed subject as she crouched
        down beside one of the animals. There was no indi-
        cation why she wanted a photograph taken.

10.58   Subject and brother left farm.

                        *

Sunday.

The weather is still hot. In the skies over the Suffolk countryside there are no clouds, just the same claustrophobic sun as yesterday – a dry glare of Provençal Van Gogh white, in a sweep of Deben Vale Constable pale-blue. All the other colours of the world are bleached from the trees and fields by the broiling light, causing the fresh green of spring to become dull and to shrivel somehow. Even the ground has started to look wasted and thirsty, and every now and then it coughs up a sparse whirl of dust from the fields, which fades into nothing before it really gets going.

The heat appears to be getting to everything that is trying to grow, or move – the crows that earlier could occasionally be seen swooping inside the thermals above the woods and copses have now sought shade and are quiet. Serena and Alex are heading home, in silence too, but for a different reason.

Serena has her window wound fully down and enjoys the sensation of the cool wind on her arm. The rolled-up sleeve of her white shirt flaps in the breeze. She flirts with the idea of it being a lover's breath as he kisses her arm.

Alex is now slowing down, and Serena looks ahead and sees the reason – a country pub. It is the sort that is found in profusion throughout the Suffolk countryside. There are small pinewood tables in the front, the hint of a gravel car park at the rear, the first-floor windows emerge from the thatch of the roof, and clearly the timbers that hold the whole structure together were old back when Nelson was alive. Serena assumes that inside, after the soul-breaking embellishments of the eighties, the owners have now ripped out the superfluous and given the customers what they really wanted: good booze, good grub and a place to waste an hour or two in chat. Serena loves places like these, and obviously her brother is going to stop here for refreshments.

Perhaps then Alex can unwind a bit.

Serena, for the tenth time that morning, tells herself that it is about time she passed her driving test. Then she wouldn't be so dependent on Alex and his mood swings – or having to explain herself. After they had visited the farm, Alex, without any warning, had brought up the subject of Annette, and Serena had been left to ponder his motivation for doing so. He knew it was a delicate and painful area of her life.

Brothers can be confusing.

And why mention Annette?

Annette Baxter had been a student at Lady Murray and had given every indication of possibly becoming a close friend. In Fresher's Week last year, Serena had gone into the drunken chaos of the student bar and had spotted something extremely unusual. The young woman sitting alone at a table in the corner did not look out of place there: she had shoulder-length fair hair, parted down the middle, a forearm full of bangles, a nose stud, a khaki slash top and trousers. It was her expression and what she was reading that made her stand out. Serena thought she had a face similar to a young and innocent child, but somehow one in the throes of addiction withdrawal. And though Serena believed herself to be the only female in Britain who read graphic novels, here was a woman intently engrossed in *V for Vendetta*, Alan Moore's and David Lloyd's apocalyptic study of revolt.

The story had ingrained itself into Serena's own psyche, and she thought it could provide a welter of interpretations. A hero in a mask and Guy Fawkes attire (like the caricature on a certain brand of fireworks), comes forth to offer a form of anarchy's rebellion against the fascist government. This man, "V", had survived a concentration camp experiment and believed that violence was a legitimate solution for overthrowing the totalitarian regime. Serena admired its distillation of what anarchy represents as a mindset, so far removed from the general public's notion of being destruction for destruction's sake.

Anarchy, in other words, is about getting rid of the rulers, not about getting rid of the rules.

V's young protégé, Evey Hammond, was an inspiration. Serena had even made herself a badge (a V inside a circle) and had worn it everywhere she went. And there, sitting hunched over the table, was another female who could obviously see the attraction. Serena, filled with a new sisterly confidence, had sat down and started talking to this waif who exuded such attitude.

Annette was about the same age as her and, as far as Serena could ascertain over the following weeks, had mostly enjoyed her childhood and teenage years, unlike Serena herself. This young woman, with the dark circles around her eyes, had grown up in Liverpool, run rings around parents, teachers, and frequently the police. She lost her virginity at fifteen to an eighteen-year-old boy, who six months later signed a major record deal, and then forgot his past. She had responded to this rejection by writing a filthy song about him that she'd given to Christian – the gay twenty-one-year old perky bald keyboard player of the band he'd dumped simultaneously. Who then went on to record a massive number one with it. Annette was pleased with the ensuing royalties, which helped her pay her way through Cambridge, and more. Besides, Christian was always available for laughs when she could reach him on his mobile.

Annette seemed completely unfazed by Serena's status. Studying literature, she couldn't give a fig about mathematics – as long as she felt sure the barman had given her the correct change, she was happy. Also, Annette had an apparent confidence that outshone Serena's fledgling dips into extrovert behaviour. She could walk into any room, ignore the undressing stares of the hope-filled young men, and carry on doing exactly what she wanted, which mostly seemed to revolve around getting drunk and reading graphic novels.

But Serena quickly came to realize that this was a front to hide a complex and unhappy personality. Annette was diabetic, and she loathed needles with a vengeance – a phobic reaction brought about by a traumatic accident at a very early age (when a needle broke in her). Easing the needle into her flesh, twice a day, without passing out, was a form of hell to her. She would sweat, become light-headed, and lose colour from the surface of her skin, but still she forced herself to inject the insulin, day in, day out, morning and evening. This ritual haunted her.

Serena later discovered that her new friend was also a bit of a manic-depressive. As the term headed towards Christmas, Annette became withdrawn for no reason. Serena tried to help on the fewer occasions they met, but Annette put distance between them.

In the first week of December, Serena had to attend a mini-symposium in New York. She was only out of the country for four days, but in that short time, without any hint of her intention, Annette overdosed hugely on insulin. Beside her body on the bed, she had left a personal note to Serena. It read: *You can have all my comics if you settle my tab at the bar.*

Serena felt completely numb until the day of the funeral. She stood away from Annette's relatives, and from the host of "friends" that had never been there when Annette needed them most, and instead took a seat alongside the only person who had ever made any effort for her dead friend.

Christian himself was the reason for a number of photographers hovering outside the crematorium chapel. He explained to Serena how Annette's ex-boyfriend had been informed by his manager that there was no publicity incentive for *him* to turn up, and then Christian commented bitterly that Annette had the boyfriend pegged correctly in her lyrics: a poor porn farce, with a right loose arse. As the first stifled giggle rose in her throat, Serena felt a heavy sorrow constrict her insides.

At the end of the service the pair of them left arm in arm, with tears in their eyes. Then, in Annette's memory, they went off to a bar and drank half-pints of lager and house-double shorts all afternoon and evening until they were thrown out.

For weeks after, besides the grieving and the ugly feeling of guilt, Serena had become fascinated by what could have driven such a bright person to end it all. What part of her mind had corrupted the rest into believing death was a solution? And in such a way? A final one-finger salute to her demons? Even as she pondered these questions, Serena immersed herself again in her work. And if it hadn't been for that, and the supporting women at Lady Murray, who knows what might have happened to her? Alex seems to sense this.

"Are you going mad?" he asks as they sit down outside the country pub.

"No, I'm going brown."

She flashes her newly acquired tan under his eyes. He takes a swig of beer, and gives Serena the eye.

"Don't be flippant. You know I'm concerned about you – and with what you're doing."

"But you've *experienced* it."

He takes another long pull on his pint. "I experienced an effect of the mind, yes," he says.

"So you're now saying you don't think it actually works?"

Alex pauses for a second before answering. "I'm sure it affects what you think, how you perceive, but to enable a person to 'slip' back in time? I have my doubts."

"But you—"

Alex leans forward and puts his hand on Serena's, interrupting her.

"Listen," he says, "be the scientist for a second, be the impartial sceptic. Consider what you're asking me to believe happened. You plugged me into your – what was it called? You wired me up to your Odysseus, while I was thinking about a time and place I've already studied well."

Serena tries, in vain, to interrupt her brother.

"Wait," says Alex, holding up his hand. "Hear me out, just hear me out. I was thinking about this all last night. Just try to be the scientist for the moment, be objective, that's all I ask."

He raps the wooden tabletop with the side of his hand, like a soft karate chop that follows the rhythm of the points he makes.

"Now, I saw in my mind's eye the unfolding of an event that I've researched thoroughly for years. I'm aware of all the different theories that have been postulated, discussed, *filmed*; involving the CIA, the Mafia, the Cubans, the military, even Lyndon B himself, and all the other mixtures and spins of what may or may not have happened. If you really want to know, I could tell you what JFK had for breakfast that morning. So, after having enjoyed nearly a bottle of vodka and some stunning sensory memories, as I did, I have one key question. How can you *prove* to me that what I saw, felt, experienced, was the actual event? I'll admit it seemed so vivid I could smell the exhaust fumes from the cars – but how can you prove that that was what Odysseus enabled me to envisage, and not just some freaky, ultra-real dream? Please, as a scientist, convince me?"

Serena sits back on the bench, her legs tucked under it, her toes digging into the grass to stop herself falling off. She takes in the scene around her, as she marshals her thoughts to answer him. The Newbourne *Badger and Set* is situated at the bottom of a broad hollow which dominates an undulating T-junction, and the rest of the village spreads outwards and upwards from the pub itself. Across one road is a freshly painted brick bus shelter that Serena thinks three small grannies would fill adequately if they sat on its concrete bench. Behind it is a low hedge of something she suspects is hawthorn, and spiralling up a nearby telegraph pole is a rampage of ivy. Beyond the hedge is a field of wheat losing its ripples of green and promising an ocean of gold within the next few days. Further around the rim of the hollow in which the pub sits, there stands a square-towered church whose black-blue flint walls cause Serena to consider the care, labour and love that went into its construction.

Off in the distance, in one of the village gardens, a blackbird can be heard bullying some other bird and further out a skylark dances and sings above the wheat, and closer by a kingfisher fishes the pond over which insects hover inches from the still surface. It is a pleasant Suffolk village scene. Life as a composite, life going on – steady, seemingly unchanging, but changing by the instant, each possibility of life sometimes depending on even the smallest decisions. The thought is both reassuring and frightening to Serena. A tiny fish rises in the pond and is snatched by the kingfisher.

Alex taps his fingers, impatiently.

"Okay," says Serena, "there's a very simple reply. Okay? I'll tell you what you can do now. You can go away and write down the precise details of some event in your life, one that I have no possible way of knowing anything about, something that I couldn't possibly even begin to guess." Serena smiles broadly as she continues. "It could even be a time in your life when you were nice to someone, like, you know, trusted them."

Alex's eyes widen. "Hey, if you're going to get mean again—"

"Okay, okay, sorry. I'm serious, though. You just write anything down that you like, then give me the date, an approximation of the time, and I'll see if I can find out what you were doing. I may even have a go at finding out what *you* had for breakfast that day."

Alex chops at the table with his hand again. "Well, do *that*, then," he says.

"What?"

"If your damn machine works, go back and find out what I had for breakfast *this* morning."

Serena sits back and starts counting on her fingers.

"Marmite on toast, four rounds, yucky muesli with fruit, and two cups of Earl Grey. I don't need Odysseus for that."

"I had something different today."

Serena stares at her brother, who is studying her intently.

"Deliberately?" she asks.

Alex takes a long swig at his beer and doesn't answer her.

"You bastard," she says. "Okay, okay," she continues, "I'll do that. I'll get inside that twisted head of yours and find out everything you did this morning before you came to pick me up."

Serena allows herself a smirk. "You know," she says loudly, "I've never before wondered who you fantasize about when you masturbate in the morning, but I may just be tempted to find out."

Alex chokes on his beer, and conversation stops at the next table. The two plaster-dust-covered builders enjoying their lunch break are staring at Serena. She raises her glass to them.

"A woman's work is never done," she calls over to them, and then downs the remains of her drink.

"You want another one?" she asks, as she stands up. Alex passes his glass to her without making eye contact, and then stares across the road at a house that is being re-thatched.

When Serena returns from the bar, she notices that the workmen have retreated out of sight, and presumably out of earshot. Alex is drumming his fingers on the tabletop again.

"All right," he continues, as though Serena hasn't been away for five minutes. He stops tapping and grasps his aluminium crutch, running a thumb partway down its length.

"All right," he says again, "you do that. Tell me what I had, or didn't have, for breakfast."

He forces a smile onto his face. Serena notices how he licks his lips, as though nervous.

Serena puts down the pints and slides onto the bench seat.

"A bit of fraternal support would be nice," she says.

Alex rubs the bridge of his nose. "Prove to me that it works, and I'll dance at your Nobel Prize ceremony."

"And?"

Alex raises his hands. "And what?" he says.

"You've got something else on your mind."

"I also have a problem with this other stuff." He gestures to the bag containing her camera.

She takes off her glasses, pulls a small bright-blue cloth from her back pocket and begins to clean them slowly with it.

"We had this discussion earlier," she says.

"Tell me, just where is the sense in what you're doing? Tramping all over the place to get photographed beside a pig with wrinkles? And for what purpose?"

"As I said, I need to have a challenge too. I feel I owe this man Lafayette some response to how I've influenced him."

"This figment of your imagination?"

"He's no dream."

"I know he *did* exist. I helped put together that dossier you have on him, I found the bloody pen he accidentally left behind in that bureau, found that story of his about a bloody humming-bird that got you really interested in him, but you haven't proved *your* story to me yet."

"I will." Serena looks around for a moment and bites her lip. "Look Alex," she says, "I know my invention works, *and* I'll prove it works, but I find I'm having to do all *this*," she pats her shoulder bag, "for deeper reasons that I don't think you'll be able to understand. I don't even know if I can express my reasons with any degree of clarity. It's a *need* thing. I simply feel as though my life is at some sort of cusp, that things are changing for me. I *have* to ask myself, what am I going to become? Where am I heading?"

Is Odysseus changing me?

"My childhood," she continues, "disappeared in a welter of expectation and publicity; my intelligence took me away from being a little girl, made me a performing freak. Now I'm taking responsibility for me again. I'm trying to be *me*, whatever that is."

"The new pop sensation?"

Another dig, another swipe.

Serena realizes that she should have let Alex joke, but no, she has given Alex another door to rattle.

Since Annette's death, Serena has concentrated primarily on her work on Odysseus, but has also found a new outlet for her musical abilities in order to give parts of her brain a breather. Christian had become interested in the music that Serena creates as a means to relax. She has not only played classical music on her flute, accompanying some of her favourite orchestral pieces, but has spent time relaxing with free-form jazz. For ten or fifteen minutes, she will sit, curled up in an armchair, downstairs in her living room, blowing note after note, lost in the sensation of making music.

What concerns Alex, and what he is being his usual unsubtle self about, is that he discovered Serena was recording these little experiments, and then altering the result on her PC. (Contracting the notes, reversing them, adding an overlay with a Jew's harp.) She has been sending the final results to Christian, who has expressed a desire to use them as backing tracks. He is hopeful he can do something special with them.

The night before, after her exchange with Phoenix, via Odysseus, in his dream, she had sat in her chair, making music, while thinking about what had happened. Looking at the file that she had assembled about her combat correspondent in Guam, she quelled her panic. Even though he was dreaming, he had been quick to pick up that his friend, Thomas Wakefield, the person whose house she was now filling with a blue-grass beat, had eventually been shot down towards the end of the war. She had then stopped playing and picked up a photo of Phoenix Lafayette, taken in Cambridge, May 1939, outside King's College. The man she gazed at looked tough, like a rugged frontiersman; like he could have taken on three other men and won. But the eyes betrayed him. Far from the dull, unfocused meanness of a thug, the eyes in the photograph glinted with sharp intelligence. And there was also compassion there.

Serena had then picked up the only other picture she had of him, dressed in a marine's uniform and looking over his shoulder towards the photographer. According to the caption, the marine was just about to head below and climb into his LVT for the invasion of Guam. His strong-looking hands reached out to grasp a rail, and Phoenix was smiling, seemed calm. Serena had found herself stroking the contours of his face. Then she had continued playing her flute . . . and thinking about how she would alter what she was improvising.

Alex hated her music.

"Look, Alex," she says finally, "it's nice that you've helped me *again* today, I *do* appreciate it, but let me handle this my way, okay?"

Alex takes a final gulp of beer, leaving half a glassful. He wipes his mouth, snaps open his sunglasses and slides them on.

"Don't forget the proof," he says, "remember I'm being Mister Sceptic."

"I won't. Aren't you going to finish that?"

He shakes his head and, in two seconds, Serena knocks back the remainder of his beer.

"Let's get back," she says.

As the workmen appear from the rear of the pub, about to return to their labours, Serena manages a mighty belch.

"It's a great pub you've got here, boys," she says.

The men shake their heads and try to ignore her.

Sunday night.

How much time has passed? Hours? Days?

No, it can't be that long.

It can only be a few hours between stopping for a drink at that pub and where she is now. But where is *now*? She is in a dream, she *has* to be. How else to explain the dark-green cypress trees, the swathe of olive groves, the pale, ochre-coloured, cliffs that slope down to the blue-green water that she *knows* has to be the Mediterranean? She can't remember the last time she visited a place where the dry heat literally took your breath away. And, except at a party, she would not normally wear such clothes as those she sees she is wearing now – a sleeveless pull-on dress in white silk, chunky golden snake armlets on both her upper arms, some sort of braided belt . . . This is the attire of the *hetairai*, those educated foreign women who acted as entertainment for Greek men in ancient times. And she is naked underneath.

How can that be?

There is also the leather thong around her wrists to consider; her hands are raised and bound to the lowest branch of a stunted oak. She is helpless, vulnerable. A part of her brain interprets her situation as being some form of Freudian self-expression, and its association with raw sex makes her want to squirm.

It is a comfortable, familiar feeling that is rising in her stomach, a fluid surge of sensation; but to Serena, the fact that she is acting out some sort of bondage fixation makes her uneasy. The feeling that she is the outsider, participating in a sexually motivated act, is so real.

Am I using Odysseus? Has the machine altered my thinking, so that I can't tell if this is a vision of some past event, or just the beginning of some horny dream?

It isn't Odysseus, however. Serena knows she has experienced this type of night fantasy before: the dreams about being tied up, being bound, being trapped. Nice ones where she perforce forgoes any sort of control. Serena relaxes: it is a dream.

But why does it seem so foreboding?

As if to answer her thoughts, a huge explosion of lights occurs right above her head. Her body shakes and she gasps; the desire beginning to surge within her is frozen – stalled. It is replaced with shock. A rocket of gigantic proportions erupts, blue and gold and silent, in the glare of the sun. It is the same as those Phoenix had been dreaming about, Serena recognizes. As the light from the firework fades, she drops her gaze down from the sky and is surprised to see a small group of marines charging past her from behind the tree. Their actions make no noise, as they run around her, one or two brushing against her body in their haste, but otherwise ignoring her. The dream then turns to nightmare.

The marines advance, giving one another covering fire – the bullets spurting from their rifles making no sound. The men signal instructions to one another as they crouch or run. From an empty, hollow space, an invisible enemy replies. And Serena finds she can't shut her eyes to it. She is forced to watch as bullets and shells rip into the marines right in front of her. Men are being killed violently, their bodies twisting into unnatural positions, clutching at parts of themselves that are suddenly not there, trying to hold in what they still retain. One man has been severed in two, and he waves his arms in futile anger, as his upper torso somehow remains upright on the ground. Another man explodes into a mist of red vapour. Vast holes slice open the chests of others. The dying men open their mouths to cry out a name, or perhaps just to scream, but the only sound Serena can hear is her own cries of terror. She aches for it all to stop.

Suddenly, the marines ripple away into nothing. Serena hangs from her bonds, limp, exhausted, drained. It has only lasted two, maybe three seconds.

Am I forever to relive that assault? In every detail?

Her breath returns in slow gasps and she tries to regain some sense of the thoughts that spark in her head.

I wish I hadn't thought of that scenario. What else might I conjure up?

Too late, she hears the grunt of the beast, well before she can see it.

In an instant, the nightmare has changed to something worse, if that were at all possible. The vision of fighting and dying men is etched on the retina of her soul, but now a creature stalks her from the shadows, just out of range in the corners of her eyes. She recognizes it to be the Beast. It isn't a Welsh Dragon, it isn't some myth of a Worm or serpent. This one has to be a corruption of all her fears, all those terrible insecurities and doubts: a hybrid of childhood terrors about what lurks under her bed, or at the top of the dark stairs. Serena instinctively knows it will never show itself – not to her. She will die unaware of what it is exactly; it will maul and savage her to death, taking pleasure in that.

Because I deserve it.

She knows such self-recrimination is stupid. But nightmares

take no account of rational thought. She deserves it because she was an ungrateful child.

Serena *had* to be bad. She was given a gift, an intelligence; and all she ever wanted, the selfish little child, was a friend, some other girl to play with, a pal to invent stories with, someone she could talk to as they combed each other's hair. Someone else to share her fears of growing up, wasn't that a small thing to forgo? It was shameful that she wanted that so much. Others have to struggle to understand a fraction of what appears obvious to her – wicked girl, wanting to trade that gift away. It would serve her right if the bogeyman got her. Now go back to sleep.

Yes, Mother.

But she can't.

The Beast is out there. It's been waiting for years. It's the one that *she's* been waiting years for. It's Red Riding-Hood's wolf, it's the snake in the Garden of Eden, and it's Nosferatu. And then, in amongst the sounds of it, as if to crush her soul, Serena hears Annette calling – calling for the help that Serena cannot give. The Beast has taken her. Serena pulls hard at her bindings. Annette cries and wails, calls to Serena again. Then she screams, and her desperate summons for help is lost amid the grotesque slobbering of the Beast. Its noises are loud and obscene, and Serena can't begin to guess what it is doing.

Is killing me the worst it can do?

It begins to move nearer, its hunger not yet sated.

As again she tries to close her eyes, Serena feels the stroke of leather on her exposed thigh. She twists to one side and looks down and away, then slowly up. A Greek warrior stands there, his identity cloaked by the expressionless contours of a bronze face-plate; all she can see is his eyes and chin, but even these are lost in the shadow that falls from the Mohican-style headdress on his helmet. He is broad in the shoulder, barrel-chested. He wears the scratched and dented breastplate of a soldier who might have seen action at the siege of Troy. He moves easily, and doesn't flinch as he strides towards the hidden monster, sliding his sword from his scabbard. The warrior disappears into the bushes.

Within moments, the din of a tremendously violent struggle afflicts Serena's ears. There is shouting from the man, roars from the Beast. There is a clash of metal on hardened scale, the zing of claw on armour. Serena hears all the thuds and the blows, and imagines the warrior being battered to the ground. There is more roaring than shouting now. Then a pause of silence, and she feels the earth shake. Something heavy has fallen. A bellow erupting from the boogie-demon of her childhood turns into a pig's squeal. Followed by another.

Then it is quiet. The sounds of the countryside return.

She watches as the warrior strides back towards her. His armour is thickly flecked with blood and now he has a slight limp. As he approaches, he drops the severed serpent's head he has been holding and raises his buckled and bloody sword towards her. With one clean sweep, he slices her free from her bindings. Serena finds she cannot breathe.

It's a dream, you stupid girl! It's a silly, trite fantasy image! What are you going to do now, then? Let him deflower you?

Serena tears the remains of the straps from her wrists.

Fuck no!

She leaps forwards and pushes the man to the ground. He collapses down easily. She stands above him, one foot on either side. She stares down at his concealed face as she lowers herself and straddles him. He attempts to reach up to touch her, but she slaps his hands away. Instead, it is she herself that gropes between their legs. There is no pain as she guides him in.

What did the girls used to say? Treat it like a giant, fleshy tampon?

He stares at her through the eye openings of his blank-faced helmet. She gyrates slowly. Then at speed. She presses down harder. She bucks wildly. Her fists thump his breastplate. She calls out. He is filling her completely. She is coming.

So soon!

My Goooooooood!

It is a perfect joy.

She is sated.

She is satisfied.

She looks down.

He is not there.

She looks up.

Her warrior is walking away. She can now only see his broad back retreating. He removes his helmet, lets it dangle from his fingertips. He glances back over his shoulder.

He is calm. He smiles.

It is Phoenix.

Serena awakes.

She is lying face down, half in, half out of her bed, with one foot resting on the floor. The bed creaks. It is a low-standing brass bedstead that she bought when she first moved into this house, and the mattress is thick and extra-sprung. One pillow is on the floor by her foot, the other, crumpled up at the head, is partially squeezed through the railings. The single cotton sheet she had been using in this heat is partially draped down one side of the bed and partially wrapped around her. Her hips are still unconsciously grinding against the edge of the mattress, and she stops immediately. She catches her breath and rolls over onto her back, pulling the sheet fully over her.

She sighs.

"Bloody hell. Bloody *hellllll*."

Serena waves a hand over her face to cool it. After a few more deep breaths, she raises herself up onto her elbows to look towards the window. Light is just beginning to appear through the curtain material. It will soon be dawn.

Serena gets out of bed, strips off the sheets and throws them in the general direction of the wicker laundry basket. She pads out of the bedroom, slowly wagging a finger at the grinning mask of V – a framed cover poster for *V for Vendetta* which she has hung by her door.

"Stop peeking," she admonishes the cartoon man.

Serena heads down the short landing, glancing into the

ghostly shadows of her workroom – the sentinels still positioned there, waiting – and carries on into the bathroom, without switching on the light. In the gloom of the semi-dawn, she starts running a shower. On an impulse, she wrenches the control over to the cold setting and steps into the torrent. Serena gasps, allowing her body to adjust shiveringly to the shock of it. The excess of the night is soon washed away and she closes her eyes, lets her face be pummelled by the onslaught. She runs both hands through her hair, opens her eyes, watches the water gurgle away down into the drain.

Without drying herself completely, Serena walks back to her bedroom, rummages in a drawer and then puts on clean underwear and a sleeveless scoop-neck top. After putting on her glasses, she pulls the curtains open. Dawn is a pale-blue light in the east. She opens the window wide, then turns and looks down at her bed.

"Bloody hell," she says again, and shakes her head. Walking into her study, she switches on her PC. For a while she writes.

It is possible that the dangers, anxiety about which I expressed earlier in this report, have begun to manifest themselves. I therefore intend to keep an in-depth diary to chronicle my impressions, my thoughts and actions as I use Odysseus from now on.

It has become obvious to me that I should be conducting this experiment under laboratory conditions with some appropriate form of monitoring. Unfortunately, I have developed such a personal interest in the man whose actions I have been following that, at the moment, I am reluctant to share my discoveries. I know this is unprofessional, but this is my decision and I will be prepared to defend it when circumstances demand. I fully recognize Odysseus' potential, and know that once I announce it to the world there will be little time for me to pursue this personal avenue, *and* the reporter, that I am so involved with.

My main concern now is with how I have, I suspect, influenced events in the past. I had always assumed – in the development phase of Odysseus at least – that my role would be merely one of an observer – retrocognition that has no impact on history. The intention, with

Odysseus, was to stimulate the mind in such a way that it would achieve a similar state to that believed to be detected in a person on seeing a "ghost". As with all known contact with ghosts, there is no interaction – the ghost seems totally unaware of the observer's presence; likewise, with there being no interference, no paradox of time travel should occur with Odysseus. It is my opinion that when Mr Lafayette was struck on the head during the landing on Guam, he momentarily achieved a synaptic resonance with myself, and this is why I am able to converse with him. This is the problem of paradox: whatever I may, or may not, have done, will be – and has always been – part of history, as *I* know it. The question remains then: what *is* the man's history? Does he live, or does he die? I haven't yet put enough effort into finding an answer to this from the records.

To expand on these thoughts, it is necessary to look at the basics of *physical* time travel. The classic paradox is explained thus: the time traveller returns to the past and somehow causes an accident that kills his/her grandmother when she is a child. With the grandmother dead in childhood, the time traveller's mother (or father) is not conceived, so therefore neither is the time traveller. It follows, then, that they would not be able to return to the past to influence it, and therefore their parent gets born and so do they. And so on, ad infinitum.

Surprisingly, especially to the lay person, this may have a solution. There is a discussion current among certain physicists which involves the postulation that there may be an infinite number of universes, and that all possibilities unfold somewhere. Results from experiments conducted on the quantum level have established cloned sub-atomic particles following the same path, even when observed at points many kilometres from their joint source. There is also the anomaly in Young's double-slit experiment to consider. If a single beam of light (for example, from a sodium lamp) is shone through two adjacent, narrow gaps, the photons interact with each other and produce an interference pattern of alternating dark and bright lines on a screen set up beyond the gaps. If a gap is closed, the interference pattern breaks down.

This demonstrates the wave-like properties of light.

However, if the experiment with the two slits is repeated, but with the strength of light reduced to its minimum (i.e. only one photon is released at any one time), and a photographic plate is placed on the screen for several hours in order to record the result, the interference pattern can still be observed. This leads to an interesting question: how can a succession of single photons, assuming each has passed through only one slit, produce an interference pattern? There is the possibility, say some physicists, that the photons are actually interacting with photons from nearby universes.

And the main question for me remains: what *is* the history in store for my Mr Lafayette?

Does he live, or does he die?

And what do I have to do to make sure everything works out the way it should?

Monday morning.

Serena switches off the PC, stretches, then stands up and goes downstairs. She unlocks her kitchen door and steps outside. The morning chorus has been finished for some time. She walks across the overgrown lawn and stops, her eyes fixed on nothing in particular.

Yesterday evening she had made use of Odysseus, in the way she had promised her brother. That clearly was the reason that the Beast had appeared in her nightmares – the reason she'd *had* the nightmare at all. The experience of tracking Alex as he fixed himself breakfast had also been intriguing. He had *indeed* not resorted to his usual tea and toast.

In fact Alex had gone to the fridge and taken out an unopened packet of bacon and a couple of eggs. He left the eggs to roll around on a plate while he sliced open the packet of bacon. As he began to tear back the wrapper, he went over and turned on the grill. He then eased out four rashers and, after inspecting each, first one side, then the other, he laid them on the wire rack and slid the grill under the heat. He had then poured a little cooking oil into a pan, placed it on a ring on the stove and, within a few minutes, began frying the eggs and was turning over the bacon. Then he opened a loaf of bread, and went back to the fridge for a pack of butter. It took five attempts before he managed to spread two slices of bread without ripping them to pieces with the frozen butter. By that time curls of smoke were wafting from the grill. He manually plucked the crisp rashers onto his plate, swearing as they burnt his fingers, then found both eggs had stuck to the pan. He swore again, and only after scraping them out with a knife, could he sit down to a breakfast of bacon and eggs on buttered bread.

What Serena found so peculiar about this most ordinary-sounding of meals, was that the bacon had been streaky, the eggs factory-farmed, the bread was white, and the butter full-fat. And her brother had been a committed vegetarian for three years now.

Serena makes her way further down the garden, trailing her fingers through the lavender and red-hot pokers. It is not cold, but for a moment, a shiver ripples down her back. Her mathematical brain has deduced that Alex must have purchased these unlikely ingredients on the same day of his 'excursion' back to Kennedy's assassination. He had been planning, even then, a means of testing the validity of her Odysseus.

Serena swipes at the stalks of lavender. She realizes that her attempts to re-create the labours of Hercules for herself must represent the elusive answer to a question she has yet to form – but they seem frustrating to Alex, which is strange in itself. (Why *isn't* she allowed to act a little haywire?) She clips the flowers again, with the distinct and queasy feeling that she may be finally growing up – taking charge.

Her romantic notions are fading like the night.

In a universe of such subtle permutations, where another universe is perhaps only a quantum step away, there is a consideration to making use of Odysseus that needs to be reported here. I have come to the conclusion that if the user begins to "interfere" with what occurs in the past, the cyclic nature of action and reaction could result in the user becoming "locked" mentally in the past, even after Odysseus has performed its automatic shutdown. That would be akin to autism – being removed from this world and existing, as it were, in another.

I could be playing with fire. But I cannot deny that the danger is exciting.

I am making new discoveries.

Some of which are inevitably about myself.

ELEVEN

Being a hero can be dirty work, and for his fifth task King Eurystheus ordered Hercules, as it was spring, to clean out some stables for a friend of his. As this order came from Eurystheus, and as King Eurystheus was becoming increasingly bitter, twisted, and devious with each labour, the impartial observer could easily deduce that these were no ordinary board and lodgings for horses. Hercules knew exactly what was ahead of him: he had heard the legends surrounding the stables to which King Eurystheus was referring. They were filthy in the extreme.

King Augeas was the proud – and some said smug – owner of more cattle, more goats and sheep, more horses than any other landowner and farmer in Greece. Was it because he was a shrewd cattle baron, some asked? Did he move in the right circles? Or was he just plain lucky? Most of his subjects thought it was a mixture of all three, with perhaps a bit of meanness thrown in; after all, he was a personal friend of King Eurystheus. On the other hand, a few brave people suggested it might have something to do with the well-founded rumour that King Augeas was the son of Poseidon. And also something to do with the curious fact that his animals were the most healthy, fertile and long-lived to be found anywhere in the known world. In fact they were the most prodigious collection of farming stock this side of Mount Olympus, and ones that any farmer might be proud to be associated with. But not King Augeas: he treated these thousands of animals that he owned (and which every other farmer in Greece envied) with the utmost contempt. His entire stock was penned up in the same place each night – an interconnecting set of large timber and thatched buildings that had not been cleaned out for years. His stables needed attention – badly.

Eurystheus felt pleased with the new task he had set Hercules. Small as he was, he stood straight and tall in his bronze jar, gripping his spear, and wanted to jig on the spot. He could cheerfully imagine how deep the dung had become. What a great idea that had been; he wished he could award himself a medal. Perhaps the sacrifice of a slave? And now Hera would be available for small favours. It was even worth a snigger. King Eurystheus made himself even happier after he recalled the herald to add the stipulation that Hercules must complete the task in one day. What fun it was being a king! His humour was clearly infectious, as he noticed a lightness of step in the herald as he departed to give Hercules the bad news.

Even in ancient Greece, the commercial and entrepreneurial world turned. Hercules, always looking out for a way to use his skills profitably, made a bargain with Augeas when he met him in his throne chamber. If the king hired him for just a day, with a payment of one-tenth of the king's cattle, he, Hercules, would clean up the king's dirty stables and remove the pungent filth that was affecting the local population. Augeas was amazed; he didn't for one moment think Hercules could achieve it, but he was clever enough to realize that Hercules could make an enormous dent in the mess of ordure. Perhaps, the king thought, he could then employ some locals to finish the rest at a cheap rate? Augeas gladly swore agreement to the deal – in front of his son Phyleus.

This labour had meanwhile attracted some interest. With his nephew Iolaus helping again, and with Phyleus carefully watching, Hercules set to work – under some duress.

There had recently been a succession of warm days – a

prelude to summer – and the smell from the stables was appalling. Hercules and Iolaus had to mask their noses and mouths with rags in an attempt to cope with the stench. Considering themselves well prepared, they then entered the walled yard to find their protection inadequate. Once inside, they could see, and smell, the extent of the problem: the walled yard was the size of the Olympic stadium and the stable buildings covered the area of a small town. One huge building was half buried in dung. But they were undeterred, for Hercules had already formulated a plan.

Phyleus, leaning against the pillar of the main gate, with servants offering him smelling salts and a quick chariot ride to the sea if the master so desired, was stunned to see the pair begin knocking down the wall on one side of the huge yard.

"But why?" he enquired.

Hercules dislodged another stone block from its setting.

"You'll see," he merely grunted.

Three hours, and one large gap, later, Hercules started on the wall directly opposite.

Phyleus began watching nervously through his fingers.

A similar gap appeared in the other wall. Six hours had passed, and the day was disappearing fast. Phyleus still could not work out their plan, until Hercules and his nephew began digging trenches. At that, Phyleus began to nod his head, realizing the direction in which they were heading. He thought Hercules was indeed a clever hero.

The two trenches that Hercules and Iolaus dug with such speed were designed as channels, leading to the two rivers that flowed adjacent to the stables. With one last simultaneous effort from Hercules and Iolaus, a conduit between the rivers was made. As the waters broke through and headed along the trenches, Hercules and his nephew, with Phyleus clapping and cheering from the sidelines, both stood back from their labour and watched a foaming tidal wave surge down the new channels.

The resulting torrents swept through the gap in the upper

end of the yard, cascaded through the open doors of the stables, flushed through the buildings, churning and boiling, then flowed out the other side towards the exit gap in the lower wall. It was a cauldron of action, wave after wave, as the water ripped away the muck embedded in the stable floor. The filth was torn up and literally carried away.

It took an hour for this flood to subside, whereupon Hercules and Iolaus blocked the flow and returned to inspect the aftermath. The place had been scoured, leaving the stables as clean as the day they were built.

Phyleus clapped.

"Well done," he said. "Well done, indeed."

His father wasn't so joyous.

As with all greedy businessmen who discover they've been outsmarted, King Augeas looked around for a loophole. Within a few hours he decided he had found one. In his opinion, Hercules had technically been in the employ of King Eurystheus – it was he who had originally ordered Hercules to perform the task – so Hercules wasn't in any position to make a business deal with himself, King Augeas. And what was this oath that he, King Augeas, was supposed to have made? He certainly couldn't recall making one.

Hercules was furious, but kept his head and, after many weeks of wrangling, took the case, and the king, to court. Hercules' prime witness was young Phyleus.

King Augeas was cocky and confident: he knew his son would never testify against him.

Arrogance is a blinding disease.

"I was there," stated Phyleus, his hand on his heart. "My father swore an oath."

"Pay up," said the judge, staring at the king.

Arrogance doesn't like to lose. King Augeas vented spleen.

"I banish you from my kingdom!" he shouted at Hercules. "And you can take my son with you!"

He stamped his foot, to make his point. And forgot to exercise his power to overrule a court's decision.

But Eurystheus didn't.

"No," the herald argued, "you were under hire to King Augeas – even the courts agreed on that – so our king can't count that as a completed task. Sorry, but you didn't fulfil the task acting for King Eurystheus."

The herald closed the gate and breathed a sigh of relief. His hair was going grey – he could do without these hero types.

TWELVE

Early Tuesday morning.

The heat of the day has stagnated into the heat of the night. In the corners of the shadows lurks a vice, a corruption that mostly hides from light. On this night a devil is abroad, seeking out converts to an unimagined disgrace – a loss, and lack, of conscience. It waits with its hot hands for everyone. It is a night when Good has to make a decision to take on Bad.

Serena finds it curious that a familiar set of buildings can look so ominous at night. It is one o'clock in the morning and she is crouched like a thief by the wall of a small, brick-built office, studying two long rows of stables lining opposite sides of a courtyard. She is clutching a shovel and a stiff-bristled broom. Serena knows the building beside her *is* an office, since she stood inside it some hours earlier, while the man in charge here listened to her strange request, then flatly refused to have anything to do with it.

Serena initially believed she had found a kindred spirit, since the office of Mr Troutfind, police horse trainer, was a mess. His large desk under the window was immersed below a cascade of forms, letters and mysterious carbon copies of documents so smudged that the words on them were nothing but illegible hieroglyphics. Serena realized she couldn't remember the last time she'd seen a carbon copy of anything. Poking out from the paperwork were two former coffee jars, one containing pens, the other pencils that appeared mostly broken; an open biscuit tin contained a stationer's store of elastic bands, beside a set of in/out trays with bulldog clips attached to their sides. Surrounding a rack of pigeonholes were pinned a welter of multicoloured rosettes, many of them faded. Put together with the wooden swivel chair, the old-fashioned hooked coat stand, and the huge clock on the wall that would have befitted a railway platform, Serena formed the impression that, unbeknown to her and the rest of the world, physical time travel already existed. Someone had obviously transported Mr Troutfind's office intact from the early sixties.

Mr Troutfind himself was of small stature for a man – forcing him to look up at Serena. For someone whose work must have been spent mostly out of doors, his skin had a distinctly unhealthy pallor. Serena had given her request her best shot, but she had already known in her heart that no amount of feminine appeal would ever beguile the likes of Mr Troutfind.

Now, as Serena glances back through the darkened windows of Mr Troutfind's office, she hopes she hasn't mistaken his departure.

Mr Troutfind runs a stable near Newmarket, breeding and training horses, primarily for the police. Serena had earlier asked him if he would let her clean out one of his empty stalls to fulfil a challenge allotted to her as part of a charity drive. Now attempting to do at night what she'd been denied during the day, she realizes she loathes Mr Troutfind and his petty unhelpfulness.

She shrugs her shoulders and gives the broom handle a squeeze. Serena shakes her head – Mr Troutfind had got under her skin. She concentrates on her task again.

The main reason she feels so nervous is that, though she'd got the impression all the horses were away elsewhere, at least one animal seems present and fully awake. Also some security lighting keeps switching itself on and off, and Serena is becoming more than ever convinced that Mr Troutfind is, at this very instant, aiming a twelve-bore shotgun in her general direction.

Serena curses silently, and scolds herself about her perennial fear of the dark.

Such a simple torment.

What youngster hasn't looked under the bed at least once in their short childhood? For Serena it had been a sudden metamorphosis. She had been a little over five years old and, up to the previous night, a Saturday, her routine had been comfortably the same. She went up to bed, her mother kissed her goodnight, then switched out the light. Serena fell fast asleep.

On the Sunday night, however, Serena's routine had dramatically changed. She had put on her pyjamas – with their one hundred and twenty-six and a half cavorting Winnie-the-Poohs (she'd counted them) – and climbed into her bed. She had snuggled down, pulling the covers up to her chin, and waited quietly for her mother to appear. As she lay there, she had cast her mind back to earlier that day and what had so shocked her – her brother Alex hitting her after she'd finished off his homework. Why had he got so angry? She had only been helping him. Serena rubbed the smitten side of her face – the physical pain had evaporated, but the tears were still waiting for an opportunity. As always, the bed felt snug, and safe.

Her mother had come into Serena's room, as she had the night before, and every night before that. She had bent down, kissed her daughter, wished her goodnight, retreated to the door and, without looking back, switched off the light and shut the door behind her. Just as she had done the previous night – and every other night. As usual, Serena was left in complete darkness.

She decided to forget about her brother, and just go to sleep. But she found she couldn't close her eyes. Minutes after the door was closed, it was still so dark. She'd never before noticed how dark her bedroom became after her mother switched out the light. She started to feel frightened. Then, for no reason at all, she was *really* scared. The precocious side of Serena told her not to be silly, the blackness of the night was just an absence of light.

But the shadows formed – and moved. It was at that

moment Serena discovered an imagination that she had no control over. What was that story about the bogeyman? A bogeyman that came for ungrateful children born with gifts that should not be wasted? Serena felt sure she could see him looming there, close up, at her bedside, whispering the same words over and over again.

Ungrateful girl, ungrateful girl.

He repeated them for years.

From then on, the Beast haunted her – every night from the age of five until fourteen. Her great secret fear. She never told anyone. As the light was switched off each night, he would emerge and stand beside her, his face never visible. There were some nights when Serena could not sleep at all. Night after night, year after year, with a stoic silence she bore the horror of the bogeyman, and his ally the dark.

The bogeyman gave his last performance on the night of her final degree exam – Serena knew she had done well – and over the years the fear that hid in the dark had become more sophisticated. This night, however, it was very different. In spite of her fear, she suddenly felt excited. Her hand delved under the covers. She slept soundly that night for the first time in nine years.

Achieving her degree had killed the bogeyman.

Serena stands at a stable door. She thinks again about her nightmare Beast of childhood. She is nervous, but feels invigorated.

Realization of the sheer stupidity of what she is now doing washes over her. The revelation that the stable is completely empty, and clean, and has no need for Serena's service makes her smile. All the stables are empty. Even the one she supposed had an equine occupant. The whinnying of a horse had been just in her imagination.

God, she wants to laugh.

Instead she takes a photograph.

Classified Secret

F2/6845/1/1

TRANSFERENCE OF AUTHORITY

AS WITH IMMEDIATE EFFECT, THIS DEPARTMENT NOW
HAS OVERALL CONTROL REGARDING PROFESSOR S. FREEMAN
AND THE DEVICE KNOWN AS ODYSSEUS.

INTERIM REPORT

Professor Freeman has apparently taken precautions to ensure that the major, or at least a crucial, part of the program she runs on her PC is dependent on direct input from herself. That is believed to be the formula for which the program mixes the sounds being generated. There is no evidence that she has recorded these details anywhere else. Acquisition of the workings of Odysseus can therefore only be successful with the co-operation of Professor Freeman or by securing the equipment while it is in use, when her PC can be examined for the information on its hard drive. This department notes that the latter course of action is desirable only if it is considered Professor Freeman is not amenable to the former option. However, this is of a high order of probability.

Classified Secret

F2/6845/1/1 (Additional)

On the question of the subject's possible instability, to which you were referring over lunch today, I've jotted down a few ideas for your consideration.

The positive symptoms of schizophrenia are recognized as hallucinations and delusions – the latter following on from the former. Hallucination is the technical term for what is commonly referred to as a 'voice'. The person believes some thoughts are so loud that they must be independent from themselves. This explanation for what is happening to such a person is known as the delusional phase, and it can take many forms. With this particular subject it could be argued that she is suffering sci-fi or paranormal delusions. The choice would be yours.

Under the Mental Health Act (MHA), a person detained is reported as being 'on section' – this refers to the various sections of the MHA. I would suggest the use of a Section 4 in this case, since only one doctor, with an approved social worker, needs to be involved and, most importantly, there is no right of appeal. I shouldn't think that you'd have too much of a problem in finding the necessary professionals able and willing to oblige you in this.

Hope this has been of help, and good luck.

It's sad to see such genius mutate to madness.

Yours

███████

THIRTEEN

W Day +1. 15.23. Ridge overlooking Asan River.

At least while we were waiting on the water there were sporadic breezes to steal and savor, instead of this fetid, muggy cell that constitutes our prison in this jungle for the immediate and foreseeable future. Some natural trigger has invigorated the insect population, and their eye-jarring clouds appear like swirls of discussion as they debate exactly where their winged tornado will touch down next. They certainly now have a multitude of warm, humid filthy corners to play with in this stockade, not least right under my nose. The insects' ominous presence bespeaks greater outrages to come, and I can hear high-pitched warnings in the primitive voice that is the tune of their rapid wing beat. Whenever they have the chance they crawl about on my face and arms. They gain sustenance from the sweat of my fear and of my body's reaction to this incessant humidity and heat.

I've sent a runner back with the roll of film I've taken – I hope they will use some of the pictures – and I've checked that my remaining stock hasn't got damp. Joe Plotkin's photograph is just for the censors – let them see the Dead Pool Poker sacrifice-gamble he made and lost. Uncle Sam is still a bit cautious about showing dead marines cluttering up some God-forsaken beach on an island with a name no one at home knows how to pronounce, let alone know which hemisphere it's in. And Uncle Sam'll probably feel just the same about Guam. But

I want to capture these moments for a collection, even if it's only a memoir. My reckoning is that the press might want to demonstrate that – while it's every bit as patriotic as the public – it remains conscious of a need to show the price of valor. The true heroes will be the ones that we leave behind here. I also sent a few paragraphs about this landing to my newspaper. I'm aiming for practical honesty: tell the public how we're spending their war bonds. This is not a place for lies. This jungle prison-cell that is my current moment of time carries the whisper of a death cell. The droning insects' buzz is like the chatter amongst workmen building a scaffold. Honesty is all, and liars do not have a right to be here.

Such thoughts keep me occupied for a time at least. And for the last half-hour I've been cleaning my camera. I'm still squatting by myself in the same foxhole as last night, but now it's been extended somewhat, and I'm cynically thinking of calling it home. There's a great view of the beach and the neighbors drop by every now and then. When they are forced to stay, such as the ones Rici and I are using as defensive sandbags, I sometimes decide to snap their picture, for the folks back Stateside. The smell of them is something difficult to convey via film, however. What Rici and I have done with them has repelled some of the incoming replacements, but I noticed Johnny and Bill – Vizi and Groucho – drag a couple of Enemy near to their own foxhole as well. Anything to provide an edge to make someone hesitate. Any attacking Enemy might recognize them and pause for a fatal instant.

If it wasn't for the fact that I risk being sent home on a funny-ticket, I would say that I've had a good day so far. Comparatively speaking. When your fundamental mission is to kill more of theirs than they kill of yours, not having the Enemy shooting at you for longer than half an hour can lead you to make the mistake of thinking you might last through the day. At least I've had time to consult my memory for another Hercules talisman, but it makes me calm and jittery at the same time. At least the resources are there to call on:

those memories and explanations of fables that I carry in my head.

My grandfather told me that for his fifth labor the hero cleaned out the Augean stables.

And now, as I wait out the long hours in this foxhole, I keep repeating in my mind that fifth task, in the hope that a solution will present itself and that I can find a way to emulate the hero's feat. But where the hell would I find a horse on this island – let alone a set of stables? No one's yet mentioned coming across such a building.

Where could I find a *stable* on this island? Or even a cowshed? But I have to work out a solution. I already have a growing list of tasks completed. I tick them off mentally as I load a magazine with bullets. I took a hat from an Enemy and called it a lion's mane; killed a coral snake as the second; found an ivory netsuke carving for my Hind of Ceryneia; and killed a feral pig for the fourth. I've been lucky so far, but I'm convinced there *are* no horses on Guam. I've got to start making my own luck – with Dead Pool Poker skills maybe? I try then to think in different ways. What has the Enemy to offer me? Have they got *anything* I could use?

I take a gulp from the flask Rici left for me. I've now got alcohol withdrawal symptoms, which is causing me to twitch and shake. At least, I hope that's the reason.

A machine-gun position? Could that count? If I rush a gun position, would it count as cleaning out a stable?

I take another swig. I think other thoughts.

We've spent most of the day sending out patrols to extend the line and, by the sound of things, we've been having an easier time of it than the other battalions on our flanks. The Enemy is repelling any attempt to dislodge them, and they appear to be making more noise about it than yesterday. I try to ignore it all. I'm adjusting to the constant din of battle, so it's the little noises that get my attention. Even as I'm thinking this, a Sherman tank chugs past me, crushing bushes, splitting palms with a creak and a sharp splinter, and squashing the remains of mashed plants, uprooted trees and dead Enemy alike. Then I hear a tiny snap as a twig is trodden underfoot. I'm bringing my carbine to bear in the general direction of the sound, am about to issue a challenge, when the person responsible trips and crashes into a bush just up ahead of me.

I hear Rici curse.

"Fuck!" he says.

I lower my weapon and cup a hand to my mouth.

"Is that the new password?" I call.

"Ha, ha, ha," he replies.

I smile to myself as Rici comes over.

"What are you smirking for?" asks Rici. "Found another pig for your collection?"

He jumps down into the foxhole, crouches onto one knee and begins to inspect his carbine. I know he could do it with his eyes shut, but I notice he's paying it more attention than normal.

"Problem?" I nod towards it.

"Damned thing jammed," he says. "Had to use my knife instead. How can one human body contain so much blood?"

I look at his hands. The evidence is still there, and on his thighs where he's wiped away the worst. Rici is a marine's marine, those blood-caked, calloused fingers can perform any brutal or technical task that Uncle Sam might order, yet I remind myself how they once held a pen to write a poem in high school. I feel a tug of realization: I would lay down my life for him, and he'd do the same for me. No question, no debate. I wonder why I thought that? He extracts a piece of the weapon and blows on it hard.

"Sand, grit or dirt – makes no odds," he says. "I thought you told me this place of yours was solid coral."

"No, I didn't. You made that up yourself on board ship, when you asked for a bed instead of a hammock."

He grunts and nods towards the undergrowth. "Keep your eyes up front," he says.

He reassembles his carbine and checks the operation. And

finally becomes aware that I'm looking at him and not at the spot where he'd emerged from the undergrowth.

"What now?" he says.

"Nothing."

He cocks his head to one side. "You thinking 'bout my sister?"

I laugh. We both know that *he's* thinking about *my* sister Alice, but I have to go along with the charade.

"No," I say, "I've gone off her. She's a lousy cook."

"That's fighting talk," says Rici, smiling.

"Yeah, I guess." I grin back.

He checks his carbine again – going through the motions meticulously, as he's been trained. I have a sudden urge to think of some way he can get off this island, be shipped out of the war, then let him go marry my sister. How he keeps his love for her so quiet I don't know. I know she thinks the same about him. And all from their first meeting. All from that first dance. *That* sort of devotion is worth fighting for.

It had been a special night when they met. Rici had been allowed a seventy-two hour pass and we'd gone into town to get drunk. Alice had been in contact with me that week and said she'd track us down – make a Lafayette night of it. I didn't doubt that she'd get there. I'd already written to her about my buddy Rici, and I suspect I may have given her the impression that she might like him. I didn't tell Rici of her proposed visit – didn't want to get him too excited.

Alice is the sort of woman I'd like to meet myself. She has that witty sparkle my mother and grandmother were granted, and that nip of intelligence that reminds a man he has only the illusion of being in charge. She acted as a sort of conduit between myself and my father while I was growing up, and I suppose both of us must thank her for that – otherwise he and I would only ever have said about six words to each other. It was Alice who, at the age of ten, pointed out to me the obvious reason for the gulf between my father and me that both of us were blind to: we were both competing for my grandfather's attention, and I was winning every time. And my father would always lose – he never had any time for the folklore of his father's country, and could never see its relevance to the country he called his home. Alice, even at that young age, could see both sides, however. It helped that she loved us both, her father and her brother, was smarter than the pair of us, and knew the advantages of controlling men.

From the age of sixteen she was surrounded by young admirers eager for her famous smile, and at her birthday party that year my father and I agreed about one thing – that the man who eventually won her wouldn't be frightened of either him or me. Only of her.

Rici and I had found a busy bar that looked as though it would sustain us for the night. It was a deep cave of mahogany, glass and low lights, hardened drinkers sitting within an eye-jerk of the bartender, the party-goers sitting or standing near the small dance floor. We were on our third beer and chaser when Alice came through the door. She is a mirror copy of how our mother looked at the same age, and has refined the same daredevil attitude – clearly a quirk of the female bloodline. As she strode into the bar, a hush cut through the din. Alice was used to it.

Rici nudged my arm.

"God, Nix," he said, "look at this babe. She's damn pretty."

The fact that he didn't know she was my sister was like manna from heaven. I let her make her entrance without telling him.

Alice was dressed in a light cotton dress, white with small red flowers printed on it. Those flowers seemed to move of their own accord – maybe some optical trick in the design. And Alice knew the effect she would cause.

"What do you think?" whispered Rici, leaning towards me. "Do you think she'll go for one of us? Oh, God, look at that body."

It crossed my mind that opportunities like this don't arise often. I had about five seconds to make the most of it before she reached us.

"Mama," said Rici, taking a deep breath, "she's coming this way. Just look at her!"

I managed to pause for effect.

"I couldn't give an opinion," I said at last, "since she's my sister."

The information appeared to snap Rici from his reverie. He stood up sharply, seemingly to grow in size.

"Don't make jokes like that," he said.

I continued sitting and waved to Alice. She waved back, fought her way slowly through the last few people, then kissed me on the cheek and thrust out her hand to Rici.

"Hello," she said, "I'm Alice. And you must be Sergeant Federici. Phoenix has told me all about you. I hope you're as *bad* as he says." And she winked.

Rici said nothing, just blinked rapidly.

I laughed inwardly. Rici had just been hit by a female Lafayette thunderbolt. And that night, for the first time, at that moment, I believed I saw a glimpse of the man who had been the boy who once wrote poetry.

The kid was putty in her hands – great fun to watch.

"So, what family secrets of ours has Nix spilled?" she asked. Alice turned to look at me, eyes wide and innocent. "Pernod, please," she said, "double."

I frowned.

"I had a hard drive down here," she said, "and before you start, I've booked into the Majestic. I'm yours for the night, so entertain me."

She turned back to Rici again and gave him that wide-open look, reaching into her shoulder bag for a cigarette case.

"Smoke?" she asked him.

Rici said nothing, just stared at her.

"Smoke?" she repeated.

Rici finally got his mouth working, and forced himself to concentrate on accepting a cigarette.

"Sure, thanks."

He took one and reached into his pocket for a light. When he'd found it, Rici flicked his Zippo, and Alice bent forward, touched his hand with both of hers, then looked straight up at him. It was so cornball but, before I could laugh and bang both their heads together, Alice started on a lengthy discourse of my worst excesses as a child.

"And he now drinks too much," she added, passing her empty glass to me. "Well," she conceded, "he drinks more than me, at least."

At that point, the bartender turned up the radio and band music filled the room. Rici stubbed out his cigarette and took Alice's hand.

"I expect you *dance* better than him, though," he said.

As he whisked her onto the small dance floor, she winked at me.

I let the pair of them get on with it. It gave me an excuse to order another drink.

Rici slaps a magazine into his carbine.

"*Another* patrol?" I ask.

"No, not at the minute."

I realize he's been checking his carbine yet again. Perhaps the jitters are getting to him, too. That's the danger of surviving the first day: you begin to reinforce your feelings of immortality – until a sudden bang makes you sit up and think about all you want to go on living for. I realize I'm going mad with Hercules and that angel voice in my head, and hoping no one notices, but how is Rici himself coping? I know he's torn between the long-term joy of having met Alice and the current dumb reality of war. It'll all be down to his luck in the end.

How much luck do we have left? How much luck can we make for ourselves?

He pulls the Dead Pool Poker hand from his pocket and,

cupping his hands around the cards, thumbs them into a small fan. He studies them, looks up at me, swipes the cards together again and jams them back in his pocket. His fingers linger at the pocket flap.

"I don't think this game was such a good idea," he says.

"Oh?" I answer, thinking that my full house probably beats what he is holding, and that he can guess so from my expression. I was never any good at poker.

"The Boys are beginning to spend too much time worrying about it," he explains. "They should be concentrating on this." He makes a sweeping gesture with his hand.

What he has said knocks me off balance for a second, but I decide to nip this rebellion in the bud.

"This is second nature to you," I say to him. "You and the Boys have trained until you can handle it on reflex. That was the whole idea, remember – get every marine acting in concert, so they no longer think of self but of squad? And of company. Of division. The Boys can bitch all they like, about whatever they like, because when push comes to shove, they'll be exactly where they're needed, and be doing exactly what's required. Joe's little gamble was just that – a gamble on life. And you're the one who's just reminded me the odds that we're playing for here. This is only the second day, after all." I spread my hands. "I'd have to be crazy to think I'll get off this island in one piece – that's what you said, isn't it?"

Rici picks up a handful of dirt and lets it dribble through his fingers.

"That's just it," he says. "The Boys are getting ideas. And Hank and the Chief nearly got themselves killed 'cause they were arguing about it."

"When?"

Rici looks down at our little collection of Enemy that we have laid out on the ground. A large number of flies are investigating their dead eyes, and Rici absently waves a discouraging hand at the nearest head. The flies move away for a second, then buzz back and land.

"Coming back just now," explained Rici. "They didn't check a dead one properly. The bastard had a grenade."

I'm surprised. "That's not like the Chief or Hank," I say. "How did they overlook him?"

"Jap was missing a leg and the rest of him was burnt to hell."

He waves his hands again at the flies. We both know what will begin soon – no, what has *already* started. The blowflies will have laid eggs, and in less than a day those will have hatched, then the maggots will begin to feed. In one of our idle moments on the LST, we calculated that over a three-week period, a man's body could support three generations of them – amounting to forty thousand flesh-consuming larvae. The body would have turned to liquid by then but, hey, everything has to eat. If we don't move on in the next twenty-four hours – we'll have to shift the corpses.

Rici sniffs and rubs the side of his nose. "Ah, shit, Nix, I thought he was dead as well. Made me jump when he raised himself up and tried to throw it."

He adds nothing else, so I spread my hands.

"And?" I ask. "How did he miss?"

"I kicked his arm to one side, picked up the grenade and threw it as far as I could."

Rici glances down at his knife.

So that was when his carbine jammed? I make a mental note to get some more details about the incident from Hank and Amos later. It seems to me that Rici should get some credit – he could have taken cover instead. Weinberg would have done.

"What were they arguing about," I ask. "Hank and the Chief?"

Rici stares at the ground for a moment. Then he decides to tell me, and looks up. Straight in the eye, that's Rici.

"The guys were debating about adding a side bet – on what *your* poker hand is."

I laugh out loud. "I told you I was never any good at it."

Rici grins, patting his pocket. "Your full house don't hurt me," he says.

"How did you—?" I start to say.

He raises his eyebrows and gazes at me as though I'm wet behind the ears.

"You've just told me so," he says.

I sigh and I reach up and try to rub some of the said wet stuff away from my ears. I assure myself I could be one of the hardest-looking men I know – if only I could maintain a poker face. I hold out my hand and Rici leans forward, reaches over to my jacket, pulls his flask from my pocket and offers it to me. I shrug; I'd forgotten I still had it. His grin is pure evil.

"Did I ever tell you how to brew moonshine?" I say. "It's all about the right combination of fermentation and distillation. There's this clever way of using a water pipe fitted inside another to—"

"Go to hell," Rici interrupts. "And don't drag me down as you go."

"Ah, isn't that just the case – one's too many and a million's not enough?"

"With you – barrels or pints?"

"Quarts – easier to lift on the forearm. Ah, a quart of Blue Ridge Mountain . . ." I say.

His eyes glaze for a moment at some memory I've jogged. At least I've taken his mind off Dead Pool Poker.

"I think the Chief has you beat," he says, smiling.

I cuss for a couple of minutes.

W Day +2. 00.03. Ridge overlooking Asan River.

I now have my stable. And also I've decided I don't like the dark. On Guam it lends itself to all sorts of imaginings. It may just be my grandfather's taotaomonas, with all his relatives and friends, but there is too much life out there in the blackness.

Every sense sends alarms to my brain, and I find it difficult to sort out the priorities.

There are no stars above me. There is no heavenly light to help my tired eyes. God is asleep. While out there – out in the cold undergrowth – is the Enemy. I strain to see them – but I'm having trouble discerning shattered palms from the ridgeline. I'd never have thought there could be so many shades of black. The sky is a distilled dark gray that has had most of its white constituents filtered out – like a somber shroud that covers us in layers of old lace mixed with soot and cobwebs. Moving in the slight night breeze are the slate-black tops of the few remaining palm trees. They fan out and wave – lamp-and-raven black against God's night-cloak. Lower down (at what I imagine is eye-level), amid the rubbish and litter of the undergrowth, extends a black that belongs to the devil. Hell could be found in that charcoal pit of zero sight – it is the ink used to write incantations of the grimiest kind on the soul.

From this same black heart, a mixture of smells rankles and drifts. It is a fetid combination. The rich texture of the jungle floor is the only scent that appears natural: all the others are man-made. Cordite and kerosene nip at the nostrils, and diesel fumes add to the illusion – and feeling – of being in a huge dockyard that is on fire. And on every level there is a fusion of the many smells of death. (Roasted pork is a dish I know I'll never eat again.) Out there in the darkness, bodies – torn apart by bullets, bombs and bayonets – rot fast in the humid air. Bodily contents and the associated torn flesh are breaking down, adding to a foul sweetness that the breeze cannot shift.

And these are smells that I can taste. I acquired another bottle of *saki* from a dead Enemy when I went up the line before nightfall. (We found an Enemy blockhouse about sixty yards up ahead. They must have got a good view from there, and I think I should do something about it soon. The Fates have conspired to give me the opportunity to clean out the Enemy from my stable. That will do for me: that blockhouse will be my stable that I have to clean.) Thankfully the sharp bite of the *saki* numbs my tongue, but unfortunately doesn't remove the sensation of smell completely. My nose and throat are gummed up and I feel constricted. There's one solution I can think of, but it requires an act of considerable self-control. I summon up the courage to try an old sailor's trick I know – I snort back, and then hawk into my mouth. Whatever it is, it feels nearly solid. I decide not to think about it longer than I need to. I pour *saki* into me instead and swill this mixture around. Instead of spitting out the contents of my mouth, I swallow. For a moment I gag, sweat rushes to my forehead, and then, miraculously, I feel better. The smells and taste are still there – may even be stronger – but they now have less effect on my stomach.

"Good one?" Rici asks.

I nod. I figure he can see *me*, so I lean forward to try to see his features. I find it good to hear a voice – one that's real and not a ghost's. A tremor flickers in the fingers of my right hand. I wiggle them, then clench my fist. I was never this bad on Bougainville. And Bloody Bougainville was where we *all* became men.

Even though nearing twenty years of age, or just a bit older, most of the marines landing at Bougainville were boys. Okay, they had been prepared as well as the Brass could train them, but these were kids hitting that island only last year. At twenty-five, so was I, of course. And upon discovering it was great to be alive after all of five minutes, great to be alive after a day, great – oh, thank the Lord – to be alive after a week, those minutes and days and weeks altered everyone. The soul can only filter out so much carnage. Seeing another human being impaled on a long bayonet, watching him die, feeling his death throes shivering down your carbine and into your hands changes you. Even if you're paid by a newspaper and not by Uncle Sam, and even if you're not supposed to be *in* the fighting, only observing it, when it comes down to either kill or be killed, there's not much of a choice in my eyes. Even if you are troubled by memories of looking into another's eyes as he wriggles and squirms and bleeds and screams, and sends those writhing contortions shimmering into your own hands and arms and shoulders and down into your soul. Kill or die – Bloody Bougainville! Your writing becomes harsher after that, more real; you photograph dead, still objects, and parts of things that once made up another human that talked, laughed and thought, but is now butchered and burnt. You bury your heroes, where you can. You try to bury your memories – when you can. You become a man. And wish there was another route you could have taken.

Other sounds have made themselves known. The daytime cacophony has dulled, now that it is night, but the dismal chorus of the odd suicidal Enemy pulses and fades, depending on how near they are. There is the crack and clump of grenades, the odd snap-crack from a rifle.

I'm staring down at my hand – some insect is crawling up my arm – and I hear another disturbance. The Enemy is shrieking. And advancing.

"Eyes front!" I shout.

Phut!

A flare has gone up. The surrounding blacks gain hazy color.

Pock!

"Incoming!"

Whoo-bang!

The mortar explodes about ten yards away. Rici and I are showered with dirt. I hear the tinkle of shrapnel pinging off my helmet.

"You all right?" I ask.

"Yeah," he answers. "You?"

Pock! Pock! Pock!

Whoo-bang! Whoo-bang! Whoo-bang!

My reply gets lost as more mortars fall. The calls from the Enemy get louder.

Phut! Phut!

Extra flares go up. I have a sudden realization. It's strange – I feel more alive now than I ever have done.

What a thing to think!

My whole body tingles. I think of Rici and Alice. I think of that wonderful female voice in my head. I think about being Hercules. I think about how necessary it is for me to do the same as he did. The tingle zips and zings inside of me. Bloody Bougainville has taken over. The sensation turns to a shudder. That dying Enemy shivers down along my bayonet again. I feel his life's energy drain away through me. In much the same way as Alice was a go-between for our father and me, I became a conduit from that Enemy to his gods. Bloody Bougainville, I shudder. I think about running – running away from this. Running out to the jungle. Running away forever.

I see my first Enemy of the night as their charge materializes out of the undergrowth. He's coming face on, his bayonet fixed. No time for grenades – again.

Tat-tat-tat!

I take him out with three rapid shots. Enemy shrieks continue along the line, as his adds to them. It's hard to gauge the strength of their attack. I take a breath. I take another. I think I can control the shakes.

I could use a drink. God, I could use a drink.

My arms jerk – and again. I can't stop them.

A drink. A drink.

I see another Enemy. And another. I concentrate. I have to concentrate. Rici takes the left one. I take the right. Mine carries on towards me.

Always towards *me*, never anyone else.

Blood is sputtering from his throat. I aim again.

Tat-tat-tat!

I put one of my bullets into his head. Nothing clean about that. Nothing fancy. I don't care. The snap-crack of rifle intensifies around us. Bloody Bougainville again. Bloody Bougainville! The Enemy continues to attack. I now find time to unpin a grenade. I toss it forward. The other boys are managing the same.

Crack-crash!

My grenade bursts open right in front of one Enemy as he emerges from Hell. Three more replace him. They scream their scream, and charge and stumble. Rici is shoulder to shoulder with me. We call out to each other our chosen targets. Less waste that way. Rici stands back. He pulls a pin and throws.

Tat-tat-tat!

I cover him.

Crack-crash!

The grenade rips into the charge and takes out more Enemy. *Less to come for me. Less to come for me!*

I may get my chance – get my chance to be Hercules again. I scan right, I scan left. Rici does the same. I repeat my actions: scan right, scan left. I don't lower my carbine. The night air is tearing my lungs apart. I still have the shakes, I still want to run, I still want a drink. More than ever I want a drink. I can't hear the banzai cries above my own breathing. I realize that there are none to hear, anyway. Not in front of us at least.

Thank God for this break. I want a drink.

"Call out!" shouts Rici.

"Turkey shoot!" replies Jim.

"Still busy, Rici," shouts Amos. "Still busy."

Ba-ba-ba!

Ba-ba-ba!

Ba-ba-ba-ba-ba!

Three chattering bursts.

"Now I'm not," Amos calls.

"Anyone hit?" I bellow.

The Boys answer in the negative.

Phut! Phut!

Under these flares, I look at the Enemy spread out in front of us.

"How many, do you think?" I ask Rici, between gasps for breath.

"Spread out over the line?" he says. "Must be battalion strength."

I scan left. I scan right.

"That's what I figure, too," I say.

Before he disappears into the dark again, as the flares gutter and fizz their last, I see him wipe his mouth with the back of his hand.

I need a drink.

"I'm getting tired of defense," Rici says.

"So am I. Let's take it to them."

"Good idea. Drink?"

"Only on social occasions."

"You don't get no dance from me."

"And normally no drink."

We both check our carbines before uncorking the bottle.

You know where the stables are, don't you?

"I'm going to clean out that blockhouse," I say.

I clench my fist. I unclench my fist.

"Yeah," says Rici, "at first light. Meanwhile, have this drink."

"No," I say, "now."

I jump out of the foxhole.

"Nix!"

"Cover me, join me – your choice!"

I must use the momentum of having cheated death once again. Use it to do my task.

I run forward – into the black. Into the dark place that I need to go into in order to survive. Into the lamp-and-raven black. Into the rubbish and litter of a black that belongs to the Devil. And leave my good friend Rici behind. Behind in the light of life.

"Fuck you, Nix," shouts Rici. "Flare! Someone send up a flare. Hold your fire, that's Nix out there. *Flare!*"

Get to the stables. Get to the stables.

I run.

Phut!

There's suddenly light. I jump over the freshly dead Enemy.
I glance down at them. *Check, check, check.* They're dead. They're
dead.

They.

Are.

Dead.

Are you sure? Take a breath, take a breath!

They're dead Enemy. Too late now anyway, I've passed
them. I charge forward into the lamp-raven-charcoal-soot-and-
undertaker black, lit now by man-made stars that the Boys are
sending up. I charge forward. I notice that where the leaves of
plants are exposed to the flares, they take on the color of
shimmering pale green.

Funny how I can admire beauty at this moment.

The black shadows continue to contrast and hide objects.

Th-zip! Th-zip!

Reality now. Bullets are fired at me. They fly over my
shoulders – they come from my rear. The Boys think I'm the
Enemy. I can't blame them – I'm breaking the fundamental rule
here.

Don't move after sunset.

But I charge forward. I have to cleanse the stables.

Crack-crash!

A grenade explodes behind me. The Boys nearly got me.
Amos must want my cards bad. I hear Rici's distant voice as he
shouts at them to cease fire. A frond of some exotic bush whips
across my face. And another. And another.

I'm getting nearer to the blockhouse.

I see a rectangle of black against the ragged contours of the
jungle. The Enemy starts shouting.

Th-zip! Th-zip! Th-zzzzip!

They fire, too. I see the muzzle flashes from their rifles.
Little rectangles of bright light against the dark shape of the
blockhouse.

Th-zip! Th-zzzzip!

More Enemy open up. I continue charging forward.

Phut!

A flare sparks overhead, and I see the blockhouse more clearly. Muzzle flash after muzzle flash lights it up for me.

Th-zip! Th-zzzzip!

Ping!

My helmet.

Th-zip!

Bullets zing and whiz around my head. I scream defiance at them. I scream at the Enemy.

I'm going to cleanse the stables. I'm going to cleanse the stables.

I duck. I weave. I'm twenty yards away now ... fifteen. I throw myself to the ground. Sometime in this mad dash I've unpinned a grenade, holding its spring closed, ready to use. I throw it towards the flashes, the voices coming from the blockhouse. The gunfire stops in an instant, as the Enemy see, or hear, what's come inside to join them. They have other priorities now. I hear shouting from inside.

Tat-tat-tat!

I fire my weapon into the slits, and bullets ricochet around inside.

Crack-boom!

The grenade goes off. Short screams – then nothing. A groan. I withdraw the pin from another grenade, squirm nearer and roll it through the opening. The Enemy inside cries out. He already knows what that sound means – that rattle and thud.

Crack-boom!

The grenade explodes. I wait and listen. There is silence. There is peace. No sounds other than war conducted elsewhere. I breathe. I breathe again. I sigh. I sit up. I rest my back against the wall of the blockhouse, deciding to wait for daylight.

I can't go back to the foxhole. The Boys would kill me for sure.

No man's luck can last this long. Not even Hercules'.

But I've done it. I've cleaned my stable.

I shudder. My hands shake.

I've done it. I've done it. I'm still alive.

I must not move.

I answer Rici's yell and tell him I'm okay, tell him I'm staying here 'til dawn.

I wait for morning.

I'm still trying to find my breath.

I'm alive.

I tremble and wait for morning.

FOURTEEN

When you're hiding in a large bronze pot that is half buried in the ground, you are inclined to look to the heavens for inspiration, especially when the reason you are positioned where you are is standing outside the gate to your city. And you've been told that he's no intention of moving until you've given him his next mission. The sun can burn hard then, and the day can loom large and long. Eurystheus looked to the skies and sought assistance from the gods. His ornate armour was heavy on his shoulders, his nose twitched at the smell of his own clammy heat, and his head was filled with constant thoughts about the good times when he could lounge about in his throne room drinking fine wines and being waited on by nubile, young slaves.

A flock of swallows flew over him, black swirls against the June sunlight. They darted about, their high-pitched song hardly audible because of their speed and height, and their sheer numbers darkened the sky in patches. King Eurystheus straightened and snapped his fingers. He suddenly had his answer.

"The king dictates that for your sixth labour," said the herald, standing casually, putting his weight on one leg, hands clasped behind his back, "you must drive away all the birds that have lately gathered on the lake near the town of Stymphalos."

Hercules adopted the same stance as the man facing him. The herald then came to attention and stared off into the distance. Hercules did the same. He counted off twenty seconds before replying.

"You mean the ones frightened away from their original home by those huge wolves from Wolves Ravine?" Hercules asked.

The herald swivelled his eyes towards Hercules, allowing himself a faint twitch of a smile.

"Correct," he said.

Hercules raised one eyebrow, nodded and began counting on his fingers.

"And, out of interest, they could be summarized thus?" he asked. "According to reports, they seem to be created from bronze, are countless in number, and are known man-eaters?"

"The very same."

The corners of the herald's mouth twitched, but he refrained himself from grinning. Hercules slowly closed his hand into a fist, then relaxed it.

"Thanks," he said.

"My pleasure."

When Hercules had left, the herald punched the air and skipped all the way back into the palace. There were some errands that made him feel youthful again. This was the way he'd been taught to do business.

Just after noon, two days later, Hercules arrived at the Stymphalian Marsh and found himself facing a serious problem above and beyond the ones he himself had outlined to the herald. The marsh – a desolate place completely enclosed by thick woods and brambles – was only just visible through a filthy-smelling off-yellow and grey mist, even while standing at its very edge. To add to the complications, the marsh was composed of a quicksand consistency. If Hercules made the mistake of approaching the birds by foot, the marsh would soon suck him down, but on the other hand its surface was too solid for a boat to be a practical option. He scratched his chin and idly tested the surface of the marsh with his foot. When, five minutes later, he had at last extracted himself from the marsh's grip, the sound of it relinquishing him was like a giant fish belching. Hercules wiped his foot on the grass. As the marsh finished its gurgling, the surface returned to its previous malignant calm: a temptation to walk upon. Hercules drummed his fingers on his spear, slipped his bow from his shoulders and shot a few arrows in the general direction of the metal birds – he could hear their muffled screeches – but not one bronze feather resounded with an expected metallic ring, since his attempts all fell short. He could just discern the faint slurp of the marsh as it ate his arrows. Hercules cursed loudly.

"What's the problem, Hercules?"

The goddess Athene was standing behind him with a wry smile on her face, the mist still curling back around her from her sudden approach.

Hercules shrugged his shoulders and turned back to the marsh.

"Just life's normal hiccups," he said.

"Would these be of any help?" she asked, holding out something for him to take. As he turned to face her again, the small muscles in her face flickered, mischievously. In her hand was a pair of krotala, forged in bronze by an immortal crafts-man, and rather similar to castanets. As the mist cleared for a moment, Hercules saw how the sun reflected off their bur-nished surface, and realized they had power. These krotala would provide a noise of terrific proportions.

"If you wouldn't mind," he said, reaching out to take her offering.

"My pleasure," she said.

She waved her hand and the mist quickly dispersed, giving Hercules a perfect view of the situation. There was a definite swing to her hips as she left him.

*

Hercules climbed up the side of a nearby mountain – he reasoned that the acoustics of the valley would amplify the sound he intended making. And so, an hour later, standing on a sheer-faced spur overlooking the marsh, he watched as the bronze birds scolded and bickered with each other. Hercules smiled to himself, raised his arm, and began to rattle the krotala. The wave of sound – like a torrent of fast drums played by giants – swept down upon the birds and, as one, they took to the air, in terror. Their wings clattered shrilly as they banged into one another, their sharp cries growing in volume. Hercules shook the krotala even harder, wincing himself at their din. The flock banked and tumbled as they flew into the echoes, panicking because they did not know where this assault of sound was coming from. They then decided, as one, to head towards the mountain, where Hercules stopped, put the krotala down and waited. The birds did not notice him standing, poised, his bow now bent in readiness. He let loose a few arrows as the birds passed overhead, heading for their escape across the mountain, and brought a number of them crashing to the ground. The rest of the entire flock disappeared from view.

As Hercules bent down to inspect one of the victims, he laughed loud and long. He had had a sudden idea that it would be fun to drop a brace of them at the feet of a certain herald – with cooking suggestions.

FIFTEEN

W Day +2. 04.03. Beside blockhouse overlooking Asan River.

There is a hint of dawn – or it could be a large fire. I stare at where the sun should rise, and will it into existence. I obviously don't have the wherewithal and, as it would appear from its lack of co-operation, I shall have to wait. As the sun is its own master (it doesn't listen to the desires of mortal men – just moves through space according to the rules of gravity) I need to be patient. I shiver and roll the clicks from my neck. I try not to blink – in case I miss any movement. There are shapes out there that my mind can suggest are moving, as there were yesterday too, and I try not to assign any more independent life to them than I have to. The concrete of the blockhouse is cool against my back, I can even believe that it is cold, but at least I am not as stiff and cold as those inside. I try to push my head further into my helmet and adjust my cradling of my carbine, my finger never far from the trigger. I must stay awake. I know that, when the sun rises, I will peer through the opening behind me to check the damage I have wrought inside. My only interest in dead Enemy is ensuring that *they* have reached that state, rather than me.

How I shall write up my insane action of last night is another matter. I am taking options that are dangerous, not only for me, but also perhaps for the men I technically have command over. Yet Hercules' labors stretch out before me – giant ancient stones that I have to push down. The Stymphalian Birds are not going to be equated with the few birds that are to be found in the hidden corners of this jungle; they will have to have a meaning that involves the Enemy. The easiest answer to the Stymphalian Birds would be to shoot down an Enemy plane, but the Enemy's planes were destroyed before we attacked.

An Enemy in the air?

The next challenge.

The talisman that is Hercules haunts my thoughts, as does Serena, the one who gave him to me. As I zero in on the hollows of darkness in the jungle with my dry eyes, I carve images of her out of mental ivory. My greatest image of fervor and passion emerges – constructed out of inventions and given a heartbeat.

I shift and alter the way I sit. My erection is painful. I press my back into the cold of the blockhouse and try to concentrate. My hands feel raw where I drag my nails over the concrete. The ache subsides, I watch the shadows again.

I think about my grandfather, I hear his voice.

Long, long ago, he says, a giant fish began eating pieces of the middle section of the island. So it was turned to stone by a woman with power.

I shiver.

The cold stone of the giant fish that tried to eat Guam is the cold concrete of the blockhouse that hides dead Enemy. The beautiful woman who saved Guam is my Serena, my voice in my head.

The fear that I dispelled when I attacked this fortification has returned in the chill just before daylight arrives.

I think of my grandfather.

I think about fear.

I think about what it is to be frightened. And yet still have to function.

My grandfather had taken me out to sea off Long Island, on a fishing trip to hunt for sharks. I was fourteen and terrified. Before we left port, my grandfather, the skipper (whittled from driftwood and kept alive with rum), and his mate (a man seemingly constructed from the driftwood shavings and the hair of some animal), told each other tall stories of sharks they had seen. In particular they traded accounts of something called a feeding frenzy. The thought of accidentally falling in amongst such a maelstrom made me tense and quiet.

"If you fell in the water in a feeding frenzy," my grandfather said, "you wouldn't have time to be frightened."

The skipper slapped his hands together – right by my ear.

I jumped.

My grandfather smiled. "That's the lesson," he said. "First make sure that you don't get into that position and second – learn how to swim fast."

He laughed.

"Use your fear," he said, "use your fear."

It was a phrase that found a resonance years later when I watched the Boys being trained. *Use your fear*, the instructors said, *use your fear*. That's what my grandfather was referring to, that's where courage finds a place to start – forcing yourself to act even though you are scared out of your wits.

Fear has a taste all of its own, that's the lesson from tonight; I feel it clogging my mouth now, a bitterness, a sour taste, a tartness that makes me want to spit.

Use your fear.

Ha! It's the one piece of advice from my grandfather which sounded so good at the time, but which I have discovered was crap. He'd never been to the places I've been, and where I am now. The Boys are supposed to use their fear and yet they know it's all down to Dead Pool Poker luck.

A better line of advice would be "Keep Your Head Down'.

I nearly wet myself when the skipper gaffed the first shark and heaved it aboard. That gargoyle eye of that large blue was a distillation of everything that torments Man. It was designed by God to instill fear. And we prove ourselves by fishing for them.

And we prove ourselves by going to war.

God must want to bang our heads together sometimes.

From somewhere out in the current world comes a familiar voice.

"Nix!" calls Rici.

"I have him," says Van Zandt again. "I have him now."

I open my eyes. I'd fallen asleep.

"Nix?" says Rici.

I've made it to daylight. Through the mist, men appear: Rici, Johnny "Vizi" Van Zandt, and the two survivors of the Marx trio – Ron and Bill – Chico and Groucho. Their eyes are obscured under the shadow of their helmets and I find myself wishing I could get a hint of how they are feeling, and what they are thinking. Johnny gets to me first and kicks my boot as I sit leaning against the cold blockhouse.

"You crazy bastard," he says.

He passes me by and peers into one of the openings. I catch a whiff of his hair cream – he's found time to do his hair, but not to shave or wash. During the last two days he's turned from being a replacement into a marine that's taken part in making death happen, but he has still taken the trouble to use his hair cream. He's different now, though. Women will no longer be attracted to him simply because of a need to mother him – Johnny Van Zandt will now have a greater depth to him, something perhaps they'll never fathom. It's possible, I think, that some of them will even feel secure by being near him.

But the softness of women is still in the future for Vizi. For him there is now more to be concerned about than two-days' worth of change to his personality.

"How many did you get?" He is still inspecting the insides of the blockhouse through the slits.

I shrug my shoulders, but I guess he doesn't see me. He clearly finds the dead Enemy fascinating.

"Nix? How many, huh?"

"I don't know, Johnny," I say. "We'll go look, shall we?"

Rici stands before me and proffers a hand. He pulls me to my feet, we share a look, and he pokes a finger into my chest.

"You stupid bastard. That was madness, you stupid rich-kid bastard Yale punk. You're here to report the war, not make it. How do you think I'd ever be able to look your sister in the eye and say I hadn't done my best to keep you alive? Huh? Do you think that just because your sorry storyteller of a grandfather came from this shit-hole that you're immortal here?"

His face is flushed. He pokes me in the chest again.

"Well?" he says. "Well?"

Johnny, Ron and Bill stand by, looking on: Johnny with a bemused grin on his face, Ron biting his lip, and Bill seemingly nodding in agreement with Rici.

Rici and I stare at each other – then we both start laughing.

"Stupid, rich bastard?" I ask.

"First thing that came to my mind," he says.

"You had most of the night to think of it."

The others realize that Rici has been hot and up, but is now down and that the fun is over. Johnny turns back to inspecting the blockhouse, while Ron and Bill check their weapons. I notice that they too are unshaven, but with their youthful fuzz it appears as if they've merely rubbed dirt on their faces. I rub my own chin – the stubble pricks my fingers. I must look like shit: a dirty, stupid, rich-kid bastard, Yale punk that is still alive somehow.

Rici leans towards me.

"How many?" he whispers.

"I just told Johnny, I don't know. Two grenades' worth anyway."

"No, no, no. How many of your – of your tasks does *this* make?"

I realize what he's saying.

"It's the fifth one," I say.

He's still leaning in close, whispering. "Out of how many again?"

"Twelve," I say.

He stands back.

"Well, next time, buddy," he says, "give me some fucking warning. If you're gonna try dying doing crazy stuff, then I want to be along. Maybe some of this hero shit protection will rub off on me. And on all of us." He gestures with his hand at the other men. I laugh out loud.

"Well, *buddy*," I say, "that sure is mighty damned nice of y'all. You're *that* confident of getting through the day?"

Rici grins his grin.

"Hell no," he says, "I just want to get through to noon."

"That's confidence."

"I'll settle for ten o'clock."

"In bits and pieces?"

Someone interrupts. "Will you two stop it?!"

It's Groucho – Bill Scott, one of the Marx Twins. The four of us turn and stare at him. He lowers his head for a second.

"Will you stop it?" he says again, as if to the ground this time. "Will you *please* stop it. We're gonna make it, you hear. We're gonna make it."

Rici snaps a glance at me, and I understand the meaning in it.

"Rici," I say, "take Vizi and Chico around to the left of this shit-pile. Groucho, you come with me."

Bill at last looks up from the ground and blinks. He glances over to Rici.

"I've only got the stripes," comments Rici, "he's the rich-kid bastard from Yale who can give the orders anytime he wants."

He nods in my direction, a grin in his eyes. "That's right, sir? Isn't it?"

"That's right, Sergeant," I say to him. I turn to Bill. "We'll go through their front door. I don't think they're in any position to answer our knock, but you never know. We must make sure there's nothing behind us before moving out today."

I point to Rici, then jerk a thumb at Bill.

"Let's go," I say.

I don't give Bill any further time to think.

"Check your weapon, Groucho," I say. "Double-check it, and let's surprise them."

As I move off, I see Rici raise his eyebrows. He mouths the one-word question: "Six?"

"Birds," I say to him. "I have to kill some birds next."

The others frown and stare at each other, but Rici gestures for Johnny and Ron to move out. Then he looks around.

"That should be easy," he says, "nothing here but us chickens."

I pat Bill on his shoulder and begin to move around the side of the blockhouse. Even as I smile, I know my obsession with myths could get us *all* killed. Perhaps I should have found some way of being relieved from attempting this assault on the land of my forefathers – the history and folklore is distracting me, reminding me of excursions into the wilds, going into the country with my grandfather.

I was fishing a river with my grandfather – three weeks after the Thanksgiving dinner where I'd tried my first alcohol, and a few days before Christmas. Though the weather was incredibly cold – we had our collars up and scarves around our mouths – the temperature had risen enough for us to be confident of finding some fish biting. We had staked a claim on some forgotten bend in the river, where the water ran gunmetal blue and eddied deep. Apart from our scarves, we were also wearing thick lumber-jackets, beaver fur hats, two sets of pants – the inner one woolen, the outer some sort of canvas – and stout boots. There was a billy constantly brewing coffee and, in-between tending our lines, we poured out clouds of steaming drink for one another, and then I asked my grandfather about his shell bracelet.

Grandfather had been wearing fingerless leather mittens, which enabled him to tie his hooks, but his exposed fingertips could also play with the cowries on his bracelet, like a Catholic counting the beads of his rosary as a comfort and act of faith. Except, instead of the incense and must that I'd always associated with cathedrals, even as a younger boy, it was the clean smell of the outdoors that I equated with visions of my grandfather playing with his cowries.

He started to tell me about the Flame Tree of Guam – the coloring of one particular petal of its flowers was much the same as the shells he wore.

"The flowers of the Flame Tree were once pure white. They are all now blood-red – with the exception of one remaining white petal, which is splashed with the blood of two lovers."

He looked out over the river for a moment.

"The confusion that lead to their deaths arose from hatred – the girl's brothers could not stand the boy being in love with their sister." His fingers counted off shell after shell as those thoughts raced through his head. "Too many people are easily convinced that it is the other person that should be dead."

I was still young, but I nodded, trying to understand. As if to reinforce my grandfather's philosophic musings, my rod began to buck and I soon felt the tremors of a desperate fight for life through my hands.

My grandfather's story convinced me that I should never be responsible for an unjust death. I believe in the necessity of what I am doing to these Enemy but, as I now chase myths, I don't know if allowing the others to be part of the pursuit is right. The responsibility for failure must be mine alone.

Bill and I do a quick check, before turning the corner.

A set of camouflaged steps, leading down into the blockhouse interior, comprise the entrance. It is constructed of several horizontal slabs of concrete supported on similar vertical slabs. The whole assembly has an array of plants growing around it for disguise. Flies swarm in a thick mass, bumping into our faces. I swat at the insects futilely, but I simply stir them around.

"After you, Groucho." I wave Bill through.

He hesitates, then crouches to take the first step into the small tunnel. I have decided he has to be first to face the Enemy. It's a bit unfair, because I'm certain that I already took them all out, but I want to get Bill back into doing what he's been trained to do, and for him to blot out any thoughts of self.

The very thoughts that are driving me along at the moment.

A ripple of the fear experienced last night, so exactly summed up by the texture of the cold concrete rubbing my back, causes my muscles to tense up again. I have a sudden image of Hercules waving his huge bronze krotala and causing those birds to fly.

What can I use?

I squeeze my eyes shut and shake my head.

What can I use? What sort of birds can I invent?

For a moment the whole world revolves around me – me and Hercules, and Serena. And here I am trying to get Bill to click back into his proper role.

I push my hypocritical ideology to one side and follow Bill downwards.

Thwack!

As I lower my head, a bullet slaps into the concrete near my head.

Thwack!

Then another.

I push Bill ahead of me and we tumble into the blockhouse. Our helmets clang against the sides of the walls. I think again of krotala. Then I'm too occupied with coughing. The sharp intake of breath I made while pushing forward means I've inhaled several flies. I choke and spit them out.

Thwack! Thwack! Thwack!

Bullets hammer the entrance, as Bill and I try to untangle ourselves. I hear Rici's muffled voice.

"Nix?"

Thwack! Th-zip!

He must have made it around to the other side of the blockhouse really fast.

"We're okay," I shout.

Thwack! Thwack!

I have another coughing fit that belies that statement, and

have to wipe the tears from my eyes as Bill squirms away from under me.

Ba-ba-ba!

"Give us a moment, will you?" I manage to yell. "We'll just get this hole cleared, then deal with whatever."

Ba-ba-ba! Tat-tat-tat! Tat-tat-tat!

I stand up. Bill joins me.

I squint, then force myself to open my eyes wide in the fog of flies. I get the impression of Bill rubbing at his own eyes. He stops.

"My God," he says, "did you do this by yourself?"

The dawn, shafting light through the various openings, illuminates the scene in a way I'm becoming accustomed to here – muted colors contrasted with the sharp line of pitch-black shadows. I make a quick judgment that in this light I can't even think about taking a photograph. But I still wish I had some flash equipment – because I'm sure my English friend Tom would appreciate yet another variation of Hieronymus Bosch. I do a quick count: there are at least eight dead Enemy. They are in various states of dismemberment – two grenades exploding in an enclosed space can do a vast amount of damage, and this blockhouse has no internal partitions to contain it. If one gets it, they all have a taste. I find it is impossible to discern where one body ends and another starts. I don't care – if there's eight of them, there's eight; if there's nine, well, that's one less to kill for some other marine coming along later. Other senses kick in, as the stench from a ruptured bowel begins to filter into my consciousness.

And not only mine.

"I think I'm—" Bill starts to say.

"No," I intervene as quick as I can, putting my hand out and gripping his upper arm, "no, you're not. Breathe through your mouth. That's it. Now start with those two in the corner. And be careful."

He mutters something under his breath that I suspect is an insult to my manhood, but I ignore it. And in the process I get distracted. I step up to one of the blockhouse slits that Johnny found so interesting from the other side. I put my hand on its bottom lip and peer out. These small windows to the outside world are bright rectangles of white light, green jungle and, beyond the ridge, as it falls away, provide a panoramic vista of war in progress. These dead Enemy here, when they were alive, had a superb view of our landing and approach. What went through *their* minds as they sat and waited for the ever-increasing flotilla to disgorge its cargo? Was there anticipation in their hearts? Or anger? *Banzai* bloodlust? Their machine-guns here are heavy caliber and must have been responsible for some serious casualties. It's easy to picture them patiently waiting, letting us get within range, waiting to impose on us the maximum chaos and damage. Watching the Boys fall. The empty shell casings from their weapons are heaped in large mounds all around. Their other gear is strewn ad hoc – whether through choice, or as a result of my violent intrusion, it's hard to tell. I'm tempted to take an object that might equate to a future task, perhaps a belt of ammunition, but I have a sudden fear that doing so will jinx the potent magic I'm trying to weave in my mind.

No, my next task involves birds – or something that I can equate with birds. So what can I do to facilitate it?

I shake my head and turn back to look at the floor with its haphazard arrangement of slaughtered humanity. I stare into the remains of their faces for a brief moment and then I poke each face, hard, with the sharp end of my bayonet. There's no response from any of them – it's as I thought, they're all dead. But it was still a good idea to check, particularly after Rici's experience. From Bill's corner I hear a groan and for a moment I think it's him about to throw up.

Snap-crack!

His rifle seems absurdly loud and makes me jump. I spin around to see him standing over a quivering body, then I step through various mixtures of soft human detritus and filth and hard shell cases and go over to him.

I stand beside him.

"How the hell?" Bill says, shaking his head, the whites of his eyes vividly pronounced.

I glance down. He's right. How life had still been possible in the remains I see there is something I can't work out either. The Enemy had even got one finger inserted in the ring-pull of his grenade, though he no longer had eyes to look out of.

"Go figure," I mutter.

I look around. Apart from the fog of flies, there is nothing else living that requires our attention.

"We're done here," I say. "Now let's see if we can get ourselves out in a better shape than they are. There's still that one out there who hurried us inside here with a slap to our butts."

Bill nods. From deep within he pulls himself together. I reckon he'll soon be able to function as a marine again – he's still breathing through his mouth, but his color has returned. I decide that, if he gets through the next few days, he might end up eating his chow right beside some split and visceral dead Enemy without a thought – like Rici and I have been doing. Bill is entering the Bougainville Blues Zone, where death in all its shades is only a curiosity when it's unusual, merely becoming background litter to war when familiar. There'll be less pain that way for him. I, on the other hand, am coming out from the other side. I'm past the stage where I wonder at the various ways it is possible to separate a man from his life. I suspect that I've entered that fool's paradise of delusion where instead of *knowing* I'm going to live (it'll always be the other guy, not me), I'm *hoping* I'm going to survive. That and going joyously mad by simultaneously trying to perform a set of tasks. This is not the right sort of thinking.

Bill and I edge up the bunker steps – me on the left, Bill on the right. I realize I've been holding my breath, so I snort and force myself to suck down some air through my nose.

It's unpleasant, but necessary. I'm functioning again.

We lower ourselves down onto the rough treads of the steps and proceed up on elbows and splayed-out legs.

As we do so, rifle fire slaps the roof of the blockhouse entrance.

Thwack! Thwack!

"Rici?" I call out.

"Yeah?"

He's just on the other side of the wall to me.

"Where is he?" I ask.

"Chico reckons he spotted muzzle flashes up in the trees ahead. And I do mean *up* in the trees."

I squirm forward some more, upward to the outside. I pause. All I can see in the immediate foreground is lush, thick-foliaged bushes and clusters of trees. Apart from the track leading into the jungle, the immediate area behind the block-house is dense vegetation. He could be anywhere from fifty yards away to just three feet in front of me – except if he were, Bill and I would have been dead five minutes ago.

"Groucho," I say, "move as far over as you can, and fire off a few rounds out there when I say so. Rici?"

"Yeah, Nix?"

"You, Ron and Johnny do the same as Groucho. Squeeze off a couple shots apiece when I say so – towards that tree line in front of us. I'll concentrate on working out where exactly he is. Okay?"

"Gotcha."

I give Rici a few seconds to pass on the message, and ready myself to watch carefully. Now that the sun is rising, the deep greens of the foliage are taking on their daylight sharpness. There should be time to appreciate this beauty of tropical growth, but the flies swarm around my face again and make me feel dirty. Somewhere, far off to my right, a bird calls – its throaty warble suddenly stopping in mid-cry – and I think again about Hercules and the Stymphalian Birds. I find myself hoping the Enemy *is* up a tree. I hope he's *perching* there, and the thought gives me sureness in what I'm doing. I carry on peering. I don't stare at any particular spot; I simply stop my eyes from focusing on anything specific – and my grandfather speaks to me again from my mountain memories of fishing that river.

"If you want to get better at hunting, merge into your surroundings," he'd said. "Return to your past, when your ancestors were hunters, and become part of the land – in the same natural way as the animal you pursue. Don't deliberately seek your quarry out – let his appearance come as a mild surprise."

I allow myself to be drawn into the surroundings – to forget expectations.

"Fire," I say out loud.

Ba-ba-ba! Tat-tat-tat! Snap-crack! Snap-crack!

The bullets from the Boys sing their lethal wasp song.

Th-zip!

There is a brief reply from the green canopy up ahead. I see the flash – a blink that is a cone of fire. A puff of smoke follows.

"In that tree!" I shout. "Thirty yards – one o'clock. The bastard's got an OP up in a tree!"

This is it, this is my Stymphalian Bird. I can complete another task here.

Rici thinks the same thing as me. "Bird enough for you?" he asks.

"Yes," I answer. "Fuck, yes."

"Cover!" shouts Rici.

I can't believe it. My buddy is going to help me – to join me in this stupid, crazy, rich-kid odyssey. He's going to help kill a Stymphalian Bird.

He's as crazy as I am!

We both scramble to our feet. The Boys here at our sides let rip.

Snap-crack! Snap-crack!

Rici and I begin to run, out in plain view.

As we plunge through the low bushes, I keep my eyes fixed on that same spot in the trees. Rici pauses to cover our advance with a burst of gunfire.

Bullets fly over our heads in both directions. Rici joins in my chase again. The fronds of plants slap against us heavily. I high-step over a patch of bamboo.

"Down!" Rici calls to me.

I throw myself to the ground and glance back at him. Rici points to the tree we're heading for. I can now discern the Enemy in his high vantage point – a little tree house that is just a bit too exposed. I see the wires from his field telephone snaking down the trunk – he's obviously enjoyed a good run at directing mortars onto the beach.

"Go on, boy – take your bird," says Rici.

It makes me happy to know that he is in on the deal – we'll go mad together. I take aim, and see the Enemy shifting about, trying to ascertain where we are. He stops moving: he can see me now. And I know he can see the barrel of my carbine pointing straight up at him. He brings his rifle up to his shoulder – a natural soldier's reaction, the human thing to do. But I don't see him as such: he is my sixth task, on a plate.

Tat-tat-tat!

I fire. The Enemy is silent – gives no last cry – but he tumbles from his perch and lands at the base of the OP. Leaves flutter down after him like spent and broken feathers.

I feel a horrible mixture of exhilaration and guilt. For an instant I wonder how old he was – he has a young man's stubble. Well, he'll never get older now. I am still emerging from the other side of the Bougainville Blues.

I could have allowed him another split second of life.

Then again, he would have killed me – or killed Rici.

He's task number six.

I go to check he really *is* dead. He is.

A noise behind me. Rici is standing there, and laughing.

"Nix, just *what* are the odds?"

The others join us (including the rest of the Boys), all panting from their quick dash towards us.

"What are you talking about?" asks Johnny. "Are you still talking about Dead Pool Poker?"

Amos, Ron and Jim all reach up to their top pockets, but

Ron and Jim quickly drop their hands when they realize the others have noticed their automatic reaction. Amos grins at me and pats his own pocket.

"No," says Rici, "this is about odds you're never going to get given in any card school that I've heard of."

I catch myself wincing as I wait for him to explain, then honestly don't care. I'm now enjoying trying to save myself like this. Even though it won't take long for the Boys to demand that I be shipped out and home.

"Go ahead," I say, "tell them."

When he's finished, the Boys look around at each other, then at me, at Rici. One or two jaws have dropped.

But Amos is grinning, and the humor spreads out and around a bit.

"It'll help us all pass the time," says Rici. "I've already started helping him out."

Bill takes a couple of steps towards Rici. "You mean, I just went into *that*," he points back at the blockhouse, "with some loon that thinks he's playing some dead Greek guy?"

"Even if he's gone cuckoo," says Jim, "I don't mind, so long as he can still shoot like this."

He reaches up, lifts off his helmet, and rubs the sweat off his forehead with his forearm.

"Hey," says Amos, frowning, "what becomes of our money if Nixy gets himself blown to bits with all this stuff?"

The arguments then break out with a vengeance, as my mortality is discussed in abstract terms and with practical implications. They don't want me to actually die – that would be against the code – but they feel they have to consider the options. Then someone asks the obvious question, the one that has been lurking in my own mind.

"Hold on," says Johnny, "what if Nix runs out of tasks before we're finished here? If Nix has done five of them already, and this Jap in the tree is the sixth one . . .?"

They all stop jawing and turn to look at me. I cough.

"I'll probably then become a legend and a dead hero," I say.

The Boys turn back amongst themselves. Bill keeps muttering, "I went in there with him. I went in there with him.'

I shake my head. *They're going to open up a side bet. God, how many more am I going to convert to my madness?*

And will I run out of tasks before we're finished here?

I need help, now.

Where the hell is Serena?

SIXTEEN

W Day +2. 06.10. Near Enemy OP on Asan River.

I need to go back and remember a drinking session I had with my grandfather when I was fifteen – it will give me a little piece of comfort, and it reminds me why I *am* the person I am. I want a breathing space. It also makes my hasty swallowing of a third of a bottle of *saki* I liberated from the treetop OP less of an event to feel guilty of; and it enables me to ignore Rici's Buster Keaton stare. I know Rici's my buddy, but he does go on about my drinking with those glances of his. He should know me better by now; I was taught to drink by an expert, I know how to handle it.

My grandfather and I were hidden away in a part of the estate that the rest of the family rarely ventured into. On a small rise stood a hexagonal wooden gazebo, with a porch swing hanging from its crossbeam, which my father had had built years before; but subsequently lost all interest in. It over-looked the carp lake and the little island that the ducks had made their home on. My grandfather had taken it on himself to renovate it as a spring-time task; I think he had in mind a place that he and grandma could sneak off to on summer evenings.

When originally built it had taken the carpenters only a day of hard work to erect the raised platform, the waist-high walls between three pairs of six pillars and the roof covering it. But my grandfather had already spent a week doing repairs before I arrived to give some support one Saturday. He called it his

Temple of Truth – God knows why. We spent the morning rubbing down the last of the rails, and I worked myself into a frenzy to impress my grandfather and so, come noon, I was glad to find an excuse to open the packed lunch I'd prepared for us. We sat together on the swing bench, with its new cushions grandmother had provided, and ate ham and cheese sandwiches.

When grandfather produced a bottle from his bag of tools, I sat up, putting down the flask of water I'd been drinking from. He told me it was Cuban rum and proceeded to fill two shot glasses. Since that Thanksgiving dinner where I'd sampled my first alcohol, and found the beauty it gave in making the world seem a better place, I had drunk wine at every available opportunity. I had recently raided my father's drinks cabinet to experiment with the wondrous range of alcohol he had acquired since Prohibition ended. But I had always used some sort of mixer, as I'd seen my father do after dinner, and had never drunk strong liquor neat. So I was excited that day to be crossing another threshold towards becoming a man. As far as I was concerned my grandfather was going to initiate me into the ways of hard drinking, and so I wouldn't have to do it on my own, as I'd been planning to.

I was instructed to knock it back in one go. I allowed the rum that same reverential pause my grandfather did, then put it to my lips. I had to force myself not to splutter as it seared the back of my throat and burned into my stomach. My grandfather laughed, of course, then pushed off hard with one foot and we swung to and fro, to and fro. After three more shots of that glorious rum, I found the world became an altered place – and I loved that gazebo, I loved the view of the lake, I loved my grandfather. I told him so and explained, with difficulty, as my tongue seemed to have miraculously grown to fill my mouth, that I thought my father would be angry at the state I was in.

"How many cents in a dollar?" my grandfather asked.

I paused, trying to work out why he asked me such a simple question.

"One hundred," I said.

"If you can still talk money, your father won't be upset," he said. And he laughed his laugh, poured me one last shot, pushed off with his foot again and told me a story about a boy who surprised his father with a demonstration of his strength.

"You see," grandpa had said, "all children have to grow up eventually. And they may well turn out to be superior to their fathers."

At that point I got up and staggered into the bushes to be sick. And that was the last time I let alcohol make me feel so ill. I'd endure the pain of any amount of monumental hangovers, but I'd never be sick again.

I would make myself fall in love with Cuban rum. I love the taste of it.

Late Tuesday afternoon.

The male swan is the biggest Serena has ever seen, and it stands far taller than the young girl it seems about to attack. As she watches, the seconds stretch and expand into adrenal-pumped aeons. Everything melts into slow motion, and Serena finds herself detached enough to observe as the swan takes another step towards the little girl. Serena still hesitates.

She had come down by the river bank at Stourbridge Common with the sole purpose of taking a photograph of herself – to add to her growing Hercules collection – standing beside one of the swans that congregate there. Instead, all she had seemed to achieve was to feed them with broken-off flakes of bread from a Farmhouse loaf for no reward. Every time she turned to set the timer on her camera, all the birds became suddenly shy and elusive, so she had had to attract them back with further investments of her dwindling bread supply. To add to her frustrations, the weather had seemingly turned from dry heat to humidity in the matter of only an hour or two. The forecasters on the midday news had predicted a forty-per cent chance the weather might later change with a vengeance. It appeared, from the way that the sky was beginning to press down on Serena, that the odds were shortening.

Stourbridge Common has more people than usual, but no one seems in a hurry to vacate the various spots of grass where they have chosen to relax and soak up the sun. For a weekday, there are considerable clusters of people gathered to enjoy impromptu picnics. They are mostly women with children, but also a few men. One man in his thirties sits with his back against a tree, drinking from a can of lager, as a young boy throws a frisbee a few times in graceful arcs that bring it spinning back to his outstretched hand, before joining his father in the shade. The man passes the can across to allow the boy a sip, ignoring the disapproving frowns from several of the mothers. In the distance some teenagers holler their defiance at an adult's listless protests and jump fully clothed into the river. Even their squeals and shouts do not intrude on the underlying tranquillity that forms the backdrop to Stourbridge Common today.

The swan arches its back, raises its wings and waddles faster across the grass, projecting its beak like the weapon that it is – rasping and sharp. The little girl with the blonde pigtails, cotton dress, and ice cream dripping from her hand stands wide-eyed with her mouth open.

For a moment more, Serena remains still, a surge of guilt washing over her because she is watching this event unfold as if she were a voyeur, and relishes not making a decision. The little girl – only five or six years old – is transfixed by the approaching bird, and even though she has her mouth open, she appears unable to cry out. In an instant of clarity, Serena recognizes the fear. It is the fear from her own childhood. She had to resolve that problem by herself, but it would only take a little effort to help here. Serena shakes herself out of her passivity and takes six quick strides to place herself between the girl and the approaching swan. As the bird turns its attention to her, it increases the volume of its hissing.

"Oh, shut up!" shouts Serena, and clips the swan about its head with a hand.

Two things then happen at the same time. Firstly, the child's eyes grow even wider, she puts a hand to her mouth as she gasps, then finally energizes herself to scamper away from danger. Once she is safe, she finds sufficient voice to yell for her mother. Her mother is immediately on her feet, before the girl can call out again. Secondly, the swan goes berserk.

It becomes a vortex of white feathers, snapping yellow beak, and powerfully beating wings. As it flaps itself upright again, its wings thrust wide, the true essence of its wild power becomes nakedly obvious to Serena. She now feels what the child felt. The reaction of the swan to being struck has stripped away the veneer of superiority that civilization gives to human-kind, leaving behind a primal fear in its place – that ancient one of being mauled or savaged by a wild animal. For most people it would concentrate the mind wonderfully, yet all Serena can think about is how the bird's reactions remind her of Alex's ranting in the early hours of that same morning when the taxi dropped her off after her nocturnal exploits at the stable yard.

"What the hell are you doing?" Alex had exploded, standing on her doorstep waving a piece of paper. The grizzled taxi driver gave Serena a look of well-thanks-but-I'm-leaving-you-to-it-missus. He blipped the throttle of his car, providing a slight squeal of protest from the tyres as he pulled away.

"I could ask you the same," she said coldly to Alex. "Why are you here at six o'clock in the morning?"

At a faster pace than normal, Alex hobbled down the pathway and met her at the gate. He shoved the piece of paper under her nose and waved it about.

"I get this e-mail," he says, "telling me that you're planning some little sojourn to add to your other stupid exploits, and I'm expected not to react? What drugs are you on? Don't you realize that what you're doing is crazy?"

The waving of the piece of paper became more frenetic. Serena stepped into it so it brushed her face as she replied.

"About as stupid as printing off an e-mail that *I* sent to you, to show to *me*?" she said.

Alex's head gave a little jerk backwards, as if he'd been slapped, and then he looked at the sheet of paper for a second, screwed it up and rammed it into his pocket. He gazed around the garden, and Serena had the odd notion that Alex had somehow misplaced his next question. His eyes re-located hers.

Ah, he's found it again.

"And why did you take a taxi?" he demanded as he tapped his one sound foot.

Serena was fascinated that Alex was so animated.

"For reasons that must be obvious," she said.

She nudged past him to put her key in the lock.

"And have you changed your locks? I couldn't get in with my spare key."

The last was a whine as he dangled his set of keys at her. Serena paused as she started to step inside.

"I'm making changes," she said. She smiled at his blank stare.

"You're going mad," he said, then followed her inside. Serena threw her hat on a coat hook and continued down the hall.

"I'm not mad enough to hang about outside someone's house when I've no idea how long they'll be out," she said.

"I don't break into people's stables in the middle of the night—"

"I'm getting together quite a collection of photos—"

"—just to *clean* them out."

"—with or without your help."

"It feels like you're shutting me out," he said, almost petulantly. "I'm here for support, you know."

"No, you're here 'cause you're pissed off and you can't believe that I've cracked one of the riddles of time."

He grabbed her by the arm. "Don't *do* this," he said.

Serena pulled away and headed towards the kitchen.

"I can. I will. I must," she says. "Tea? Or are you more into coffee these days?"

"I don't drink coffee."

"You did on Sunday morning."

Her reply froze him to the spot, and Serena thought his expression quite comical. She would have laughed if she wasn't filled with such mixed-up emotions; tired after having been up all night, excited at what she had done, yet confused at her motivations. Now here she had Alex, bleating as though a favourite toy had been confiscated. She considered the possibility of getting drunk, just for a change. It would have been nice if she could have invited Phoenix over, then they could have got to know each other better and got blitzed together. Shame they lived in different times, and separated by God knows how many decades. She reached for the kettle, feeling a tension headache coming on.

Serena blinks. It is the afternoon again, and she stands on the river bank, rubbing the back of her neck. The swan begins to quieten down when she turns and walks back to collect her camera. Serena doesn't know how long she's been thinking about the events of that morning, and it worries her that she's losing contact with the present. She *is* aware that the various conflicts she is dealing with are all vying for her attention and distracting her. Checking the settings on her camera for another attempt, she wonders if the sky isn't becoming too hazy. Serena glances over at the other swans on the river. In the usual way that the mind leaps to connections, that of her Greek myth of

Leda, mother of Helen of Troy, with whom Zeus had had sex after metamorphosing into a swan, springs into Serena's consciousness. She latches onto the incongruity of the story.

"I don't care if it was Zeus disguised," she says to herself. "How the devil did she manage to be seduced by a *swan*? Make the mistake of just lying comatose by a Spartan riverbank?"

She wished the swan would waddle back for another go at her, so that she could be justified in clouting it again.

Leda became famous in works citing Greek mythology for two reasons. Firstly, this was one of the numerous cases of mythical women having sex with animals. Secondly was the popularity of this particular story with artists. Picture after picture, down through the ages, from Correggio and Michelangelo on to Cézanne and Dali, they all continued to paint their interpretations of a beautiful naked woman with a lecherous swan in attendance. Serena, on first seeing some of them, thought them damn near pornographic in tone.

Serena turns back to the river, puts her hands on her hips and leans towards the offending bird.

"And why do artists and poets involve themselves obsessively with such a minor Greek myth? What does it represent to them? Violence wrapped up in beauty? The attraction of the bestial? What is it about woman being fucked by animals that seems to spark their creativity, hey?"

Serena resets the timer on her camera. When it clicks, the picture it captures is of Serena remonstrating with an inflated swan. Afterwards, the bird continues to spit at her as she collects her belongings.

Serena mutters under her breath as she works. "Be careful of swans, they warn. If you get them angry they can break your leg with their wings. Strange, but you never actually meet anybody with first-hand evidence for that belief – do you?"

This question is directed at the swan itself.

"Be careful of swans, they say – they might fuck with you. Or fuck you."

She tries to laugh. It had been a mistake to commemorate the Stymphalian Bird task by getting photographed with an angry swan.

Maybe that's what Leda and the swan is all about – giving in to animal passion, and seeing a beauty in doing so.

Serena crouches down to pack her shoulder bag. The Beast is back, the thing she had thought she had dispelled all those years ago. The Beast seems larger now, more defined. It has her mother's heart, and Alex's anger. The Beast possesses the vitriol of Alex's outburst of that morning.

"No. I don't want fucking coffee," he had repeated.

Serena still went to the sink to fill the kettle.

"Why do you want to put all you've won at risk with these stupid games of yours?" he asked.

Serena turned off the tap and put the lid back on the kettle.

"I didn't *win* anything," she said. "I seem to remember being coerced into achieving academic goals that other people had set for me. I certainly don't remember it being voluntary."

As she plugged in the kettle, her hands were trembling.

"Look," she said. "I'll now do what *I* want – even if it's not okay with you. I think that's a simple enough proposition to understand, isn't it?"

God, it's taken me years to say that.

"You don't know what's at stake?" he asked.

Before she could answer, the phone rang.

"Excuse me," she said, and went into the hall to pick up the receiver. It was Christian – a welcome relief. She could now think about music for a moment.

"Hi," he said. He was like a breath of air, the complete change of thought she needed.

"Christian, it's early for you."

"Late, actually. I've just got in."

"So have I."

"Naughty girl."

"So my brother has been telling me. What can I do for you?"

"Great news, girl – but hold on to your bladder. The suits at the record company are definitely interested. They think the sound is new, out-there, trend-setting."

Serena heard his tinkle of a laugh.

"In other words," he continued, "they think we're going to make a packet of dosh out there with the kids. What do you think of that?"

Serena didn't answer.

"Serena, girl, did you hear me?"

Everything at once, everything at once.

"Yes, yes I did. So, you'll be wanting some more tracks?"

"All you can dream up. We'll thrash out the royalties thing when we next meet. Talk soon, okay?"

"Sure."

He paused. "Hey, it's good news, Serena – so cheer up."

"It's good news, Christian, and you've cheered me up."

He laughed. "Ciao, girl."

"Ciao, yourself."

And she stood there, phone humming in her ear, trying to work out how it is that life can change just on a whim. She hoped that somewhere, somehow, Annette herself was watching and smiling.

She returns to the present, returns to Stourbridge Common. She looks up at the sky. Clouds are beginning to form, dotted everywhere across the sky, and they grow in size as she watches. The shapes they take on all seem grotesque to Serena, and when she looks away, out over the common, all her thoughts rush into one and she is hit by such a violent sensation that all the muscles of her body seem to contract at the same time. It startles her, and she staggers, putting a hand to her face, and reaching out with the other hand for support that isn't there.

She finds herself suffering from a series of flashbacks. They are Odysseus sharp.

Oh, my God!

There is a repetition of her experience in the landing craft on Guam with Phoenix. The incident repeats three, four times. Just as the vehicle she is riding in makes contact with the beach, another one beside them is hit. Serena watches it explode, again and again – feels the whack of concussion, smells the stench of diesel, of fire and burning, sees men disintegrate, their bodies erupt into fragments and flames. Then there is the rush of terror – the absolute conviction that her life will never be more in peril than it is right now. It comes as a chill in her bowels, a seizure that constricts her chest, causes her heart to thud. A flush shivers for an instant over her face; she feels clammy as all the blood drains away. She tries to swallow, but finds she can't – her mouth is too dry. Serena finds it is so peculiar to feel fear manifest in a man same as in a woman.

Then she is back in the dream – Hercules' fireworks party that Phoenix wanted to get away from. She supposes it similar to a bad LSD trip – people changing shape, distorting, fading in and out of focus. There is little structure or permanence – as in all dreams – but there is also that hint of nightmare. She looks around. The giant that is Hercules holds sway over everyone – he is confident, calm, and conscious of her own presence. When he looks at her, she can't tell if he wears a proud smile or not. And she repeats her error again and again – giving Phoenix information that he shouldn't know about the future, telling him again about Tom Wakefield's death. Phoenix's dream could be her own disaster.

Oh, God.

It feels exactly as before, as though she is operating Odysseus again, as though she has moved back in time. Then, in between the rapid electric sensations that tingle and zip within her, she decides that it is all because of her lack of sleep and the excitement of what she has achieved, rather than a result of having successfully used Odysseus. That and what Alex had told her that morning. It had been Alex who had added to her fears. It had been Alex who pushed aside the rock that let the Beast out again.

When she had returned to the kitchen, Alex gripped her shoulders between each hand. He squeezed, and it hurt.

"So your music is going well?" he said. "That's good. Now listen, you know what I found when I got home?"

Serena shook her head, just wishing he would leave so she could crawl into bed, and not get up for a week.

"I found I'd been burgled," he said.

Serena was jolted awake and was immediately alert.

"Oh, that's terrible," she said, reaching out with a hand to touch her brother's face. "Are you all right—?"

"Listen to me," he interrupted, avoiding her probing hand.

Alex limped to one corner of the kitchen, turned and leant his back into the angle of the storage units. He slid both hands out along the work surfaces and glowered at her. It gave him the air of a patronizing lecturer confronted by a naive student.

She stopped attempting to talk to him, instead becoming fascinated by the intensity in her brother's eyes.

"There were only a couple of things taken," he continued. "They threw a few books around and scattered the contents of my filing cabinet everywhere as if to demonstrate they were making some sort of effort, but they removed only certain very specific items. I've heard about this sort of incident before, Serena, so I know what's going on. I've lost my laptop and quite a few of my floppy disks – the ones with my records. There was nothing else gone of any value, not a thing that any normal thief would take. They couldn't have made their intention plainer."

"You keep saying *they*. What are you implying?"

"I think I've probably just been done over by some" – he spits the words out – "*defenders* of our *realm*. And they've been deliberately obvious in the way they've done it, so that I get the message – and now I'm passing it on to you. That's why I've been standing out there on your doorstep for hours."

"What do you mean?"

He gave her his best condescending Big Brother smile.

"Serena, you've never been, how shall I – you've never been *discreet* about your research, have you? Your proposals for what you wanted to invent? I know you've taken precautions to stop intellectual theft, but anyone would've been a cretin to miss what you were trying to achieve. And the inevitable has now happened: your ... your mind-travel machine has somehow become hot news. Why do I know that? Because the government is now interested. They already broke into my place and lifted what little information I had about your research."

"But why do you assume that? Criminals are stealing PC equipment all the time. And, anyhow, no one apart from yourself knows Odysseus has actually worked."

"The disks they took were mainly the research I'd done for *you*. That's their message – they're so cocky they don't care if I work out what's happening. And it's my belief that they're having you constantly watched. You've probably been under surveillance for some time now. *That's* how they know how far you've progressed. You know, I still have some doubts about whether it genuinely works, or if it's simply a sophisticated trick of the senses but, one way or the other, your mind-game machine is potential dynamite, so they want to get their hands on it. And they won't be wasting any time either. If they can break into my place and leave a calling card so obvious, and not *care* that I twig, then they are *not* likely to waste time. You should give serious thought to the implications of that, Serena!"

Serena cleared her throat. "Which are?" she asked.

Alex folded his arms. For a moment Serena didn't know if this simple action was a measure of how pompously *right* he was feeling – or how scared.

"Anyone who can't be bothered to ask first," he explained, "but moves straight to some sort of covert action, has to be bad news."

"Oh."

"Yes, oh, indeed."

Returning to the present, Serena stares at the camera still on its tripod, and feels the spasm of fear ripple away from her.

Is this the worst? Can the Beast do more to frighten me?

She looks, trying to see if anyone is watching her. In her present paranoia she figures that everyone is suspect.

Even that man under the tree allowing his son to sip lager.

Serena wonders exactly what forces she has instigated against herself.

I have to find an answer, a way out of this.

She gathers up her equipment and begins to walk home. A few minutes later, she is hurrying as hard as she can, trying not to drop anything.

She repeats a mantra.

An answer, an answer. Please, let me find an answer.

SEVENTEEN

Myths can weave and intertwine. The warrior and adventurer Theseus is best known for his fight against the Minotaur in the Labyrinth. But this occurred only after Hercules had set wheels in motion with his seventh task.

Some years earlier, King Minos had angered Poseidon, the god of the oceans. This was generally considered a bad idea – the Greeks thrived on sea-going trade after all. What had happened was that Poseidon had brought forth from the sea a spectacular bull, which he intended Minos to sacrifice to him, but King Minos made the mistake of not doing as expected and had put the bull out to stud with his cattle. Such are the errors that mortals make. Poseidon, furious, and in the throes of planning storms to wreck the shipping around Crete, stopped himself in time, and, in the wicked, evil way that gods sometimes continue to make themselves happy, conjured Minos' wife Pasiphae to fall in love with the beast.

Upon setting eyes on the animal as it strutted around a field, Pasiphae became enthralled with the bull, removed all her clothes, opened the gate, and entered the field to give herself to the creature. Hence the Minotaur was conceived. (As mentioned, bestiality was a common sexual liaison then, where the gods were concerned.) King Minos thereafter had to deal not only with his wife's somewhat unusual offspring and the fact that she had cheated on him with an animal, but also with the fact that the same animal was now rampaging around, crashing and barging all over Crete. Either Pasiphae had rejected its further advances or had left the gate open. Anyway, Poseidon was using the bull to wreak havoc.

The years passed.

In Mycenae, the day was like any other summer's day. The sun shone and the olives ripened. Old men told tall stories of their youth to impress each other, young men talked of their own exploits to bored young women, and King Eurystheus stood in his dusty jar, one hand shielding his eyes from the sun's glare, looking up at his herald. The herald, as is the nature of such relationships, stood with his face hidden respectfully in shadow and looked down on him.

"Tell Hercules," Eurystheus said to his herald, "how we provide tribute every year to King Minos." The king shrugged, momentarily lost in thought. "Zeus alone knows what Minos does with all the young men we send him."

He shook his head and continued with his instructions.

"It now seems appropriate to me that Hercules should capture this bull which has spent the last few years ruining the Cretan countryside. You see, I know about diplomacy and this will stand us in good stead with the king."

Without even allowing the king to pause for breath, the herald answered, "I will so instruct him your highness."

Eurystheus tilted his head to one side and put a single fingertip to his pursed lips. He slowly nodded his head. "I'm glad you enjoy your work so much," he said.

"The pleasure is mine," the herald said, and bowed to take his leave.

"Oh," called out the king, patting his hands impatiently on the rim of his jar, "warn him that there are also reports that the beast breathes fire. I might have forgotten to mention that."

The herald remained devoid of any emotion. "What a shame," he said to his king.

"Indeed."

The herald bowed as low as he could – then giggled.

The king slapped a brief rhythm with his hands on the jar. The two men smiled at each other.

Hercules sailed to Crete, where King Minos was help personified once he heard what the hero intended to do. He promptly offered all sorts of assistance, but Hercules needed to work alone – he had a point to prove, especially to the herald of Mycenae with the newly broken nose. So he set off in the direction of the loud bellowing he could hear from distant valleys.

Hercules soon found the bull. It was as big as both kings had promised, and it did indeed breathe fire. The bull lowered its head, pawed the ground, and snorted. Such a creature didn't like people who eyed at it the way Hercules did, and it intended to trample this man to the ground for his impertinence. But when Hercules ignored its preparations and walked straight up to it, the bull stopped pawing the ground and looked up. This was not what usually happened. By now Hercules had got quite close to it.

Their struggle was short and brutal, it was over in seconds. Before the bull could even begin to think about lowering its head to charge, Hercules had used his favourite wrestling grip – the headlock – and forced the beast to the ground and into submission. It was so surprised it forgot to breathe fire over the victor.

After succeeding in controlling the animal so quickly, Hercules had a small feast with King Minos, just to be sociable, then boarded his boat to take the chastened bull back to King Eurystheus. As the crew cast off, Queen Pasiphae stood at the quayside and waved Hercules goodbye. But he noticed that she was looking longingly at the bull as she did so . . .

When Hercules returned to Mycenae, the sun was still shining, the olives were bigger, the old men were now sleeping, and the young women were beginning to weaken to the young men's advances. King Eurystheus, for all his confidence in his diplomatic skills, then made an error. After initial annoyance that Hercules had succeeded yet again, he dedicated the bull to Hera and set it free. This was not a wise decision, and the goddess was not happy. This animal was yet another symbol of Hercules' glory, and that stupid King Eurystheus had only gone and just given it its freedom. Hera smiled bitterly, waved a hand, and cast a spell on the animal. She forced it to express her fury by rampaging throughout the countryside, as it had on Crete, until it ended up in Marathon. This would be where Theseus would eventually kill it, prior to his own magnificent adventures in the Labyrinth.

But that's another story.

Hercules, meanwhile, had a homecoming feast to celebrate the completion of his seventh labour. The old men woke up and chatted to the young women, while the young men asked Hercules to describe his tale again and again. And the party went on for five days – showing that heroes take easy tasks in their stride.

EIGHTEEN

Serena just makes it back home as the storm crackles into life. She strides through her house, throws her hat to one side, opens the kitchen door and stands there, her arms wrapped around herself, marvelling at this sudden change in the weather. In the short time it has taken her to return home, the empty sky has filled with dramatic clouds that have now merged into one tremendous expanse of deep colours, awash with vigorous energy. There are shades of purple and even yellow in the folds and cracks of the clouds, but the over-whelming hue is something akin to oil-smoke. Serena has the impression she would choke if this ever-changing eruption of thunderclouds were to lower itself to the ground. It attempts to do just that with the first flash of lightning.

The bolt is so close to Serena that the intensity of the flash makes her cringe. It's as if some deity is personally upset with her. Before she can fully appreciate the shock of it, the sound of the thunderclap envelops her, like a huge slab of rock tumbling to the ground. Ten seconds later, the thunderstorm does it again – only brighter and louder – and then again. The rain arrives in a tumultuous flood. One second the air is charged with energy, the next and the entire power of the storm is unleashed in a violent deluge. It is the fiercest storm Serena has ever witnessed, and she steps outside to welcome it.

The torrent whips every part of her skin exposed to it. In an instant she is drenched, and for a moment considers stripping naked, to be baptized in this unholy tempest, but she settles for stretching out her arms and pushing her face towards the heavens – to be washed and cleansed in the stinging downpour. As the thunder trembles, Serena knows this is a moment of rebirth. She is surprised at how easy it is to jump away from the complexities of her personality, and to land in a new and different version of herself, where the world appears less confusing, carries less doubt, is now filled with purpose. St Paul had his revelation on the road to Damascus; Archimedes while climbing into his bath; Professor Serena Freeman has hers a couple of steps from the shelter of her kitchen. She finds the sensation of renewal is almost sexual.

She now knows what she has to do – even if it means becoming lost in a past mostly consigned to books. There is an attractiveness to the past that she has always been drawn to. It is not a nostalgia for a supposed era when summers are imagined as warmer and longer, followed by winters bringing drifts of snow for Christmas Day; it is that sense of protection to be found in a foreign country where they do things differently. And in an odd way, Serena considers, this security arises from knowing that you are not part of a present constantly foreshadowing a future that no one knows; instead you are existing in a past where you *do* know what will happen. But the past that Serena finds herself desiring is not one that includes her own childhood.

She opens her eyes at last to the downpour and blinks as the raindrops speckle her face. For all her precocious intelligence, she had never before had the common sense to see the obvious – not until this moment.

Alex's betrayal.

That one component of her personal history that she had never guessed existed. And now that she can see it for what it was, what it *is*, she is determined to crush it whenever it is conceived, born and recognized.

Alex had been pushing his sister towards academia for most of her life, because he knew that would take the parental pressure off him. If she was the one under the parental spotlight, then he could escape to do what *he* really wanted. At her expense, always to her cost. If that had not been the case, she would undoubtedly be in different circumstances to where she finds herself now: a person who has to catch up on wasted years. A person determined to turn back, leapfrog the pain of childhood, and find solace in a time and place known only in history books. She has been there, and wants to return.

She feels she *has* baptized herself – she is new. Serena heads back inside to dry herself off, before getting ready to use Odysseus again.

W Day +2. 08.17. Asan River Ridgeline.

We make final preparations before the day's attack. The weather fits my mood. As if the Enemy hasn't got enough natural defensive advantages on this island, a gentle rain now falls to form swathes of mist. There have been regular showers ever since we landed, but they have been brief, a sort of mild reminder that this is the tropics, and that rain and intense heat are buddies here. This, though, is sullen stuff. We hide inside our ponchos and try to stave off the worst of it. I check that my camera is wrapped up tight. Around me, the leaves jitter and shimmer under the droplets of rain – the light spangles and jumps, green, from bush to bush. It looks lush and verdant, but this movement could be hiding something more sinister. It makes everybody jumpy. I'm not the only person obsessively checking my equipment – we've been resupplied and marines up and down the line are busy fiddling with the best positions to fix and carry the extra weight. I find places to stick a couple of extra magazines for my carbine, and another for my Colt. I also "acquire" one of those cardboard tubes with metal ends that I've seen some marines carrying, and I stuff it full of grenades. The Boys' activity alternates between shifting the loads on their bodies and wiping water from their rifles. There isn't much talk, just standard Marine Corps bitching.

"Shit, this rain's as warm as fresh piss."

"Least I can drink it."

"Hey! My boots keep cutting cheese every time I move."

"Why didn't I volunteer to be a fly-boy?"

"Yeah, why didn't you?"

"Hey, guys, you'll have to leave me behind – I can't swim."

"Shit, boy, *I* have to keep moving just to stop sinking."

"Sinking? Oh, sorry, buddy – thought you said *stinking*."

And so on, and so on. Remorseless, like the rain.

But before it started, the Boys and I had continued our conversation. It involved Hercules and his seventh task, a bull – and the odds of getting to kill one in the near future.

I didn't get the strange looks I half-expected, but a fierce debate with me as a sideline.

Amos, the ex-cowboy, opens the discussion.

"A bull is a bad thing to have to kill with your bare hands, Nixy. 'Cause you'll never do it, no matter how strong a guy you are."

"No," I say. "In fact I want to seek out something that might *represent* a bull."

Amos shakes his head. "There's nothing to represent a bull other than its own mean, vile self," he continues. "You try sitting on one at a rodeo and then tell me they don't hold a grudge. You fall under a horse, it will do its damned best to avoid treading on you. Do the same with a bull, and that evil spirit will tramp your head into the dirt, then turn around and do the same with the rest of you."

I try to interrupt.

"Chief—" I start to say.

"Hey," says Jim, "you did a rodeo, Chief?"

"Sure thing, Babe," says Amos.

I feel like throwing up my arms and surrendering.

"Wow," says Jim, "I'd never want to get near a bull, let alone annoy it and then try to sit on its back. You're right, Chief, they're just plain mean."

"You can say that again," says Amos, rubbing his chin.

"You'll never show it who's boss; the only thing it understands is some sort of brute."

Johnny laughs. "Well, that's sorted things for Nix then."

The Boys all laugh.

Rici wraps his arm around my shoulder. "We've established he's crazy, but I'm all for following him. Nix needs a bull next to keep his luck going – maybe *ours* as well. So any ideas what will do instead of a bull? A fat Jap who's just the same size as Nix?"

"Yeah," says Jim, "if Nix can jump on a big Jap's back and stay there for ten seconds – that will count, won't it?"

I have the sudden feeling that I'm in some sort of surreal comedy – or I'm suffering alcohol withdrawal. It's the fact that they're *having* this debate at all.

The surreal feeling fades in a trice, and in its place arises a horrible, gnawing fear that I'll not be able to find anything. I'm *certain* now that I *have* to do it.

Rici and I share a look as the Boys eventually fall silent – they are all imagining performing the deed. I nod to him. At least the Boys have their danders up, and are focused on what needs to be done here – death without compassion.

We are due to start the attack at 0900 hours. Moving onto office hours, Rici said. I told him I hoped that we *would* also be finished by 1700 hours, since I have some after-hours drinking to catch up on. He says he'll join me.

The idea is to assist the 3rd Marines' efforts to gain control of the high ground lying on the left of the line. Elements of the 9th will fight to join up with us on the right.

I think to myself that it doesn't seem proper somehow to sum up so briefly what will be required from the Boys in the next few hours. This will not be work for the faint-hearted – this is the point where I believe the Bougainville Blues will turn into Grisly Guam. All along the line we are moving up supplies for the men possessing the demolition charges and the men with the flame-throwers – "spit and roast" is a phrase one of the Boys has coined.

Our replacement fireman was moved up earlier this morning. He looks as though he managed to get a wash before he landed, but it doesn't seem to have been the morning for his monthly shave. He's nineteen, from Maine, and has a large nose. He introduced himself to Rici and me as Foglong, after Foghorn Leghorn the cartoon rooster. The steel in his eyes gives us the clue that he has done his fair share of Work, and neither Rici nor I are tempted to josh with him. If he can kill, and doesn't give a shit about having a joke name, that's his affair.

Foglong, too, is now checking his equipment and, as I've never taken too close a look at a flame-thrower, I decide to ask him about it. Anybody prepared to carry such pressurized hell on his back has surely got to have a story to tell.

I squat down beside him, reaching for a cigarette under my poncho, but then I remember and my hand stops halfway to my pocket.

"My Pa has a theory that those smokes will kill you one day." Foglong grins on observing my frozen stance. "Especially if you light up near me."

I decide I like him.

"So," he says, "what do you want to know?"

"What makes you think I'm interested?"

"Everyone is – eventually. I assumed it was my personality at first."

I like him even more.

He pats the tanks, which look like the cylinders you'd find alongside welding gear in a workshop.

"The M-Two-dash-Two backpack flame-thrower," he says. "Uncle Sam's choice of inferno."

He takes a breath and gets into his stride.

"This one has compressed butane," he says, pointing to the tank with an obvious valve on top. "And this here," he taps the screw-top of the second one with a finger, "is the jellied juice. Imagine thick snot, like after a bad cold, that you can put a match to – this is just as sticky, just as difficult to remove."

As I make mental notes, I decide I'll have to find some other way to describe it when I write it up.

The rain stops – as quickly as that. As if a faucet has just been turned off. We look at each other, shrug and remove our ponchos – at least we won't be fighting in the rain.

"Here," he says, "give me a hand."

Foglong stands and hitches the harness of his flame-thrower over one shoulder, and I help him get his other arm through. He grunts as he takes the strain.

"So," he says, after adjusting a strap, "this is the business end."

He holds out the nozzle connected by a tube to the cylinders. It's as though he's presenting a rifle for inspection.

"Two triggers," he says. "One in front ignites a bleed-off from the gas."

"That's why you carry a Zippo lighter?" I interrupt, letting him know how I've seen others get these things working.

He smiles. "The M Two's better than the M One – still need a Zippo as a back-up, though, if the sparks fail. The second trigger lets the shit get going – the compressed butane forces it out. Gas and shit then pass through the ignition system, and one sheet of sticky flame takes off into the wild blue yonder. Burnsville."

Foglong makes sure he is comfortable and wiggles his right-hand trigger finger at me.

"Mustn't be too heavy with little Joe here – just short squirts, or after ten seconds you're pissing in the wind with nothing but your pecker to wave at them."

Now I *really* like him.

He doesn't tell me it all, though, not about the disadvantages, but I know that this thing has about the same accuracy and effectiveness as my Colt 45 – fifty yards tops.

You have to get in close.

So close that you can see the expression on the Enemy's face as you squeeze that trigger.

That close?

I turn and look around wildly, then I stop. I'm not dreaming this time: her voice is as sweet and as clear as before. I nod to myself – my little insanity, my taotaomona ghost, my Greek-English diva. She's back, she's back!

You're back?

Yes, yes I am.

God, I'm not dreaming. My grandfather was right, ghosts are real. You certainly pick your moments. I'm tense, tired and scared, so you turn up – any connection?

It's deliberate. I'm trying to be chronological.

But don't get in the way of what I have to do here, will you?

I understand.

Umm, chronological? What are you talking about?

Timing, I'm talking about timing.

As I said, I'm tired, confused and frightened. Yes, you have timing, okay.

"You all right?" asks Foglong.

I'd forgotten he's there. I hope I haven't been talking out loud.

"Yeah," I say, "I'm okay. Rici and I will act as your cover."

"That's good." He continues to give me a strange look, then turns away. I can smell a hint of petroleum on him.

You have to get so close, that you can actually see their faces?

That close, and it isn't pleasant. But then, I think that's the idea.

God, it's modern-day Greek fire.

And just as scary. Those Byzantine guys had it right – the thought of this being fired at an enemy could make the opposition stick up their hands and give up. That's if they're not this Enemy.

I have to ask. I think I don't want to know the answer, but I have to ask. Have you seen it working – close up?

I've seen it working.

My God.

God has nothing to do with this, Serena. This is Man's work – with the devil riding on his back.

"Okay, Foglong," I say. "I think it's about time."

What's happening?

It's an attack. Jim and Hank are out on the left. Johnny and Bill are out on the right. Rici, Amos, Ron and I will give Foglong support in the middle.

"Let's go," shouts Rici.

You staying?

I'm staying – do you mind?

Do I have a choice? 'Course not – the Boys think I'm on my way to being shot to pieces, in both mind and body, as it is. A little disembodied voice between friends can't do any harm.

Where are you now?

Where? What do you mean?

With Hercules? Where are you now with his labours?

Ah, I've got to find myself a bull. The Boys know about it. Except for our fireman. Everybody in the squad is now aware that their tame combat correspondent is after something representing a bull. They really appear keen for me to get it.

Pardon?

The Boys know what I'm doing. But I haven't let on that I've been prompted by you. That would be too much for them.

You're halfway through, then?

Plain sailing – I think I'm charmed.

I'm glad.

I see the Boys moving, so I check my carbine again and follow Foglong.

We start the advance.

W Day +2. 10.36. Asan River Ridgeline.

The terrain rises in places, and that's the least of our difficulties. While there are pockets of undergrowth that have been altered by naval bombardment into rough, circular gaps, the thick jungle growth prevents rapid forward movement. I feel as though I've shrunk and been thrown into some verdant greenhouse constructed by Boris Karloff, portraying a Transylvanian botanist. Thick-stemmed, broad-leafed plants tower above me like giant green rhubarb stalks; there are shrubs with leaves the texture and shape of water lilies, but tens of times larger, casting more shadows into the gloom. As always, the swarms of insects seem to find their way inside our uniforms. This lack of visibility makes us all nervous – there has been little contact yet with the Enemy.

Over to my side, and just ahead, Rici raises a hand beckoning us all to stop. I seize the opportunity to take a few deep breaths. Then Rici gestures for me, and Foglong, to make our way over to him. There must be an Enemy position visible up ahead. One that needs spit and roast. I glance at my weapon, as if to confirm I've still got it in my hands. Foglong and I crouch down beside Rici, who points and we look. I squint, and see, about twenty yards ahead, just as the ground veers up, there are plants growing in seemingly abnormal ways. It's obviously a concealed entrance to a cave. You'd miss it altogether if you hadn't been to Bougainville.

We'll have to clean it out; it's a simple enough technique. We'll move closer, giving protection to our man with the flame-thrower, lob in a grenade, then let the fireman give anybody still alive inside a squirt of fire. Unless the cave runs deeper into the hillside, anything near the entrance will not survive. After the smoke disperses, we'll climb inside to check. That's the theory, and I know it works.

So why do I feel a rush of unease?

I haven't yet found this bull, that's why. I haven't yet worked out a viable equivalent.

Am I going back into action without the proper talisman?

Foglong fires up his M Two and we move ahead, me in front and partly to one side. I brush the leaves of a bush away from my face, then do it again to remove the rainwater it's left behind.

We are soon in position, with Foglong to the left of the cave entrance, myself to the right. Rici is further back down the slope, amid the vegetation. I edge nearer, at a crouch, then slowly push a knee into the soft earth, bracing my other foot to make myself comfortable. I take a slow, deep breath, turn to nod briefly to Foglong, then I pull the pin and toss a grenade inside the cave. I breathe out again, and get my carbine ready. I can hear several thuds as the grenade bounces around inside. There is immediately the sound of scuffling, and some excited shouts erupt from behind the leaves covering the entrance.

"Live one," comments Foglong.

"Check." I ready myself to let loose with my carbine. I imagine the same panic in the cave as I generated at the blockhouse.

The shouting from inside gets louder, and it seems they're crashing into one another in their panic. There's more than three voices, and they merge into one high-pitched cry. But the Enemy leaves it too long to decide what they should do.

Crack-boom!

The grenade explodes, and a plume of smoke gushes out and upwards, with leaves, dirt and shards of shrapnel whizzing alongside. Foglong moves quickly after the faster-moving fragments have shot over our heads. He's done this before, and it's second nature. He clambers up the slope in front of me, rams the nozzle of his flame-thrower into the cave opening, and lets loose one swift blast.

Shriek-whhhhosh!

The flame surges out of the nozzle, the howl of its eruption intense and painful to the ears. I think of dragons roaring: a primeval screech, a sound generating a basic terror.

Shriek-whhhhosh!

Foglong licks the flame from left to right. Below its high-pitched roar can be heard the cries from inside the cave. That will stop soon, or the Enemy will be breathing in the flames.

Shriek-whhhhosh!

The screams cease, but Foglong continues for a fraction of a second longer. The remnant of the liquid fire wanes and dribbles to a finish. I take another breath, and relish the humid, jungle air filling my lungs – before the gruesome smells of the flamethrower and its consequences hit me.

We wait, listening. A second passes. And another.

Foglong turns to me and starts to say something, but is interrupted. We instinctively move backwards, unintentionally providing an open stage for what is happening. The burned and shriveled remains of the plants surrounding the doorway are thrust to one side, and a fireball, with the rough outline of a man, staggers outside. Somewhere inside this blaze, inside this fierce flowering heat, inside this Halloween dance of spluttering inferno, is a single Enemy. This man inside the heart of the fire makes a sound no human might recognize. He takes another step towards us, bending down into a crouch, his burning hands still clasping his rifle. The face I glimpsed for a split second, as he emerged from the bunker, melts into the mist of enveloping flame, and he begins to blacken and crackle.

Though his face disappears, he brings his rifle to bear on us, still functioning.

Before his fingers seize up, he lets loose a couple of shots.

There is no chance at all of him being able to see us anymore – but he's snatching his opportunity to take one of us with him. He staggers forward another step. We say nothing.

Shriek-whhhhosh! Foglong sprays him with another half-a-second's worth of extra hell. The flaming, shambling gargoyle drops his rifle and brings the remains of his hands to the stub that is his head. His action galvanizes the rest of us.

Ba-ba-ba!

Tat-tat-tat!

The Enemy jerks and squirms, finally collapses to the ground, then issues a long sigh.

We move nearer. There is some terrible compunction to witness what is left. The choking stench deters no one – our desire to see is all. The distorted shape of the Enemy emerges from the smoke. A claw of a hand twitches.

Oh, my God.

He's dead, Serena. That's just a death spasm.

I put a few bullets into the remains of his head.

He's dead.

Oh, my God.

Yes, oh, my God.

We move on.

I feel sick.

Death is never pleasant.

But that is obscene.

I know, so tell it to the same guy you saw getting cut in two on the beach.

I don't need reminding. And that doesn't make this right.

It may not be right, it may not be moral, but this is war, and people get killed. They're people who have every intention of doing the same to us.

Us or them, then?

That's it, simple math. If we kill more of the Enemy than the Enemy kill of us, we win.

You shouldn't talk to me about mathematics.

Okay then, how about chess?

Chess?

That's right, chess. You can still win a game with just a king and a pawn, you know, but the best likelihood of success comes by overpowering in numbers. That means using skill, tactics and strategy.

Is this just a game to you?

Don't insult me. I have never taken a life that I've felt ashamed of. This is how wars are conducted and won. They shoot, bomb and bayonet us; we shoot, bomb and bayonet the Enemy. The Enemy attack us with as much barbarity as the Enemy can muster; we do the same and use fire as well. They torture, behead and defile any soldiers or marines they capture, since they don't take prisoners; we take no prisoners either. That is war. That is my war. And if I compare it to a chess game, it is my right. Only a combatant can judge another. And, notwithstanding my seeming indifference to incinerating another human being, I want our side to win this game. We have to.

At the price of losing your humanity?

Don't patronize me.

Oh, I'm not. Please believe me, I'm not. But aren't there other options?

Not here – not with this war machine. I'm doing what I can here so that we win – it's all about duty, country, family and justice. There can be no appeasement here.

But to force men to witness things like that. Surely those sights will turn men's minds?

So that they hear voices in their heads?

Yes.

On that I can agree.

No, I didn't mean it like that, I didn't mean it like that.

I suppose I am at the limit. I'm tired, confused and scared. Now, I'm intending to record all this savagery, because, I concur, it would have been terrific if this could have been avoided, but the Enemy gives us no choice. There are some things that you have to stand up to.

The truth? You'll record it?

I will, and I have.

Be careful, Phoenix. History seems to indicate that those in power hate people revealing the truth.

Ah-ha, death clears away the bullshit.

"You okay, Nix?" It's Ron.

"What?" I ask him.

He comes over to me and peers into my face.

"You've gone pale," he says. "You going to be sick?"

He nods back to the bunker that the rest of the Boys have finished clearing out.

"I thought you'd seen worse," he says. "At Bougainville?"

I nod, it seems the easiest response.

"I have," I say. "It gets to me sometimes."

Really?

Yes, really.

I had the impression it leaves you unmoved.

It affects me.

"Come on, Chico," I say to him. "I'm okay, let's move."

We advance some more into the jungle, with our weapons of fiery death, and with the sound of a sudden gentle weeping that tears my heart apart echoing in my head.

W Day +2. 14.21. Asan River Ridgeline.

Progress is still slow: we have had to destroy three more bunkers. Serena has stopped talking to me and I can't say I blame her. The insides of those caves, when we have finished with them, are not places to discuss even in abstract terms. But I take notes, and photographs, because it's my job and it's the target I set myself. There has been no repetition of the Enemy still standing up to fight as he burns, but the dragon-roar of Foglong's flame-thrower has left other objects that I inspect and take pictures of. Someone, somewhere, will want to use them, I hope. There's nothing worse than reporting the truth, only to find that someone else decides the public shouldn't have the choice of passing judgment. Not telling the true story, as it is, provokes more anger in me than anything the Enemy has done. The public should be allowed to see what we are doing in their name, see what fires we are setting to cleanse the world of the Enemy.

We are on level ground again, and I stop to wash my mouth out with alcohol and spit away the soot. All the boys are a shade darker in color than they were this morning; we don't voice it, but it will be good to wipe the smoke and grime from our skin. It would be helpful if it were to rain again. My hand shakes, so I lower my elbow to my chest – it reduces the jitters as I drink. Another swig, another spit. My throat is dry.

I slowly replace the cap, roll my shoulders, fiddle at my lower lip with my tongue. That damned panic is back. I still haven't seen anything that I could count as my next task.

Am I up to this self-imposed test?

I think about deliberately losing, about not completing what I'm engaged in, and I start to wonder how the end will turn out. A bullet in the head, like Joe? A mortar strike?

Getting wounded and then being left to be discovered by the Enemy?

I notice Rici as he casts a glance in my direction. I grimace and he frowns, but I'll not bother telling him what I'm thinking. I swear to myself; I don't like my imagination sometimes. I look around to check the situation. Rici's now moving ahead with Foglong, Amos and Ron. To my left I can just about see Johnny and Bill, and Jim and Hank. Everybody has fanned out; we are advancing cautiously. The Boys place their feet with care. In combat you get attuned to unexpected sounds or silences.

Jim and Hank wave me over. They are now about twenty yards ahead, crouching down, and they are both grinning.

"Look." Jim, points ahead into a clearing. "Who'd have believed it?"

For a moment – with that sparkle in his eyes – I see him as he should be at his age, a seventeen-year-old surprised by the wonder and beauty of life. Not the hard-nosed killing-machine he actually is, not the man who has seen the things I've also seen.

I stare through the gap in the trees.

"Who'd believe it?" he asks again.

I can't, for one. My grandfather had once told me that water buffalo were left to roam wild on Guam, but I'd forgotten all about it – until now.

It's a bull!

Oh, Serena? Ah, of course, it's a Hercules moment. Yes, it's a bull – but it's a bloody big water buffalo, and I'm not going anywhere near it.

"Jesus," I say to Jim and Hank, "the Chief used to *ride* things like this?"

Thirty yards away, in a patch of tall grass, the bull stands with its square head erect, its large ears pricked. It is a massive animal, of genuinely mythical proportions, and its huge stubby horns – wider at their base than I am across my chest – curve off the center of its skull and out to each side. It makes the average oxen look like a child's toy. I can't begin to imagine anyone controlling such a beast.

"This is easy," says Jim. Before I can do anything, he brings his BAR to bear on the animal.

Ba-ba-ba!

The BAR coughs with its customary blast. I have doubts about the caliber of bullet needed to do the job – I think an elephant gun would be more appropriate. The first few rounds Jim fires into it cause splotches of blood to appear along the bull's flank. But these merely seem to annoy the animal; it snorts, paws the ground and lowers its awesome head as if to charge. We all look at each other. Hank begins to move away. I don't blame him.

Ba-ba-ba!

Jim aims more carefully. This time he hits it in the head, just below the juncture of its horns. The bull stops moving, the muscles in its legs trembling – then the animal wobbles, tries another step towards us. It collapses, blasting a last snort from its nostrils.

"There you go," says Jim to me, with a seventeen-year old's beaming smile. "Saved you the trouble."

Beside him, Hank is frowning.

"I don't know, Babe, I don't know," he says. "I thought Nix was supposed to do it."

"Oh, shit," says Jim, giving me a worried look. "For real?"

Before I can answer, from the other side of the clearing comes a familiar sound.

Pock! Pock! Pock! *Mortars!*

Snap-crack! Snap-crack!

An arsenal of weapons opens up, and the Enemy is firing at us in force.

"Take cover!" I yell.

We all dive and love the ground.

The onslaught is tremendous – the Enemy has been waiting for us in a planned ambush, and they want to take out every one of us. Jim, Hank and I are too exposed – none of us has the inclination to raise ourselves into a position where we can attempt to answer the Enemy's fire. We wriggle backwards to get some distance, a bit of cover, between the Enemy and us.

Pock! Pock!

Whoo-bang! Whoo-bang!

The mortar rounds begin to explode around us. One lands about twelve feet from us, in a clump of bamboo so that, along with the earth and hot metal, splinters of bamboo threaten to tear us apart. The Enemy's bullets continue to provide singing metal rain. As we struggle towards a dip in the ground, Jim's helmet wobbles and begins to fall off. Hank reaches across to bang it back on firmly, and Jim grunts his thanks.

We make it to the hollow, where Jim sets up his BAR and promptly starts to send off rounds in the general direction of the muzzle flashes in the undergrowth. The clatter of firing on either side of us indicates the rest of the Boys are letting loose. I catch a movement in the corner of my eye and see someone hurl a grenade across the clearing. I fire off a few shots, and try to remain single-minded.

Phoenix?

Leave me alone, Serena.

Phoenix, please.

Shut up!

I stop to change the magazine of my carbine. The absolute din shows no sign of abating; in fact the Enemy seems to have found more men. I squirm around and see, through the foliage, Foglong retreating as quickly as he can. I realize that though his "jellied-juice" tank must be empty, his cylinder of butane could still tear him apart if a bullet caught it. Even as I think this, there is a sharp metallic thwack as a bullet does indeed slap into one of his tanks. I wince, but the cylinder holds and doesn't rupture. Foglong continues ducking and diving, while I see that he's trying to unclip the flame-thrower from his shoulders. I turn back and give him covering fire until I figure he is out of sight, and I make a quick calculation that we're all getting low on ammunition and cannot hold up for much longer. Rici dashes across twenty yards of open ground and slides down beside me.

"Phew," he says, "and on the eighth day the devil created the ambush."

He then jerks a thumb over a shoulder. "Vizi and Groucho will give us cover. Let's move back and regroup."

"Okay," I say.

We all rise to a crouch and begin to weave our way back. Bullets still zip and buzz around us, and I can't help feeling that one will soon find a home somewhere in my body.

The Enemy sends us more mortars.

We run faster. Jim starts shouting. "I'm sorry. I'm sorry."

We crash through something resembling a giant cabbage, and finally begin to slow down.

"What is Jim going on about?" asks Rici.

I shrug as we stop. "He shot my bull."

"What?" he asks.

"Babe shot my bull."

"You're kidding me," Rici says.

He turns and cuffs Jim on the top of his helmet.

"Bad boy," he says, trying not to laugh as he looks at me, "I'll write your mom. Now let's get out of here."

"I'm sorry," repeats Jim as he inspects his BAR. "I'm sorry."

I pat his back.

"Don't worry," I say, "don't worry. Let's move."

"I'm sorry, Nix, I'm sorry. This is all my fault."

"Move it," orders Rici, and the cuff on Jim's helmet is much harder this time.

As the mortars continue falling where we lay moments before, the bullets somehow continue to miss us. We beat our retreat in a more organized way.

But even though Rici is laughing, and Jim himself is beginning to smile, I can't help wondering if he is right – that he's broken the spell and that our luck is changing.

It should have been me who did it. It should have been me.

NINETEEN

Horses are no longer what they used to be. King Diomedes owned a stable in which he kept four savage mares, who didn't eat oats or hay – they were fed the bodies of his guests. It should be noted that the act of visiting friends had a slightly more dangerous edge to it, in those days, but that was not the concern of Hercules, who was instructed to bring the mares to Eurystheus to complete his eighth labour. How he accomplished that was to be his own problem (secure horseboxes being an invention of the future).

The wind blew a September breeze of salt, seaweed and foam across the docks on the day Hercules set sail with a crew of volunteers all eager to be associated with yet another noble exploit from the legendary maestro of tasks. They were not disappointed.

After travelling for many days across the Aegean – the wind on their backs, fresh polish on their armour, jokes and banter on their lips – they landed on shore and the expectation of action became immediate. As the crew jumped down onto the beach to make their boat secure, Hercules immediately set off on his own towards Diomedes' stables. The men he left behind nodded amongst themselves as they coiled ropes and pulled in flapping sails – Hercules on a mission was like a storm-force wind.

The acquisition – or theft – of the nags was over quickly.

Unarmed men tend to get short shrift from Greek heroes, and the grooms who tended the stables were no exception, giving up their charges with little more than a scuffle. The mares were enormous, powerful-looking animals – each needing three grooms to hold them still. And as each was brought from its stable, Hercules approached it and slapped its hindquarters. Each time the said mare would rise, strike out at the air with its hooves, then pull at its halters, dragging its grooms around the yard. This did not appear to upset the grooms; there was a small possibility they were going to be glad to see the back of these beasts that eyed them continually with naked hunger. The hero even wondered if they were being just *too* cooperative.

As Hercules arrived back at his ship, the four snarling mares pulling his chariot at a speed he'd never travelled at before, the crew pointed over to the horizon behind Hercules, and he looked back. The grooms he had mercifully spared had obviously alerted the king's soldiers, and they were gaining upon him. Hercules nodded to himself, brought his chariot to a stop on the beach with a lurching skid, and left it in the charge of a young man. Hercules then headed back on foot to assist the rest of his crew, which had run ahead to engage the approaching force.

But Hercules had a better plan than fighting while outnumbered. Remembering his lesson at the Augean stables, with lightning speed, and a strength that left some of the oncoming soldiers dumbstruck and stationary, he broke down a dam that had been constructed to rescue low-lying land from the sea. The subsequent deluge swept down onto the plain, engulfing most of the army and sending the remainder back the way they had come. And then, when Hercules chased after them, it being the wont of Greek heroes to finish the job with a flourish, he found Diomedes to be among their number. Hercules was not as sympathetic to the king as he had been with the man's grooms. (Even though he was technically stealing from him, Hercules thought Diomedes trod on shaky moral ground when it came to the question of using his guests as sustenance.) Hercules walked up to him as he floundered in the mud and clubbed him back to the ground, then dragged the body back as food for the king's own mares.

He discovered that they had been impatient for their next feed time.

Alas, there was little left of the youth put in charge of the mares and, after the second bonus meal of the king, the animals remained placid enough to endure the voyage home without incident. Surprisingly, they stayed that way even after Eurystheus rashly set them free.

Fortunately for the tourist industry of that time, the mares made their way straight to Mount Olympus, where they were promptly eaten by the other savage beasts that roamed the countryside.

TWENTY

W Day +2. 19.44. Asan River Ridgeline.

We're dug in and licking our wounds. With all the strange, magical things that have been happening to my mind and my memories, I shouldn't have been surprised, but it turns out that Jim's killing of the bull water buffalo was actually a piece of good luck. It meant the Enemy opened up on us sooner than they did elsewhere along the line. The Hercules influence continues to work, and the death of a bull saved us.

On our left flank the 3rd got put under tremendous pressure, those on their extreme far left having to deal with a counter-strike of evil proportions. Sounds of their battle filtered through to my senses. Even though Uncle Sam's marines were using everything available to them (clattering and roaring Shermans, stomach-thumping artillery, a crashing crescendo of naval rounds and swooping waves of aircraft), they were pulled to a halt and nearly beaten back. The sounds of their struggle echoed and boomed all day.

It's good that we're starting to reach high ground, as it means we can have the beachhead secure and thus be able to land more equipment. More chess pieces for us? If it weren't for the ferociousness of the Enemy's play we'd probably get cocky and make mistakes.

Casualties have been high today, but the Boys have got away with only a few scratches and nicks. So, as far as they are concerned – and for me – the Hercules winning streak continues.

Except for our foxhole position, maybe. The terrain has the advantage of being more open (all the palm trees around here having been slashed to pieces) which gives us a clear view of any potential encroachment. The panorama has its downside too: I can see at least forty dead Enemy amongst the broken palm roots and crushed bamboo, though I count only six dead marines. It seems the Enemy had fought as they always fight – with savagery until the end.

This is the most dead Enemy I've ever seen in one go, as now the war moves on without them. The flies build in clouds over each body and the stench heralds a night of uneasy sleep. You can get pissed with the dead sometimes.

I take a photograph, and I debate whether to take one of Johnny and Amos as, before dusk closes in, they move methodically among the clusters of dead. None of the Enemy here has a sword, but Johnny finds an 8mm Nambu – the rubbish equivalent of the German Luger – and he holds it up for me to see. I lower my camera and cock my head to one side. It's not Johnny's pose that attracts my attention, it's just that I can't understand what Amos is doing. He is down on one knee and has opened the mouth of one of the corpses. He reaches in with his fingers, but doesn't seem to have any success with what he's attempting, so he draws his bayonet and works at the Enemy's mouth for a minute. I hear him swear, then Amos stands up, clips his bayonet back onto his rifle, stamps a boot hard down on the Enemy's chest, then smashes his rifle butt into the corpse's face and jaw.

He does this again and again, then reaches down and pokes his fingers into the resulting mess and pulls something out. Amos wipes it on his jacket and holds it up and I catch the glint of gold. Johnny wanders over and inspects the Chief's find, then they turn back to their work with renewed vigor, clambering over the shattered palm trunks and into shell craters, where they find eight more bodies that need to have their jaws cracked open. Then Johnny and Amos return to their foxholes, strolling as casually as if they've just been out on the town.

Meanwhile I sit in my foxhole and tremble. I have accumulated a day's-worth of sweat, there is dirt and muck in every corner of my body, I am covered in the thin, buttery coating of smoke that the flame-thrower has generated, and I have spent ten minutes watching corpses being broken open for a fragment of gold. I long for my fabled river of moonshine.

Phoenix?

Phoenix?

Serena. Hello.

Are you – are you okay?

Okay? Take a look around, Serena. Welcome to the golden land of my forefathers.

I'm so sorry, I'm so ... I never ... I could never have imagined what it's like to be here. Never.

What did you expect? This is what can happen to men when they have to kill other men. I'm just like everyone else here; we're doing our bit, which will mean someone else won't have to. We know the price and we're prepared to pay it. The price we pay here is to lose a little humanity from our souls and have it replaced with a different variation. I doubt any man who survives this will ever want to fight anyone again. That's the cost and payment for our being here. What we will take home is a host of demons that will hopefully take away our rage at the smaller things that irritate. But tell me, you sound intelligent, you sound wise, Serena, tell me, how much is a man expected to take? How much of his soul does a man have to exchange before he is set free by becoming totally mad?

I don't know Phoenix. I really don't know.

Well, I can tell you: it's the sum total of all I have seen, all that I have done. And I don't think I have anything more to give.

You have Hercules.

I have Hercules, yes. I have convinced myself – and the Boys. I have convinced myself I have some stupendous collection of tasks to complete to save my life. That's how it seems to me, anyhow, but what's next? Some wild tale about some damn horses, I seem to remember. God, that makes a lot of sense.

You have me.

Yes, I do. Yes, I do, Serena. But what are you? An imagined beauty of my own invention? Is that the trade I'm making? I get to see all this, but I'm granted you as a prize? What do you have to offer my poor eyes in return, Serena? What's your beauty?

I wish I could show you.

Yes, I wish you could, too. Tell me about yourself, Serena. Talk to me.

No, you tell me about you. Tell me *all* the good things, tell me the stories of your youth. Take yourself away from here by taking me with you and telling me about your life.

You have a crafty way of changing subjects.

It's given as a birthright to all us girls.

Is that a fact?

That's a fact. It's a safety device — keeps you boys on your toes.

As we should be kept?

As you should be. You're quite enlightened for a man of your time.

My time? I'm a man of the moment.

Of course. Who taught you that?

My grandfather.

Grandfathers are always wise.

It's the age thing. It's about being closer to death and therefore taking delight in the life of youth. My grandfather and I would have great conversations now — we both of us now know about death and life.

Tell me about him.

You're changing the subject.

Maybe, but tell me about your grandfather.

He took me on trips all around America. I think he was amazed at how big the States were compared to Guam. He said he owed it to his new home to see what made it what it was. It was a contagious enthusiasm, and I must have traveled more around the States than most any American I know. Before the war, the majority of the Boys here never made it out of their town or city, let alone their State.

Tell me your favourite adventures with him.

You don't like the subject drifting back to this place, do you?

Not if I can help it.

You have a lovely voice, you know.

You've told me that before.

It's worth repeating. You have a lovely voice.

You've said it three times now, and according to some fairy tales I seem to remember, I have to appear before you now.

I wish you would.

"Hey, Nix," interrupts Jim.

You're wanted.

I know.

"What's up, Babe?" I ask. ·

Babe?

It's a nickname.

"The Boys have been having a talk," Jim continues.

"A bitch more like," I mutter.

"Yeah, yeah," says Jim. "It's this Dead Pool Poker game."

I notice that the rest of the Boys are gathering in a group around me. Rici is saying nothing – just staring, being Buster. I shake my head; I must look a sorry sight if the others are anything to go by.

All this filth we have wallowed in.

"What's Dead Pool Poker?" asks Foglong.

"It's a game Nix shouldn't win," says Bill.

I look at Rici – he still says nothing. Bill carries on.

"The Chief says if we're helping you do this Hercules thing you've got going, then you should forfeit your part in the poker game."

I look over to Amos. He is standing there, cradling his BAR, his usual easy smile on his face, as if waiting for all this to be sorted out so that he can head off to the range and poke some cattle. He spits a wad of tobacco to the ground, and I think of him collecting teeth.

"That's only because," I turn back to Bill, "I've got a better hand than him, maybe the best hand of the lot."

"Well, have you?" asks Ron.

"Why not let's see," I say. I reach for my cards.

I pause.

"Shall we?" I ask again. "I mean, what have we got to lose?"

Hank steps up. "Isn't it too soon?" he says.

A couple of the Boys nod.

"I don't remember any time limit being mentioned," I say. "But it's not me driving this issue, it's you guys. So, shall we, just to make it all the more exciting?"

I take out my cards, and Bill quickly follows, then Ron, then all the others in a flurry, and then finally Rici, still standing Buster quiet.

We flash the cards and work out who's got what. I don't think Amos has told anyone how he and I have collected some other sets of cards, so there are still some confident glints in a number of eyes.

Bill fans his hand. "Here."

He has two Jokers, the Jack of Spades, the Nine of Spades and the Six of Clubs: Three of a kind – Jacks.

"Damn, Groucho," says Ron, "you got me beat."

Ron has a Joker, the Two of Clubs and the Two of Diamonds, with the Nine and Four of Diamonds. Three of a kind – Twos.

Hank, Jim and Johnny are shaking their heads.

Johnny laughs. "I've got a measly pair of Jacks, even with a damn wild card."

Johnny shows his Joker, Jack of Diamonds, Eight of Clubs, Seven, and Five of Hearts.

What have you got?

A full house, Aces over Queens. Jim and Hank aren't the worry. But let me concentrate and work this out.

I'm rooting for you.

So am I.

Jim and Hank confirm the obvious.

Jim has a Joker, but only the Ace of Clubs, the Ten of Diamonds, the Seven of Spades and the Four of Clubs to back it up. A pair – Aces.

Hank has a Joker, the Jack and Ten of Clubs, the Five of Spades and the Five of Clubs. Two pairs – Jacks over Fives.

This leaves just three of us to show. Foglong leads the interest, and the rest of the Boys circle Amos, Rici and me. Amos is first to weaken, since he knows what I've got, and he thrusts his cards out into the open. Hank whistles and Johnny curses, then laughs.

"That's some high flush," he says.

Amos has put together a Joker and the Ace, Ten, Nine and Eight of Hearts. It's a dangerous hand if he gets anymore Jokers.

"Well," says Rici, "I got your full house beat, mister."

He's still guessing, but Rici plays cards better than I do. He flashes the King of Clubs, the King and Queen of diamonds, and the King and Queen of Hearts: Full house – Kings over Queens.

You've got him beat!

I know.

"I've got you beat," I say, and show everyone my beautiful full house. Rici smiles, but some of the Boys explode with a volley of curses in my direction.

Amos leads the assault. He's known for some time what I've got, but he's pretending he's just found out – like the rest of the Boys.

"Fuck you, Nixy!" he says. "How much money do you rich sons of bitches need? That's *it*, you bastard! You can fuck around with your stupid tasks, labors or whatever damn fool thing it is you've got going. You can do that shit all by yourself now."

He addresses the rest of the Boys. He is actually shaking.

God, he's angry.

Tough, I got him beat. Ha!

I see you like winning.

Too right.

"The only way any one of us is going to beat him," says Amos, "is when one of us gets hit and someone takes his cards to make a better hand. That's if Mister Death Fingers doesn't get to them first."

Not everybody is with him, but I see a couple of nods and sneers in my direction. I can't help remembering what Amos had said about Joe's and Frank's hands – low and busted.

Ah, this is not what Joe had planned.

Joe?

A good man. He's dead, shot in the head on the beach.

Oh, that was him?

Yes.

Rici coughs. The Boys fall silent and turn to face him.

"I seem to remember that's the idea, isn't it? It's why it's called *Dead* Pool Poker, isn't it?" he says. He puts his cards back into his top pocket, and pats it.

"Just so you guys remember where I've got them."

Except for Amos, everybody else glances at one another, then does the same as Rici. Amos suddenly laughs – one of those big-belly-booming cackles that must have frightened the horses on the ranch where he worked.

"Ah, fuck it, Nixy," he says, "we'll see each other in hell."

"Sure," I say, "but not if I see you first."

Amos puts his cards away, shakes my hand, and nudges Foglong at the same time.

"Here, Foglong," he says, "this idiot thinks he's a Greek god."

Foglong cocks his head, purses his lips and puts a finger to them. He shakes his head. "No, you're wrong, Chief. This man looks like a card-sharp."

"Well, fuck you too, Foggy," says Amos.

The pair of them wander back to their foxholes to wait out the night, and they continue to bicker as Amos passes a nip of his chewing tobacco to Foglong. It's good, we're all buddies again.

I jump in my hole and wait for the night.

I even think about the possibility of sleep.

I need to dream of horses. And to contemplate a tension in

my stomach that I get every time I think about Serena. It's maddening – she seems so real.

You cannot desire ghosts.

I need to dream of horses.

Serena says nothing.

I need to dream of horses.

W Day +3. 07.14. Asan River Ridgeline.

I have taken a short walk just to check out the narrow road nearby and I squat down to one side of a bend and stare along the long straighter part that runs away to my left. I thought I heard a motorcycle earlier. *That* could represent the horse I need. But my reconnaissance is also an excuse – I have come here to clear my head because I am still troubled by the intense dreams of last night. I am now certain that coming to this island has made them frighteningly clear and brought confusion in a multitude of forms. During most of the night, and into the early hours, I spent my time waiting for Enemy incursions – listening to the odd firefight in the distance and drinking a bottle of *saki*. When I finally managed some sleep, the images that sliced through my head alternated from stark through to bizarre, and then beautiful. It was as confusing as hell.

At one point I saw a woman's face. The way it jiggled and shifted slightly every now and then, coupled with a comprehension that she was trying to hold her image steady, convinced me that I was seeing her face in a square bathroom mirror she was holding up in front of herself. It therefore appeared to me as if I was that woman. And while it was unsettling to think of myself transformed into another person, I had a suspicion as to who it was I was looking at. She had short dark hair, high cheekbones, and a style of circular boffin glasses that I didn't much care for, but this was compensated for by her having those cute sort of lips I love. I even changed my mind about the spectacles. For some reason, I knew instinctively that it was

Serena. While I immediately found myself excited and pleased at seeing her, it was the build-up of glimpses I had of where she was sitting that disturbed and frightened me.

Coming to this island has sparked peculiar states of night-mind.

She appeared to be in the same room where Tom used to paint, and where I used to spend time when taking breaks from my writing. (I had a tantalizing moment, as she moved the mirror, when I saw through the huge open French windows towards the green of the park and the golden buildings of Cambridge outside.) The positioning of the windows and the *size* of the room were identical, though there was something altogether alien about some of the items in the room.

For a start, Serena appeared to have her head clamped inside some sort of brace so that she could not turn her neck. Behind her, over her shoulders, there stood objects whose function I couldn't work out. But they reminded me somehow of the movies of my youth, with Boris Karloff and his instruments in a mad scientist's lab.

As if to reinforce the mad scientist analogy, behind these technological pieces of furniture on the wall behind there was a white board with symbols on it which I wouldn't even have understood if they were the right way around.

The room, and Serena, seemed so real – I could just see a glimpse of a rug on the floor, a door with the same large brass doorknob I remember; but the unfamiliar objects convinced me completely that I was in some sinister nightmare.

The final touch was recognizing the same watercolor Tom had just about finished on the day I heard my grandfather had died – except it was obviously now framed and hung on the wall. It was also fading with age.

Then Serena appeared to move and the room suddenly snapped into distorted and sliced variations of what I had just witnessed. I had that night terror of knowing I was dreaming but being unable to move.

And then I dreamt of jungle forests: dark, terrifying places where goblins called my name and things slobbered and panted in the shadows. Again and again I heard, in the distance, a whinnying, and I felt I must pursue this horse that lurked out of sight. I discovered I was wearing a suit of armor. As the goblins jeered and giant boars consumed the remains of other knights, as gigantic snakes rose out of murky slime pits and fearsome birds crashed their way through the upper branches, I struggled through thorny plants and slimy foliage to find this horse that sounded so powerful.

And then I did.

Only it wasn't a horse.

There, on the other side of a murky pool, fading in and out of vision because of the thick mist, stood a unicorn.

And I knew it to be evil.

Deadly evil.

This was no beast that demonstrated God's ability to create beautiful and wonderful things; this was a thing the Devil himself had tamed and ridden.

It was a huge stallion – no longer God's pure white, but soiled and gray, its coat matted. Its eyes were aflame with Hell's orange heat and it snorted fire from its nostrils. And, as if to exemplify an ultimate blasphemy, the huge horn that spiraled from the crest of its head was cracked and broken off at the tip. All dignity had been stripped from this ancient symbolism; the unicorn I saw in my nightmare was a mutation, a distortion of all the good that it might have represented.

And I knew I had to kill it. I had to remove this abomination from the world and so free the jungle from the monster's corruption and the iniquity of its very existence.

As it pawed the earth one last time, snorting flame, I steeled myself to look into its eye and we stared at each other. As I did so, I became aware that I no longer stood facing the beast in my knight's armor, but that I was now clad in a lion's skin and some sort of gladiatorial breastplate. I also realized that if I killed this beast I would become immortal. As I made my advance, with the clamor of what I knew to be a Greek army behind me, it turned and ran. So I ran after it. I ran after it with the usual slow progress of dreams. I ran for a long time, hunting it down, getting ever closer, seeking it out to its lair . . . until Rici shook me from the nightmare, handed me a drink, and told me to go for a walk just up the line to calm down before the new day's push.

The Unicorn was both Diomedes' horse and the Enemy combined.

This is a battle I *must* win.

Where is this damned motorcycle?

The road is nothing but a track that has been widened and abused by the heavy loads carried by Enemy vehicles. Pools of stagnant water lie in the deeper potholes, with their own colonies of mosquitoes, and, in places, the muddy ruts are so severe that the axles of anything lower than a lorry must get caught in them. On either side, and meeting above to make a roof for at least half the distance I can see of the track (about four hundred yards), the jungle encroaches, its presence a physical fact. It is making a rapid attempt to reclaim the empty spaces, and I get the impression that if I were to close my eyes for ten minutes, by the time I reopened them, not only would the track be covered with a plethora of new shoots, but also vines would be sneaking their way up my legs. Just looking down this road, where dirt alternates with mud, depending on whether the soil has remained in the shadow of this dense jungle or not, convinces me that whatever we think we are doing here, it is all just a transient effort in the end. Our follies, our mistakes of good intent, our dead – they will all be consumed by this vibrant life-force, which pays no heed to Man's frantic endeavors and pitiful struggles.

A thin layer of smoke wafts out of the undergrowth and I can tell by the smell that somewhere nearby a marine has recently employed a flame-thrower. I must have been so lost in my thoughts that I didn't hear it roar. Nor the resulting screams.

I dig my hand into the soil to scoop up a handful and sniff it. It's the second time I've done this since I've been here, and I try to uncover the reason. I find myself thinking about how much of this land would have been fertilized with the bones of my forebears. Even though America is where my blood now stirs, there is an attraction to this world of giant plants and murky pathways that calls to me through my grandfather. If it wasn't for the fact that my memories of the last few days would then haunt me, I think it's possible I could live here. At least for a while? Somewhere on the beach, where the winds wash in and blow away the heat. Where the unicorns are white.

I tense up, listening past the echo of distant gunfire. The sound comes faint at first, but it is so unlike anything I have heard in the last couple of days that it is easy to latch on to. It is regular, deep – an engine of some machine with a heart. It's also very familiar in the way my childhood memories are.

The engine is revved. It's the motorcycle.

I stare down the length of the track. I'm certain that we Americans don't have any bikes here and, besides, this guy is coming from the direction of the Enemy. I feel a flutter in my stomach as I get ready to fire.

The engine is revved again, then he comes around a distant bend and into view. He is standing up on the pegs so as to gain more control as he passes over the ruts. He looks for all the world like one of those guys on dirtbikes that race each other in the desert, always concentrating on the ground – taking quick glances to assess the next dip or rise. I take aim.

He's defenseless.

He has a gun.

He's riding a motorbike. He can't shoot you. It's just as if he's unarmed, Nix.

He's the Enemy. He's one of Diomedes' man-eating horses.

He gets closer. I hesitate.

I see the expression on his face. There is a slight smile, like he's enjoying the challenge of riding a bike on such an awful road.

He's thirty feet up the road, and he looks up to check the

bend he's approaching. The bend where I am crouching, aiming my weapon at him.

He sees me.

I hold my carbine steady.

Nix! Don't!

Sorry.

The smile has gone. He's so surprised he doesn't even slow down.

He's less than fifteen feet away. I can see a smear of grime on his forehead where he's mopped his brow with a dirty hand. He seems to seize up. He can't act.

The Enemy on the motorbike is twelve, ten, eight feet away when I open up.

Tat-tat!

Two quick shots.

Tat-tat!

Another two. The carbine gives those hard-kicking shoves back into my shoulder that I've never managed to get used to. Even as the thumps of it pulse into my neck, the bullets hit their target. Whether it is from their impact or simply an instinctive reaction, the rider jerks backward and the bike is raised onto its rear wheel. For a moment it contains all the theater of a circus act. But I can't smile. Before the bike becomes completely vertical, his hands release their grip on the handle-bars, his arms fly out to his sides, his hands scooping the empty air. He tumbles off, and the bike crashes down, flips over, and brushes past me as it careers into the undergrowth. The Enemy rolls into one of the ruts in the track. The bike engine splutters behind me, then suddenly stops. I go to check whether I've killed the Enemy or not. When I see the damage to his chest and his unblinking eyes, the pupils of which have already relaxed, opened wide enough to allow me to look into where his soul departed from, I know he is dead. He is dead and no longer one of Diomedes' horses, and I chalk up another Task completed.

As I walk back to join the Boys, I think I hear that sobbing in my head that I'm becoming accustomed to, and a soft whisper that repeats a lament:

Be careful, be careful.

Wednesday afternoon.

Serena switches off her PC and lingers there as it whines to a halt. She notices a similarity in sound to how she heard the exhaust and engine of the motorbike cooling when it lay in the ditch and was no longer running. She looks over at Odysseus, glances at the bathroom mirror discarded on the floor, runs a hand through her hair, then goes out to the balcony and sits down on the chair. Serena congratulates herself on the idea of using a mirror while Phoenix slept and dreamt. She thinks she might find a way to integrate a camcorder to record her remotely and then to mix the signals into the equation. The problems involved in planning this take her mind off her most recent experience, for a short time at least. When she shakes herself out of her reverie, she instinctively takes a few deep breaths.

It's good to be alive.

After the heavy rain of the day before, the sun has returned and the earth is steaming – the horizon shimmering into haze – but people are already out in the parks again, enjoying the weather.

People rarely stop to consider how society has been shaped by what soldiers endured during the war.

As far as Serena is concerned, there was no need for what Phoenix had done; he could have simply stopped the soldier as he rode past, and taken him prisoner, but she is acutely aware of how differently they each view the situation he was then in. There must be a mammoth gulf between their human values.

I don't know if we haven't all lost something since then. Certainty, perhaps? From what I know of that war, if it hadn't been for

Winston Churchill being such an obstreperous and persistent renegade, one half of the coalition government would have sought to negotiate a settlement with Hitler in May 1940. I bet that wasn't common knowledge then – or if it was, it wasn't reported in any history book I have read. When is it possible to form certainty, if the very people who govern you don't think you're able to handle the truth? And the truth then, during the Phoney War, was that many people just didn't want to fight. My God, we don't want all those Johnny Foreigner Jewish immigrants over here, anyway, do we? Quite a few people in this country didn't possess that certainty that you apparently need in order to kill. And then again, why should I be right? I've never been forced to defend myself in war.

It seems that every time she closes her eyes, that Japanese soldier engulfed in flames staggers into view. He raises his gun to fire, his eyes stare out for a second, then disappear in the fire that consumes him. He falls as Phoenix, and the marines, shoot him. Then he staggers back into view and does it all over again. Serena gazes out at the groups of people enjoying themselves in safe, modern, homely Cambridge, and she begins to sob again. The doorbell rings.

She stands up and goes down to the front door, stumbling twice on the stairs. When she opens the door, Alex stands there grinning, waving a buff-coloured folder in her face.

"Hey, sister," he begins to push his way in, "you'll never guess . . . What's up?"

He hobbles back a step, as if her grief will contaminate him.

Serena wipes the tears from her eyes and sniffs. She waves away his concern as she recovers herself.

"I'm okay, it's nothing. Come in, tell me what's getting you so excited."

Alex frowns. "Hmm," he says, the knots on his brow disappearing.

The excitement flashes in his eyes again and he follows Serena into her kitchen, where he takes a seat at the table and waits until she has blown her nose, before he speaks.

"I've found out something more about that marine – that

combat correspondent you were interested in. The writer that lived here for a time?"

Serena catches her breath. "Phoenix?" She sits down, leaning forward over the table.

He smiles at her eagerness and pats the folder. "I did some more digging around."

"Did he survive the war? I never did the obvious thing of finding that out. I chose him because, well, he once lived here, and I've got his pen, and . . . oh, damn to all that. Did he survive? Is – is he still alive today? I hadn't even considered that possibility."

"That, I don't know – on both counts."

"What are you saying?"

"Concentrate, Serena. I was looking through the wrong records. He wasn't actually a marine, was he?"

"No, he was a war reporter."

Alex gives a patronizing nod and reads from a sheet of paper he pulls from the folder.

"Honorary Lieutenant Phoenix Lafayette, combat correspondent to the *New York Picture Post* was reported, by that newspaper, as being MIA – missing in action."

Serena's nails dig into the surface of the table.

"How?"

"He went missing on twenty-sixth of July nineteen-forty-four – five days after their initial landing on the twenty-first. It happened during a Japanese offensive. By all accounts it was quite a battle, and, like all those situations, it was very confusing. It seemed a number of men cracked under the accumulated strain of what they'd been through, and went temporarily AWOL – meaning Absent Without Official Leave. Perhaps that's what happened to Lafayette. It's all I can offer you at the moment. His body was never found, Serena, so maybe he could have just run away. But I doubt it."

"My God," says Serena. "Oh, my God."

She slumps back into the chair, hangs her head for a moment, then quickly raises it and stares at Alex.

"But that's less than two days away."

Alex grunts at her. "What are you saying?" he asks.

Serena shakes her head. "But he can't die," she says. "He can't die. I won't let it happen, I won't."

Alex hands her the sheet of paper. "I didn't say he *died*, Serena. I said he was listed MIA. There is the small possibility he buggered off to live in the jungle."

"But there's nothing about him? No other details? You say – you said, that there was no body found?"

Alex slips the paper back into the folder.

"Well, there were an awful lot of men, on both sides, who never found a proper grave, Serena."

She ignores his words, and shakes her head.

"I'll not let him," she says. "I'll not let him."

Alex frowns, apparently confused, and Serena begins to cry again.

How could I have let myself fall for someone so completely, obviously, physically out of touch with me? He was supposed to be just an experiment. I can't believe I let myself forget that I can't alter what's already happened.

Her world seems to be crashing into numbing oblivion.

She discovers that her nails have prised loose a splinter of wood from the old table, and a spot of blood drips from where it has cut a finger.

But Serena decides to ignore it: she has other things on her mind.

TWENTY-ONE

The ancient Greeks had scant regard for women. This should come as no surprise to anyone, given how the men and boys of that time were taught to think about others. They could ponder philosophy: "A life without asking questions is no life at all," said Socrates. They could explain and discuss how to construct an argument and could ask the eternal question: why? But feminism? In those days, women were sold off with a dowry, aged fifteen, to be wives of men twice their age. They were expected to stay indoors and keep house, and they died in droves attempting to give birth, hopefully to a boy, as a "man's life was worth thousands of women". Females were merely considered a necessary accessory.

Except for the Amazons.

These women had a different approach to life: the warrior code. A *female* warrior code. It went a little way to balance out the injustices that their sisters elsewhere had to bear. These women were renowned for their lack of respect for justice and decency. Any boy born to them, when he was an infant, had his arms and legs broken, thus rendering him incapable of growing up to fight, or even to escape them. As the women saw it, the males of their tribe were in servitude (including the bedroom) for life, and they, the Amazons, didn't care about their men's feelings one bit. Aside from being the first military force to use cavalry, they removed their right breasts to enable them to shoot their arrows cleaner and to throw their spears further.

These women *lived* the warrior code.

And the queen of this unusual sisterhood was Hippolyte.

Hippolyte was an Amazon among Amazons: tall, fierce and intelligent. She had the aura that only some exceptionally regal people can exude – and she also wore a special belt. The war god, Ares, had given it to her because Hippolyte had proved herself the best woman warrior there was in the world. Queen Hippolyte wore this calfskin leather strap, emblazoned with the purest gold and garnet medallions, across her chest, as a means of carrying her weapons – namely her spear and sword. It was seen by all as a symbol of her skill and courage on the battlefield.

It was a pity, therefore, that King Eurystheus thought it would make a nice present for his daughter.

"And that's your ninth task," declared the herald, speaking through an inspection portal in the main gate. He had learnt his lesson – Hercules delivered a vicious punch.

"Okay," said Hercules, scratching his nose, "but when I return you know you'll have to come outside the gate again to accept it on behalf of your king. That'll be a shame, won't it?"

Hercules nodded to himself, as was becoming his habit of late. It was as though the groan that could be heard from the other side of the gates was something he had been expecting. He headed off to round up some volunteers.

The crew from his voyage to capture the man-eating horses of Diomedes re-enlisted to help Hercules this time too, and Iolaus joined the band as well. Then they set off.

After numerous detours (some adventures seem to hover between quest and journey), Hercules and his sailor-soldier-friends made port. Queen Hippolyte herself came down to the harbour to visit the well-known hero, and he made quite an impression on her – all muscles and lion-skin armour, so when he told her of his latest task, she replied that she would gladly give him the belt as a present. This would have been a grand

and sexy gesture, except that the goddess Hera was getting annoyed at how Hercules seemed to be so easily achieving all that was asked of him, and she had been circulating among the other women, spreading a rumour that Hercules had come to steal the belt. This trip was about to reach its climax.

The Amazons then became outraged at what they were told, and swarmed down to the harbour on horseback, howling their war cries. As they approached, Hercules realized that Hippolyte would inevitably side with her own army, whatever their misconstruing of events, so he instantly drew his sword and killed her on the spot. He preferred Prudence over Diplomacy. Then he bent down, unclasped the belt from Hippolyte's dead body, draped it over a shoulder, and readied himself for battle. (Hera had been correct after all, since Hercules *was* taking the belt without permission. She just hadn't specified the chronology of events.) In the carnage that followed, Hercules put to the sword all the major leaders of the Amazons.

Feminism would have to wait a while.

As he headed back to Mycenae, Hercules hoped that the king's daughter would treasure this spoil of war. Her sisters had paid dearly for it.

TWENTY-TWO

W Day +3. 08.11. Ravine leading to Fonte Plateau.

We have to advance up the ravine and clear out the extensive defenses located in the caves.

Oh well, another day, another buck.

"How many more?" growls Rici.

The prospect of what is in store for the day ahead, and what that means, doesn't really register with me; for some reason all I can see is that Enemy tumbling off his motorbike. Task number seven is completed; number eight is now on the horizon.

I am back with the Boys and, as I've said, they have been briefed on their objective of the day: to advance up the ravine and link up with the 3rd on our left. That's what Uncle Sam wants from them. They have also now been told, by me, that I'm on the lookout for an Enemy ammunition belt – task number eight. Judging by the look on their faces, this appears to leave most of them a little perplexed.

"I'm losing track here, Nix," says Johnny, nipping the end of his nose with his fingertips. "Didn't you tell us you wanted something you could say was like a horse? How do you do that with an ammo belt?"

His fingers leave his nose and he raises his eyebrows in a gesture of "Well?"

Rici comes up and stands beside me. He puts his arm around me.

"Nix here is ahead of the game." He nods towards the road. "That guy he took out on the track over there half an hour ago, apparently he was on a motorbike. The bike is now a write-off, so Nix reckons that's the equivalent of a dead horse."

That's not exactly the way I explained it to him, but I doubt whether a full explanation would alter the questioning stares the Boys are giving me. I merely shrug.

"Was the bike an Indian or a Harley?" asks Jim.

"A what or a what?" says Rici.

Jim looks aghast. "Only the best makes of bikes around," he says. "American, of course. I'm saving some of my money to buy one – I haven't decided which – to ride around and visit all of the States once this shit is finished."

"Oh," I say, nodding, as if I knew that's what he intended doing all along. "That bike was the best America had to offer the world, Babe. It must have been shipped in before the war."

"Well, that's okay," says Jim, smiling broadly now. "That Jap had no business riding it then."

"So, about this belt?" says Johnny, still standing with his eyebrows raised.

"It's another of Hercules' tasks," I explain, "but since we're just about to haul ass out of here, I haven't the time to explain, so all you need to know is that if you help me find an ammo belt I'll be happy."

Johnny salutes me with a finger to one nostril.

"Job done, buddy," he says.

And we quickly busy ourselves, sort our equipment, and make ready to move out. Johnny deems it necessary to slick some cream into his hair and Amos and Jim explain the niceties of American motorbikes and motorbikes in general when Rici doesn't seem to show enough interest. I don't think he's ever ridden one. Come to that, neither have I.

I finish before the rest of them, and take time to have a smoke. I extract a Lucky, light it with my Zippo and, as I inhale, I look around and appraise the terrain. The run the Boys and I did up from the beach had constituted quite a rise, but where the line is meant to advance today invites even greater trouble. It is not so steep that we can ignore the possibility of climbing it and make our way around, like we did with the cliff, and it doesn't have the comfort of any flat land allowing easy support from our tanks. It is just enough of an incline to put us in serious trouble. And the Enemy has removed the thin covering of jungle – helped by our bombardment.

So we will be fully exposed, with only some tree stumps, outcrops of sword grass and the odd shrub as cover, while we advance into the ravine with the Enemy being able to rain down mortars and bullets from both sides. It is a fantastic defensive position for the Enemy, and I wish we could bypass it, sneak past them somehow, and leave the problem of the ravine to someone else. We will have to cover our backs as we attack the left side. The top of the rise looks far away, and I wish, for my peace of mind, that there were more vegetation to disguise that fact. It is going to be a race: a day of rapid movement it has to be. And I will follow, and do my bit to help. I don't have a choice, as I am locked into being here and performing my duties for my newspaper and for Serena and myself.

The elation of achieving my previous task has long gone, and I am now approaching the next, and all the rest, with a grimness and determination I have never felt before. There has been a change within me, as if ideas have solidified all the while I've been thinking I'm falling apart. I can't say when it occurred (I still feel that my body is just one quiver away from shaking to pieces), but I am filled with a resolve, a terrible resolve. Even though my own private motivations are steeling my intent, I've noticed that the Boys, just as tired and probably as dubious about personal survival as I am, are also thoroughly determined. The initial impact of our landing is fading, and we are all now focusing, and forgetting any personal consider-ations. Perhaps it is the prospect of today, but I find I can't really take any pleasure from that Enemy on the motorbike. It was as Johnny said, a "job done".

The Boys spread out as before: Johnny and Bill and Jim and Hank off to either side, with Rici, Amos, Ron, Foglong and myself up the middle. There are other squads with us, and if any one group comes across unusually stubborn resistance, we are all to aid one another. But as I expect that's exactly what we'll *all* be coming across today – stiff resistance – we may as well be fighting just for ourselves. If the demolition charges, bazookas, grenades and flame-throwers don't do the trick, we can always call in other assistance from behind. And we must watch our backs; we will cover ourselves.

We get the call to move out.

We check our bayonets one last time.

The race starts.

W Day +3. 08.46. Ravine leading to Fonte Plateau.

Th-zzzzip! Th-zip!

My God!

I throw myself to the ground.

Love it, love it.

Leaves and dirt jump in spurts around me. I don't feel any bullets hit my body, but they are close.

Thwack! Thwack! Ping!

The last of some piece of metal.

I wriggle forward into a better position to respond. A hand taps my right ankle, then grips it and gives it a slight pull. I squirm and move backwards, without removing my eyes from checking ahead, and then I get dragged in beside Rici when he gets a better hold on me. He's found a bit of cover. I mutter some thanks. He tells me to fucking forget it. I tell him I already fucking have. He tells me I have a fucking foul mouth. I tell him he has a fucking foul face. More bullets hit the ground. Rici and I return fire.

The day has begun in earnest.

Ba-ba-ba-ba-ba!

Amos has found a higher position to our right, and he lets loose a volley of shots with his BAR.

Ba-ba-ba!

The BARs of Jim and Johnny open up to our left. The Enemy's quantity of return lessens. I pitch up a grenade.

Crack-crash!

As it explodes, Rici gestures to Jim to get higher and nearer. Jim picks up his BAR, and he and Hank rise to their feet as best they can and maneuver up the slope. Rici turns to Amos and Ron, and signals for them to do the same. We give covering fire.

Fifteen seconds of frantic scrambling later, and they are twelve to fourteen feet nearer the cave. Rici points to Foglong, to Johnny and Bill, and to me, and indicates to us that we're going straight up the middle. We get ready.

Rici and I throw a grenade each, and Jim and Amos open up on either side again. The grenades explode and fragments rattle off our helmets. As the last bits pitter-patter away, we force ourselves upright and push forward and up, and run as hard as we can.

Go, go, go! Touchdown, touchdown! Fuck, it's hard to weave. Go!

We grunt and huff. Rici is first to reach the entrance. He jumps over three or four contorted Enemy that the grenades have taken out. Rici misses his footing for an instant as he lands. He regains his balance and, as he does so, an Enemy comes rushing out of the cave, screaming a battle charge, his bayonet leading the way. Rici shoots him at point-blank range and, as the momentum brings the same Enemy on, Rici steps to the left, jams his right foot into the earth to bolster his stance and drives his own bayonet in past the Enemy's lethal thrust. Rici catches him just under the ribcage and heaves him over as if he's pitching hay. As he twists under the effort, Bill gets level with them, and he gives Rici a helping hand to flip the wriggling body off Rici's bayonet and down past us. Bill takes aim and puts a bullet in the Enemy's head.

So we are here at our first cave of the day. We take a few seconds to regain our breath.

Foglong positions himself to the right of the entrance, and Johnny, Bill and I all toss grenades into the dark, jagged opening. We don't bother with charges and we don't have a bazooka to hand.

Crack-boom! Crack-boom!

As the grenades go off, with the usual human reaction from inside, Foglong steps up and gives a couple of quick squirts – those screeching howls that I know I will never get used to – then he moves cautiously into the cave and we follow him.

The Enemy are still screaming and burning, those that are still upright stumbling around like Halloween torches in the pitch black. We all open up on them – including Foglong.

Shriek-whhhhosh!

For two or three seconds the human shapes roll and scream out and wave their fiery arms, and die their deaths in the ferment that is their hell.

Rici gestures for us to spread out.

The flames begin to subside and, in the smoky light from the still burning bodies, we move further into the cave, checking that it ends where we think it does. Bill finishes off one Enemy who has crawled behind an open wooden ammunition box that is burning fiercely. He then realizes what he's looking down at. So do I.

"Out!" Bill shouts. "Out, out, out!"

We all turn and stagger as best we can through the smoke, back to the entrance. I push Foglong ahead of me to protect his back. I feel a hand shove me. It is all a mad hustle. As we burst outside, to the surprise of the others just reaching the entrance, the bullets in the ammo box begin to go off.

Th-zip! Th-zip! Th-zip-zip-zip-zip!

There is a thunderous rattle as bullets zip past my ears. One ricochets off my helmet.

How many more times?

There's a cry behind me. "I'm hit!" calls Johnny. "I'm hit!"

Foglong leaps down the slope and lands on his butt. I manage to stop myself from following him and turn back, even as I'm diving for the ground. I slap the slope with my chest and blow the wind out of myself. Bill jumps over me and then tumbles into Foglong. I try to look up.

"I'm hit," says Johnny. "I'm hit."

Th-zip! Th-zzzzip! Th-zip!

The cave entrance still spits volley after volley of bullets over our heads. Rici, Amos and I finally get to Johnny.

"I'm hit," says Johnny.

"You're okay, Vizi," says Rici. "You're okay."

We all grab a handful of Johnny and yank him a few yards down the slope. The bullet hail seems to increase in volume, and then they cease as though they've been switched off. Johnny has frozen to the ground, clutching his upper left chest.

"I'm hit," he says.

Amos reaches down, moves Johnny's hand aside and rips open his jacket. Blood spurts up, and Amos slaps his own hand over the wound. Johnny becomes animated and thrashes his legs and tries to punch Amos away. I clasp his ankles and manage to get a grip on his flailing fist, as Rici fixes a dressing in place.

"I'm hit," says Johnny.

Amos clamps his hand over Johnny's mouth and squeezes Johnny's jaw shut.

"Vizi," says Amos, "it's a meat wound, straight through, you're okay partner, you're okay. Tell me you're okay."

Amos releases his grip. Johnny stops trying to jerk around. He nods his head several times.

"I'm okay," he says, "I'm okay." And he inhales a deep breath which, by the look of pain that flashes across his face, he won't be doing again in a hurry.

"That's it," says Rici. "Let's get him off here."

"Wait," says Johnny, shaking his head. "Wait."

We pause, all puzzled. Johnny reaches up to his top pocket and pulls out his cards. I can't believe it.

"Forget that shit," says Rici.

But Johnny brushes him aside and holds his cards out for Amos to take.

"Here, Chief," he says, "I'd rather give them to you now than have you scalp me later."

"Fuck you, too," says Amos, and he whips the cards away in one swift movement. As we move Johnny down the slope, Johnny tries to twist his head back towards Amos.

"What does that make?" he says. "What does that give you?"

Amos fans Johnny's cards.

"Hey," he says, "this is useful."

He flicks away four cards into the dirt – the Jack of Diamonds, the Eight of Clubs, and the Seven and Five of Hearts. Amos then gets his own cards out. He smiles at me and shows me his Ace of Hearts.

"Bet you'd like this, huh, Nixy?" he says.

I purse my lips and watch him rip the card in two. He snaps his cards together, then slowly fans them under my nose. With his two Jokers and the Eight, Nine, Ten of Hearts, he has a Straight Flush – Queen High. I could have used that Ace.

"Let's go," says Rici.

The race restarts.

W Day +3. 09.16. Ravine leading to Fonte Plateau.

Jim, Hank, Bill and Rici lead the rush to the Enemy's position – out of all the remaining men, these Boys have found they have a knack for getting up slopes the quickest. Not by much, but enough to make a difference. The rest of us are about ten yards behind now.

Pock!

Whoo-bang!

The Enemy in this cave has a mortar positioned outside.

Pock!

Whoo-bang!

I don't bother turning my head to see them land. Their explosions come as a waterfall of thunder.

But we have continued to rush forward – we are no longer where the mortars were aimed at. The Boys have run through the last defensive line settings of the mortars.

We reach the slight hiccup of rock that guards the entrance, and Jim, Hank, Bill and Rici continue with their charge, firing as they go.

Ba-ba-ba!

Tat-tat!

The Enemy mortar team reaches for their rifles, but they're too late. They've made the rookie error of not being continually covered by one of their number.

Tat-tat!

Tat-tat-tat-tat-tat!

Bill and Rici cut them down with short bursts. I go up over the lip of rock with Foglong, and I realize I'm becoming his unofficial support for the day. It's not a position many favor, not with what Foglong carries on his back.

Th-zip!

As Foglong takes up his stance at the right-hand side to the cave opening, and Bill and Hank start unpinning grenades, an Enemy rushes out, firing his rifle. Jim cries out and I see him fall backwards, clutching his abdomen.

Snap-crack! Snap-crack!

Tat-tat-tat!

Shriek-whhhhosh!

Foglong, Rici and I return fire, but our bullets don't seem to halt the Enemy, and Foglong's efforts have only turned him into a running fireball. The Enemy plunges over the lip, and I hear Amos let rip with his BAR at close quarters.

Ba-ba-ba-ba-ba!

Bill and Hank both blow out their cheeks and throw into the cave the primed grenades that they have been forced to hold onto longer than is healthy for one's sanity.

Crack-boom! Crack-boom!

"Thank fuck I didn't release the lever," mutters Bill, turning his back on the explosions.

"You and me both," I say.

As Foglong jams the nozzle of his flame-thrower into the entrance, Rici gestures for me to help Hank attend to Jim.

Shriek-whhhhhosh!

The dragon roars and Foglong, Rici and Bill, followed a second later by Amos and Ron, disappear into the smoke.

From the sounds coming immediately from our right, the next squad is just as busy as we are. So is the one to our left. The ravine seems to reverberate with concentrated exchanges of bullets, mortars, and the whoosh of our flame-throwers. I turn to move.

Jim is writhing on the ground while Hank is holding Jim's intestines in place. I stop hesitating and go to help him, calling out for a medic. Jim says nothing; he simply keeps looking from Hank to me, and back.

Hank is whispering to him. "It'll be fine, Babe, it'll be fine."

Jim fixes a stare on me and grasps my hand with his.

"Look after him, Nix," he says. "Look after him."

Shriek-whhhhhhhhhhhosh!

Above the echoing roar of Foglong at work inside the cave, Hank has to shout at Jim. "You're going to be fine, Babe, you're going to be fine."

My hands are now covered in a mass of blood. I call for a medic again. Jim's hand leaves mine, whips across and snatches Hank's collar.

"Hank," he says, "look after Nix, will you? He'll need a stupid fucker like you to get him by."

And with that he tenses for a moment, then goes limp.

Damn, not Babe, not Babe.

I say nothing out loud, but reach over to close his eyes. Hank stops me and does the job himself.

"I'm sorry," I say.

"Not as much as me," he says.

He blinks a couple of times.

"Sorry," he says.

"Forget it."

Hank then begins to reach into Jim's top pocket.

"No, Hank," I say, grabbing a hold of his wrist, "enough is enough. We have to stop this."

Hank pulls away from me and takes Jim's cards from his pocket. He glances at them, then hands them to me.

"I'm a man of few words, Nix," he says, "so pay attention. I don't know what's happening here, don't know what law of God we've broken by taking on this bet, but by my calculation, if you take Jim's cards, you'll have top hand."

I look down at the cards – a lovely Joker, a lovely Ace of Clubs, the Ten of Diamonds, the Seven of Spades and the Four of Clubs. I look back up at Hank. He nods. I look down again at Jim's cards – I can ditch my two queens and use Jim's Joker and Ace to make top hand: Five Aces.

"Why?" I ask Hank.

"You're going to win anyway," he says, "and when you do, you can write about us, about Babe, about all of this, and I know you'll do it right."

As I reluctantly take out my cards, rip up the excess ones and tuck Top Hand back into my pocket, Hank reaches down and wipes the grime from Jim's face.

"Fuck," he says, "he wasn't even a kid. He was just a child."

"No, he wasn't. He—" I start to say.

Fuck!

Th-zip! Th-zip! Th-zip!

I give Hank a hard shove sideways as the Enemy I just caught sight of, out of the corner of my eye, opens up from twenty yards away.

The bullets hit Jim's body and it seems as though life has returned to him. I roll to the right, grabbing my carbine. Hank is scrambling for his rifle as well.

"Not yet!" shouts Hank. "I'm not ready to be killed yet! I'm not ready!"

Th-zip! Th-zip!

Ba-ba-ba-ba-ba!

The Enemy has us nailed.

Before we can fire, Bill starts shooting from the cave entrance. The Enemy staggers and falls down on top of Jim.

I feel my shoulders droop.

Fuck me.

Fuck me, that *was close.*

"Thanks, Bill," I say.

"No problem," he says, and he and Hank pull the Enemy off Jim, and push the Enemy's body over the lip to join his burnt friend.

I look at Hank who is wiping his brow.

"You've got top hand now," he says. "You've got top hand."

"What do you mean?" I ask, thinking back to what he'd shouted just before the Enemy caught us out.

"You'll be the last one," he says. And he checks his rifle and moves off, taking a last look at Jim.

I'm scared – I have a feeling I know what he's talking about.

W Day +3. 11.34. Ravine leading to Fonte Plateau.

We carry on fighting our way along and up the narrowing ravine. The intensity of the Enemy fire has increased now we are reaching our goal of the summit: Fonte Plateau. And the Boys are now getting exposed to crossfire from the other side of the rise. Whatever bombardment the naval guns and the air strikes put down here, it did little to remove the number of Enemy emplacements. The ferocity of incoming fire is as bad as anything we've encountered so far – including the landing itself. Pausing in the open is fatal, and we all do our own variations of the college football weave.

Find cover, give covering fire.

Get up and run, run, run!

Hit the dirt. Find cover, give covering fire.

Try to catch your breath.

Get up and run, run, run!

Curse with the foulest worst words you know.

Hit the dirt. Find cover. Struggle with a new magazine. Give covering fire.

We move on and up – weave, duck and dive.

Hank crashes to the ground. "Shit! Shit! Shit!" he says.

He rolls onto his back, throws his rifle to one side, and slaps both his hands to his right thigh. Before he can get a good grip I see a dribble of blood. It's small: vein, not an artery. The Enemy keeps up its assault of fire. Bullets are hitting everywhere; I hear a couple of wasps whizz past my ears. I quickly raise fingers to test one ear, but there is no blood. The collar of my jacket has a hole in the top right side, though. It still feels warm from where the bullet passed through it.

"Shit!" Hank says, as Amos gets to him. He puts his BAR to one side, kneels down on one knee and gets both his hands on Hank's leg.

"Medic!" shouts Amos, looking over his shoulder. "Get your asses here!"

"Let me help, Chief," says Ron, joining him and stooping down.

"No, cover us," says Amos.

Pock! Pock!

The sound is distant – they're coming in from the other side of the ravine.

Whoo-bang! Whoo-bang!

"Cover!" shouts Rici.

Love the ground, love the ground.

The mortars whistle down, then throw clumps of earth at us. I feel the sting of hot metal on my neck and quickly brush it off.

No blood, no blood.

"Move aside. Let me at him."

It's a medic. He's a small ferret of a man who probably hasn't started to shave once a day yet.

So this is what angels look like these days?

He gets on his knees beside Amos and starts tearing into Hank's trousers. He produces sulfa, shakes some onto the wound, and then gets Amos to help him fix a dressing onto it and around the leg.

Pock! Pock!

Whoo-bang! Whoo-bang!

More rounds hit the ground.

Shit, it's raining shit.

Ha, ha.

Amos turns on Ron.

"I said cover us!" he shouts.

Ron turns, still in his crouch, and returns fire.

"Sorry," he says, "sorry, Chief."

"Don't be sorry," says Amos, helping the medic pull tight the ties to the dressing. "Just do your job."

"Watch it, Chico," says Hank, his voice shrill and high, "you're next, you're next."

Ron glances across at Hank as he changes magazines. "What's that, Hank?" he asks, ducking at the mortar explosion less than twenty feet away.

Hank pushes the medic to one side, to look at Ron, and then at everyone else within range.

"Haven't you guys worked it out yet? You haven't worked it out yet? By God, don't you know we're getting hit in order?"

"Take it easy, Chico," says Amos.

"Chief," says Hank, "you're okay – so's Nix over there. But Chico is next, he's got the next lowest hand."

"What's up?" says Rici, as he finishes a running slide down into a position beside Hank. "How is it, Hank?"

"I'll be okay," he says.

Rici looks at the medic. The medic nods.

"I'll go organize a stretcher team," the medic says, and gets up into a running crouch and heads back down the line, holding his helmet firmly on his head.

Amos has his hand on Hank's shoulder. "Say that again, Hank."

Bill joins the group. "You okay Hank?" he says.

"*I'm* okay, Groucho," he says. "I've got away with it – it's just a wound. But you guys still have to face your Dead Pool Poker hand."

"What?" says Bill.

"Hank," says Rici, "stop this shit."

"Let him go on," says Amos.

"Yeah," says Ron, coming back into the group, "I want to hear what he has to say."

I shut my eyes for a moment.

"Nix has worked it out," says Hank.

Fuck.

I open my eyes. Everyone is staring at me.

"I can't," I say. "It's stupid."

"As stupid as doing tasks like Hercules?" Hank asks.

I can't answer.

"Who got it first, Nix?" Hank asks. "Who got it first, huh?"

"Bob did," says Amos, "on the beach. We all know that."

"That's right," says Hank.

"Stop this," warns Rici.

"What did he have, Nix? What hand did he have?" asks Ron.

I shrug my shoulders for Rici's benefit. Rici rolls his eyes and shakes his head slowly.

"Eight high," I say, "the lowest hand out of all of us."

"Go on," says Hank. "Go on, tell them."

I sniff and draw a breath. "I took Bob's cards," I say, "so I know he had the lowest hand. He died first. Joe had a queen high – and he was next. I took his, so I know. Frank had a pair of tens, and he got hit next. And so on."

I wave my hand as though I'm conducting an orchestra.

"Tell it all, Nix," says Hank.

Ron is looking around at everyone in turn. I know he's trying to remember what we all had that time we showed our hands.

"Barney," I begin. "Harpo fell to the bottom of the list because I took Bob's, Joe's and Frank's cards. So Barney's king high made him last on the list. And, as it happens, he was next."

"Oh, for Christ's sake, Nix," says Rici, "this is shit."

"I know," I say, "but that's the way it's working."

"That means I'm next in line," says Ron, grabbing my collar, a collar with a new hole in it caused by a bullet that missed my jugular by an inch. "Is that what you're saying, Hank?"

Hank looks up at him.

"Remember," he says, "Johnny had a pair of Jacks, Jim – my buddy Jim had a pair of Aces. I've got two pair – Jacks over fives. They were the hands they had, and that is the order they got hit. That's the order for all of us that got hit – lowest first, then up."

He laughs.

"Jesus," he says, "ol' Joe Plotkin didn't know what he was doing. Dead Pool Poker – what a great name for it."

"Give me your cards," says Ron.

His request feels like ice water on my heart. I suspect everyone else has also stopped breathing.

"Sorry?" I say.

Despite the bullets still cascading down on us, Rici stands up.

"This," he says, "this is where it *stops*! Have you got that?!"

"No," says Ron, "I want his cards. I can make a full house. With my Joker I can make a full house. I can live a bit longer."

He is already down on his hands and knees and reaching out to Hank's top pocket. Amos pulls him off.

"I'd like to win myself," says Amos, "but no, Chico, you can't do it like this. Rici's right, this is where it stops. Fuck this game – give me a Jap's bullet any time, instead of this weird crap."

"No," says Ron. "*No!*"

And he pulls away from Amos.

"No," he says again, "not me. *Not me!*"

He takes two steps, staring us down with a glare, then he turns and starts running, back down the slope.

"Ron!" shouts Rici. "Get back here you bastard! Get back in the line and do your job!"

Pock! Pock! Pock!

Love the ground, love the ground!

"Take cover!" shouts Rici, but we're already going there.

I pull my helmet down over my head and wait. For some reason, I know – I know with an absolute certainty – that every one of the Boys is thinking the same as me. And there's nothing we can do – it's as if Fate is spitting in our hearts.

Whoo-bang! Whoo-bang! Whoo-bang!

When the mortars go off there is not even a cry of pain.

Ten seconds pass. When we look for Ron, there's nothing but pieces. At least it was quick.

"Fuck," says Bill. "Fuck, fuck, fuck."

And we all know he's not just talking about losing a buddy.

Pock!

We start running and weaving.

Find cover, give covering fire.

Get up and run, run, run!

Whoo-bang!

Hit the dirt.

Find cover, give covering fire.

Including Foglong, there are now only five of us left.

W Day +3. 13.15. Ravine leading to Fonte Plateau.

This fortification is big. It must be a system of interlinked caves, where the Enemy can retreat from concentrated fire at one entrance and move across to hit us from another angle. Whatever we throw at it just seems to wash off and have no effect.

I've noticed that it has a number of machine gun nests, and I'm thinking of Hercules again.

That's good.

Serena.

If I can help anytime, I will.

I think I'll need it.

Whatever. I'll try not to break your concentration.

I could kiss you.

Don't say things like that.

"Nix?"

It's Rici.

Must go – kiss, kiss.

Stop it.

"Yeah?" I ask Rici as he joins me in my patch of cover behind a tree stump and swathe of tall grass.

"The Captain says we're to wait up here. We're taking too many hits so he's calling up an air strike."

He pats my shoulder, takes a look around, then gets up and moves on to spread the word. I settle down to wait.

You could use the distraction.

What do you mean?

You could go and get your ammunition belt after the aeroplanes have completed their attack.

I'll think about it.

Don't think about it too long.

Ah, huh. Okay.

Good.

Yeah, good. Now, let me think.

Okay.

I have difficulty working out if I'm tense or relaxed.

And there's a good reason for this confusion.

There's something about an air-strike that makes me feel as though I'm watching the *coup de grâce* of a man being shot at the hands of the officer in charge of a firing squad. *We, the men at arms, have been summoned, at the appointed hour, to the courtyard where the execution is to take place. We will have been* anticipating this moment for some time (it may have been over days or weeks), and our feelings of apprehension as we stand at the gate are incontrovertibly mixed with our imaginings of what the man about to be led to the stake will be thinking. The gate swings open and we march to our place in the courtyard. We wait. In line. After some moments the prisoner is brought from the cells. A drummer begins to mark time. The prisoner looks up at the sky, around at the buildings, at the men accompanying him, at the ground, and finally, yes he has to look, he turns from his brief inspection of the stake to the men who are waiting for him. We know what he is thinking as he looks candidly at us. He spits. The condemned is led to the stake and his hands are tied behind his back. The officer reads out the charge sheet, the verdict and the sentence. He doesn't allow the prisoner any last statements. A blindfold (more for our benefit than for his) is placed over the condemned man's eyes and a square piece of white paper is pinned to his chest – just over his heart. The officer marches away to one side. The drum beat stops. We are given our instructions.

There is that awful pause.

The prisoner tenses and tries to arch his back, as though getting braced for the impact might protect him. We fire. The crack of our rifles causes the pigeons in the courtyard to whoosh into the skies. We stand easy. We wait. We wait for the man in command to walk up to the slumped body and deliver us from the necessity to still be here. We saw our bullets hit, but there is still that outside chance that we haven't completed the job. We need assistance. And that's how it is, that moment when the officer marches back to the prisoner, withdraws his revolver and takes aim, those moments of expectation are what it is like to be waiting for an air-strike.

I look across at the remaining Boys and the other men from other squads.

I can feel the sense of excitement.

The request has been radioed in, and we become like schoolchildren awaiting the arrival of our older brother to sort out the bully. Somewhere, not far out to sea, the order is passed. The aircraft may already be in the air, but I imagine the men climbing into their cockpits nevertheless. They have bombs to load. I think of Tom and those Mosquitos he's now flying, and consider his lot in his war in Europe – the war in the air must be so different to that on the ground, with altogether different attitudes. And, of course, there are different planes here in the Pacific. From the carriers, the Navy Boys mostly launch those big-tailed Curtiss Helldivers these days – 1000lb bombs and 20mm cannon from the pilot, and something else from his gunner at the back.

We wait for them. And we count the minutes.

We try to estimate how long they will take to reach us.

We scan the skies.

It is like that moment in the courtyard, awaiting that single shot from the officer in charge.

Just like those seconds that melt into days.

Someone from one of the other squads shouts. We look in the direction he is pointing. An echelon of three planes is silently swooping in ahead of their own engine noise.

They are high. As we watch they begin their run.

Then they begin their dive.

I wonder what it must be like to see dive-bombers coming for you.

I'm glad we have air superiority.

For a moment I think the planes are moving quite slowly – but I am so mistaken. They are suddenly above us, a radial roar from their engines blasting down into our ears, the howl from their descent so guttural. They are so close I can see the faces of their pilots and the gunners. Then the cannons of the planes spit and strafe the Enemy, as an initial insult; then the planes pull up and release their load, and a bomb whistles in. Even before it smashes into the ground, the planes have banked and the gunner in the rear is letting loose with his machine guns, then waving to us when he has finished. Yes, the war in the air is so different to that on the ground: different attitudes, and different perspectives.

The bombs explode.

There are three huge thunderous bangs that mix together, and nothing is recognizable in amongst the yellow and black blast-clouds of debris that mushroom into the sky and across the ground. There is undoubtedly Enemy amid this swathe of destruction, but I can't worry about that. I just take a photograph. I didn't even realize I'd taken my camera out. One or two of the Boys give a cheer at the fireworks. This will have lessened the odds.

Do it Nix, do it now!

What? Oh, fuck, I'd forgotten.

Do it!

Fuck, yes!

I struggle to get my camera put away. I look up. The results of the explosions are still billowing and glowing with their heart of fire. The camera is packed and sorted.

I start running.

You can do it!

I don't bother to weave.

I hear someone I don't know calling out "Let's go!"

I grunt, stumble, and grunt again.

Watch yourself! To your left! Go to your left!

I sidestep left and take the easier route. I run. I try to focus.

The tree! The tree ahead!

I see the Enemy taking aim.

Tat-tat-tat!

I give a short burst from my carbine. He drops his rifle and clutches his chest. I get to him. I use my bayonet.

God.

I help him die. As I move on, I glance back. The other squads are following me. I also see Amos and Bill and then Rici. They are all grim-faced, all running hard.

Get going!

I run harder.

Up that way! Up there, straight ahead!

I grunt up the easiest way – straight ahead. The smoke from the explosions begins to drift around me. It's acrid and has a bitter taste. I pause, I try to catch my breath. My vision is becoming obscured. I can't remember the route I'd planned.

Move left again! They were up that way!

I run left. I can hardly see now. Visibility is down to about ten yards. It's a fog of gray and black smoke.

You've missed that rock. That funny shaped rock is too far left. Veer right. Edge to your right, Nix.

I sidestep – change direction. I unpin a grenade.

It was just—

Shut up now!

The machine gun emplacement emerges into view. Every step increases the clarity of the position. I see the Enemy peering through the smoke. I throw my grenade. As it flies I skid to a stop and begin to open up.

Tat-tat-tat-tat-tat!

After a quick burst, I drop down and pull the lid of my helmet over my brow.

Crack-crash!

The grenade goes off. I leap up and run forward. I jump over the sandbags. Two Enemy are moving. I save ammunition and lunge into them with my bayonet. As I begin on the second Enemy I hear movement behind me. And my bayonet is stuck. I ram a foot on the Enemy's chest and try to wrest it free. I look over my shoulder – and relax. It's Amos. He lowers his weapon. The bayonet comes free, following another grunting effort from me. Amos stands there, catching his breath.

"Jesus, Nixy, you're a bastard," he says.

Rici emerges from the smoky gloom. He jumps into the pit. He does a rapid check and kicks an Enemy.

"Nine?" he asks.

"Who cares?" I say.

Amos bends down and picks up an ammo belt.

"Yours, I believe, buddy?" he asks me.

I take it from him, study it for a moment, and remove a bullet – which I tuck into a pocket – then throw the belt to the ground.

"That's another one down and out," I say. "Now let's go down and help the others."

Just as Bill emerges next from the thinning clouds, we turn him around and head towards the cave complex, where the sounds of a clearing-out assault have begun.

The air-strike has given us an edge. So has the fact of the completion of my ninth task.

I think about the next one.

Classified Secret

F2/6845/1/3

Authorization is hereby given for black project as requested and formally outlined here.

1. The device known as Odysseus shall be acquired while it is in actual use and shall be disabled in such a manner that analysis of the program can be made by our scientific and computing experts.
2. Operations shall be carried out with extreme prejudice.
3. The recovery team is being assembled.

TWENTY-THREE

There had to come a time when circumstances would dictate that one of Hercules' labours would become a labour within a labour. This type of annoying occurrence would later develop into what is known today as Sod's Law. When Eurystheus demanded that Hercules bring him the cattle belonging to Geryon, the king set in motion a task of colossal proportions. Even the herald had no idea what was about to unfold – if he had realized how long Hercules would be gone, he might have considered doing a little jig. For life was about to become harder for the man who was the bane of the herald's career.

While the cattle themselves were ordinary cattle writ large and noble, as would be expected in a labour about to be undertaken by Hercules, Geryon himself was monster writ nasty. He was disgusting to look at and had an infamous pedigree. Geryon had three heads, six arms and legs, and surrounded himself with useful associates.

He didn't look after his cattle directly, but made sure they were protected as if he were there in person, seven days a week. Geryon had his cattle guarded by a large and ferocious two-headed dog, and tended by a centaur. Geryon felt he had nothing to fear, especially from heroes on quests.

Hercules set off for his rendezvous.

Now Geryon lived on an island near the boundary between Europe and Africa. This was the End of the Known World – thus an apt place for Geryon to live. And Hercules celebrated his arrival in the vicinity by promptly splitting a mountain in two. He never fully explained the reason why, but this neat trick resulted in the formation of the Straits of Gibraltar and that chasm's sides being renamed as 'The Pillars of Hercules'. Leaving his mark on geography as he travelled, the hero sailed on.

As soon as he had arrived at his destination, Hercules despatched in quick succession: the guard dog, with a swift smash of his club on both heads; the centaur, with the same club, and an even mightier swing; and the monster Geryon himself with a volley of arrows. So, task completed.

Or so Hercules thought, as he rounded up the cattle.

The trip home proved a little more difficult.

First Hercules wandered through Spain, leaving a few of his camp followers to set up new outposts in the wilderness, until he arrived in the Pyrenees. Here he sought the attentions of the princess Pyrene – who gave her name to that mountain range – neglecting to mention to her that he was still technically married. After leaving his mark in this territory also, the Hercules–Geryon cattle train proceeded north to Gaul.

Since the Gauls had a practice of killing strangers, Hercules first had to convince them that this was a pastime they should no longer indulge in – at least not with him. The Gauls changed tack and gave him the bonus of some leisure time spent with a princess. From then on, the Gauls claimed themselves descended from the resulting offspring.

Greek heroes enjoyed some payback for being heroes.

Hercules then departed with his cattle.

As he proceeded home, two sons of Poseidon cast their eyes on those fine animals and wanted them for their own. Hercules quickly killed the pair of them – he had his labour to complete and needed to get back to Mycenae. Unfortunately, an army, which had joined Poseidon's sons, began to overwhelm Hercules and he found he was soon out of arrows. Wounded, exhausted, and weeping with frustration that there were not even any stones to fling at the enemy, Hercules fell to his knees – his hands to his face. Dark clouds formed in the sky, and everyone looked up. Zeus, taking pity on his son's tears, rained down a shower of rocks for Hercules to use. And Hercules did so, with deadly force, smashing the foe apart.

Zeus decided to commemorate this event with a new constellation of stars named after his son – it's still up there in the northern night sky if you care to look. The field of the battle is also still to be found: on the plain near Marseilles, the land is covered with apple-sized rocks, and the springs that well up there are of brine – from the salt in Hercules' tears.

Which all added to his recent trend of stamping on any local geography: HERCULES WAS HERE.

And he still didn't stop.

A bull escaped from the herd and swam to Sicily.

Hercules pursued it and had to kill a three-headed monster that stole another of his two bulls after he had arrived there. The original bull swam back roughly the way it had come, and where it touched land, the country there was renamed Italy – from the native word for bull: *italus*.

At the next stage of his journey, Hercules had to wrestle with another of Poseidon's sons – everyone seemed to want possession of Geryon's cattle – and Hercules duly dispatched him with a killer throw. People cautioned him that, alongside previous actions, this was an interesting and provocative attitude to take with Poseidon's children, considering how much travelling over water Hercules needed to do.

One day, ages having passed since his departure, with the Greek sun turning the olives brown, Hercules finally returned to Mycenae. He was tired and fed up – even the herald knew enough to keep his mouth shut. But there was one last insult to be played out. Eurystheus promptly sacrificed the whole herd to Hera. And reminded Hercules (via the herald of course, as King Eurystheus wasn't *that* stupid), that he wasn't acknowledging the second and fifth task that Hercules had performed. Hercules would have to do two more.

Hercules sighed to himself. A hero's work is never done.

TWENTY-FOUR

W Day +3. 17.20. Fonte Plateau.

We've made it to the plateau, I've dug a lovely deep foxhole, and I'm hunkered down for the rest of the day, and the night to come, waiting for my latest wave of fear to subside. It's been increasing in frequency during the last hours. And in magnitude. I'm still filled with a resolve to finish this, but the shakes I'm experiencing are nearly constant, and I dare not try to take any photographs at the moment. The Boys are avoiding my eyes now – they're letting me deal with my problems my way. It's odd, but here I am supposedly reporting on the vicious front end of a brutal war and, just to stay alive and do my job, I have to take part in it. Where's the Holy Grail of truth in that, which I once felt was so important? I'm interfering in the events I'm paid to be impartially recording. Haven't I read somewhere that a physicist has stated that you cannot observe anything without affecting it in the process of looking at it? Is there no degree of absolute certainty? God help me if there isn't. And God help *us*.

The Boys have dwindled to a meager four in number, and that's including me. Foglong has been required to go back and help with some mopping-up jobs in the caves, so we form a little line of two foxholes and, for all the link-up with the 3rd (we finally encountered them), Rici, Amos, Bill and I could as well be on the moon. Amos, with Bill as his assistant, has his BAR at the ready; and Rici has set up another one, with me to help him if he needs me. I hate even to do the calculation, but two-thirds of our number have been removed in one way or the other. Eight down – four to go.

Anything but the Enemy has become life to be respected. Even the flies, who seem to be thriving. Out of all the strange and peculiar things I have seen crawling, scuttling, flying and scratching a living here – big beetles, small beetles, things that appear to be hybrids of giant ants and leaves, caterpillars that could be scraps of fur given life, twigs that have eyes, fat hard-backed worms with a surplus of tiny claw-legs, pieces of moving bark that feed off the twigs with eyes – it is the flies that have welcomed our presence the most. There seems to be ten for every breath I take. And it pays not to speculate too clearly about what they're feeding on.

I sit with my back resting against the rear wall of our foxhole, staring out front, and I de-focus – as my grandfather taught me – and I let my senses take over. I do it to try to calm myself. It's difficult to believe my eyes though.

Standing about one hundred yards away are three water buffalo. I think they are suffering from some sort of shock, as I have not seen them move for over an hour. They do not eat, they are not even drinking from the small pool of water at their feet – they simply stand, not even flicking away the swarms of flies that must be a plague for them.

They are so obviously the ingredients for my fulfilling the Tenth Task (I'll be damned if I'm going to look for an Enemy equivalent when I've three gift buffalo in front of me), but how to use them? It would be a shame to waste the opportunity, but I hesitate about the best way to go about it. Simply mowing them down with a burst from the BAR, as Amos suggested, wouldn't achieve anything strategically against the Enemy, but it would put the animals out of their misery.

Their loss of will is spooky – especially as they are not creatures especially known for being conscious of what is happening around them.

What to do with them? How do I use them as a task?

"So, do you reckon Hank had it right, then?" asks Rici.

I blow out a sigh, sagging where I sit, and look across at him. He has on his inscrutable Buster face, which is appropriate I suppose. Ever since Ron got shredded to kingdom come, I have known we were going to have this conversation.

"Yeah, Nixy," says Amos, "what do you think?"

Bill glances across at us as well.

All for one, and one for all.

It's the Three Musker-Marines.

I bow my head slightly, getting my thoughts straight, then look up at them.

"It's undeniable," I say, "that from day one, whoever has had the lowest hand at that time has been the next one hit. Hank is absolutely right about that."

"So I'm next?" says Bill.

Before Rici or Amos can say anything, I get my answer in.

"The way things have been going," I say to him, "I wouldn't want to be in your boots. Or anywhere near them."

Bill closes his eyes and swears.

I give a sour little laugh – to let him know I'm joking.

"But, Groucho," I add, "it's all just shit. I know the odds against something happening this way must be astronomical, so it's easy to get the feeling we've been caught up in the greater scheme of God's displeasure, but in the end it's all shit."

"Yeah?" says Bill, obviously not convinced. "It's not you sitting here holding the crap hand."

"Yeah," I say, "but that's the shitty way of things, and I could be wrong."

I thrust a thumb into my chest. "*I'm* as superstitious as the rest of you, I mean, *I'm* trying to survive by emulating Hercules. How stupid is that? And what's even crazier: the fact that I'm actually trying to do it, or the fact that I *believe* I'm succeeding? Or of you idiots helping me whenever you can? Perhaps Hank was right, maybe we have tried to piss in the face of Fate by taking part in Joe's game – but there is a way out." I give him a sly smirk.

"How?" asks Bill.

"Quit the game," says Rici.

As Bill and Amos turn to look at him, I grin at Rici and nod. Rici and I often think alike.

"That could stop it," I say. "Throw in the towel, call it evens and we split the pot."

I pat my pocket that contains the money. "That's one hundred and eighty bucks each," I say. "Quit the game, and Fate might look in a different direction."

"Oh?" says Amos. "And what if some of us don't want to finish just yet? What if *I* want to risk it?"

"Chief," Rici says, "I know you want all the luck you can get, but listen up."

Amos whooshes a spurt of tobacco onto the lip of his foxhole. Rici doesn't blink, nor does he even look down at the mess – I sometimes think it's a special secret course that sergeants go through in the Marines: Stare Down the Troops.

"Chief," he says, "tell us what you got again? What have you put together?"

"Straight flush," Amos answers, wiping his mouth. "Queen high."

"And everyone else? What have they got?"

Amos nods to each one of us in turn. "Groucho's got the lowest at three of a kind – Jacks. *And* he has two Jokers. You've got a full house, Kings over Queens, and flash Nixy here has five of a kind – Aces."

"So, Chief," says Rici, spreading his hands, cocking his head to one side and finally smiling, "how are you going to win?"

Bill nods and I jut out my lower lip – Amos has already spent some time working out all the permutations and it will be interesting to see what he has to offer by way of a solution. It doesn't take much.

"If all three of you guys get hit," he says.

I have to admit it, he's right. I don't like how matter-of-fact he sounds, but he's right. Though I know he has missed something – and the gleam in Rici's eye tells me *he* has worked it out already.

Amos' hand twitches as he begins to reach for his cards.

"But," says Rici, "you're below Nix and me. Even if you get Bill's cards, even if you get *mine*, you can't beat Nix. And if we go along with Hank's prognosis, if we get hit in order of value, then that's what will happen. Nix will win. You apparently threw away your chance of drawing with him when you ripped up your Ace."

"This is shit," says Amos; but the way his eyes flick and dance about demonstrates to me that he's doing the mental arithmetic.

"That's what *I* said," I remind him. "Didn't I say it was shit?"

"Go fuck yourself, Nixy," says Amos.

"I wish I could," I say, "then I'd be in a freak show on Coney Island rather than out here. And getting some pleasure out of it, too."

Amos kicks the side of his foxhole.

I just can't be fucked with this crap anymore.

"Split the pot," I urge, knowing the response. I notice that my hands are shaking – I put one on top of the other.

Amos has a fit of cursing, the volume of it amazing. Bill, Rici and I simultaneously fold our arms and stare at him.

Amos stops ranting, his mouth still half-open. He kicks the earth again.

"Ah, fuck it," he says, "I'll go with the majority. I don't like it, but I'll go with whatever you guys want to do. Let's split it – I'm only going to end up losing it all in some game anyhow, so losing less makes some sort of sense. Do it, Nixy, split the pot."

As I reach for the cash, I notice he is also fingering his top pocket. It's where he stashes his loot, as well as his cards – the gold teeth he's collecting. He'll make more money out of that little scam than what he will have in his hand when we split the pot.

I divide out the money, then wrap up my own share again

and replace it in my pocket. Bill and Amos attend to their BAR. Rici makes a big point of kissing his bundle before folding it away into his pocket. He gives me a brief smile, as if to hint that's one problem out of the way.

"That'll go towards my first date," he says.

"Alice comes expensive," I say.

"She seems worth it."

Good, he has his mind on other things.

Now, what to do about the buffalo?

I lick my lips as I think.

A mistake. The taste of the carnage wrought today lingers like rancid meat on my palette. It is a foulness that I could remove easily in some New York bar with the money that's now squarely mine; I could line up small cold beers and large chasers and swill that sweet alcoholic nectar around into all the corners of my mouth. The saliva I produce is bitter, but it provides enough to perform the trick I did the other day. I sniff hard, hawk the mess into my mouth, suck on it for the barest instant, then swallow. The reaction of nausea sprinkles sweat on my brow, but once again I feel better. The simple action has also cleared my ears.

I hear the brutal conversation between Amos and Bill as they inspect their weapons. An outsider would be hard pushed to discern its friendly undercurrent. Amos is describing some brothel he knows in Houston, and Bill is relating the story of a night out before he left home. The way they describe the women involved, and what they did, it seems as if it was the same woman. I now miss Johnny's comments about his successes – they had a bit of class at least. With the constant clink of metal upon metal being generated as they take things apart to clean them, then slap them back together, I could imagine myself in a blacksmith's. But only for a minute or two. I glance upwards when I hear planes approaching about three-quarters of a mile away, and I watch as they dive to release their load. The aircraft peel away, and seconds later explosions roll and rumble like war-thunder.

I grip my hands together again to stop the trembling.

Then I'm startled as Rici suddenly throws me a bottle. I whip out a hand and manage to catch it. I study it as I hold it aloft. It seems we have an endless supply of *saki*. No wonder the Enemy are never sober. I look into the liquid's depths – I could swim my life away in it.

"You earned it," says Rici.

"Yeah, I'm touched."

"And if you're good, you can have another."

I raise my eyebrows. "Another *bottle*?"

"Anyone else and I wouldn't trust them to be able to function."

"But me?"

"You're an experienced drunk."

There's no animosity in his observation – we both know it's true. And we both know that sometime it's going to be up to Rici to sort me out. That or some smart girl I meet.

I unscrew the cap and sniff. It is a lovely smell. I wish I'd had it a few minutes earlier to wash the grunge down. God, I love to drink. To be on some mountainside, the remains of snow in the shadows, the air sharp and clean, the sky cloudless, a bottle of crystal moonshine wedged between the rocks of a stream fed by melt-ice from the higher slopes, and nothing to do but drink that liquor till my mind slurs – that's heaven for me. A cold, clear drink in a cold, clear space. As I raise the bottle to my lips, my brain registers other smells – the familiar ones of the war in Guam that give it its unique flavor – and in an instant I find myself thinking about the death of my grandfather. I counter that with thoughts of Serena.

Serena will sort me out, like she helped me today – as she has been helping me ever since I landed on this island. I have a thick sensation in my gut and I simultaneously feel lust filling my groin. I add another object to my mental heaven. Along with the moonshine and mountain air, I now have a down-filled sleeping bag – one that will fit two, if they snuggle close. And she is waiting for me. That's what my grandfather told me love was all about – a terrible lust and a terrible need. There were times when you'd feel both at the same time, he maintained.

But there was an aspect of love that my grandfather was wrong about. He'd often talked about love between a man and a woman, where desire was a natural part of it; he didn't mention the love between a grandfather and a grandson. Or of men that have known each other and are risking their lives together.

His death affected me greatly. I think again of the Boys who have died – Bob, Joe, Barney, Ron and Jim – and I feel a sadness at their passing (one that I must harden myself against if I am to continue to function); but my grandfather's passing was the first scar on my life. There's part of me that screams because that is so trite.

I did not know what to do then, but I wouldn't have trouble now.

Even though my grandfather taught me well, he never communicated that facility that enables men to grieve when they lose someone they love. It's a common fault. Men are seldom instructed in the way of sympathy; in fact there is a culture in some male quarters of cutting off all contact from any friend that has weakened or stumbled. It's the sort of bully mentality that leads ultimately to becoming the Enemy and their outlook. When compassion is looked upon as a weakness, then the world and its peoples become impoverished.

But perhaps my grandfather *did* teach me well after all. If he hadn't taught me his lessons, then I wouldn't be here, in the land of his birth, having grown into a man that some others respect, thinking about a spirit called Serena.

And I suddenly remember the Sirena of his stories.

A long, long time ago words possessed a magical quality on Guam. A person had to be careful what they said, because spoken wishes had a habit of coming true – which could prove to be very inconvenient.

Now, there lived on Guam at this time a young woman – barely grown from a girl – by the name of Sirena who was considered to be the most beautiful maiden found anywhere. Once a day, more often if it was possible, Sirena would go and swim in the sea. This she loved to do and, after some time, she began to decipher the sounds of the waves – she found their words bewitching and enticing.

And Sirena would undress and enter the water, enjoying that refreshing sensation of being free. She would swim for hours, neglecting the chores that her mother had given her – much to her mother's consternation.

Each time that Sirena forgot to finish washing the family clothes, or omitted to help with the household work, her mother would grow more upset with her, until one day she could take it no longer. When she found that Sirena was missing yet again, Sirena's mother ran down to the sea and, before she could think what she was saying, she vented her anger with a mother's forceful outburst.

"Sirena, you are impossible! You should have been born a fish – that's what I wish had happened to you."

Sirena's godmother was nearby and overheard this yelling. She realized instantly what Sirena's mother had not understood in her anger, and quickly added her own words: "Half of Sirena belongs to me – let that part stay human."

Sirena felt strange sensations course through the lower half of her body and she discovered her movements through the water becoming even more fluid and easy. Then, glancing down, she found that from the waist down her body had turned into the tail end of a fish.

Realizing that her life had changed forever, she waved goodbye to her mother and godmother and slithered into the depths to enjoy a different world. Sirena was the first mermaid and, ever since, the men traveling the oceans have reported seeing this captivating water angel, who often lures their companions to their deaths.

I look for something to do about those water buffalo. I must stop thinking about the many ways to die.

Too late.

That's why I know it was my fate, my destiny to be here. If ever there was a symbol mixing attraction with danger, it is the folklore about the mermaid. All over the world, wherever land meets water, men will talk of such beautiful creatures from the seas and oceans – wondrous women who can lure you to places of danger.

It seems as though some horrible joke is being played upon myself, that I am indeed being lured onto some torturous mental reef by an enticing mermaid who sings her song for me alone. She talks to me. She offers advice. She is in my dreams. While I am standing in the surf, longing to wade out over the coral to be by her side. Serena, my English Greek mermaid. It is a magic of extraordinary proportions. What are the songs we humans sing to each other, which can mean a man will pass one woman in the street with barely a nod, and be stopped in his tracks by another? Is it down to biology? Chemistry? Fate?

Was I born to be the sort of man who must seek mermaids all his life?

Can mermaids rise up from the sea to live with a man?

Questions, questions, questions.

And those three water buffalo have still not moved.

I set up some digital recording equipment (many thanks to Ms Frances Driver of our media department), and have recorded a number of stationary and moving images of myself. I am of the opinion that seeing me was unsettling for Phoenix, and therefore I am trying something different. I feel like Princess Leia, in *Star Wars*, recording a hologram message for The Rebels, but without the silly hairstyle.

I have attempted to ascertain what became of Phoenix by using Odysseus to bypass the days following our last encounter, but I cannot latch onto him. So I have decided to follow him, as best I can, on a real-time basis – I *must* help him live. To assist me, I have travelled further back into his past to see if there were any clues about his personality that might help me to help him. I did this in little five-/ten-minute spells – vignettes of his life as it were.

It was as if I'd been given the keys to his history, i.e. what makes this man. From the snippets I allowed myself, I gleaned a tremendous amount about the character of Phoenix Lafayette. I have spent some time with Phoenix in a bar, and discovered he treats alcohol like a substitute for water. The only way he appears to maintain some balance is to consume large quantities of coffee. I got the impression that he sees intoxication as a method of assisting his writing – at least that was what I've heard him say to others. I believe it is a smokescreen, however, some act of rebellion that he hopes will diminish him in other people's eyes, none more so than his father's, so they will consider him merely a drunk and leave him to sink or swim in a future of his own making. Which is all he has ever really wanted.

I could see why Phoenix loved his grandfather telling stories – the old man's voice had this beautiful pitch and lilt, and I could have listened to him for hours myself.

It is these stories from his grandfather that shaped Phoenix. They gave simple explanations for how the world works: those in power dictating what is right and what is wrong.

It seems as though great clouds have been lifted from my mind.

I will choose my own destiny.

It's surprising how similar my thinking is to that of Phoenix. I dread to think that we may be influencing each other's thoughts.

But then, isn't that what couples do – isn't that what we have become?

Following Phoenix has changed me – all my romantic illusions have been brushed aside by the reality of his war. I have seen him working hard at his journalism, as if to prove himself to his father. I saw him following the raw recruits through their training and how they grew to respect him. I witnessed episodes of fighting elsewhere in the Pacific and heard his words of comfort to men who had lost their friends. I saw too many young men – boys really – calling for their mothers as they died. It would be lovely if life could just be a fairy story with a happy ending, but, while that is something worth aspiring to, if you accept the odds are against it in the first place, then you'll not end up disappointed.

There must be a way to counter this fatalism.

Phoenix *must* be affecting me. I was *never* this pessimistic. I *must* invigorate him. I *must* help him strive for life and happiness for himself. He has his tasks, while I have completed mine.

Propped up on my desk are twelve Polaroid photographs of myself with my prizes. There they are: the mane from an old toy lion; a china frog; a muntjac deer; a Vietnamese pot-bellied pig; an empty horse's stable; an angry swan; a child's farmhouse plastic bull; and a plastic shire-horse from the same set; a big leather belt from a shop called *Just Hyde*; plastic cows, also from the farmyard collection (the shop assistant gave me a funny look); an apple; and a Dalmatian dog walking in the park. (Not quite a hell-hound, but the muzzled Dobermann pinscher I encountered looked too emasculated for my purposes.)

Phoenix has less than two days left to complete his tasks.

Meanwhile I must return to work.

W Day +3. 17.48. Fonte Plateau.

I look closer at the still stationary animals that could represent my tenth task. I even feel my head twitching now – the muscles in my neck writhing and buckling. I blink several times, trying to concentrate. I can spot movement in the undergrowth right behind the water buffalo. Between the legs of the cattle I see slow-moving Enemy legs.

I pat Rici on the arm. He turns and, before he can say anything, I put a finger to my lips. I point to the buffalo and imitate a walking man with two fingers. He shades his eyes and stares, then turns back to me and holds up four fingers. I nod agreement. Rici picks up a stone and tosses it at Amos. Amos jerks around, spits some of his unending tobacco to the ground, and is about to sound off big time when he realizes what Rici is indicating to him. Bill catches the exchange, and both Amos and he appraise the situation unfolding behind the cattle. Amos turns to me, gives me the thumbs-up, and grins. So does Bill. The change in them is complete; they are now marines at Work. I tap Rici on the shoulder again, I point to the water buffalo, then to myself, and then I cover my eyes with one hand. I point to Rici and to Amos and Bill, and do my walking fingers again – only faster. They all nod.

I check the Enemy's position.

I'm going to use the water buffalo as cover to attack the Enemy.

That will be my tenth task.

So I ease myself out of my foxhole, signal for the others to follow, and start running. But seeing a beautiful imp of a woman standing twenty feet away, between my "cattle" and me, is not what I want just then.

She seems to have stepped out of some raunchy twenties' silent film and has short hair, glasses and is dressed, if I'm not mistaken, in black leather.

She's gorgeous. And it's Serena.

Hello, Nix.

You pick your moments!

I glance back at Rici, Amos and Bill, and the image of Serena flashes across my vision to become center stage again. I hesitate.

What the fuck?

I shut my eyes. She's still there.

I have my eyes shut and she's still there, in my head. She's still there.

I open my eyes again and the Boys are moving forward, following me.

She's still there. Everywhere I look, she's still there.

I shake my head.

I'm sorry, Nix. I'll switch it off.

I ignore the voice. I try to ignore the vision. I start to run again. This is to be my tenth task and I can't back out now.

Run, Nix, run!

Shit!

The Enemy is beginning to emerge from behind the buffalo furthest to the right. They'll spot us for sure. I run harder to try and put the animals between the Enemy and us again. Serena still stands dead center.

Shit! I've dropped the switch!

Pick it up, then!

Grunt, gasp, run.

Harder!

Grunt, gasp, run.

Run!

As I cover the ground, I trip and nearly fall. I can hardly focus.

Nix!

I run harder.

Leave me! Let me see! Let me see!

I've got it!

I try to ignore the voice. I run, I run and I run. I keep the buffalo between the Enemy and us. I'm nearly at them.

God, they're big.

Th-zip! Th-zip!

Shit! The Enemy has seen us!

Love the ground!

Serena shimmers and disappears.

We all hit the ground together. Almost at the same time, the water buffalo join us there. They stagger and crumble to their knees as the Enemy try to kill us, but hit the beasts instead. The three buffalo roll over dead, without a sound. But they serve the same purpose as before, becoming a cover to hide behind. Amos rests his BAR on the belly of one, Rici slaps his down on another. Bill and I give them assistance. We just have the edge – the Enemy is exposed. The exchange of fire increases as Rici and Amos get their BARs working. I hear a cry and the return fire lessens. Another cry from the Enemy, then a scream. One by one we are picking them off. Then the Enemy fire stops.

Amos and Bill rise to their feet and run, at a crouch, off to their right, while Rici and I cover them. There is definitely no return fire now. Amos and Bill have reached the Enemy. They do a slow-sure check. Bill rolls over one Enemy with his boot and pulls out his .45. I think of that image of the firing squad. Bill administers last rites, while Amos saves himself a bullet and smashes the butt of his BAR into another Enemy's face. I turn away as he reaches down to the broken jaw and reaches inside with his fingers. He can do it with just one blow now he has had some practice.

Rici is grinning, and pats his dead buffalo.

"Thanks, guys," he says.

"Number ten," I mutter to myself, "number ten."

As Rici goes over to talk to Amos and Bill, Serena's image reappears.

Hi. You know how to torment a guy, don't you?

Sorry about that.

I snap my eyes all around, but she still stays in my view all the time.

I'm getting used to it, now.

Did I hear you right? Number ten?

That's right.

I keep my eyes steady.

God, you're pretty.

Stop it, you'll make me blush.

I still want to take you out.

I wish you could.

I want to hold you. I want to hold you and kiss you.

I take a step forward, but she stays out of reach.

I wish you could. Nix?

Yes?

I love you.

I know.

I don't want you to die. I want you to live.

I know.

You mustn't die, Nix.

I know. I love you, too.
Oh God.
Yeah, oh God.

Classified Secret
F2/6846/3/
Final Instruction Notes.

1. Subject is reported to be now using experimental apparatus on a full-time basis. It has been observed that she does take occasional breaks where she appears to be reading World War II history books, but to all intents and purposes, she can be said to be continuing her experiment around the clock. This has obvious advantages for us, and is most welcome.

2. The situation is being closely monitored and our team will keep in radio contact with the observers. It is recommended that we proceed quickly before the current situation changes.

3. Entry will be made via the rear door with a duplicate key already acquired from a locksmith. Mortise locks are never used by subject. Otherwise, if circumstances are different (subject has been noted taking extra precautions), the team will force entry and proceed as quickly as possible to workroom as per plan. Estimated time in this worst-case scenario is five to six seconds. Subject will probably be alerted by this forced entry, but will have no time to switch off equipment.

4. To reiterate: Subject will be prevented from switching off equipment by whatever means available. Weapons to be silent.

5. The team is instructed to begin operation within forty-eight (48) hours of receipt of this message.

TWENTY-FIVE

So far Hercules had spent eight years and one month completing his ten labours. He wasn't pleased to be reminded of the decisions made by Eurystheus.

"The king doesn't count the Hydra or the Augean stables as being satisfactorily concluded," the herald said through his hatch in the city gate.

"Mmm, and so what does he want now?" asked Hercules, drumming his fingers on the metal surrounding the hatch opening, knowing from the herald's tone that the following words would give pleasure to one of them, and it was unlikely to be Hercules.

"The apples of the Hesperides," said the herald.

Hercules stopped his tapping. "What? Hera's wedding gift to my father?" he said.

"Those are the ones, and I understand that Atlas' nymph daughters, the Hesperides, guard them. There's also the hundred-headed dragon Ladon, which sleeps curled around the roots of the tree, to consider."

Hercules sighed. "Did King Eurystheus happen to mention where this garden could be found," he said. "Because I've always been told that it was magical and therefore a bit difficult to get to?"

"Sorry, no clues. You're on your own – I think that's the general idea."

"Thank you."

"My pleasure." The hatch slapped shut.

*

Hercules wandered through the known world: around Northern Africa, then to Asia and back. On his way he fought a sea-god, who did know the whereabouts of the garden. The god told Hercules that he would have to find someone else to help him obtain the apples, and refused to give up the secret location. So, the search continued. Hercules was forced to fight another two of Poseidon's sons. (Poseidon was apparently prodigious in his frolics – all foam and salt.) He beat another Poseidon child in a wrestling match, after Hercules lifted him off the ground which diminished his power. And he killed yet another such son, who tried to use Hercules for a human sacrifice. The world was paved with problems – and sons of Poseidon.

As he searched, Hercules discovered a man called Prometheus chained to a rock – sentenced to his terrible fate by Zeus for stealing the secret of fire. Every day a vulture would swoop down, rip out his liver, and then every night his liver would grow back, ready for the morrow. This cycle had been repeated for many years. When Hercules killed the tormenting bird, as a reward Prometheus told him the trick needed to obtain the apples.

"Take the load from off the back of Atlas," said Prometheus. "He'll be so grateful, he'll go get you the apples. Mind you, be careful, he hates holding up the world so much, that he's likely to try to find a way to make you take his place."

And so it happened.

When Atlas returned with the apples, he offered to take them to Eurystheus himself. Hercules sighed and agreed, but then asked if Atlas would mind taking the load back while Hercules put some padding on his shoulders, since they weren't as strong as Atlas's.

A few minutes later and Hercules was heading back to Mycenae with the apples of the Hesperides and Atlas was left with the world on his shoulders, shouting all sorts of abuse after him.

*

"The king says to remind you that we can't keep these," the herald explained.

"What? Then why . . .? Have you any idea what I've . . .?"

"They belong to the gods."

Hercules paused, then spoke slowly. "I suggest you get yourself one of those semi-submerged bronze pots your king likes so much."

As Hercules left to find his friend Athene, to hand her the apples to take back, he thought he could hear a faint whimper. Perhaps it was the wind.

Next time, the herald achieved some sought-after revenge.

"The king has given this last task an awful lot of thought," he said, from his own new pot behind the gate, after Hercules returned.

"And that would be?" asked Hercules.

"Bring back Cerberus."

There was a thick silence.

"Bugger," Hercules then said.

There was another thick silence.

"I don't envy you," said the herald.

There was a noise as he clambered out of his pot, and then the gate swung open.

"I wish you all the best." The herald held out his hand.

Hercules took it, clasping his other hand to the herald's other arm at the elbow.

"Thank you," said Hercules. And then he set off.

The herald watched the hero depart, and was of the firm opinion that Hercules would be killed this time. He realized that he could never have himself done what Hercules had done already.

"Bugger," he said, echoing Hercules' sentiments, and returned inside the gate to head for the palace.

*

Cerberus was a monster belonging to Hades, and guarded the entrance to that part of the Underworld where the wicked were punished, called Tartarus. He was not a beast to be approached lightly. At the front he had three heads, each one similar to that of a vicious dog; his rear was like a dragon tail with a huge scorpion sting, and his broad back glistened with a line of darting snake-heads. This was no ordinary guard dog, so Hercules decided it would be a good idea to take some precautions.

Hercules went to see the priest who had started up the Eleusinian Mysteries. These were sacred rites, and whosoever got to know them would enjoy happiness in Hades (the Underworld being named after the god who ruled it). After purification, Hercules was granted the privilege of knowledge of these Mysteries. Then he set off to that place from which no mortal had yet returned.

Approaching the dark and jagged entrance to Hades, Hercules paused long enough to give praise to his father Zeus, then headed on down. Into the depths of the Underworld he walked, past dead monsters, and down past dead heroes, down past wronged ghosts. Hercules helped out where he could. Once again he was made to wrestle, once again he won. He was filled with a terrible resolve: he would not be stopped. This would be his *last* task – one way or the other.

His journey finally came to its end.

The god of the Underworld, Hades, not being averse to taking a gamble, said that the hero could take Cerberus away with him, but only if he did not use his weapons to subdue him. Hades pointed out that this would be some fight.

Hercules thanked Hades for allowing the opportunity, and then made his way down into Tartarus itself. The residents of the Underworld followed to watch, and it did not take long to get there. The crowds paused and stood back, while Hercules proceeded on. And he could hear Cerberus even before he saw him.

"So this is what hell sounds like," said Hercules to himself.

And then, there stood Cerberus.

Waiting for him.

TWENTY-SIX

W Day +4. 09.11. Fonte Plateau.

We've had a lie-in, while most folks back home will be in the office, the shop or the factory by now, or on their third cup of coffee, and they'll have discussed the morning's news as heard on the radio or read in the newspapers. They'll have talked about the war, no doubt expressed opinions on how "our boys" are doing, what "our boys" *should* be doing, what *they* would do about it. Well, I'd like to be there, to tell them *exactly* what has been done on their behalf. I would explain it all in minute detail, hand out photographs, give them names to put to the faces and corpses. There'd then be that cold silence that happens at parties when an unexpected and unwelcome guest turns up. I'd quickly be shown the door, since there's only so much truth that anyone can take.

Nevertheless, I write it all down during this glorious early-morning intermission I have been granted, during which I try to dry out my equipment as I am forced to wait for others. It's either that, or start thinking about it.

Most sane people will have spent a night of quiet dreams that faded as soon as the alarm clock sounded to start their day. I suspect a few more than usual will have perhaps been troubled by those nightmares about missed loved ones away at war, which awoke them in the early hours.

I have spent yet another of *my* nights in an extended quasi-state of disbelief, where sleep means an odd moment when physically the body cannot stay awake any more. A night when the sky is not lit by the stars, but flares going up from both sides. Flares from our ships which have moved closer into shore, so that they can shine their searchlights more effectively across the ground that we have had to leave empty because there are too few of us left on the line to defend it. And flares from the Enemy as they try to kill those that remain. A night when insects that you wouldn't want to look at in daylight are finding their way in under your clothes.

Much time is spent thinking about dry deserts and dry air and not contemplating the total number of days that you have felt damp and been covered in a foul-smelling mixture of dirt, smoke and sweat. It has been a night when you wonder which poor fool is whimpering, only to realize it is yourself – a black corruption of the mind when you know you are filled to overflowing with images you would love to forget; when you pray for daylight because it will ease at least some of your demons that thrive only in the dark.

The debate about whether the drink is helping me continues on a minute-by-minute basis in my head. Why stay sober? With the alcohol I consume, I transport myself to regions of this earth that are otherwise beyond my reach, places that are not *here*, at least. They may be high-school cardboard cut-outs of events in my life, but, they're not Guam, they're not *here*.

Images of drink . . . A cut-glass crystal tumbler, with a base over half-an-inch thick, that holds a fifteen-year-old malt. It's the West Coast of Scotland, standing on a crag with purple heather flowering up and down the mountains. A stag stands defiant on a cliff edge, a golden eagle swoops in a never-ending circle over the glen. The lights are being lit in the hotel below, with the prospect of a meal, a hot fire, and more of the glorious whisky, more of the stomach-warming, mind-changing nectar from the peat.

A dimpled pint mug filled with that deceptively warm, typically English beer. A village pub with Tom and some friends, gentle jibes about one another between the English and the Americans, an endless game of darts in the corner, stories from old men who can stand upright forever in one spot no matter how much they drink. That sensation, coming halfway through the third pint, when everyone appears to emit a cozy glow of friendship.

A frosted beaker, held in a cork container, filled with Jamaican gin and some ice. A boat off the Florida Keys, fishing for those big marlin that cruise up from the cold depths of the Atlantic, and feeling that frozen nip as the drink slips over the tongue, knowing that the change to come will be slow and mellow and lingering and full of pleasure.

A rum, a vodka, a tequila ... A tequila? I'm there in that desert, dry and losing myself in the delights of a drink that fires the mind and helps end the day in a frenzy of delightful cravings. With tequila you can see things that are not normally visible.

Why stay sober? Spirits for a spirit.

But not wine – wine is not drinking, it's life.

There's part of me that is fascinated by my present decline. By the very nature of my work, I've seen more action than any one of the Boys, and that's including Rici, while this constant drumbeat of war has become louder and more dramatic in the last few days. No wonder I crave those other worlds that drink provides for me. Even though I've made it my aim to concentrate on just one group of men in the job they have to fulfil, where if I've had the opportunity, I have gone elsewhere to report – to try to cover as much as I can, providing contrast. I decided last night that there must come a time when you become so numbed by the brutal experiences that you lose any shred of humanity, or else accept your mind is going to rebel. It sometimes takes time to see the obvious.

I'm in love with a ghost?

I'm in love with a goddess who has a flash of wit in her eyes, who can do that sultry thing with a tilt of the head that women have perfected to indicate they are interested in a man.

I'm in love with a woman who looks like she intends to

dance away her time, laughing with the joy of life. I'm in love with a spirit.

That must say something about my state of mind. At least it means I still have my humanity, I suppose.

It's been easier to make progress to where we are now than it should have been. The Enemy is continuing to yield the lower ground to us – as I pointed out to Rici shortly after we landed – but I still do not understand their reasoning of their continued use of such tactics. They fight with the utmost ferocity, yet they give up good positions in obedience to some order. Why? This can only mean one thing: the Enemy is continuing its policy of defense against our island hops, and is planning a massive *banzai* attack sometime. It is a loser's strategy that will enable us to win Guam if they don't overwhelm us. And that's the key question, however mad it seems: can they overcome us in suicidal attacks? The longer they leave it, the better equipped we will become. But *they* don't seem ever to worry about dying.

We now have a good supply of water from the Asan Spring, which means less dependence on marines hauling cans up from the beaches. The relief of having fresh water whenever needed is a perfect boon (I have noticed a discernible increase in morale); it eases the pressure of working in this heat and humidity. I'm contemplating using some of my ration for a wash; that always makes me feel better.

I suddenly have a sacrilegious idea. As Rici watches me, I take off my helmet, upend it on the ground, and pour the remains of a bottle of *saki* into it. I dip my hands into it, lean forward, cup a handful of the liquor and splash it onto my face. I bend down to do it again, my fingers dabbling like birds in a birdbath.

"Good God," mutters Rici. "I've seen everything now."

I ignore him and try to dismiss the electric reaction of the alcohol on all the small cuts that I've picked up by fighting in the jungle. As I rub away the filth, the bristles of my beard prickle my palms. The heat from my skin evaporates the *saki* as I groan in pleasure. Sod the pain, sod Rici's laugh, and sod the fact that I'm not keeping it to drink, I'm getting clean and I'm getting cool. I then dig out another bottle (some guys from 2nd battalion liberated an Enemy store they uncovered), and I pour its entire contents into my helmet. I scrub myself with a vengeance, splashing happily with my new luxury. The *saki* turns a filthy undrinkable color.

Rici has picked up another bottle, and he wriggles it in my direction. The contents slosh from side to side – I find it mesmerizing. It would be lovely to swim inside that bottle, and chase the air bubbles.

"Go ahead," I say. "I'll only drink it."

He grins, takes off his helmet, upends the bottle, and the contents gurgle out as they did for me. Rici swirls the precious liquor around in his helmet, sets it on the ground and pulls up his sleeves. He winces at the first splash on his skin, but he carries on. So we wash, we get clean, we get cool for a while. After we're finished we hurl the muck into the air, put our helmets back on, sigh contented sighs – and listen to elements of the 9th advance on our right.

It's pleasant to listen to war when you're not taking part: the guns, the mortars, the artillery fire. As we sit and contemplate our little bit of peace, I inevitably think about Serena, and about my sister Alice.

She and Rici remind me of the Guam love story about a girl from a rich family who falls for the son of a poor fisherman – only *those* two ended up throwing themselves off the cliff at Tumon Bay because the girl's father wanted her to marry someone else.

Two such diverse backgrounds, that's Alice and Rici. How often does this sort of thing happen? Two halves of a relationship, from worlds that normally never have contact, have by some quirk met and fallen in love. Perhaps it's this war, stripping away all the pretence. Live and let live and, given the chance, Rici and Alice could have a pretty good stab at enjoying life together.

So could Serena and I. But that *is* a fool's paradise.

Live and let live? The paradox is that's why we fight the Enemy: to enable us to do just that.

"So, Rici," I say suddenly, "are you in love with my sister?"

I don't think I've ever seen Rici flustered before, but he now gives a good imitation briefly. He looks at the ground for a whole minute, without saying anything. Then he slowly nods his head.

"Yes," he says, looking across, "yes, I am. I've been hit by the Thunderbolt. You okay with that?"

I fold my arms, parodying the stance of the righteous.

"Why shouldn't I be?" I ask. "My best buddy has fallen for my sister – they make films about situations like that, don't they? You'll probably be played by some mean and moody Humphrey Bogart."

"I thought you said I look like Buster Keaton?"

"Right, but I've never heard him talk."

He glances down at the ground for a second again. "I really *do* love her," he says.

"I know. And I'll dance at your wedding."

"If we get back."

"You had to bring that up, didn't you?"

"You know I'm practical."

"Stick with me and you'll be lucky as well."

"Still believing in your Hercules, then?"

"Couldn't believe more."

"You know you're going mad?"

"From day one, Rici. From day one."

"I'll even let you date my sister."

"No need."

"Why?"

"Don't get upset – I've fallen in love with another."

"Tell me, bud, how you manage that thousands of miles from civilization and . . . Hey, you've not, you know, gone over to the other side?"

"No, Rici, I've just gone mad, but she's lovely."

"Yes," he says. "Yes she is."

I leave him to continue thinking about Alice.

W Day +4. 10.41. Fonte Plateau.

It takes the 9th about an hour to achieve their objective. And in that time I have thought about many things and come to some conclusions. The most important is that I'm running out of tasks, and so I'm also running out of time. That is *the* dilemma – *the* panic. The fear chews on my insides and beats its fists in my chest. But I still have Serena; that's my alternative Dead Pool Poker hand. She seems the one constant companion I can depend on – apart from the Boys.

What's that sound?

She'd asked this about a quarter of an hour ago.

That's the ninth, they're getting to grips with gaining more ground. That rumble of tanks means they've likely freed up a road somewhere.

And that's good?

Oh, yes. If the tanks are up and running, it will mean more protection, more men from the reserve and more equipment.

Sounds like the endgame; you know – your chess metaphor?

Nowhere near, we've barely finished the opening moves – let alone entered the middle game, for that matter.

So, you're going to be stuck here some time?

God knows. But I'm likely to totally crack up first.

I'll look after you.

I'm sure you will.

No, I mean it: I'll look after you.

Serena, if I could hold your hand, if I could touch your face, if I could kiss you, make love to you, I would find some sort of peace. But as that's impossible, I shall just have to dream.

I wish you could—

You wish I could do what?

I wish you could make love to me. I'm sure it would be good.
I know it would.

And as I sat with this incredible heat surging in my loins, I listened to the 9th fighting, knowing that sometime today our period of rest will end and the advance will continue.

So I sit here and think, and try to pretend that the pounding in my chest is just an over-exuberant heart and not due to some gargoyle-demon of fear.

How the hell can I find anything that can be an apple?

Phoenix is under such duress from his current circumstances that I have doubts about how much longer he can carry on. I'm sure he is not aware of it, but he keeps looking at his hands, seemingly fascinated by how they tremble and shake. In these days of Post-Traumatic Stress Disorder it's easy to look back and say that the men fighting WW2 were put under too much pressure; but while it was the dead who paid the ultimate price, how many more had their lives blighted by the memories? As always, that's the benefit of hindsight. I try to think of ways to calm his thinking, but the mental onslaught on him is relentless. In many ways I'll need to fight for his sanity as well as his physical well-being.

I wish I could hold him, tight.

W Day +4. 14.00. Fonte Plateau.

We're going to seize more of the plateau. To this end some softening-up is taking place from the navy, and from our own artillery, along the whole extent of the front. It will be another one-and-a-half hours before they finish and we can begin to move. It is like listening to, or conducting, some crazy synchronized symphony, where the percussionists are not following the conductor but are playing just when they feel like it. The only predictable note is the explosions following the shells as they hit.

They start as a low whistle from somewhere behind, already high in the air, yet soon coming down fast. And each time you think it's not going to make it, that the damned thing is going to fall short and is going to hit you. Then the whistle turns into a wail, and it disappears in a cloud of fire and smoke, and returns a dull yet sharp-faced boom that cuts through your hearing. Over the space of one minute, I try to count how many are landing.

One whistle chased by another.

Two-tone whisper equals howitzer.

Another whistle.

Thud, thud.

Crash!

A whisper.

A whistle.

Thud.

Crash!

Thick cloud and flame.

Canvas is ripped – a low trajectory.

Thud, crash, thud, whistle, whisper.

And so on, and so on, each noise overhead causing me to flinch, so I tense my shoulders and lower my head.

I soon give up counting.

How much more?

I don't know how much more *I* can take, let alone him.

The noise of the shelling has a terrible foreboding. It seems as though the devil is speaking.

I tense my shoulders along with Phoenix.

There's nothing I can do in this situation, except convince him to get away. But his sense of duty would prevent him.

If this is just a matter of luck, what if one of the shells were to fall short?

To distract myself, I must seek out opportunities for his quest. He hasn't completed the tasks yet.

He'll be okay.

He'll be okay. I'm there to help him.

*

W Day +4. 15.35. Fonte Plateau.

Lieutenant Bowlsure issues the order and we begin to move the line further onto Fonte Plateau. I take a photograph, and no one smiles. We are all weary but we keep the advance going. It doesn't take us long (three to four minutes – we were that close) to reach the outer limit of where the bombardment hit, and some of the craters we discover still smoke and smolder. I am indeed heading towards Hades. I take another photograph to prove it. I am yet to find my apples of Hesperides, but suspect I could be encountering Cerberus before then. I take a drink whenever I have a moment. And chain-smoke cigarettes whenever we pause.

Unfortunately the Enemy is still here in force and the resistance is as fierce as anything we've encountered. We hit the dirt, we return fire, we maneuver. We signal to the guys with bazookas where they should aim. We run forward a few more yards and we hit the dirt. We throw grenades, we return fire, we take hits, but we kill many more of them than they do of us. We move on. Our battalion is ordered to bypass a ravine where the Enemy has a particularly strong hold, and, as the Boys give it a wide berth to save on casualties, our artillery opens up again, with support from the air this time.

I can't even begin to imagine what it must be like inside that defensive trap the Enemy has built for itself.

We have a break. I have a drink. I have a smoke.

I see twelve planes circle above us, looking for the entire world like buzzards waiting for something to die in the desert. Instead, they are seeking Enemy in the diminishing remains of a jungle, knowing this Enemy has no way out. The pitch and whine of the aircraft changes – the birds announcing they have spotted something – and they peel off, one by one, and swoop down. I am conscious of becoming detached from everything, as though what is happening is only of any consequence to others and has absolutely nothing to do with me. The first plane roars down like a lion on its prey in some remote African savanna. The pilot lets the Enemy have several seconds' burst of cannon before he releases his bomb and then banks up and away. The second plane rushes down, reminding me of some serpent from the depths pouncing on a victim running along the shore. The third aircraft appears to me as some sort of vicious fighting buck. On and on they come – each one dancing through the sky as though their mission is not only to destroy the Enemy but to remind me of the tasks of Hercules. I watch them, my mouth open, my hands on my ears, witnessing the demolition of a defensive position in a whirlwind of destruction that is annihilating the Enemy.

They roll away into the sky, each cutting a vortex through the smoke, and meanwhile the artillery ceases its deluge of shells, and my view of the ravine fades in a mist of hell-clouds and dislodged vegetation fluttering in the wind. Yet another part of my grandfather's world is slashed back to a distressed version of what was there before, and its soil now enriched with the blood of the invaders that are the Enemy.

I try to take a photograph. I find I can't.

W Day +4. 16.23. Fonte Plateau.

It has begun to rain. Some of the Boys stop to put on their ponchos and this joint action prompts a break. Rici, Amos, Bill and myself gather in a little group to have a smoke. Bill and Amos discuss whores again. What fascinates me is that I know they're telling the truth. I cup the cigarette in my hand to keep it dry, and to help pass the time – it seems so normal to do so now – I watch an Enemy die. He is lying in the mud, less than ten feet away from me, and surrounding him on the ground are most of his insides as he holds in what he can of the rest to prevent it from falling out. He doesn't seem to care too much about the pain, and he appears to spend his last few minutes watching us enjoy our ten minutes' relaxation. Perhaps he would like a last smoke.

His eyes meet mine. No, he doesn't want a cigarette; his soul is beyond my understanding.

I notice his head is trembling, so he *is* feeling pain. The rain falls gently onto his face.

I smoke my smoke. He looks away from me at the others.

Nix?

Serena, hello.

Nix, what's that near his arm?

I look down.

What do you mean?

There, about two feet from his right arm.

I keep looking, then I see it. The rain has washed the dirt off it and now I can see it. It's the pin from a grenade. I look back at the Enemy. He is staring at me; his soul is still beyond my understanding.

Shit!

My cigarette falls from my lips.

I leap towards the Enemy lying in the mud. I fling my body at this Enemy who has set himself up as a booby trap. His eyes grow wider, and he begins to take his hands from his gaping stomach. I get to him, throw myself down, grab both his upper arms, and press them to his sides. He bucks and twists and screams insults at me. He even tries to bite me.

"Nix?" It's Rici.

"A grenade," I say, "maybe two. I think the bastard's hidden one in his armpit. Maybe both armpits."

For a man who is dying, this Enemy makes a good attempt at getting me to loosen my grip. I pray that the grenades are where I think they are – if they're hidden under his back, I'm already finished. His spittle hits my lips and I grimace, trying to squeeze the life from him. I press his arms as hard as I can against his body, and summon up strength I never knew I had. I hear one rib crack. He thrashes even more wildly.

Thwack!

Rici drives his bayonet into the Enemy's throat. I'm showered in a momentary gush of blood. The Enemy goes limp. I wait – I'll not be conned. I count to ten, but there is no life here; the Enemy is dead.

"You okay?" asks Rici.

I nod. "Take over from me," I say.

Rici crouches over the Enemy's head and continues pressing the elbows to the corpse's chest. I release my grip and force my fingers into his bloody armpits. After a second of groping I feel metallic objects in both. I enclose my hands around both of them, making sure each lever doesn't spring.

"Jesus," I say, "they feel like they're ours."

"Probably got them off some dead marine."

"Ready?" I ask.

"Okay, boys," Rici announces to everyone else, "get ready to hit the dirt."

As I stand up, the Boys have already backed off. I don't blame them.

I pick a good direction, lob the one in my right hand as far as I can, then carefully pass the one in my left hand to my right, and repeat the operation. I hit the mud myself.

Love the ground.

Crack-crash! Crack-crash!

Both grenades go off.

They were your apples of Hesperides, Nix.

Grenades, apples? Who cares? Is God counting?

Hopefully.

A hand clobbers me on the back as I begin to get to my feet.

"Well done, Nixy. I thought we'd be burying *you*." It's Amos.

I give a sigh of relief, smile at him, and look down at my shaking hands. I come to a decision – Amos has given me an idea.

The Boys begin to move off.

"You go ahead," I say. "I'll catch you up."

Rici frowns, but I grin to show I'm okay, and he turns to join the rest of them.

What are you doing?

Keeping my options open.

I reach into my top pocket.

How do you intend to do that?

I take out my winnings from Dead Pool Poker, and look around for a good spot – one I can remember.

I'm going to bury my winnings.

Why?

It'll give me a little something to come back for. I'm going to run out of all things Hercules any time soon, so keeping an incentive seems the right thing to do.

Perhaps.

Definitely. Look.

The grenades I threw into the remains of the undergrowth have ripped down still more of the jungle foliage, exposing objects that I heard my grandfather talk about, but I never expected to see.

What are they?

Latte Stones.

It is a formation of ancient pillars, each one constructed from a six-foot tall rectangular base stone, of what appears to be limestone, surmounted by a huge circular capstone made of coral. They look like rows of giant mushrooms.

Latte Stones?

The Chamorro – my ancestors – put them there, thousands of years ago. Don't ask me why.

I step over the remains of the dead Enemy and make my way to the nearest standing stone. It doesn't take me long to dig a hole in the rain-soaked earth. I take out my cigarette case, remove the last remaining smoke, put my small bundle of money into it, place it in the hole, and shovel the earth back on top of it. I stamp the earth down to conceal it.

Good luck.

Thanks.

The rain becomes heavier, but I try not to consider it a bad omen. Wiping my lips clean, then checking the operation of my carbine, I hurry after the Boys.

*

Cerberus was no puppy: he was the guard dog to the Underworld. And as soon as he spied Hercules, he rushed towards him, intent on ripping him to pieces. Hercules did likewise. The pair leapt at each other, each grappling for the best hold, and they rolled over and over – it was vicious fighting. The three heads of Cerberus snapped at Hercules, each and every way they could, and the snakes' heads along its back nipped at him when they had the chance. As their violent tussle grew in strength, they crashed into rocks, they smashed up the ground. Then Cerberus had his opportunity: for a moment, Hercules lost his grip. The hound whipped its tail round for a killing sting. It was then that Hercules' cloak, made from the Nemean lion, came to his rescue. The sting glanced off him and, in the ensuing confusion, he was able to get a proper grip around Cerberus' thick neck. Hercules applied pressure. Cerberus yelped in pain. Hercules began to drag him along the ground. Cerberus struggled. Hercules pulled. Upwards and onwards. Upwards and out. And on to Mycenae.

The herald stared, terrified, at Hercules.

"Go tell King Eurystheus I have a little something for him," said Hercules.

Cerberus snarled, continuing to try to escape.

The herald ran to his master.

In awe.

But laughing.

W Day +4. 17.02. Fonte Plateau.

Not many stories from Guam have a sequel, the meaning is usually contained within the initial fable, but the tale of The Two Lovers has an extra layer.

The bodies of the two dead lovers were found to have turned to stone: two human-shaped marble rocks are to be found lying side by side in the white sand floor of a cave at Tumon Bay. The islanders give thanks to their ancestral spirits for providing this monument to reflect upon, and yet more thanks that it is there for their children. In the end, life is to be lived, life should be protected, and, above all, life should be enjoyed.

And that is how it should be.

That's how it should be for Rici and Alice.

That's how I'd like it to be with Serena and myself.

Such are dreams.

We're advancing yet again and the world has altered into an entity that is monstrous and disturbing in the extreme. I have been cast into an environment the like of which not many people can ever have experienced in their most fevered nightmares. Now I am Hercules searching for Cerberus. I have a spirit guide and she is known to me as Serena. I exist in the surreal landscape of myth and fable, where even the imaginative highs released by alcohol are slight compared to living through this adventure that is my final quest.

The world is now different. There are few plants left intact in this universe of mine. Trees are like giant tooth stumps with jagged splinters. The bamboo plants have become simply cane cocktail sticks without leaves, broad-leaf plants are now shredded green hooks, the sword grass is like a frozen sea broken into areas of empty space, save for the bodies that the ghosts have left behind.

Warriors from the land of my birth do battle here, and sacrifice much. They slog over ground that has lost touch with what nature intended for it. They use everything at their disposal to eliminate an army sent from the land of the rising sun.

A machine of war passes me. This is no Trojan horse – but a modern implement of destruction that needs no disguise. The dragon that lives within it howls with fiery breath, and I feel the wave of heat it exhales washing over my face.

I check that the spear on the end of my shooting stick is still firmly attached. I ignore the memory of a life recently quivering its last on the lethal tip of it. One of my companions warns me to keep on the lookout for samurai with explosives bound to their chests; it seems they are trying to reach the beaches where the ships unload our cargo.

But I give them another name: Cerberus.

How *else* to name someone prepared to die in such a way?

The stench, ever increasing, begins to become attractive. I have doubts that I ever really found it distasteful and now seek out the source. My friends may try to deter me from the peril that is Hades, but I am Hercules and I must finish my final task.

Nix!

My spirit guide calls to me.

Yes?

Nix, are you alright?

Couldn't be finer. I know what I need to do.

Nix, did I hear Rici correctly, that there are Japanese soldiers now carrying TNT strapped to their chests? Like suicide bombers?

That's how some of the Enemy have armed themselves, yes. And I intend to find one. That will be my last task.

Cerberus?

Yes, and one is nearby – I can sense it. The other Boys have missed him.

How can you be sure?

Look there.

My God!

My Enemy is cunning, he moves with stealth – just like Cerberus. He creeps along, hiding in the rain and the broken trees, like a hunting dog sneaking past, carrying its prize. The undergrowth conceals him, and I crane my neck as I seek him out. Then Cerberus reappears. Around his chest he carries pouches containing fire and brimstone. He crouches lower; he will be out of sight soon. I begin to stalk him, as I have hunted before. I duck and dive, moving slowly, slowly – then I quicken my pace. I'm hidden from his view, so the tables are turned. I ready my shooting-stick, and then run past the clumps of grass that hide us both. Now he's twenty feet away. I hear shouting behind me. My soldier-friend's concerns for me alert the Enemy, who turns. I run straight at him, laughing my hero's laugh. As he sees me, he points his shooting stick at me.

Tat-tat-tat!

My shots miss him, so I carry on running.

Th-zip! Th-zip!

His shots miss me, too. As I reach him, I manage to brush aside his stick with my own. I laugh loudly again.

Nix! No!

He tries to spear me, and our shooting-sticks clatter hard against each other. We juggle for position, then he jumps away from me. He throws his shooting-stick to the ground. When I point my own at him and squeeze the trigger, it doesn't work. His hand goes to the detonator, and my mind clears. In this instant of wrestling with Cerberus, my life becomes unimportant and yet at the same time so precious, and all the fog vanishes from my mind. I am Phoenix Lafayette, not Hercules. I become suddenly sober. I swipe at the Enemy with the butt of my carbine. I hit him on the jaw. His arm comes up and knocks my carbine away. It slips from my grip.

Phoenix!

I have a split second to react – while he's still surprised that he's made me drop my weapon.

Hit him, Nix! Hit him!

I do the only thing I can think of and I punch him hard. He staggers back and falls to the ground. I go for my knife and leap on top of him. He reaches for the detonator again, but I beat him to it. I've had the practice. He screams in my ear, but I cut off the noise. I press down on top of him. I stab him once more. I press my hand over his mouth and stab again – and again. I stop myself, sit up and kneel over him. I sever the wires to the TNT.

Cerberus is dead.

The last of the twelve challenges has been overcome.

I look up to the heavens. It is gray upon gray. The sky has melted into sea.

The rain has increased to become a torrent and the night approaches.

I have finished my tasks but I have yet to face the night.

I have to face another Darkness when the Enemy appears, and I will need to repeat the struggle I have just been involved in. Only more so.

I have killed the guard dog of Hades which prevents the dead from leaving the imposing Underworld.

Tonight they will surely come.

I kneel here in this downpour of rain, washing away the blood from the Enemy I have killed, and I am filled with a terrible premonition. All that has gone before will be as nothing as to what happens tonight. I feel as though I have been given prior knowledge. Bloody Bougainville was merely an induction. This assault on Guam was merely a process of wearing me down further. I have performed as Hercules did, yet now I must face a night of suicidal *banzai*.

They'll come for me. My luck has run out.

TWENTY-SEVEN

W Day +5. 00.06. Fonte Plateau.

Warm night-rain tumbles from the sky. The deluge seems to form and materialize twenty feet in the air, in some mystical cloud, before falling rapidly to smack anything it can with its liquid touch. It doesn't sting; the rain only irritates. There is no part of me that isn't wet; the first foxhole that Rici and I dug turned out to be right in the path of a stream that started as a trickle, then gushed into our trench with gurgling glee. I could never have imagined how a hole that took twenty minutes to dig could fill so quickly with water, and sound like it was laughing at the same time. The second one fared little better. In an hour the rain had filled that up as well. So we have decided to take the risk of one of the Boys taking shots at us, and we are now camped on the mud, ponchos pulled up tight, listening to the rain and debating if it is concealing other noises that we ought to worry about.

Plink, plink. Plink, plink.

The sound of rain here is all twisted about. Water pelting the remains of a broad-leaf plant seems to echo memories of a stream rolling over a rock in the Blue Mountains. Puddles laugh (water has always had a private joke against me) as though they are being filled by an irate barman preparing a cocktail in a shaker. And the rain ricochets off our helmets with the same zing and ting as from a barn's corrugated iron roof.

Plink, plink. Plink, plink.

Rain can sound lovely if you're sitting on a porch, wearing warm clothes and with a cozy living room and rum within reach, but out here there is menace in the tunes it plays. The raindrops dance and sing their requiem, and I think of nails being shaken in a tin. It's that sort of song exactly. From way off I hear a jeep growling and grinding gears – it must be down near the beach – and now and then machine-guns issue their burping cough. The war envelops everything with its percussion accompaniment. We continue to fight to keep our positions; we carry on in our relentless pursuit of success, careless of the din we make.

I have a deep satisfaction from having completed my tasks – for some seconds out of most minutes, I dream of a fanfare welcome of return, a hail-the-conquering-hero New York pat on the back for the man whose personal odyssey has finished. But the remainder of those same minutes is filled with a dread that I *have* finished them. Now all that remains are the remembered stories my grandfather told me, my shell bracelet – and my fear. It pays not to think in this place, but I think I have used up my entire talisman.

Somewhere, and to someone, I am in debt. I have borrowed much, with my luck acting as collateral.

The line is thin, and we are weakened. Most of the Boys have paired off, to ensure maximum use of the BARs, so there is about fifteen yards between each foxhole. We all secretly wish for at least double our number. *I* wouldn't be content if the men were *ten* deep. I wonder if my wish can be granted by praying to the god of rain.

I close my eyes. And open the door to my fears.

The rain becomes a million insects scuttling and slithering around me. They whisper and chirp as they move and scratch. It sounds like some hive of nameless things. So that's my answer?

One of my insect demons splashes too hard into a puddle.

I snap open my eyes. I hear another splash. And another. It is a man running. It is an Enemy coming in from the right.

"Chief!" I call. "Up front! Near you!"

"Gotcha, Nixy."

Phut!

Someone pops up a flare. The Enemy starts shouting as he runs in.

"Cops-man!" he cries. "Cops-man!"

He's picked up some words. He's calling for a medic.

I see him. Out of the rain he comes. He is snarling – lips back and teeth exposed – and his eyes are wide. His skin is pinched taut on his face. He has quite a high-bridged nose for one of the Enemy. He appears to be made up of hundreds of raindrops. His helmet has fallen off. He slips and slides in the mud, but keeps his rifle pointing towards us. Towards *me*.

"Cops-man! Cops-man!"

He's drunk. He fires.

Th-zip! Th-zip!

His bullets fly over my head.

Th-zip! Th-zip!

He's coming for *me*.

Amos lets loose two quick rasping bursts.

Ba-ba-ba! Ba-ba-ba!

It's overkill.

The rounds all hit in the same place; the Enemy's chest catches them. He staggers one last time, falls face-first to the ground and twitches, with his right hand bizarrely reaching out as though he wants to touch me.

The flare fades and the image of him sputters from view. The last thing I see is the Enemy's hand.

I compliment Amos on a job well done. Bill tells him to save his ammunition. They bicker, but I refuse to get involved.

I can't get that last gesture from the Enemy out of my mind.

I hope the mud will suck him down quickly.

Phut! Phut! Phut! Up go the flares.

*

W Day +5. 00.38. Fonte Plateau.

The rain has turned the soil into a kind of slime – it feels unlike any mud I have ever touched. I press my hand into it and it oozes between my fingers, as I expect, but when I pull my hand away from its sucking grasp, there is none of it to be found on my palm. Yet the same stuff sticks to my clothing and equipment with the utmost ease. It is curious, as if the very earth wishes me cleansed – or desires no contact with me. I make the mistake of leaning too far forward to try this experiment again, and the rain gushes down my back. I react sharply.

"Okay?" asks Rici.

"Getting wet," I say.

"Aren't we all?"

Phut! Phut! Phut!

I look at him for a moment, trying to think of some insult to toss in his direction: something along the lines of how wet and pathetic he seems, and how he is looking so like Buster Keaton in *The General*, awash amid a thousand gallons of water. When I turn back to watch my front, the Enemy who has been approaching is only ten yards away. He's been silent and his arrival is helped by the downpour. He could well be a duplicate of the last Enemy, and for a heart-stopping second I think he must be a ghost – summoned by my ancestors to scold me for how I spill blood on their bones. My carbine comes up from under my poncho, and I'm squeezing the trigger before I can think anything else.

Tat-tat-tat!

Tat-tat-tat!

I don't believe he is even aware I am here before he realizes he's dying. Through the falling rain he looks me in the eye. I'm the last human he will ever see. As his legs give up supporting him, he ends up kneeling before me, head slumped on his chest and hands in his lap.

I move over to him and push him onto his back.

I give zero consideration to the fact that I'm moving about

at night – the constant flares give more than enough light. Besides, I don't think I care.

They're coming for *me*.

W Day +5. 01.07. Fonte Plateau.

The water has released yet more smells that I endeavor to ignore. Humid olfactory waves of jungle moisture are tolerable, because they are natural, but, with the diesel fumes, oily smoke and cordite mixed in, there is now a sweetness that you find yourself thinking about too much.

I shake my head, blinking the rain from my eyes.

Phut!

I look up.

A flare going in the rain is both beauty and the beast. The sky is filled with streaks of silver, and each drop of rain catches the light and becomes, for a marvelous instant, a shooting star of glittering white. In a quirk of magic and physics, the flare becomes like a broken sun – its bright core surrounded by a halo of exploding comets. The light floats down, illuminating the whole of our front. Here and there I can see marines dug in, most with their ponchos spread over the lip of their foxhole to try to stem the ingress of rain, while others are merely poncho hillocks crowned by helmets sparkling with rain. They exude a kind of misery, and they hint at the beast that comprises the downside of this firework show.

As I watch, two of these little mounds jump to their feet, bring their guns up, and fire red and gold flashes into the cold white cloud of shooting stars – aiming at the small group of four Enemy charging in their direction.

Ba-ba-ba!

Tat-tat-tat!

Rici and I lend a hand, Rici with the BAR and me with my carbine. Two of them fall straight away. We have to stop firing when the Enemy gets too close to the other Boys. Rici and I leap to our feet – intending to run over and help them. We slip and slide – exactly as I have seen others do – and I am forced to watch a six-second hand-to-hand fight take place without being able to help.

We stop. Our Boys have won. They wave us away.

Rici and I look at each other in understanding. We both know that these are just probing attacks from the Enemy. There is a major assault on its way.

We head back to our position. They're coming for *me*.

W Day +5. 02.04. Fonte Plateau.

I feel the ground tremble. For a moment I have the delightful sober idea that, to add to our woes, one of the extinct volcanoes that originally helped form this island has been jolted into life by our activities. As though the god Chaife has taken this opportunity to seek more souls from the many that are now so readily available. I glance over my shoulder, only to see the silhouette of a Sherman coming up behind me, making its way to our position. There are four more following, plus several squads of marines. It's obvious that someone with Brass has decided we need extra help – and the fact that they've taken the risk of sending men up here in the dark and rain is not reassuring. A tank is a tank is a tank; but just how many of the Enemy is Brass expecting to pour on to our position from the remaining heights? I shake my head and smile to myself. It doesn't matter – I love to see Shermans within spitting distance. If it wasn't for the fact that their potential attracts attention from every piece of artillery the Enemy can point at it, I'd quite like to go to war in one. Perhaps it's a power thing; but their being so much stronger than anything else you might encounter can make you want to throw your weight around a bit. Advance fifty yards, pushing down trees, rolling over foxholes and barbed wire, keep the Enemy moving back, then slowly spin that turret and barrel to a target and fire. Send a couple of extra rounds in for good measure, and advance another fifty yards. That's if your weight doesn't bog you down in the mud, and if the Enemy doesn't line up some big piece of their own in your direction, of course.

The men inside keep the engines running.

Something's about to happen, something soon, something big.

W Day +5. 02.31. Fonte Plateau.

At first I think it is a new variation of noise that the constant rain is making, but as it happens again, I can place it. Someone up ahead is breaking glass.

Smash! Then the tinkle.

A voice screeches a drunken bellow. "Ree-treat!" an Enemy calls in broken English. "Ree-treat!"

Ting, ting, ting.

I can't work that one out.

Ting, ting, ting.

It's metal upon metal – but what on what?

Ting, ting, ting.

I brush my fingers along my bayonet right down to its tip. I slip my hand back, unhook the bayonet, cradle it for a second, and then tap it on the barrel of my carbine.

Ting, ting, ting.

I smile to myself for the second time this awful night. I reattach my bayonet and listen with confidence. Another mystery solved.

Ting, ting, ting.

Smash!

Tinkle.

If I weren't already crazy, it would drive me mad.

*

W Day +5. 02.41. Fonte Plateau.

I start to take a long gulp of water and spill most of it down my chin or into my lungs. I splutter, cough, grip the canteen harder, and force the shaking in my hands to stop. I breathe deeply. I take another gulp.

Phoenix?

Hello, princess.

Are you okay?

Possibly.

You spilt your water.

I missed my face – that's all.

Really? So, it would be unfair of me to say it was a nervous response to the prospect of your being brutally slaughtered?

Ah, the Queen of Understatement is back.

I take another long gulp, noting the shakes have diminished. This woman is good for me.

You know, Phoenix, there is one aspect of all this that I still have trouble with.

What's that specifically?

How you can function? How *any* of you can do what you have to do? The terror you feel must be impossible.

It can be ignored.

But *how?* You're spilling your drink again.

I can function – because I need to. You can't ever let the terror win, Serena. If we did that we'd all find ourselves cowering before any idiot that stands up and shouts boo, let alone anyone with a gun.

It makes me sad.

What, standing up for yourself?

No, the need to. And the fact that you're lying to me.

Until the time comes that medication can remove that part of some men that makes them want to dominate and bully, the majority of us will still have to carry on stopping them.

That day might be sooner than you think.

Terrific. There's only one flaw.

Oh?

If we do that, we'll probably take out the rogues that make life exciting.

Like you?

I couldn't comment, Serena. Can you imagine a world where nobody did anything wrong?

Sounds nice at the moment.

That's just perspective.

It saddens me that the final answer always appears to be war. Why?

Why go to war? We've had this discussion. And this is the easy answer: this war has to be fought. But how much are we expected to take? I'm beginning to realize that a breaking point comes to everyone – that's the danger. There's only so much violence that one person can participate in and still recover from and pretend to be normal. I wait here for an inevitable attack, and yet it is what I'm imagining is going to happen that is terrifying me most. Demons dreamt are worse than demons encountered.

I know about that. I spent my childhood suffering from the attentions of a night-time beast. I still fear many things: I worry about you, I also worry about my brother.

You have a brother?

Oh, yes. His name is Alex.

Doesn't sound mystical enough for a deity.

He's no god.

But what about you, then?

I'm no goddess – I've told you that. Could you believe that I'm a scientist?

Serena, at this moment you could tell me you were the Pope and I'd believe you.

You might think it's as far-fetched, but I *am* a scientist. I teach mathematics and look into mathematical solutions to physical problems.

No Greek connections, then?

Only with Pythagoras and Euclid and other such luminaries. I love the myths, but this is where I must tell you truths, not fables. And you must do the same.

Shame. I love stories.

Phoenix, do you remember your dream?

Which one? I dream a lot.

The one where you first actually saw me?

That was a nice one. You have such a pretty face.

Phoenix, do you remember the room you saw me in? Do you?

Well, it seemed familiar.

It was that house in Cambridge you stayed in before the war, wasn't it?

Well, it seemed close. It seemed like Tom's home, but it was only a dream – that's why it was different.

How would you feel if I told you it had to be different because it is how the house will look many, *many* years from now?

How do you mean?

How would you feel if I told you that the room where you saw me is how it will look, in the future?

I'd say you're mad. And if you're not, I'd prefer you telling me you were the Pope.

I'm breaking a fundamental law here, Phoenix, but I want to keep you alive – that's why I'm telling you this. I figure I have always told you this: that this is some causal time-loop, that it doesn't *matter* what I tell you, because I have *always* told you.

You're nuts. I'm nuts. I'm holding a conversation with a vision of my own making and—

Phoenix, I'm not a vision. I'm not a ghost. I'm not some memory of your grandfather's. I am a scientist in mathematics, and I have discovered some of the mathematics of time. I am from the future. Phoenix, I know what is going to happen.

This is a game of my own making, isn't it? I'm panicking about my future, so I invent someone from the future to help me protect myself.

Phoenix, believe me, please. My name is Professor Serena Freeman. I am a mathematics don pursuing a career in Cambridge, England. I have devised a technique whereby I can experience the actuality of events in another person's life. I chose you, in particular, because I knew you once lived here; that it seemed to provide an easier stepping stone, as it were, to get inside — well, to get inside . . .

My head?

Yes, that's how Odysseus works.

Odysseus?

It's the name I have given the equipment I use — the equipment I *am* using.

The name I gave it, you mean?

No, Phoenix. I *must* convince you.

Yes.

Yes, what?

Yes, you must. You must convince me. Prove it. I've only got a few minutes to spare and to stop myself from thinking about what is to come.

It's difficult.

Really? For a professor of mathematics?

Ironic humor in times of stress is something I adore.

Well, future princess, anything to say?

If I went back into your past and discovered something you did, some event only *you* know about, this might seem to demonstrate to you I'm telling the truth. But there is a problem.

Uh-huh?

Since you think I'm some sort of spirit of your own creation, *you'd* obviously say that *of course* I'd know your past, as you think I'm part of you.

That's right.

You hadn't thought of that, had you?

That's right.

You lie and tell the truth with equal ease, don't you?

I'm a writer.

Okay, well . . .

Yes?

If I told you something about the immediate future, and it subsequently happens, you'd believe me then, wouldn't you?

I'd consider it.

Consider it?

I might be lucky with my predictions.

It will be *my* statement of what will happen.

Convince me.

Okay, I've had my brother Alex do some research about today. I've read quite a bit of the detail.

Uh-huh?

At three o'clock this morning, the Japanese will launch a major offensive in your area.

That's five minutes away.

Phoenix, these Japanese soldiers will attack the tanks with their bare hands. Your friend Rici will be injured in the hand-to-hand fighting that follows.

Rici?

He'll survive, but the field hospital you both go to will then also be attacked. *That* assault will happen at six-thirty. And you will go missing.

Thanks.

The timing of events, Phoenix. The times — even you couldn't guess them.

Phut! Phut!

The Enemy fires an array of flares into the night sky. I glance at my watch in the bright light. It's 03.00 hours.

Shit!

Shit, shit, shit!

W Day +5. 03.00. Fonte Plateau.

Phut! Phut!

We send up our own.

Hell opens its doors and ushers its devils out into the world. Through the spangled rain they come, weapons at the ready, Enemy after Enemy moving forward in an uncoordinated and frantic rush. Most are screaming their fear into the night, as a last exultation that they are still alive, repeated and repeated, with the knowledge that what they are doing is intentionally, desperately suicidal.

What timing, Nix. What timing.

Rici and I throw off our ponchos so we can move more easily. Rici nestles into the stock of the BAR and I unclip a couple of pouches, ready to hand him replacement magazines. Marines start firing along the line and the fight is engaged.

Rici doesn't hurry himself. Five Enemy rush towards us. Only two have rifles, the other three are simply carrying bayonets, and one of the three has a bottle of *saki* in his other hand. I have a perverse wish that a whistle could be blown for half time, so that this Enemy and I could share his bottle. At least two Enemy have dark patches around their crotches – I can't say I blame them. They are all shouting.

Rici hits the group with two one-second bursts.

Ba-ba-ba-ba-ba! Ba-ba-ba-ba-ba!

They stop, they weave and stagger, and they fall. I glance right. Amos is hunkered down – he's not hurrying himself either.

I quickly look ahead again.

Three more Enemy emerge out of the rain; firing as they run. Rici swears – he needs a new magazine for the BAR. He'll have to get it himself. I bring up my carbine and fire.

Tat-tat-tat! Tat-tat-tat!

I get two of them. As I fire on the third, another group of maybe five or six Enemy runs at us – as if the star-lit rain is molding them from the wet air. Rici gets the BAR working with a new magazine, and opens up again.

Ba-ba-ba-ba-ba!

Tat-tat-tat!

He hits the majority of them, while I pick off a straggler.

And still they come, another squad of six. They are closer to us than the last group. They're getting nearer before we even see them. I have a sudden need to open my bowels.

I'm sorry I lied about being scared, Serena. I'm sorry.

Ba-ba-ba-ba-ba-ba-ba-ba-ba-ba!

Tat-tat-tat! Tat-tat-tat!

We hit them, and I see yet more.

I glance to my right as Rici changes magazines again.

I turn back and fire.

Tat-tat-tat-tat-tat!

Rici fires.

Ba-ba-ba-ba-ba!

Two of the Enemy rush past me, and I look over my shoulder. They are heading for the tanks – armed only with rifles. They fire at a Sherman and their bullets ricochet into the night. There are other Enemy already swarming over the other tanks, thumping at them with their bare hands. The marines inside the tanks open up with their forward machine-guns.

Brrrrrr! Brrrrrrr!

Serena was right!

Brrrrrr! Brrrrrr!

I stop gawking at the tanks and look forward.

Phut! Phut!

More light.

To add to the incredible noise, a howitzer opens up.

Whistle.

Th-whoop!

The shell explodes less than thirty yards away. The Enemy are ripped apart. Pieces of them land at my feet.

Jesus, how near are the Boys intending to fire those things?

Th-whoop! Th-whoop!

Th-zip! Th-zip!

Ba-ba-ba-ba-ba!

Phut! Phut! Phut!

Everything is a madhouse of noise, lights, obscene sights. Flare after flare rises into the night sky; the rain turns to shards of silver; tracer fire flashes past. Bullets hit the ground, bullets hit the tanks, and bullets hit marines and Enemy alike – with the Enemy taking practically all the casualties. I see Enemy hit in the chest, the gut, the face – with all sorts of rounds, including armor-piercing. I see Enemy blown asunder with howitzer shells. I see a tank fire point-blank into a group of twenty Enemy – who vanish. But still more come.

The devil bellows out in his ecstasy, and we are all finally pitchforked into his lair as the battle melts into the second-by-second moments of life and death that are the chaos of hand-to-hand combat.

Two Enemy get near to us. Rici takes the one on the right; I take the left one. Rici makes three more shots before he runs out of bullets; but I don't see what he does next as my world is filled with the Enemy that is on me. I'm luckier than he is, I've had practice at this type of charge and I deflect his bayonet to my right with my own and let mine slide down his rifle into his chest. I grunt with the effort.

He carries on fighting.

Shit!

I can't remove my bayonet. He screams at me. I'm so close to him I can smell his breath. He has a bad front tooth. He hasn't shaved for days. I make the mistake of grasping the barrel of his rifle with my right hand as he begins to bring it around to slice at me. I still have hold of my carbine with my left hand. He grabs my collar and goes for my throat, but before he can, his head jerks sideways as Rici clobbers him with the butt of his BAR. I kick out at the Enemy's groin, jolting him enough to get my bayonet out of him. Rici turns to deal with another that's reached him, but mine hasn't finished yet – he brings his rifle up to butt me. I've now got my carbine in one hand and my .45 in the other – I'd cocked it earlier – and I fire into his face as he starts his move.

He dies.

Whistle-crash-boom!

Ba-ba-ba-ba-ba!

Phut! Phut!

The orchestra continues with its deadly music.

Rici is struggling with his next Enemy, his BAR now on the ground, and both men have bayonets in their hands, and both have their free hand on the other's wrist to try to prevent a fatal strike. I ram my Colt between them and stick the barrel under the chin of the Enemy. The shot takes the back of his head off. I holster my .45 and, at last, get both my hands back on my carbine.

Th-zip!

This round hits my shoulder. I'm surprised at how much it hurts, but as I've other things on my mind I decide to ignore it. Brave me. It still feels as though someone is grinding their foot relentlessly on my shoulder. Three new Enemy fall upon us – the one at the rear has a saber – and I manage to swipe my bayonet into the lead one. It pierces his guts on his left side, but he doesn't stop his impetus – he carries on charging towards the tanks. Rici manages to reach for his BAR, while I strike the other two Enemy with the butt of my carbine: in the face of one, and slicing with the bayonet across the chest of the second – the Enemy with the saber. I manage to do the same again. This gives Rici time to get a new magazine in his BAR. He then uses the BAR butt on the one I've already done the same to twice, while I kick the second on his right knee. When this puts him off-balance, I shove my bayonet into his belly.

Tat-tat-tat-tat-tat!

Rici kills his one with close-range shots but, before I can drive my bayonet further in, the Enemy pulls himself off and manages to catch Rici in the chest with the saber. I stick the Enemy again, but he pulls himself off one more time and barges past me, waving his blade to and fro – another Enemy on a mission for the tanks.

I find time to take a breath, and it feels good.

"Fuck it, Nix!" shouts Rici. "We're still alive!"

"Speak for yourself!"

Rici and I can see a break of about five seconds before the next wave of Enemy reach us, so I get a magazine into my carbine and Rici finds a better position with his BAR. We turn back to the fight, bloodied but not down. I catch glimpses of the Boys doing much the same as we are – staying alive simply by not wanting to die.

It brings out the animal in us all.

Ba-ba-ba-ba-ba!

Tat-tat-tat! Tat-tat-tat!

Three other marines slide into position beside us, but we don't get the chance to say hi. We need to maintain our barrage and try to stop the Enemy before they get to us.

We fail.

We are overwhelmed.

And once more I am dueling with bayonets.

I deflect one blow at the last second – the tip nicks my cheek. But I am getting better at this. I take him off his feet with a swift kick and then a blow with the butt of my carbine. The Enemy fighting Rici is jarred by his comrade falling, and without thinking turns and catches him with his bayonet. He freezes at his mistake and Rici and I kill them both. One of the marines who has joined us starts shouting. It's Lieutenant Bowlsure.

"Nix! Rici! You're both hit. Get some attention!"

Rici and I look at each other. He is bleeding from the chest.

"Do I look as bad as you?" I ask him.

"I think we need fixing," he says.

"Medic!" shouts Bowlsure. "We need a medic here!"

He tries to smile at us.

"Get patched up and come back if you feel up to it," he adds. He gestures to the other two, and they move across to reinforce Amos and Bill's position.

Rici and I look at each other again, and then we both start to help one another away. It's obvious that we need to do something about ourselves. A medic appears out of the rain and rips open his bag. After a quick judgment call, he decides Rici is the worst hit. He gets me to press a bandage to my shoulder as he attends to Rici first.

I have seen everything that has happened. It was worse than the initial assault on the beach. When the men on the landing craft were blown up by the Japanese shells or torn apart by murderous machine-gun fire (though there was an ineffable sadness and an absolute terror and horror to it all), there was an air of it all being chance, fate – that indeed, their lives *did* depend on what Dead Pool Poker cards each man was dealt before the attack began. A full-scale banzai is a far different chamber of hell for a person to be forced into. I didn't dare say anything to Phoenix, though, lest I broke his concentration. Because, in the end, that's what kept him alive: his skill and practice at dealing with such close-in chaos. It was a fitting way for me to have the romance of my Greek myths placed into context. The men who took those Pacific islands were real warriors. True, they had weapons that could put distance between them and those they were expected to kill, weapons with far more lethal force than any which Greek soldiers could imagine, but those men went through the same face-to-face experience of living by the second whenever involved in close-quarter battle.

I stayed there as Rici and Nix were helped away to the field hospital. They were wounded, both had lost blood, but neither was seriously hurt.

Which, in some respects was unlucky, since the serious cases were apparently being evacuated to the beach for transport out to the big ships. If that had occurred with them, neither Rici nor Phoenix would have had to fight for their lives again.

I was right: the Japanese attacked the field hospital at six-thirty.

W Day +5. 06.16. Field Hospital.

I put down my notebook.

Rici and I turn to listen to the familiar sounds.

Someone shouts that the Enemy has found our CP. Men run past the tent – men from the motor pool, men from head-quarters. They are getting ready to use weapons they've prob-ably only ever had to fire in training.

Rici and I leap from our cots and get our jackets on. We divide our ammunition.

Other men grab what they can.

I could tell by the way Rici and Phoenix were talking that they thought they had already done their bit. As they discussed their situation earlier, I know from his hesitant responses that Phoenix was remembering my warning – perhaps that's why he insisted on them keeping their guns close by. Along with the other men in the hospital, they went into battle again.

W Day +5. 06.28. Field Hospital.

The Enemy fights their way to the hospital. Serena was right. Instead of striving to kill, and not die out in the mud and rain, it looks like this will be a barroom-type fight of tables, chairs, cots and tents, but with a deadly difference.

Tat-tat-tat!

I shoot an Enemy as he hurtles through an open gap.

This is not the peace I so much desired.

I laugh as I fire.

The marines all fought with the same passion – as if I could have expected anything different after what I have already witnessed. There was a savagery to the fighting that I wish I'd never seen. Most of the men there were in pain from their wounds, but they had no intention of dying after having endured so much.

These men had no time to be petrified.

Phoenix saved Rici, and Rici did the same for him.

Everyone helped one another.

W Day +5. 06.48. Field Hospital.

We take the fight further out.

We fight hard.

I am shaking so much now that two out of three of my shots miss their target – even when only feet away. I am becoming a liability. I have to pause and compose myself. Up ahead I see something happening. I find it disturbing.

I can see evidence that hell is the creation of Man.

All I crave is a little peace.

When some of the Japanese soldiers realized that their attack on the headquarters was failing, they decided to end their lives in a fruitless and pitifully bizarre way. They sat down on the ground, still getting hit by bullets, and they each took a grenade in their hand, removed the pin, and then placed the grenade on their heads under their helmets.

Through the eyes of Phoenix, I witnessed at least ten men do this. They committed suicide rather than surrender.

The whole episode affected me deeply, and it finally pushed Phoenix over the edge.

Classified Secret

F2/6901/2

EXTRACT OF INFORMATION PROVIDED BY A. FREEMAN TO HIS SISTER REGARDING COMBAT CORRESPONDENT PHOENIX LAFAYETTE.

At approximately six-thirty in the morning of the 26th of July 1944, elements of the 3rd Battalion of the 18th Regiment of the Japanese army defending Guam attacked the field hospital set up in the US divisional head-quarters. Medical staff, including doctors, and even the wounded men who were able to do so, fought off the attack with whatever weapons they could find.

According to witnesses, this was the time that contact was lost with the combat correspondent Phoenix Lafayette. Marines were apparently dealing with the aftermath of some unusual suicides by Japanese troops, when Mr Lafayette was seen running off into the jungle. He was pursued by a number of friends he had made while reporting the actions of 3rd Battalion, 21st Regiment,

3rd Division, but they were subsequently unable to find him.

His loss was reported back to his employers at the *New York Picture Post*, who subsequently ran an article on his courage whilst under fire. He was later mentioned in dispatches along with the men he had effectively served alongside.

Along with other personal effects recovered from the hospital was his notebook. It contained his last known report. The following is that statement.

A man can witness only so much. I have seen many terrible things that men can do to one another in the name of an ideal. I have no doubt, though, that Man has the facility to surprise me still with new inventions of horror. How ever much I am convinced that we are right in what we do here; every time I kill a man, I find myself wishing there were some other solution.

I crave for peace. I lust for the beauty of its quiet so much that I would sacrifice anything to drift in its tranquil waters. Just a little bit of peace, that's all I crave.

There may come a time when men cease to wage war on one another – I hope so. When I hear young boys call out to the only woman they have ever really loved, their mom and her healing hand, as they squirm and die in shuddering pain, I know that a future of peace will only occur when men cease in their desire to dominate. Or when the women, who have borne those children that are expected to fight, are allowed to decide their own child's Fate.

There have been men I have written about who are now just memories, my descriptions of them gathering dust in some cuttings library, my photographs standing on some shelf. They will stay forever young. I lament what we have lost and what we are losing. Children that are boys,

boys that are men, they all would have said that they were
ordinary people doing extraordinary things because they
had to. I hope I have made you understand that.

I think of their faces, I think of their laughter, and
I think of their death and unfulfilled promise.

My soul craves a little peace. I desperately need some
help to find it.

It was shortly after this passage was written that the
Japanese attacked the hospital.

An extra dimension of this unfortunate development,
which was censored later from the reports his paper
released, was that, as his friends chased after him
(feeling he had put himself under too much strain, was
suffering from battle fatigue and thought he was trying
to save them from his own supposed madness), he was heard
repeatedly to call out a woman's name: "Serena".

He was also warning her to run.

Classified Secret

F2/6901/3

REPORT FROM BLACK PROJECT TEAM OF THE RECOVERY OF
ODYSSEUS.

Action was prompted by the closure of the curtains of the
objective room by Professor Serena Freeman after the
setting up of Odysseus. This had never been observed to
happen before. After allowing for the amount of time she
normally took to attach herself to the equipment – plus
five minutes – the back door of Professor Serena Freeman's
house was discovered locked, with both dead-bolt and
mortise, therefore entry was made by destruction of its
hinges with a sledgehammer. Progress was quickly made to
the upstairs objective, via the kitchen and stairs. This
took approximately thirty seconds. Professor Freeman
was not found in the room, the equipment seemed in a state

of disarray, and some important components were missing
or destroyed. There were various books on contemporary
history scattered about, and a peculiar set of twelve
Polaroid photographs beside the PC display.

The team dispersed but she was not to be found anywhere in the building. Following investigation, it is
apparent that Professor Serena Freeman managed to make
her escape during the six minutes we waited outside
before entering. We feel that if we had been given more
information, and better back-up, we could have procured
the equipment in working order.

Attached is a transcript of the Odysseus diary she
left on disk, with a copy on her laptop - specifically
addressed to your department.

Classified Secret
F2/6846/4
Transcript of file left by Professor Serena Freeman with
annotations for clarification.

Hello, gentlemen. I trust you will repair all damage you have made to
my home. Though I will not be returning to it, I'd like to think that my
brother doesn't have to spend too much time cleaning up. You will
notice that Odysseus is no longer operational. This fact causes me great
amusement, and doubly so when I articulate your reaction. In fact, it
cannot be repaired, and I have destroyed all executable program files
and various data files — just as you had feared. (Waste bin was filled
with shredded and burnt disks. They cannot be recov-
ered.) I have also removed and destroyed the hard drive of my PC.
(This too is correct.) I know you will ignore this advice, but I
would not bother seeking any information on the laptop you have
found. Your team should be able to report to you that it was only
purchased this morning with the sole purpose of writing this document.
(It was.)

I'm sure that you will have worked out by now how I was aware of
your intentions. Odysseus would be a powerful tool to people like you,

and I am proof of that. Ever since I used Odysseus to sample the life of my brother, I have been aware of his duplicity with regards to me, and his involvement with you. This does not surprise me. He has always resented the gift I was given, and has done many things to bring about my dishonour. Though he has protested many times throughout his life against the sort of organization you represent, and indeed paid the price with his disability, I have always had an inkling that he is deeply attracted to power and that such a failing would make him easy to manipulate. Having discovered his treachery – there is no other word for what he has done to me – it was only a matter of time before I was able to investigate your assassination attempt on me. I have investigated all of you and I am aware of everything you had planned for me. That's how good Odysseus is. As I *know* you now know.

It must be really hard finally to realize what you've missed, isn't that so?

And to make the pain worse for you, I believe I've found some other uses for Odysseus. Picture this if you will: it is not too many years in the future and Man has visited the planets; Man has travelled outside the solar system and investigated other stars. Indeed, Man has discovered other worlds possessing intelligent life – with all the ramifications that *that* will eventually entail. (Religion will have to indulge in some pretty drastic self-examination. And who will tolerate people like you with your obsession about borders?) That is the other use of Odysseus – to be able to travel to the stars without leaving the comfort of your armchair. We will then become travellers to the stars – and beyond – via our minds. Such developments can be made through Odysseus. As can others.

So I have now departed for other shores. I believe I know where Phoenix ran to and how I can keep him alive, how I *will* keep him alive. Because some time in *my* future, I will affect the outcome of his dash into the jungle. I was so involved in his life and death struggles that I missed the obvious – there's no rush. *I* have all the time in the world. I don't believe he died in the jungle – I believe that the history of his disappearance is *because* of me. You see, there are avenues in the development of Odysseus, that I haven't yet explored, that hold great promise. I don't think I'll be short of money to buy the necessary equipment; I've always got my musical skills to fall back on. (We believe this to be a reference to her recent involvement with the pop industry, and we shall be keeping tabs on those connections.) Beside which, I'd like to travel. I fancy Guam – it sounds marvellous. I will, of course be doing my best to avoid you all. Oh, to prevent any misunderstanding, the information necessary to build another Odysseus is only to be found in *my* head.

That fact makes me so happy.

A friend of mine showed me that unhappiness is only a thought away. (We think the person she is referring to here is Annette Baxter. See pop reference above.)

I need to live my life.

Happiness is only a thought away.

Oh, could you water my plants please? I always forget them, and I don't think they should pay for my sudden disappearance, do you? Thanks.

I'm just a silly little girl in love. It's glorious to be so sloppily romantic. Don't women like me just piss you men off? Ha, ha, ha! We women can move mountains when we want to: Eat your hearts out, you sad boys.

(We believe she actually succeeded. While there is *no* evidence in the archive to establish exactly what happened to Phoenix Lafayette, there is every indication that some outside interference caused his bizarre actions during the assault on the aid station. Our only option is to await any information that may arise after further investigations. We must establish the whereabouts of Professor Freeman. We *must*.)

PART TWO
THE FABLE

Her Achilles

I once watched a midget at a freak show eat a light bulb, then push six-inch nails up each nostril and, for an encore, hawk gobbets of fiery spit over twelve yards at a scantily clad girl while she was doing cartwheels. I gathered later it had been some sort of record. I myself had also been drunk for a record memory-deluding fifteen days. And also doing far more drugs beyond the prescribed amount of what most sane junkies would consider safe. Still, that was at an opening to a bondage sex shop in Soho, London, in the mid-eighties. And London, as some of us remember, was a strange place then, even for us Venice beach bums from California covering the latest Rolling Stones reunion concert – before the next last one. And for me that circus act in that street on that day was especially beneficial, because it led on to two distinct life changes. Firstly, I was offered a job including an airline ticket to the Pacific island of Guam; and secondly, because of the job itself, I was able to buy, outright, an old house in a small town in Suffolk, England. One that provided a wicked answer to a question I always receive at book launches: *"Tell me, Mr Chillwood Davies, where do you get your ideas?"* And to which I always reply – after a knowing sigh – with these immortal words, *"You'll never believe me if I tell you."*

I inform them that, shortly after I first moved into my house in '87, Great Britain suffered a rare hurricane that tore up much of the woods and forests on its south-east coast. No twisters, but a mighty blow nevertheless. I tell them how I spent much of that night awake, feeling my house shake, and fearing that I'd been sold a shack that could wobble in the slightest breeze. I must have been the only person who got up the next morning and jumped for joy to find that it had been just a cheap storm.

That following day, I went up to the attic, to check the roof for damage, and found some interesting detritus left by previous owners. In an otherwise empty suitcase were some photos, and, surprisingly, a tiny artificial Christmas tree. Beside it stood a plastic bucket containing thirty straight sections of OO gauge Hornby toy railway track. (No train, no carriages, no curved track, no explanations.) Next to that, a five-foot Styrofoam Rupert Bear; and a Cabbage Patch doll hanging, all cobwebs and moth holes, from a rafter with a noose around its neck. And, in a corner, the innards of seven electric lawnmower engines, with "I am happy, I love grass" spray-painted on the side of their cardboard container. (Don't ask – I've spent *years* trying to work that one out. The possible drugs connection my only interest.)

Along with all this junk, I discovered a few dusty old books from the thirties. One of which was a copy of *Webster and Brown's Plot Thesaurus*. It works like the alternate word version that is *Roget's Thesaurus*, only this book provides plots, characters and technical help in writing. So, now I use it for every story I write. I don't ever have to suffer writer's block – I just flip to the index. It's made me what I am. Oh, and the tips in the book's Foreword are terrific. One of these, I tell the curious questioner, is the imperative of starting a story – of whatever length – with a hook. And the hook to *my* story – this fantastic Machiavellian construction of mine that I get all my ideas from an old leather-bound book I found in the attic – was my initial *You wouldn't believe me if I told you.*

That's what sucked them in: they *wanted* to believe.

They then generally go red in the face, while everybody else laughs in relief that *they* didn't ask The Question, and I get to look cool and appear to be an utter bastard at the same time.

This sort of thing pleases me – gives me an excuse to light

up a King Size Marlboro and blow ego smoke-rings. Interestingly, quite often some people will come up to me afterwards and ask confidently, with a whisper and a nudge, if it's still in print. There are days, I have noticed that you *need* drugs when you have to deal with the gullible proportion of the world. So, as they're suckers and I'm a bastard, I give them the personal telephone number of a presenter sometimes appearing, as a critic, in an arts program on British television and who, I claim, has published an updated version.

Never could stand that accent.

Guam was good to me. While the world was going crazy with greed in the eighties, my English editor, at the magazine I sometimes worked for, having a delusion that his morals were finer-tuned than those of the herd, would occasionally send me off on projects to investigate possible sleaze, and damn the expense. That sort of attitude appealed to me. It still does. The reason I succeeded (if there was anything actually to tell) where others had failed, was that, with my drink and drug habit and my natural affinity with the "low life" that swim in the pools that surround celebrity and power, I was able to cruise through the flotsam that knew the dirty little secrets. And my editor Paris Blackstone – bald, small, with a Freddie Mercury moustache – thought I'd be ideal for Guam. Anyway, I was usually dressed in clothes that he considered wouldn't be out of place there. I once made the mistake of asking why his parents had hated him so much at birth as to give him such a Christian name. It was a bit disheartening to hear, not that he'd been conceived there, as I had expected, but that his *mother* had been conceived there, in the lift ascending the Eiffel Tower in fact. He thought that it was cool, but it means I can never go to Paris ever again, knowing I'd always be looking for that bloody lift going up or down, and wondering. The fool also claimed my Hawaiian shirts gave him migraines.

Anyway, Blackstone sent me to investigate the past of a

certain Alfonso Federici, one-time many-decorated sergeant of
our glorious Marines who battled their way across the Pacific.
Married – since his return to the States after the war – to the
heiress Alice Lafayette and proud father of three grown-up
boys and a teenage girl, he had put together one of the best
electronic technical companies America had ever conceived.
Blackstone's sixty-cigarettes-a-day, two-quarts-of-coffee theory
was that Federici had Mafia connections and that he, Blackstone, had uncovered a regular pay-off that Federici was making to a contact in Guam. Believing there was some great exposé
in the offing, he handed me an expenses package, bade me
adieu and pointed to the door.

It only took me three phone calls at Heathrow to friends
living back over the pond, to establish that Federici had as
much in common with the Mafia as the Lincoln Memorial does
with a Henry Moore sculpture. And another five calls to find
that Henry Cutteran – Our Man in Guam – was an old Afro-
American diver, eking out a living at Apra harbor by showing
tourists the underwater war-sites around the island, when not
arm-wrestling at his local bar in the evening. (And he was quite
a tourist attraction himself.) I decided anyway to use the ticket
so thoughtfully provided by Blackstone, and would give him
the bad news about his theory when I returned. Beside, he'd
been extra generous with my expense account, and I'd even
been given my own stash of coke. Hell, in the eighties it was
my experience that you could be slipped a toke off an air
stewardess if you flew first class and you asked nicely enough.
I hit Guam running.

God created Guam late on a Saturday afternoon. He'd done all
the messy business of creation, was drinking a cold one in his
garden, and was looking forward to a night out at a club and
some girls to follow. On a whim, He decided to offset all the
nasty, little brutish things that the happy-clappy, church-going
crowd doesn't like to be reminded of that He had conceived –

tapeworms, bubonic plague bacilli and estate agents – and so He fashioned Guam from a piece of love, and skimmed it out onto the ocean the way a kid zips a stone across a pond. A tropical island big enough to take an airport? God has had some pretty trick ideas when it comes down to making life great.

One of which was Our Man in Guam himself.

Henry Cutteran had been carved from cracked ebony sometime in the Bronze Age, and had been given special dispensation by God to live forever. I exaggerate, of course, but he was the oldest person I had ever met, the color of ink, and under that good-humored, many-wrinkled mask there was vaguely concealed a character that had seen too many fools already and had forcefully decided that he would no longer tolerate any shit. He had me in one, and the light reflecting off his sunglasses sparked at me.

"So, now the dope fiends have come to play on our beautiful island?" he said. "With their novelty shirts, too." And he poked me hard in the shoulder with his index finger.

I was standing on the quay, six-foot-two in my socks, looking *up* at this thin straight-backed rod of centuries-old pensioner, after inquiring if I could hire both him and his boat. And then *knew* I had found one of life's kindred spirits.

The sun was somewhere overhead, in a sky stolen from a David Hockney painting. In the distance, an absurdly green thicket of palms did their coconut-growing over beaches so white they had to be false, and the colors of everything else were so bright, I felt as though I'd just taken some serious drugs. I noticed, for instance, that some careless person had taken a rainbow and smashed it over the boats that rode slowly on the pool of gin that was the sea. I could never live here, I thought; this place inhibited the use of amphetamines. One had to *slooooow* down here.

"That's right," I said, winking up at this wonderful man I had just met, and poked him back in his chest.

His punch to my face knocked me to the ground.

"We not that close, yet, Misty Davies," he said, looking down at me.

I grinned as I spat the blood from my mouth. I *loved* the idea of being called *Misty* Chillwood Davies. I held up my hand. Henry pulled me to my feet and dusted some of the dust from my clothes.

"Good, Misty," he said, "we've now cleared up who gets to hit who. It seems *I* win. You can call me Misty Cutteran when we're on shore, and you call me Misty Henry when we're on the boat."

He leant forward to whisper in my ear. "That's where we'll smoke the good shit," he said.

I had fallen in love with the man there and then, and decided he was about seventy years old. I found out later he was eighty-three.

So there we were, the next day, bob-bob-bobbing on the ocean half-a-mile from Guam, me now dressed in colonial pants, shirt and Panama hat, Misty Henry in baseball cap and similar garb, our bare feet up on the gunwale, and smoking the most incredible marijuana I have ever put to my lips. We were in Henry's classic fifties game-fishing boat, but though it was an old vessel, it had every modern convenience. He'd owned it for years it seemed, and a large amount of money had been spent on it since to make the punters happy. I felt like I was Hemingway, and Henry knew why I was there. He also knew that he could tell me everything, since I wasn't going to tell Blackstone anything.

"You tell this after I'm dead." Henry blew smoke rings into the breeze.

"You'll live forever," I protested.

"Don't talk shit, Misty Chillwood. We all have to take that walk someday. But *mine* will be of my own choosing – if I get the chance. I'll wake up, see it's going to be a day like today, decide that's it, then I'll take a bottle of Uncle Jim Beam and head out, drop anchor, soak up the sun," – he raised the joint – "smoke a little weed, drink that whole bottle, then go for a long swim in the sun. Let the sea rock me to sleep."

It was easy to imagine. I decided I liked it.

Misty Henry then spent the next three hours telling me all about his life – longshoreman, chain-gang fugitive, gold prospector (in Australia), bigamist, Cuban gun-runner, sailor, heartbreaker, his suspect deals that led to him "retiring" to Guam in the late fifties to start his current business. And in there somewhere, in all that great life's story, somewhere he included his dealings with ex-sergeant Federici of the US Marines.

It appeared that Federici, and his wife Alice, had come to Guam in '69 to commemorate the twenty-fifth anniversary of the island's liberation. They had hired Henry to take them to the landing beaches – where the three raised glasses of neat Appalachian moonshine to the memory of the fallen, discussed the war and wept a little. Alice had then gone on to Tomhum to lay a wreath at the plaque commemorating her ancestors (her grandfather had come from Guam, it seemed) and then, many more weeks later than they had originally intended, they had said their goodbyes. A month after that Misty Henry Cutteran received his first cheque in the post. And then he received another the next month. And so on, and so on. Not great amounts – just enough to make his life less of a struggle.

Why was he given this money? Misty Henry had an answer.

"It was what Miss-Hess Federici laid down on that plaque," he said.

"Which was?"

Henry got up and went to his cabin. I waited, watching the world relax and be happy with itself. I didn't even stir when I thought I saw a shark's fin pass. Even sharks, and estate agents, have to eat. A few minutes later and Henry came back on deck with a color photo – the print was old and faded. Smiling into the camera were a young man and woman both in bathing suits. She had her head resting against his shoulder, one hand up to touch his barrel of a chest. He had his arm draped over her shoulder. They seemed very happy.

"They had nicknames for themselves," said Henry. "Vee and Evey they called themselves. It ended up with them staying with me for ten weeks, and they were a special couple to see together – some folks 'round here said you could physically touch their love. I got kinda envious, but I sensed a secret. They weren't having all the right light there, and I soon saw through to the darkness beyond, especially with that Vee man. Okay, he was having trouble quitting smoking like Evey wanted him to, and on cutting down on the drink, but that don't explain everything. He helped me on the boat some – a quick learner that man was – but I'd catch him occasionally listening to the radio, listening to the music, just as I did, and I saw the fear that would flash in his eyes. Especially that day that Evey's bet came through.

"She'd got me to put a few hundred dollars on those English boys, The Beatles, and I went and made a bet for her that they'd have the top five singles in the US charts on a particular week. You would not *believe* the odds I got for that. When Vee heard the news, he turned to me, just 'bout where you're sitting now, Misty Chillwood, and he told me, no color in that face of his – he told me that with Evey by his side, with what she knew, and with his own knowledge of how the markets worked, they'd soon be millionaires. He said they'd already decided to use their fortune to make a difference to people. Scared me that did, Misty Chillwood, scared me a lot. He was *so* sure of himself. So absolutely sure."

He stared at the ocean for a moment, lost in his memories, then grinned and carried on.

"They used some of the money they won on that bet to get some forged papers, they gave some money to me, then they headed back to the States. Now, you take a look at her wrist, Misty Chillwood." He handed me the photograph.

I looked and saw she was wearing a bracelet. It appeared to be made up of red and white shells, probably cowries.

"That's the item that got laid down at that ancestral plaque of hers. And there's the problem," he continued.

I interrupted, as I knew my music history.

"You've got more than that problem, Misty Henry. You said Federici and his wife Alice came to Guam to honor the twenty-fifth anniversary of the liberation. That would make it sixty-nine, but The Beatles made the top five in sixty-four. Plus they wouldn't need false documents to get away, if they were home-grown Americans."

Henry poked his finger at the photograph.

"Not them. *That's* Vee and Evey. Her surname was Ham-mond – never did get to find his. They're not Misty Federici and Miss-Hess Alice. That's the problem. That's the question that bothered me stupid all these years."

He flicked at the photograph and then continued. "How come Miss-Hess Alice in sixty-nine got a one-of-a-kind bracelet from a couple I was kind to back in sixty-four? I saw that bracelet so many times. One of a kind, as those shellfish are long gone. You couldn't make another if you tried. So how did they all get to know each other? And I figure they *must* have known each other, *must* have been close. Miss-Hess Alice sure was particular about that bracelet; said it was proof about the magic existing in the world. And that's why I get the money – that's only thing I *can* figure. 'Cause I'd been good to their friends Vee and Evey, when the pair of them washed up here. Neither of them with papers, her with her strange clothes and English accent, and more brains than anyone I'd ever met, and him with those old-style marine fatigues that looked like they hadn't aged a month from being issued, that wicked, fresh gunshot wound to his shoulder, and that huge fistful of dusty dollars that I used to place that bet for them. I even got the impression he'd dug up the bills from someplace he'd hidden them.

As he recovered from his bullet wound, he told me beautiful stories about Guam – told me tales about the war here like they were only yesterday to him. But he couldn't have been there as he was only in his twenties. That boy was a true storyteller. I cared for them proper and so they paid me back."

He giggled, in that self-satisfied old-man way of his.

"They sure loved each other – and they knew it. Evey told me that Vee was her personal Achilles, you know, that Greek fellow that could only get killed by being wounded in the heel. Well, that's what Evey thought of Vee: he was her one weak spot."

I'd sat back and reached for a bottle, and smiled. Ol' Misty Henry Cutteran was being, as has been observed elsewhere in this life when you can't be accurate because it will get you into trouble . . . well, he was being economical with the truth. You see, I knew how at that time, in the eighties, a new art form was taking hold – graphic novels. And one of them, strung out over a series that damned near spanned the decade was *V for Vendetta*, in which the lead character was known simply as "V" and his sidekick was a girl named Evey Hammond. Ol' Misty Henry had slipped up. There was no way a person in '64 could have known exactly what some English writer and artist would have dreamed up to some twenty years later. It's the sort of thing that SF writers like me just get off on: too much of a coincidence. And probably too much weed on Ol' Henry's part. I left him to his stories and his plans, and headed home.

And then didn't the old coot just go and do what he'd said he'd do. One fine morning, Henry Cutteran wrote a note to go with the letter and test results received from his doctor, took his boat, his bottle, and I suspect a big joint, and he anchored off the coast, drank a bit, smoked a bit, and then went swimming. A month after I got the news, the first cheque arrived. Followed by another the next month. Nothing special, just enough to live on, just enough to save up and buy my house. And it's still being sent to me. I don't ask where it's coming from, and suspect I'm supposed to keep quiet, but what the hell has an old drug fiend like me have to keep quiet about? Those strange and wonderful stories from an old Afro-American who spent the last of his days sailing turquoise seas? I can even imagine what his last thoughts were as he slipped into the warm water and started his swim. It was what he'd once told me about his Vee and Evey. That young couple he saw in '64.

"Misty Chillwood, I once saw them two lovers walking down the white beach, hand in hand, talking ten to the dozen and sharing a laugh about some fool nonsense. I knew then, seeing them two young kids, that that was what life was meant to be about – love between two people, however it happens. I missed my own chances over the years, but they were my own fault, I can't blame others. But seeing those two walking that beach, the palms overhead and the sea lapping at their feet, they made me feel jealous and warm at the same time."

Ol' Misty Henry Cutteran could always talk up a good story.

As I try to do the best with mine.

And I never did ask what odds he got on that insane bet on The Beatles.

> *Here lie the remains of Chamorros from*
> *Times past, ancestors who have*
> *Bequeathed life and spirit to those*
> *Who have followed them. We carry that*
> *Spirit with us now, and into times*
> *Yet to come. At this place let us*
> *Remember those who came before, honor*
> *Their remains, and resolve to honor*
> *Their spirit by our action now and*
> *Through the challenges of our future.*

Plaque honoring Guam's ancestors at Tomhum

Afterword

Al Jolson sang at my wedding. Well, it sounded like it. The mayor of our town at the time was my uncle Don and he demonstrated how easily he could conjure 'The Jazz Singer' into a room. The guests were amazed – this was no tenth-rate karaoke, this was someone who could *sing*. But, as I stood and listened, it begged a rather unique question: exactly how many people can say they had the mayor sing at their wedding?

Which, when you think about it, leads to questions of deeper, if apparently simplistic, philosophical values. What are the special moments in *everyone's* life? What makes *yours* different from mine? What has given *you* pleasure?

Tonight, after an evening with friends at the Royal Oak, I sat out in my garden at one o'clock in the morning, with cold beers to hand, lying back in a comfortable, adjustable beach chair, and watched the Perseids meteor shower that always happens along in early August. Perhaps it was the beer, but as I stared up at the shooting stars, I *really* became aware of how individual we all are – when we look at the night sky and the photons from stars, millions of light-years away, crash into our retinas and register in our brain, no one else can say they've experienced that moment as you have, can they? Things like that make us *all* different. And I reflected, just how many ghosts from the past can stand up and say 'I was there' when the *big* events of history took place? How did it actually affect them? Yet how vastly many more, throughout the millennia, have discounted the *small* things that make us who we are?

Take this half-a-second of time.

I saw a Perseids meteor explode tonight, and it shattered and sparkled and shone in a way only few celestial objects do. I applauded, but then, I was drunk on beer, and from the insights emerging from this personal experience.

How many others simultaneously saw that beautiful transient incident?

How unique am I?

How often do *you* ask that question?

The fact is that we are all star-children and will return our energy to the greater good of the universe, some day, when we die. That's physics, and that's also religion and philosophy. Bugger taxes as being inevitable, at a basic level it's how we live our lives that should matter. And how we let events affect us.

For instance . . .

Ipswich, Suffolk, England, in the mid-sixties could still be called a market town. During the school holidays, on Thursdays, my friends and I would take our thin sycamore sticks with the special string binding on the end (God knows what it was for, or whether it represented merely some archaic tradition), and we would head down to the cattle-market to play at being farmers, among the adults who actually were. The place reeked of the countryside. Cow shit, pig shit, and urine from both sets of animals – smells that clung in the throat. The men – and by Jesus you'd better address each as Sir – would always smile and let us help with the herding, though our timid swipes and self-conscious yells never amounted to much. But reality always hovered somewhere nearby. The genuine *men* – unlike us – moved their cattle and pigs using vicious blows and harsh calls. And, when I think about it now as I write, I remember that the one end of the stick had string wrapped around it to stop it splitting. That's exactly how hard the farmers wielded their sticks. And, if those men were questioned about the savage force of their blows – perhaps by the person I am today – they would have replied that they had a job to do. One that sometimes bit back.

I recall a day when a huge boar somehow managed to climb out of its six-foot-high enclosure. This was no little-piggy-went-to-market; this was an honest-to-God monster: The-Pig-That-Ate-The-Wolf. One that was somehow aware of its intended fate – and was having none of it. Grown men were scrambling to get out of its way, as it rounded a corner and hurtled into view. To my child's eye, as I goggled over the top rail of a pen, it seemed as though the Devil himself must have let loose a demon. This pig was of mythical proportions. And pissed off too. I slipped back and down, retreating to cower in a corner of the pen, terrified that it was coming for me. And get me it surely would; nowhere was safe. Hadn't it just escaped from an identical pen to the one I now trembled in? It barged against the gate, banging the latch off as it charged past. I stopped breathing, realizing the gate to the pen I was hiding in lay open. I was vulnerable. I was frightened. Then a deep challenging voice echoed around the shed. From my stooping position I could just see a man (turned-down Wellington boots, flat cap) vaulting the rail of another pen and deliberately landing in the boar's path.

For the next twenty to thirty seconds all I could hear was this man's incredible bellowing, the pig's snarls and grunts, the hellish roar from the other panicked animals, and other men's cries as they reluctantly joined in to help.

After closing my gate securely, but very gently (that pig would surely hear anything louder, and come back to investigate), I climbed up the side to watch. The pig now stood in the alley, screaming at the flat-capped man. But *he* was having none of it. As the boar decided to charge him and bite, the man gave it a solid back-hander around its foam-covered jaw, then manoeuvred the beast into another holding area.

I had never seen such courage before.

*

And another thing . . .

I also remember a series of TV programmes about WWII from those formative years. Apart from the visceral torment of viewing footage of liberated concentration camps and their terrible secrets, there is another image that sticks in my mind. The Americans were recapturing the Pacific islands. It was brutal – it was total war. One of their main weapons, and the one that primarily stuck with me, was the flame-thrower. Time after time I witnessed the spit-and-whoosh of burning liquid being squirted into holes that the narrator explained contained Japanese soldiers. Then, finally, one emerged, covered in a dancing maelstrom of fire. As he staggered forward, mouth open, uniform and skin ablaze, a nearby marine shot him dead.

There was no cheering from the American soldiers.

Oily-looking smoke and guttering tendrils of flame continued to engulf the corpse for a few more seconds of TV time.

There were still no cheers, and the marine carried on with his advance, perhaps wondering about the last thoughts of that fireball of a man – still alive as his flesh cooked.

I was staggered that one man could do that to another, even though I knew it was war. What it must have taken out of that marine's soul to carry on performing such a horrendous duty is at the limit of my imagination.

But more importantly, and this took many years to sink in, I still think of the man who took the pictures – without the benefit of a telephoto lens. He was in a war zone at the time (undoubtedly with some sort of weapon, but obviously not using it at that moment), and he was trying to report the truth. For us.

This novel, and this five minutes of thought, was written for those three men: the Farmer, the Soldier and the Witness with his camera.

They'd know why.

And so would all the world's heroes – on *whatever* side. Because the enemy too must have once looked to the heavens and considered themselves uniquely chosen. In particular, my heroes are all those who had the courage to say no to their own leaders and paid the ultimate that anyone can: in the ovens, in other sordid mass graves, or in some lonely forgotten spot. As some still do today.

It is up to each person's own god to define what makes a hero.

And to remind us that all men are mortal.

Remember that all this was won by courage, a sense of duty and a feeling of honour. Take them as your model, for happiness comes from freedom, and freedom comes from courage.

Pericles speaking to the Athenians in 430 BC, at the funeral of those killed in the war with Sparta

OTHER PAN BOOKS
AVAILABLE FROM PAN MACMILLAN

NEAL ASHER
GRIDLINKED	0 330 48433 8	£6.99
THE SKINNER	0 330 48434 6	£6.99
THE LINE OF POLITY	0 330 48435 4	£7.99
COWL	0 330 41158 6	£7.99

ANDY SECOMBE
LIMBO	0 330 41161 6	£6.99
LIMBO II	0 330 41162 4	£6.99

JEFFREY FORD
THE PHYSIOGNOMY	0 330 41319 8	£6.99

All Pan Macmillan titles can be ordered from our website,
www.panmacmillan.com, or from your local bookshop
and are also available by post from:

Bookpost, PO Box 29, Douglas, Isle of Man IM99 1BQ
Credit cards accepted. For details:
Telephone: +44 (0)1624 677237
Fax: +44 (0)1624 670923
E-mail: bookshop@enterprise.net
www.bookpost.co.uk

Free postage and packing in the United Kingdom

Prices shown above were correct at the time of going to press.
Pan Macmillan reserve the right to show new retail prices on covers
which may differ from those previously advertised in the text
or elsewhere.